## People Rave about

## THE DIE IS CAST

"Omigod, there was a love story? Really? Because, like, all I remember was my cameo appearance. Which was totally a-maa-zing. So entertaining! The best cameo, like, EVER!"
— *Kitty Lightly, host of Entertainment Now*

"Heights and Woodhouse had the audacity to cut scenes from my novels and paste them into their book. That's copyright infringement. Those two will be hearing from my lawyers soon."
— *Steve Finder, author of the bestselling Bucky Browne adventure series*

"A pack of convoluted Disher lies from first page to last. Obviously, Heights and Woodhouse were students in one of Professor Adam Burke's crazy alternative history classes."
— *Michael Mistral, reporter for Unearthed*

"I loved it! Really exciting! One of my favorite novels. That Lady Xenia is something else—wait, what? I thought you were asking me about Steve Finder's Bucky Browne and the Cave of All Fears ... no, I've never heard of this Lady Jane character."
— *Pope Boniface X*

"Whitaker Corporation, America's premier retailer, denies any involvement with the incidents portrayed in this novel. We have no further comment."
— *Patricia Whitaker, founder and CEO of Whitaker Corporation*

"Another silly adventure novel about the search for the Last Supper Dish? No, of course I didn't read it. I already know where the Dish is—Vatican City."

— *Rupert Winters, professor of archaeology, Oxford University*

"Just another vile Catholic propaganda piece. Just more of the Pope's fake news, smearing the integrity of the Orthodox Church. One day, the Last Supper Dish will be found, and the world will know the lies of the Vatican!"

— *Jimi Bowler, blogger for TrueDishers.net*

# The Die Is Cast

Heights & Woodhouse

H & W Books

U.S.A

Betrayal,
loss,
hopes dashed.
The game
begins when...

# The Die Is Cast
### Lady Jane and the Last Supper Dish, Book One

## Heights & Woodhouse

*The Die Is Cast* Copyright © 2021 by Heights & Woodhouse Books

Copyright notice: All rights reserved. No part of this book may be reproduced or transmitted in any form or by any means, electronic or mechanical, including photocopying and recording, or by any information storage and retrieval system, without prior written permission from the publisher.

Published in the United States of America by Heights & Woodhouse Books, https://heightsandwoodhouse.com.

Authors' Disclaimer: The world of this novel is fictional. Names, characters, locales, historical events, business entities, government agencies, and religious institutions and offices are either imaginative creations or used in a fictitious manner, and the characters involved are imaginary. People often think, speak, and act in ways that are less than ideal—sometimes intentionally, sometimes not. Our characters participate in this enduring human mystery, and in that sense only do they resemble real life. If our characters think, speak, or act in ways that offend the reader, then we want to assure you that they have often offended us. And yet, they have also endeared themselves to us—even the nasty ones. We are entertained by their story, and we hope you will be too.

Title page image: Unknown, *The Last Supper*, late 13th century, tempera colors and gold leaf on parchment. The J. Paul Getty Museum, Los Angeles.

Book Layout © 2016 BookDesignTemplates.com

Cover Design by Heights & Woodhouse Books

The Die Is Cast/Heights & Woodhouse, 1st ed.
ISBN 978-1-954864-00-9 (eBook)
ISBN 978-1-954864-01-6 (paperback)

When evening came, Jesus was reclining
at the table with the Twelve. And while they were
eating, he said, "I tell you the truth, one of you will
betray me." They were very sad and began to say to him
one after the other, "Surely not I, Lord?"
Jesus replied, "The one who has dipped his hand into
the bowl with me will betray me."

The Gospel of Matthew, chapter 26, verses 20-23

# SCENE LIST

The Fall of Constantinople ............................................. 1
A Promising Strike ........................................................ 8
Lights, Camera, Action ................................................ 13
8 Ball Productions ....................................................... 17
Attempt for Atonement ................................................ 25
The Dream Team ......................................................... 40
Outlook Not So Good ................................................... 53
A Package Examined .................................................... 76
Tonight, We Dig ........................................................... 94
A Bridge of Sorts ........................................................ 104
Family Secrets ............................................................ 122
Panikos the Youth ...................................................... 141
A Case of Projection ................................................... 158
The Secret Order of Andronicus ................................. 183
Nature Calls ............................................................... 205
The Prodokleis ........................................................... 227
Halo Effect ................................................................. 240
Not Getting Anywhere ................................................ 260
What's on Our Hearts ................................................ 276
The Blinded Seeker .................................................... 286
A Change of Fate ....................................................... 308
The Mystic 8 Ball ....................................................... 316
Whitaker One View .................................................... 342
Treasure Hunting ....................................................... 367
Adventure Is My Destiny ............................................ 387

Scruuuum! ....... 395
Intrigues ....... 418
Confessions ....... 450
The Whitakerware Crusade ....... 477
A Persian Sword ....... 489
No Answer ....... 516
The Dream of Istanbul ....... 537
Anathema ....... 545

# Prologue

Scene A

## The Fall of Constantinople

*May 29, 1453*

 Giustiniani was slain. Constantinople's heroic Genoan commander—struck down by the great Ottoman cannon while defending the northwest wall, the Mesoteichion. Like a dark wind, the rumor of his death swept from regiment to regiment and chilled the heart of every man who heard it. The Mesoteichion had not held. It was all but smoking rubble. And Giustiniani had been dragged from the battle, his boots leaving twin trails of blood. So it was said.
 At the southwestern wall near the Golden Gate, Sultan Mehmet's janissaries began a fresh assault. Jakab gripped his spear, trembling. He was no warrior. He was a monk, conscripted in a desperate hour along with children and old men to defend the city's walls. He'd already seen what no man should. "Slain, slain! Giustiniani slain!" shouted a frantic youth racing past. Jakab only just glimpsed the boy's fearful eyes.
 If it were true ... their leader ... lost ...

# THE DIE IS CAST

To Jakab's left were several archers—Genoans like Giustiniani—who sought to defend their adopted home. Upon hearing of the commander's death, they dropped their bows and fled from the ramparts back into the city. Others followed their example. Commands to hold the wall went unheeded, and the trickle of retreating men soon became a stream. As it swelled, the stream swept Jakab up with it. He had no choice. He dropped his spear and fled.

But where was he to flee? The city was surrounded. The Mese, the city's main street, was churning with people, all uncertain which direction to run. Many simply stood huddled together weeping, clinging to their last possessions. Some rushed south to the harbors to try to escape the city by boat. A scant hope, Jakab surmised. He had seen the masts of the Turkish fleet. The Sea of Marmara was no longer a sea but a floating forest.

In the tumult Jakab was pushed north. He kept his feet moving lest he be caught in an undertow and trampled. At the aqueduct that spanned the city's third and fourth hills—Constantinople was built on seven hills like Rome—the current of the crowd slowed, and Jakab broke free. A shadow fell over him. He looked up. It was the Church of the Holy Apostles towering above him from the fourth hill. There some of the nobility had taken refuge, and many priests had gathered to pray. Perhaps if God would not spare the city from the Turks, he would at least spare his churches. Jakab crossed himself and prayed it would be so. Then he turned east. There was only one place to go. Only one place he wanted to be when the Sultan's army took the city. There they would find him.

# THE FALL OF CONSTANTINOPLE

On he went, avoiding the main thoroughfares now. He did not wish to see people, their fearful countenances, and he wanted to hide his own for shame. The houses he passed were silent, the windows empty. Doors had been left open. Endless rows of darkened, gaping mouths.

At last his destination lay before him. He slowed as he neared it, taking in everything one last time: the amber brick walls, the central dome, the tympanum that crowned the red, wooden doors, and the words carved into the lintel.

He pushed the door open. The shrine was empty save for an aged and bearded monk kneeling in prayer before the altar in the apse.

"It is finished," Jakab announced. "Giustiniani—" his knees buckled as he spoke, and he slumped to the floor.

The aged monk rose and went to him. "Then ... they come?"

Jakab covered his face and wept.

The old man knelt and gently grasped Jakab's shoulders.

"I am sorry, Laomendon," Jakab sobbed, rocking back and forth. "Our Brother Thaddeus--I could not save him."

"Killed?" Laomendon asked, his voice full of grief.

Jakab nodded. "We were on the wall. The janissaries—"

"Say no more, my son. He is with the Lord."

Jakab put his head in his hands.

"Come," Laomendon said, "let us pray that the Lord will likewise receive us."

With determined strength, Laomendon gripped Jakab's arms and pulled him toward the altar. Blood on Jakab's waistcoat stained the old man's wrinkled hands. Silently, he looked at the blood. His hands shook, and he clenched them hard. "Come," he commanded and began to chant.

Jakab tried to obey. Laomendon was his spiritual elder. Often in the dark days of the Sultan's siege, Jakab had taken comfort in Laomendon's uncommon serenity. But now as his voice united with the aged monk's chant, with the din of war echoing all around, Jakab despised his need for comfort. "What good is it?" he shouted. "God does not hear. He will not save us. Soon we will be nothing. Our city, our people—lost forever!" He pounded the floor with his fists.

"Not lost. Only ... hidden, perhaps. When our Lord was crucified, the apostles also feared they had lost all. But they endured. The truth of God will endure. We must believe."

"Endure?" Jakab shouted. "Thaddeus is dead! I held him in my arms. And we will soon follow him. Do you not understand? So few have come to our aid. When many could. Especially the Latins. May God judge them for their betrayal. For betrayal upon betrayal!" Jakab shook his fists in the air. "Once they came to plunder us, to rule us, to steal our sacred treasures. Now, what does Pope Nicholas do? Merely stands by watching as these sons of Muhammad do the same. The janissaries will plunder our churches. Take our sacred relics for their hoard. Plucking fruit from every tree. Everything they see."

"It is as our Lord wills. And he is just. We must place our faith in him."

"Where is he now? I cannot see him."

Laomendon turned his eyes upon Jakab. They were not serene eyes now, but stormy. "Enough! My son, you must cleanse your heart of doubt. It is only the pure in heart who shall see God."

Laomendon's rebuke made Jakab weep afresh. How could this have happened? How could it be that this was the end? Jakab stood, and as his elder's chanting filled the shrine, he walked about it, taking in once more its sumptuous beauty. He wanted its images to remain before his eyes to the very last: the frescoes of the apostles in the north aisle, and of the Christ in the central dome, and finally, the four mosaics in the west aisle—as beautiful as any mosaic in Hagia Sophia, Emperor Justinian's matchless church.

The four vivid figures stood proud and defiant, as Jakab himself wished to stand. Each of the four men held an identical treasure—a golden dish. Jakab stepped toward the nearest image. The saint's fiery halo and cold, ebony eyes could of themselves inspire many seekers to become penitent. Ministering in the shrine to pilgrims, Jakab had often witnessed it. He touched the golden dish in the saint's right hand, then pressed his lips to it, kissing it. "Until the wages of sin are paid," he murmured.

Shouts beyond the walls of the shrine made him gasp. Hastily, he returned to Laomendon at the altar. "Father! Have we done enough? Have we sufficiently protected the Legacy? Justice must prevail. It must!"

The old monk ceased his chant and lifted his eyes. "Tell me, Jakab, what do you see?" He pointed past the altar to the bare wall of the apse.

"Nothing," Jakab said. "Nothing at all."

"And thus it will be for the Turks. We made certain of that."

"But do you not think, in time, they will discover the chest?"

"No."

"But how can you be sure?" Jakab knelt beside Laomendon once more, his anger spent.

"Because as you have just said, they will take only what they see."

"But how will the Legacy of Andronicus be passed on? What if Alexander and Demetrius do not reach Athos? They carry our Order's secret texts. What if the shrine is destroyed? What if—"

"My son," Laomendon interrupted, shaking his head sadly, "these are questions we cannot answer. The fate of the Legacy, like our own fates, like the fate of our Order, we must leave in the hands of God. Perhaps, in the fullness of time ..."

Jakab opened his mouth to speak.

Laomendon stopped him, placing one hand on his arm. "No. No more questions for this poor, old monk. You, Thaddeus, myself—all of us have suffered long nights of labor, and we have done all we could with the time God gave us. Rest your mind in that knowledge. It is true we ... will not live to see divine justice prevail. But we must believe—" Laomendon's hand trembled. Beyond the walls could be heard a clashing roar. He gripped Jakab's arm firmly. "Believe, my son, that the Lord will exact punishment upon those who have betrayed us." His voice rose. "Believe that his justice will run like water, his righteousness like a mighty stream!"

The clashing roar grew near, now punctuated with shrieks and curses. It hammered the walls all around.

# THE FALL OF CONSTANTINOPLE

The shrine's red doors burst open. One door, screeching, swung wildly, broken from its hinges. They had come, the soldiers of Sultan Mehmet, and with them, swords dripping with blood.

Scene B

# A Promising Strike

*University of Pittsburgh*

*Pittsburgh, Pennsylvania*

*February 15, 20—*

"I must admit," Professor Adam Burke said to the phone receiver cradled between his shoulder and his ear, "this dig sounds promising. Very promising." He scribbled down names, phone numbers, and dates on a notepad.

Burke was an active listener. "That's good, he's highly able," he interrupted as the woman he spoke to went on, and "yes, I'd thought of Stoltzfus too," and "of course, without question, Dr. Foo."

"Oh, other names?" The smile on Burke's freckled face grew wide as he considered the question. He'd been waiting for a chance to mention a person's name—a woman's—in particular. But he didn't want to appear too eager. He leaned back in his chair and ran his fingers through his thinning, brown hair. It was a routine, unconscious gesture, as if to confirm to himself that his hair was still there.

"Let's see," he began, pretending to be without a ready answer, "if you believe the structure might be a church or a shrine, then I'd recommend Dr. Calvino at University of Bologna. I worked with him in Croatia. Yes, on the grounds of the Euphrasian Basilica. Very knowledgeable man. And, uh, perhaps—I've never met her, you understand—but you might consider Dr. Elena Hromadova at Moscow State. She's new to the field. I've reviewed some of her work here and there. In the latest Journal of the History of Ideas she has a brilliant essay on eighteenth-century Dishing. I believe the article is called The True Origins of the Cappadocia Theory. I'm quoted in it extensively."

Burke paused, listening to an interjected question. He responded with a self-deprecating chuckle, a chuckle he'd perfected over his many years as Miller Family Chair of Byzantine Studies at the University of Pittsburgh and as the director of the Keslo Museum of Near Eastern Archaeology. It was a chuckle that not only inspired his graduate students to work harder to edit his manuscripts, but also persuaded wealthy patrons of the museum to empty their pockets.

"No, Hromadova isn't a former graduate student. As I said, I've never met her. Truly. It's just an instinct I have. Her work is exceptional. Those would be my top recommendations." He shifted from the subject quickly: "Say, I'm sorry you had trouble getting in touch with me. I've been on sabbatical. Didn't my assistant give you my cell?"

Another pause. Another chuckle. "Yes, that's right. Getting good help these days. Hey, did I ever tell you about Stoltzfus? No? Well, he once uncovered an ancient

Egyptian tablet. Written in hieroglyphs, naturally. When he translated it, all it said was—Kids never listen, and it's hard to find a good servant. True story! Yes, some things never change. But anyway, I'm glad you found me. What have I been doing on sabbatical? Writing my speech for the conference at the National Archaeological Museum in Bulgaria, of course. You didn't know I'm the keynote speaker? Not that I have anything to talk about. Just the, oh, interesting trinket I found in the dig in Sofia a few years back. Ha-ha, yes—interesting trinket—that's what I said. The Saint Nil icon. The museum will have it on public display for the first time. A big event for sure."

As Burke spoke, he reached behind him and lifted an object from his bookcase. It was a wooden panel the size of a book and bore the likeness of a thin monk with a scraggly beard and golden halo. Only half the monk's face appeared, as the entire upper left corner of the icon was missing. Near his heart, the monk clutched a dish in both hands. Gently, Burke felt the cracks and pits in the panel. They weren't ancient cracks and pits. The icon was a facsimile. Burke had paid quite a bit to have it made, and it was excellent work. Small differences between it and the original would only be clear to an expert—such as himself. Saint Nil's irises, for instance, were just a touch too white. No replica could approximate the natural aging process that over the centuries inevitably turned white paint yellow.

"The anticipation for the Nil is at a fevered pitch," Burke said. "After all, it's still the only one in existence."

Carefully, as if it were his child, Burke replaced the facsimile on its display stand. The conversation devolved into professional gossip of little interest to Burke, which allowed him to plan his exit in a way that would still convey collegiality and charisma. He decided to cap off the exchange with one of his favorite lines, one that guaranteed a laugh: "Well, Zainab, if giving my life to history enables me to make history, I guess I'll just have to suffer the fame and fortune." A nice way to wrap up a conversation with a fellow archaeologist, especially one lesser known in the field. Burke hung up and reclined in his chair for several minutes, contemplating the future. Then he dialed the Archaeology Department secretary: "Sandra, Burke here. Yes, I'm fine. Would you check my calendar for me? I need to clear out all my appointments for the next, oh, ten weeks. I'm going out of the country. Reschedule what you can. Nothing before May."

This task accomplished, Burke stepped around his desk to make sure his office door was locked. Then, from the top drawer of his filing cabinet, he took out a small dartboard and three steel-tipped darts. He hung the dartboard from a hook nailed to the back of the door, a hook reserved just for this purpose. He stepped off five paces, readied his first dart, and faced his target.

"Ah, Winters," he said a bit too cheerily. "Winters. Winters. Winters." He flicked the first dart and struck a glossy photograph thumb-tacked to the board. The photograph—already full of holes—was of an old man in a gray suit standing at a podium accepting an award. The dart hit Winters, puncturing tufts of thick, white hair. Burke rarely missed.

"For so long you've eluded me," Burke said, flinging his second dart. "Even though you haven't published one thesis worth a damn in over a decade." The dart hit the podium where Winters stood. "And without your sycophants at the Journal of Near East Antiquity, you'd have sunk into scholarly oblivion long ago." With his fingertip Burke plucked at the tip of his third and last dart.

"It's just so easy for you, eh, Winters? Pass off your unthinking, banal skepticism as real scholarship?" Squinting as he took aim, Burke readied the third dart for a finishing strike. "But I've got you now. Once I get to Istanbul, it's over." The dart stabbed the old professor's heart with a satisfying thunk.

Scene C

# Lights, Camera, Action

*Göreme, Turkey*

*February 15, 20—*

    The day was calm, without a trace of wind. It was as if the little town held its breath. Nestled among the rocky cliffs, the white stone houses were like tombs, the ruins of an ancient people long forgotten. The arid valley below lay in shadows, as thick motionless clouds absorbed the weak rays of the late afternoon sun.
    But the little town wasn't forgotten. At its central market, vendors were closing after another busy day. Several late customers still haggled with a woman stacking woven rugs. Near them on the main street, a man carried a mountain bike with a flat tire back to the rental shop. Overhead, a blue and white striped hot-air balloon gently descended. ANATOLIAN TOURS—read the balloon on one side—THE BEST LIFT UP.
    As dusk settled in, Jane Whitaker stood in a shop at the far end of a dead-end alley. She was on a secret mission and had dressed accordingly. Her face was hidden by the brim of her white Barmah hat and by the fox fur collar of her vintage Versace gray-silk bomber jacket.

# THE DIE IS CAST

Her hands trembled with excitement as she received a brown-paper package from the proprietor.

"Only you would have been able to choose such a rare treasure," he said to her. "It must be, as you say, destiny." His eyes twinkled as he spoke, and he grinned broadly through his beard.

"Oh, I'm sure of it," Jane said, tucking the package into her jacket. "I almost didn't come in 'cause I wasn't sure this was a shop. Like, the sign isn't in English and stuff, ha-ha. But then, I saw that tailless cat in the window, and I just had to see it, 'cause, like, I've never seen a cat without a tail. Destiny works in mysterious ways, y'know what I mean?" Before the proprietor could reply, Jane added, "Cats give Baby Girl the shivers, don't they Pookums?"

Grudgingly shifting to share space with the package was Baby Girl, Jane's long-haired teacup Chihuahua. The little dog had one blue eye and one brown. It was dressed in a baby-blue monogrammed sweater. Jane lifted the dog and kissed its ear. "You're so brave," she cooed encouragingly.

The proprietor chuckled. "Kübra, that old stray, cannot even kill a mouse. He is so fat and lazy."

"Ha-ha. Kübra, huh? What's your name?"

The proprietor paused as if searching his memory. "Er, you may call me Babu."

Jane giggled. "I'll always remember you. Like, I can't believe the secret to the Dish was here all along," she blurted. She touched the brim of her Barmah hat in a parting salute.

Babu meekly inclined his head. "I am richly blessed by our meeting. May you find the reward you seek. Farewell!"

## LIGHTS, CAMERA, ACTION

Exiting the shop, Jane surveyed for spies. Seeing none, she ducked into an alcove and unzipped her jacket. "Wait here for Mama," she instructed Baby Girl, setting the little dog down. She secured the brown-paper package in one hand and reached into her jacket pocket for her phone.

It took her a minute to pose herself. She shook her head twice to get into character, pushing her long blonde hair back behind one ear, lowering her chin and parting her lips in a half kiss. She snapped several pictures with this facial arrangement, making sure both the package and the shop were visible in the frame. It was a frustrating procedure, because she wanted Baby Girl in the picture too, but it was hard to manage everything at once, and the package was the most important thing, besides herself.

Eight tries later, she finally got The One, and it was super cute. But choosing the best filter before posting her picture to *Dishpix.com* would make it even cuter. The choice came down to Electra or Xanadu. She chose Xanadu.

Where was Baby Girl?

Peeing in a lonely patch of grass.

Jane swept Baby Girl up with kisses and re-tucked the little dog and the package into her jacket. Then she turned onto the street without looking and collided with an old man riding a donkey. He shouted at her in Turkish. Giggling mightily, Jane scurried up a steep incline and pushed her way through the gated arbor to her hotel just as the last brushstrokes of day faded away.

Guests had gathered for happy hour in the hotel café. Entering the lobby, Jane lowered the brim of her hat and hastened to the stairs, hoping Baby Girl wouldn't betray their presence with a yip. She just had to get to her room. Once there with the door locked, she'd be safe. She could allow herself to believe it was hers. Wouldn't Pope Boniface be furious! But what could he do? Truth was on her side. Just like in all her favorite stories. She was one step closer to fulfilling her dream. Soon, the world would know.

As Jane climbed the stairs to the second floor, she imagined walking on red carpet through a sea of cameras, their flashbulbs shimmering in wave upon wave.

Scene D

# 8 Ball Productions

*CBS Broadcast Center*

*Hell's Kitchen, Manhattan*

*February 15, 20—*

Natalie habitually bit her lower lip when she was nervous. But standing off-stage next to Ray, she tried hard not to for fear of smudging her lipstick. Usually, she didn't wear lipstick, but this was television. And as the makeup artist had explained, bold lips and eyes would help her hold her own next to Kitty Lightly.

Kitty was the show host. Tall, blonde, luscious—she stood awaiting her cue opposite the stage to Natalie and Ray. Upon meeting Kitty backstage, Natalie had immediately disliked her. Kitty reminded her of someone.

Ray usually didn't wear suits. As he fidgeted, a production assistant fluffed the handkerchief in his breast pocket. The last time Natalie had seen Ray in a suit, the two of them had also been about to walk across a stage. Natalie couldn't help but remember because hearing their names called out had been a dream come true. They'd arrived at the peak of professional achievement.

But after the awards show, neither of them had lingered long at their own party. Ray had left first. She'd watched him go, not knowing if she'd see him again. Not knowing if she cared to.

All at once, the countdown began. They were about to go live. Theme music blared; the studio audience cheered. As well as she could in pink stilettos, Kitty rushed to center stage. The spotlight quickly found her. She blew kisses at the front row. "Hello, hello, hello! Welcome to Entertainment Now," she squealed. "I'm Kitty Lightly, and have I got the scoop for you."

"I'd rather be behind the camera," Ray said to Natalie.

"Me too."

"We have to do it."

"Remember what Reggie said."

"I know what to say."

Natalie clenched and unclenched her hands; her fingers were so cold. She sought reassurance that they could pull off the interview and glanced up at Ray. His lips were pinched in a hard line, his gray eyes fixed on Kitty. It was his game face. Kitty was nearly through her opening bit:

"... and did you know soap star Amber Lane's on-screen romance has continued off-screen? Well, now you do! And tempers flare on the set of Another Superhero Movie. Did you know producer Jude Muckenfuss told Pepper Richards that if he wanted such bad acting, he would've cast his cat? Well, now you do! So, hold on, people—I've got all these stories for you and more. Let's get entertained."

Kitty hopped up the three steps to the host's chair. Next to it were two empty ones. The audience clapped on cue, and Kitty smiled with glossy, full lips as she perched herself on the chair's edge and crossed her legs. Her platinum bob needed no adjustment, but she brushed her fingertips along her bangs. Her bracelets twinkled in the spotlight. "But first, we begin with our surprise celebrity interview," she announced. "We welcome two guests who've never, ever appeared on Entertainment Now."

The audience murmured.

"I know, how could anyone not love me?" Kitty ad-libbed. "I mean, look at me!"

A few in the audience whistled and hooted.

Natalie rolled her eyes in disdain—and envy.

"I think you look great," Ray said to her suddenly.

Natalie didn't hear him right. "Kitty? Yeah, nice body work, but her brain needs a fill-up."

Ray turned his head sharply. "What did you say?"

Natalie frowned, puzzled.

Kitty read from the teleprompter: "Tonight's guests first met at New York University Tisch School of the Arts, where they studied documentary filmmaking at The Maurice Kanbar Institute of Film & Television. Their first joint project, The Full Chester, a documentary about the fast-food industry, won top honors at the inaugural Tribeca Film Festival. Their second documentary, Monica's Dress, won the Audience Award at the Sundance Film Festival. And most recently, their much-acclaimed The Tent at Ground Zero got them their first Academy Award for Best Documentary Feature. So, you might say these two are super good at what they do. Just like me!"

"Marry me, Kitty," a man in the audience shouted.

## THE DIE IS CAST

Kitty pretended to swoon. The audience roared. Fanning herself with her hands, Kitty told a production assistant to get the man's name. Then she read again from the teleprompter: "After pursuing solo projects the last three years, our two guests have reunited. So, cheer up film fans. Here to tell us about their latest project are—from 8 Ball Productions—it's Ray Cozart and Natalie Ashbrook! Let's give them a warm Entertainment Now welcome."

Listening to Kitty's introduction, Natalie suddenly realized what she'd just said to Ray. *Solo projects.* She hadn't meant to imply anything. It was a joke, and one not totally meant for him—or Kitty. Natalie had meant it for another woman, the one who resembled Kitty, the one she hated. That woman was Staci.

As Natalie stepped with Ray into the spotlight, she felt him take hold of her hand. She knew it was just for show, just part of the game. But still. Her emotions flitted between hope and sadness. Her body seemed to melt away; she was all mind, formless and floating, inhabiting the past and present at once. She felt an uncanny merger of time and place. Back in the past, six months before she'd walked across the stage with Ray to receive their Academy Award, there had also been a marriage proposal. Geoffrey had proposed. And she'd accepted. Those days should've been days of exhilaration and triumph, but they weren't.

Feeling her hand in Ray's, Natalie remembered the first time their hands had touched. That was so long ago. They'd still been in film school then. She felt fresh regret about what had happened between them three years before. She wanted to communicate her grief by squeezing Ray's fingers, but they reached the chairs next to Kitty, and he let go.

THE DIE IS CAST

Natalie remembers the first time she held Ray's hand. We'd love to share that touching story with you. It's our gift. And we want you to be fully in-the-know before joining the adventure. Download your free copy of *When the Pirate Met the Princess* by following this link:

https://heightsandwoodhouse.com/get-pirate/

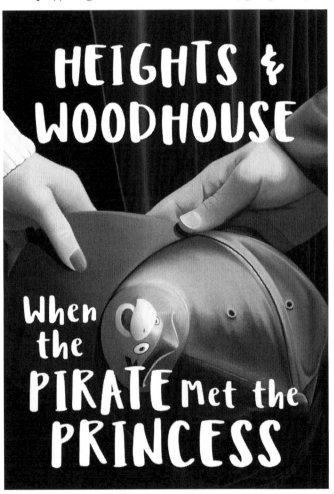

Latin supplicants, study the message of Panikos:
Present yourselves at the gathering of the Twelve.
Kneel before Andrew and pray for your souls,
For you will soon enter the earth.

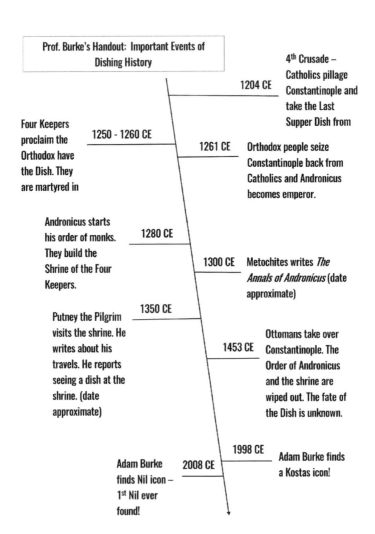

Scene 1

## Attempt for Atonement

*Hall of Pontifical Audiences*

*Vatican City*

*Thursday, February 18*

"... thus, considering our desire for greater Christian unity, especially with our Orthodox brothers and sisters, I propose that on my trip to Istanbul in March to celebrate the Feast of Forgiveness with Ecumenical Patriarch Philotheos, I will return to him the Last Supper Dish."

As Pope Boniface X ended his speech, he leaned his broad shoulders forward and crossed his forearms on the table. Before him in the conference room sat thirty men who held various positions in the Catholic hierarchy. Boniface had hand-selected them from the general Synod of Bishops to hear this announcement. The annual meeting of the Synod to discuss the state of global Christian unity had already ended—three days before. The international media and the throngs of laity who'd gathered in St. Peter's Square had already left the city. Thus, from Boniface's perspective, the real work could begin. He'd invited two additional guests to this special, closed-door meeting. They were not Catholics but Orthodox archbishops.

Hearing Boniface's proposal, the men murmured among themselves. One of them, Cardinal Carlino Betori, the Prefect of the Congregation of the Causes of Saints, called out, "But Your Holiness, the Dish is ours!" A man seated next to him, Bishop Louis Fortier, Apostolic Vicariate of Istanbul, agreed, "Yes, it has been safely held by the Papacy for 800 years. There is no reason to change that. None!" Across the room, Cardinal Eduardo Donizetti, President of the Pontifical Council for Promoting Christian Unity, dissented, "Ours? There was a time, you recall, when our two churches were not divided."

And so, the debate began, a debate centuries in the making. Catholicism. Orthodoxy. Christianity's two largest churches, born in the first century during the height of the Roman Empire. Cardinal Eduardo was right— there had only been one united Church back then. But differences in culture and language had slowly divided the western Christians loyal to Rome from their eastern brothers and sisters, loyal to Constantinople. Still, the two might've formed a great friendship. After all, the bishop in Rome was the successor of Saint Peter, one of the Twelve Apostles of Christ, and the bishop in Constantinople was the successor of Saint Andrew, also an Apostle of Christ—and Peter's brother. But it had not turned out that way.

Cardinal Carlino requested permission to speak. He was granted it. He stood and addressed Boniface. "Your Holiness, as Prefect of the Congregation of the Causes of

Saints, it is my responsibility to protect the Church's holy relics. What you propose would put the Last Supper Dish at risk. I voiced the same concern three years ago when you first suggested giving Patriarch Philotheos the Dish and the relics of Saint Kosmo the Dignified. The future of Orthodoxy in Istanbul is tenuous, at best. They are under constant pressure from the Turkish government. Their seminary has been forcibly shut down. Most Greeks have left the city. The Church of Saint George is not invulnerable. They cannot arrange the continual security needed. And they lack the facilities to accommodate the influx of tourists."

"But three years ago when Philotheos visited Rome, he left with Saint Kosmo's relics. You agreed to their return," Boniface said.

"I did, but the Dish is different," Carlino countered. "It is the only object we have that is attested to in the Gospels. The only object that Jesus himself touched. Our Lord even performed a miracle with it when he revealed Judas Iscariot to be his betrayer. The Last Supper Dish has been venerated by Christians for 2,000 years—first in Jerusalem, then in Constantinople, and now here. And here it belongs—safely guarded by the strongest Church on earth. Holy Father, what you propose—giving it away—it is a scandal."

"I wouldn't be giving it away. I would be giving it back," Boniface said. He didn't go on. He didn't need to. Carlino knew what he meant. All the men did. According to Church tradition, the Last Supper Dish had been given by the Apostle John to his disciple Polycarp in Smyrna. Before Polycarp was martyred in 140AD, he gave the

## THE DIE IS CAST

Dish to Felix, bishop of Byzantium. When Constantine formed his empire and renamed Byzantium after himself, he kept the Dish in his throne room. Later, Emperor Justinian placed the Dish in his great church, Hagia Sophia. For nearly a thousand years, the Dish was the great jewel of the Byzantine Empire.

"But Your Holiness," Carlino hastened to reply, "if not for the Fourth Crusade of 1204, the Dish may have been lost. When the crusaders took Constantinople, they saved it. Along with many other holy relics which can still be seen in our Vatican museums to this day. If we had not saved the Dish, no doubt it would've been destroyed when the Ottomans conquered Constantinople in 1453. That basilica where the Dish was kept—Hagia Sophia—it's now a mosque. Can we not say that God used the crusade to transfer the Dish to our care? What men perhaps meant for evil, He meant for good, as in the ancient story of Joseph being sold by his brothers into Egypt, only to have Joseph preserve Egypt and his brothers during a famine. As many of us believe, God executed judgment on the Orthodox for failing to recognize your ecclesiastical authority. They still do not accept it. Do you have the right to absolve them of their sin of separation, especially when there is no repentance? We returned the relics of Saint Kosmo three years ago. A great offer of peace since he is one of their saints. What has Patriarch Philotheos done in return?"

"Giving the Dish back is no absolution of *them*," Boniface said strongly. "And Philotheos has done something. He has invited me to Istanbul. Our co-celebration of the Feast of Forgiveness at the Church of Saint George next month—it is a genuine step forward in our

Dialogues of Love, not merely symbolic. That is my hope. My belief."

There were murmurings among the assembled men. None louder than that of Bishop Louis. He was, as many said, a quintessential French snob. He stood up next to Carlino and looked down his long nose as he spoke. "Your Holiness, your American naïveté is touching. You think ancient disputes can be resolved merely with charisma and eloquence. Believe me, returning a relic taken during the Fourth Crusade is no means of healing their ancient grievance against us. And the Dish is sacred. It is not a tool to be used. I agree with Carlino. You would only put the Dish at risk. As a resident of Istanbul, I can confirm the pitiful state of the Orthodox Church there. The Ecumenical Patriarch will even have difficulty finding his successor. Turkish law stipulates that the patriarch must be a Turkish citizen by birth. But there are few qualified Greek men who fit that description. What will happen to the Last Supper Dish when the ancient bishopric of Saint Andrew is no more?" He nodded toward the two Orthodox archbishops who sat to the side of the room. "Of course, we would never wish for such a profound loss," he added, barely disguising the insincerity in his voice. "But it is a conceivable scenario. Would the Dish end up in Moscow with the Russian Orthodox? Or in Sofia with the Bulgarian Church? The situation in Istanbul makes the future of the Dish too unstable."

Boniface glanced to his right at his secretary Victor Santorini. Victor's obvious scowl wasn't surprising. Months before when Boniface had told Victor the names of the men he wanted invited to the special meeting, Victor had openly scoffed, "Carlino and Louis? Hardliners?" Boniface had assured him that true unity could never be gained simply by excluding disagreeable people. "I want a frank discussion, not a supper party." So far, he was getting the frankness. He heard rustling from the seats along the wall. The Orthodox archbishops—Chrysanthus and Leronymos—whispered between themselves. The younger Leronymos appeared about to stand. Chrysanthus held him back. Their long, flowing beards failed to hide their fuming countenances.

Carlino retrieved a folder from his chair. "Your Holiness, you should know—three years ago when you first suggested returning the Dish, I started a petition. I thought if the hundred or so members of the Synod could not convince you to abandon your design, then sheer numbers might. There are thousands of signatures from members of the Curia and the priesthood—from all over the world. The laity will not take kindly to seeing Mother Church stripped of her most precious jewel. The Dish alone draws over five million visitors to Vatican City annually—*five million*. Many affirm that beholding it is a profoundly moving experience. You must answer to your flock. What will your answer be?"

The folder was passed from hand to hand up to Boniface. Several men who themselves had signed the petition handled it as though it were scalding. Soon, what they had confidently done in secret would be known by the Vicar of Christ. But it was too late to erase their names. When Boniface received the petition, he thrust it at his secretary Victor who, try as he might, couldn't hide the "I told you so" look in his eyes.

Across the room from Carlino, Cardinal Eduardo spoke, "I ask the Holy Father to recognize me."

"We recognize Cardinal Eduardo," Boniface said.

"I have not yet yielded the floor," Carlino complained.

The aged and frail Eduardo struggled to rise from his chair. Father Frederico, a young priest seated next to him, gently assisted the man to his feet. Boniface gave Carlino a look, daring him to shout down the eldest of the College of Cardinals. Louis tapped Carlino's arm to signal he shouldn't take the dare, and the two men grudgingly sat down.

Although frail, Eduardo's mind was sharp, and he used his natural seniority strategically to sway—or cow— opponents. As President of the Pontifical Council for Promoting Christian Unity, he ranked below Carlino in the Curia. However, the council organized the Dialogues of Love, the name Boniface had given to his outreach to the Orthodox Church. As part of those Dialogues, Eduardo had prevailed upon Carlino to return the bones of Saint Kosmo the Dignified to the Orthodox three years before.

"I must apologize to our two revered guests—if you will not do so." Eduardo looked sharply at Boniface and gestured toward Archbishops Chrysanthus and Leronymos.

Boniface hadn't expected to be rebuked by an ally. But he saw Eduardo's eyes twinkle and did not interrupt.

"Carlino and Louis describe so eloquently the degraded state of Orthodoxy in Turkey as a reason not to return the Dish," Eduardo said. "Why let them go on this way, Your Holiness?"

"I'm trying to be polite," Boniface said with a slight grin.

"Polite! You are such an American. Equal parts aggravation and charm. You have too much faith in democracy, so you are pushed around at your own meeting."

"They do call me The Yankee Pope," Boniface said.

Several men chuckled. Boniface was from New York. Ten years prior, upon his election as the first American pontiff, he'd been called The Yankee Pope by a journalist. It'd been meant as an insult, but Boniface embraced it.

Eduardo's face sobered, and he went on: "How ironic that we must have a clandestine meeting so we can speak the truth openly. Let us not pretend the vulnerability of Orthodoxy in Istanbul is merely a vagary of history. *We* are the cause. Who made the Byzantine Empire ripe for Sultan Mehmet to pluck? We did—our Catholic crusaders. The Empire never recovered from the Fourth Crusade. We occupied Constantinople for fifty years, oppressing the people and supplanting Orthodox clergy with Catholic priests. The people fought back, of course. Four Orthodox monks—Kostas, Zoticus, Panikos, and Nil—led the revolt. And what did we do? We killed them! But their martyrdom rallied the people, and we were driven out. Two centuries later, when Sultan Mehmet besieged the city, did we seriously try to help them defend it? No! Your Excellency, how many Catholics are there in Istanbul?" Eduardo waggled his finger at Louis, who rightly understood that it was a rhetorical question and made no reply. "The fact that we possess the Last Supper Dish is not God's provision, nor a judgment on Orthodoxy. Our possession is a legacy of our sin. We have betrayed or abandoned our eastern brothers and sisters again and again."

"That is why I seek a tangible sign of our commitment to them," Boniface said. "The Dish will be that sign."

"You think giving the Dish back to the Orthodox will atone for our many sins?" Carlino asked Eduardo. "Will the Dish be sufficient payment, do you think? Who will calculate the reparations, and how shall they be distributed? Perhaps we could direct all the revenue from our museums to the Orthodox in Istanbul. Or let us just empty all our museums and, oh, tear down Saint Peter's Basilica while we are at it. Surely, that would be enough?"

"To hear a cardinal scoff at the idea of atonement," Eduardo replied, "is shocking." He resumed his seat.

Carlino was unembarrassed. "It is a valid question, Your Holiness," he said to Boniface. "Would Patriarch Philotheos accept the Dish as payment for our sins? Shall we ask our Orthodox guests for their opinion?"

Boniface inhaled deeply and looked to Archbishops Chrysanthus and Leronymos. The two bearded men waited for permission to speak. Boniface exhaled; he drummed his fingers and glanced at his secretary. Victor appeared confused by Boniface's delay, as did all the assembly. Boniface looked up at the ceiling as if in prayer. "How can I clean the speck from my brother's eye when there is a log in my own?" he said quietly, eyeing the two archbishops. "You may speak, friends."

Chrysanthus and Leronymos stared back at him coldly. The elder Chrysanthus stood. He had a long gray beard and wore a black cassock and kamilavka, a cylindrical clerical hat with a veil in the back. About his neck hung a panagia, a medallion bearing the image of the Virgin Mary. He lifted his chin haughtily. "No." He sat back down.

"No, you will not speak?" Boniface asked.

Chrysanthus stood again. "No, Patriarch Philotheos would not accept your bowl as payment."

"Why not?"

"Because it is worthless. A bowl used to feed the emperor's dog."

The room erupted.

Above the clamor could be heard Bishop Louis: "You are steeped in delusion, believing children's fables!" Only Carlino sat unperturbed. The words of Chrysanthus had been sweet music to him. After all, if the Orthodox didn't want the Dish, Boniface couldn't give it back.

With difficulty, Boniface restored order. "Your Eminence," he said to Chrysanthus, "you know the story that the four monks were keepers of the Dish isn't true."

"Do I?" Chrysanthus smirked. "Then why do we Orthodox venerate them as saints? Why do archaeologists search for their memorial shrine? Why are scholars writing books about the lost Dish, teaching their students the history? Why are novels written and films made? Why do Dishers the world over still search for it?" He glared at Boniface. "Not true, you say. Hmph. Why are you so sure it is not?"

Boniface made no reply. "The story" to which he'd referred was known to everyone in the room. Eduardo had even referenced it obliquely when he'd mentioned the four thirteenth-century Orthodox monks, Kostas, Zoticus, Panikos, and Nil. The revolt they'd led against the Latins who occupied Constantinople after the Fourth Crusade had been incited by their claims to have hidden the real Last Supper Dish from the crusaders. The crusaders had been thwarted in their greedy triumph, tricked into taking a dog dish back to Rome. So the monks said. After their martyrdom, which brought about the defeat of the Latins and the restoration of the Byzantine Empire, the new emperor—Emperor Andronicus II—had constructed a memorial shrine in their honor, The Shrine of the Four Keepers, for so the four monks had come to be called. He created a new order of monks in his name—The Order of Andronicus—to maintain the shrine and create and disseminate icons bearing likenesses of the Four Keepers. Written on the icons were riddles encouraging seekers to come to Constantinople to behold the Dish of Christ. The shrine had, indeed, drawn many curious pilgrims from the West who'd heard tales of four monks martyred for the true Dish. This was according to some historical accounts (a few more reliable than others) which intimated that the Dish was kept at the shrine. Unfortunately, in 1453 when Sultan Mehmet conquered Constantinople, the Shrine of the Four Keepers was destroyed, and the true Dish—if it were the true Dish—lost.

Over time, the story of the Four Keepers of the true Dish had gained traction in the medieval world. People who believed it came to be called "Dishers." Some accounts traced the origin of the moniker to a pottery-throwing incident in the year 1295 that had resulted in the Archbishop of Cologne losing a tooth. Their numbers had grown too rapidly for the Catholic Church's comfort. Accusations multiplied that the Church knowingly displayed a fraudulent bowl to deceive the laity and garner wealth and power. Efforts were made to snuff Dishers out in the mid-fourteenth century when two of their most vocal members—Sir Robert Houghton, the Earl of Salisbury, and Philip the Fortunate, the Comte de Maine—had been denounced as heretics and excommunicated by Pope Gregory XI.

Louis's voice filled the void created by Boniface's silence. "Mere accusations are not evidence," he said to Chrysanthus. "The Last Supper Dish—a dog bowl! Preposterous! Perverse! A vague belief, as Pope Pius IV said—in the sixteenth century. One would think you Dishers could have produced evidence for your story since then. But no, that is too hard for you. You have not even a scrap. All you demand of yourselves is to hold your beliefs sincerely."

Eduardo nodded in agreement. "You cite novelists and filmmakers," he said to Chrysanthus, "proof that you chase your own imagination, and that is all."

Louis and Eduardo, on opposite sides when it came to the fate of the Last Supper Dish, were in firm agreement on one thing—the bowl on display in the Pius-Clementine Vatican Museum was genuine.

"How dare you," Leronymos said, pointing at Eduardo. "Our saints did not die defending a lie."

"May I speak, Holy Father?" It was Father Frederico, the young priest who acted as Director of the Press Office for the Holy See. Due to his position, he was a man in touch with public opinion.

Boniface gestured for him to stand.

"In my role for the Holy See, I am very much a storyteller—in the best sense. A craftsman. You understand what I mean," Frederico said. "So, let me tell you a story. Supposing you were to take the Dish with you to Istanbul next month and offer to return it to Philotheos? And supposing, as His Eminence Chrysanthus has said and for the reasons stated, he rejects your offer? What would be the result?"

Boniface leaned forward in his chair, intrigued. "Go on."

"Well, as a result, Philotheos would be proclaimed by the public as a hero. He will have thwarted the Evil Empire. Us! The Four Keepers are featured in bestselling novels and blockbuster films for a reason. Haven't you all heard of Steve Finder? Or of Bucky Browne, the great adventurer?" Frederico looked about at ignorant faces. Except for Boniface's face. "I see the Holy Father knows what I mean."

"What?" Boniface said defensively as all eyes turned to him. He kept Finder's novels on a bottom shelf in his study. "Finder is an American adventure novelist. Bucky Browne is, er, the hero of his books. Of course, I've heard of him."

"The story of the Four Keepers excites the imagination because they're freedom fighters," Frederico said to the group. "In Finder's novels, Bucky Browne heroically searches for the Dish to right history's wrongs and to protect it from evil conspirators—cardinals and popes. Don't you understand? Despite our charitable labors for the poor and the weak of our societies, people view us—especially youths—as perpetrators of injustice."

# THE DIE IS CAST

"Surely even the young can discern fact from fiction," Louis scoffed.

"You have no idea how popular modern Dishers are," Frederico countered. "It's cool to be one. Searching for the lost Dish—or Dishing as it's called—has been taken up by many youths as a social justice cause. It's a global phenomenon. There are Disher websites that report archaeological progress in search of the lost shrine. Like a play-by-play of a sporting match. Dishers flock to famous religious sites, not for their spiritual or historical value—rather, they hunt the Dish. One social media site alone—Dishpix.com—has 80 million subscribers. Surely, you're all aware, at least, that Disher protests have been on the rise the last ten years?"

Several of the cardinals mumbled in grudging acknowledgment. As they all knew, Disher protestors had on occasion even been chased out of Saint Peter's Square.

"Believe me, Holy Father, if you make Patriarch Philotheos a hero by enabling him to publicly reject you, Dishpix.com will grow to 120 million subscribers by the year's end. Dishers will stage a grand protest in Saint Peter's Square demanding you admit the real Dish is still out there, and that our Dish is a fake. And next year's summer blockbuster in America will be yet another Bucky Browne adventure in search of the lost Dish." Frederico sat down.

"And ... what if I do nothing?" Boniface asked Frederico.

Frederico shrugged. "Look around you." He gestured at the assembly to indicate the status quo. "The game between our churches will go on."

Archbishops Chrysanthus and Leronymos leered at Boniface as if in triumph. They stood. "We will make our report to His All Holiness Philotheos," Chrysanthus said.

"Please, do," Boniface said, his face clouded with disappointment. But his gaze was still firm and unwavering.

The two archbishops strode out, leaving behind a silent room.

Scene 2

## The Dream Team

*Istanbul Museum of Ancient History*

*Monday, February 22*

"Ladies and gentlemen, I am Adam Burke." The man who made this pronouncement smiled wide, enjoying the applause from the thirty or so professors and students crammed among the tables in Girard Lab, the artifacts processing workroom at the Istanbul Museum of Ancient History. He pointed to a few people who clapped longer than the rest. "Thank you, Dr. Foo—and yes, Dr. Calvino, I see you. And Dr. Stoltzfus, of course. Thank you." After signaling Stoltzfus to resume his seat, Burke said, "I also thank Dr. Zainab Ayhan, curator of the museum, for the hospitality extended to us today." Seated off to the side, a beautiful, raven-haired woman wearing a red scarf accepted a much smaller smattering of applause with a slight tilt of her head. Burke continued: "And why are we here today? Some of you, no doubt, are here to share drinks with your old archaeology buddies." He paused for the obligatory chuckles. "However, for the rest of us ... well, I suspect we want to dig up some old stuff."

## THE DREAM TEAM

In the back corner of the lab, young Giulio Makarios sat very still, absorbing everything. Shaggy, black hair framed his stubbly face, and his brown eyes darted about the room. On the table before him lay artifacts from a previous excavation recently undertaken in Istanbul. There were potsherds, hand-size crucifixes, and a few wooden panels in various states of decay. Figures with somber faces framed by halos were painted on each panel. These panels, Giulio recalled from his class notes, were icons of saints venerated by Byzantine Christians. The icons looked very old, perhaps dating back to the thirteenth or fourteenth century in Giulio's not-quite-yet-expert opinion. All the artifacts on the table were in plastic bags and labeled with dates, locations, and identification numbers. Such information, Giulio knew, established an artifact's provenance, an official record which authenticated it as a true piece of antiquity.

Next to Giulio sat his graduate school professor of ancient history, Dr. Papadopoulos, who was himself an ancient fixture at Phanar Greek Orthodox College in Istanbul. He was a serene and dignified but good-humored man with white hair swept back from a forehead lined with age. His gray, pinstripe suit was a bit too big for his thin frame. At one time Papadopoulos had regularly conducted field research in and around Istanbul, but a surgically replaced hip had long ago ended those days. He did no digging now; that was Giulio's job. Papadopoulos sat leaning forward, his wiry hands resting on the handle of his cane. Giulio had never seen Papadopoulos without his cane. It was made of bloodwood and crowned with an ivory handle, intricately carved. The carving depicted a basilica, the windows of which were painted green, red, or blue and the dome, a deep gold. Curiously, however, the basilica was upside down. Giulio had once asked Papadopoulos about it; his professor had smiled and replied that it was a mistake in the cane's manufacturing but that he liked it too much to have it corrected.

"What do you think of the celebrated Adam Burke?" Papadopoulos asked quietly, inclining his head toward Giulio.

Giulio shrugged noncommittally, not because he didn't have an opinion but because he wasn't sure he should say what he was thinking. That Adam Burke was celebrated in archaeological circles was an understatement. As Miller Family Chair of Byzantine Studies at Pitt University in the United States, he was one of the premier authorities on Byzantine antiquities. And he was a Disher. The Golden Boy of Dishing. He believed the Dish used by Jesus Christ at the Last Supper had yet to be found. He'd devoted his academic career to proving the Vatican's Dish a forgery. Most archaeologists believed the real Last Supper Dish was already on display at the Pius-Clementine Vatican Museum and had been in the possession of the Papacy since the early thirteenth century. Burke's opinions put him in the minority among scholars but in the majority on social media.

As even Giulio knew, Burke's work had been fueled by two finds related to the Dish: the first, in 1998, was his discovery of an icon of Saint Kostas in a dig near Zadar, Croatia. Saint Kostas, a Byzantine monk of the thirteenth century, was rumored to have been one of the Four Keepers of the Last Supper Dish. Though the Kostas icon

Burke found wasn't the only such icon known to exist, Burke's was in mint condition. Kostas, with his dark beard and eyes, stood holding a bowl, his halo aflame. On the icon's reverse side was a jagged line drawn next to two half-moons and a triangle. Theories abounded about what the markings signified. On the front side was a tantalizing Latin inscription. Every Kostas icon had one. In English, the inscription read:

Latin invaders, remember the words of Kostas:
God still guards the Queen of Cities
And her most precious treasure.
If you dare desire the Dish of Christ,
Go and find my brothers.

Kostas's brothers had to be a reference to Panikos, Zoticus, and Nil, the other three Keepers. Dishers believed the icons of the Keepers were the key to finding the real Dish, for an icon of Panikos in the British Museum also bore a Latin inscription:

Latin supplicants, study the message of Panikos:
Present yourselves at the gathering of the Twelve.
Kneel before Andrew and pray for your souls,
For you will soon enter the earth.

When that icon had been discovered (years before Burke's discovery of Kostas), Dishers had swarmed all the Saint Andrew churches in Europe, searching for a trap door somewhere, any kind of underground vault hiding the Dish. But they didn't find anything but catacombs.

Then, recently in Bulgaria, Burke had uncovered an icon of Saint Nil, the fourth member of the Four Keepers. No icon of Saint Nil had ever been uncovered, nor any of Zoticus. Regrettably, Burke's Nil was only partially intact, with its Latin inscription damaged. What was left of it read:

```
................................. Nil:
................ [ac]ross the sea
.................. the Queen of Cities
....................... sail again
............................. the rocks
..................... the port
................... ready.
```

Though two years had passed since then, the archaeological community was still reacting. Did the icons of the Keepers truly contain clues to finding the Dish as Dishers believed? Giulio had written a paper for Papadopoulos offering an interpretation of the inscription on the Nil icon. If he played his cards right (that is, if he ingratiated himself to Papadopoulos enough) he hoped to have his professor recommend his article to Burke for publication. Burke served as general editor of *The International Journal of Underground Knowledge* which promoted innovative Disher scholarship.

"In National Geographic, Burke looked taller," Giulio said to Papadopoulos. He knew his professor liked cleverness, and his joke brought a twinkle to Papi's eyes.

What Giulio wanted to say was that Burke's appearance disappointed him. The Golden Boy who posed with his artifacts in magazine photos was more dashing than this real-life, paunchy, freckled, balding Burke who gazed at people over the rectangular lenses of his wire-frame glasses. Those glasses were permanently planted halfway down the bridge of his round nose. The long sleeves of Burke's beige dress shirt were rolled up, exposing his pasty, hairless forearms, and his khakis were vintage 1980s—pleated and cuffed.

"Let's get to it," Burke said. He opened his laptop which was plugged into a projector set up on the front table. After tapping a few keys, he waved to his assistant, a young man seated by the back door. "Duffy—the lights."

A square field of bright blue appeared on the wall behind Burke's head. The blue field was crossed by red lines that broke and blurred in places. "Here we have a digital image from ground-penetrating radar. This is on the northern shore, the Fatih District, under what used to be the Sirkeci Rail Station. It has recently been demolished to make way for a passenger station for a new subway. If this were an overhead photograph, you'd see Halah Street running along the front entrance here." As Burke said this, he swiped his finger across the bottom edge of the image. He picked up a laser pointer.

"I believe—in consultation with Dr. Ayhan, of course—that these lines represent the walls of a Byzantine shrine." Burke paused to let his fellow Disher scholars take in the significance of his words. Among all the shrines in the world, only one mattered to Dishers. Was this the one? Had it finally been discovered? Burke grinned, hearing these murmured questions reach his ears, but he dared not mention the prized shrine by name. Hope could prevail, but it could also disappoint. And in any case, as an academic, he knew it was better to hedge and defer rather than to declare. Hasty, definitive statements could sink a career. So, with the laser pointer, Burke traced several thick lines near the left, right, and top borders of the image. The lines met at distinct right angles. "These outer walls suggest a Greek cross, each arm being of equal length. The southern walls don't appear to be intact. These red patches in the center must be portions of the collapsed central dome. It's just a guess, of course." *But my guesses are usually right.* He thought this but did not say it.

Burke returned to his laptop and punched another key. A zoomed-in image of the central red patches appeared. "The entire structure is eight meters below the surface and, oh, roughly 180 meters square, which is a size consistent with what we know of shrines built in the late Byzantine Empire—perhaps the thirteenth or fourteenth century." He turned toward the image as he spoke and crossed his arms. "Many shrines were constructed in that era as a last gasp of imperial greatness. The emperors sought to refuel the tourist industry after the Fourth Crusade of 1204. Pilgrims were a source of revenue, and they flocked to shrines, many traveling great distances. Recall the pilgrimage undertaken in Chaucer's Canterbury Tales. Medieval Christians believed shrines were portals to the heavenly realm and that the relics of the saints contained therein were touched by divinity. And for a small fee, a pilgrim too could be the beneficiary of a heavenly touch. Shrines where miracles were reported to have occurred grew in size and opulence. To visualize an equivalent structure to the one represented here, recall Saint Peter in Gallicantu, a Byzantine-styled shrine par excellence. The shrine is built on Mount Zion, south of Jerusalem, where according to biblical accounts, the disciple Peter denied knowing Jesus. Although the current construction dates from the 1930s, Gallicantu was rebuilt upon its original fifth-century foundations which—"

Burke had been speaking toward the image with his face upturned as if reciting a lecture set in his memory, but tittering in the audience made him pause. It was Dr. Stoltzfus wanting to know if they should be taking notes.

"Yes, you should be, Stoltzfus. This is all for you," Burke responded good-naturedly. "But these others," he gestured toward the rest of the audience, "I know are already well-informed." Everyone chuckled. Burke set down the pointer. "I can take a hint. But there'll be a quiz on your way out."

In the back of the room, Duffy flipped on the lights. Down in front Dr. Ayhan stood, and Burke with a gracious bow yielded the floor to her.

"Thank you, Adam," Ayhan began with a prim smile. "The prospects before us are immense. Istanbul is a city built on treasures waiting to be found. The monetary value of what we uncover may be considerable, but the historical and cultural implications are, of course, incalculable." Ayhan's smile grew as she spoke. "It is my pleasure to offer the facilities of the Museum of Ancient History for the duration of the excavation to process all recovered artifacts."

There was a smattering of appreciative applause.

# THE DIE IS CAST

"Having said that," Ayhan continued, her face sobering, "we will be beset with a few difficulties. I must speak to you now, not as a museum curator but as a representative of the excavation's proponents—the consortium of investors in the Marmara Metro Project as well as Turkey's Ministry of Transportation and Ministry of Culture and Tourism."

She paused, adjusting her red scarf. "First, some background on the Marmara Project for our international guests. The project—named for the Sea of Marmara, of course—will be an underground, high-speed rail connecting the European and Asian peninsulas of Istanbul. It will be a major transportation route for both people and freight and is vital to the future economy not only of Turkey but also of the surrounding nations in Europe and Asia. The construction of the massive tunnel beneath the Bosporus Strait has regrettably met with setbacks, and the project is already four years behind schedule and three billion dollars over budget. This state of affairs affects this excavation, not just because it was Marmara engineers who alerted us to the presence of a structure beneath the old Sirkeci Rail Station, but also because Marmara contractors cannot brook further delay on a project whose operating budget is already astronomical."

"What are you saying?" someone in the audience asked. It was Dr. Calvino.

Ayhan cleared her throat and glanced at Burke. "I'm saying we have ... only six weeks to complete the dig."

Calvino leaped to his feet. "Impossible!" Others seconded his sentiment, and concerned talk rippled through the assembly.

## THE DREAM TEAM

Ayhan raised her hands to quiet the room. "I assure you, we do have the full support of Marmara managers and the Ministries of Transportation and Tourism. In fact, it was Ahmet Öztürk, director of the Ministry of Culture and Tourism, who succeeded in negotiating a delay for us with Istanbul's Rail Bureau Chief, Feredun Pasa. Both men are sensitive to the cultural value of such a promising archaeological find, so we must be sensitive to their interests, which are—much as we would wish otherwise—time and money."

Dissatisfied muttering spread through the group. Ayhan gestured for Burke to rejoin her. "I hope you will agree at least that we have chosen the best principle investigator to coordinate our efforts?" With a quick smile to Burke, Ayhan retook her seat.

"Here, here!" Stoltzfus cheered, rallying several in the group to spontaneous applause.

"That's a nice touch, Stoltzfus," Burke said, grinning, "but there will still be that quiz."

Several in the audience chuckled, and the mood lightened. Burke signaled Duffy for the lights, and the radar image of the shrine again shone forth. "The truth is," Burke began, reaching for the laser pointer, "you've all been carefully chosen. Zainab and I have assembled the best team in the business. Look around you. You know why you're here. We all share the same passion, the same desire. We all share the same quest. You're here because you're Dishers. That should tell you something about the significance of this dig. Some of you I've partnered with before. A few of you I've wanted to meet—er, uh, Dr. Hromadova, for instance."

As he spoke, Burke forced a smile and nodded toward a young woman in the front row, the woman who'd cited him so extensively in her latest scholarly essay. Burke lived with a perpetual hope—the hope that a woman who approved of his mind might also be inclined to approve of him in other ways. He believed if such a woman were smart enough to recognize his genius, then she might be more willing to overlook his several physical deficiencies. It went without saying that a woman of such brains and inclinations would also be a woman of great beauty. Upon seeing Hromadova, however, Burke was disappointed on this latter point, and he winced as he smiled at her, relieved that the room was dark. "Each of you can be trusted with an undertaking of this magnitude," he went on, "and I'm grateful that you've spared no expense to make the journey." Burke twirled the pointer in his fingers, feeling in his element. "Given our time constraints, I've devised a plan that will get us to those walls with maximum speed," he paused for effect, "but I can't promise a miracle."

Burke began a technical disquisition on trenchers, industrial scrapers, and back hoes, which Marmara contractors were graciously lending to the excavation team to expedite dirt removal. Burke's plan was to advance toward the interior of the shrine through its destroyed southern face. Machinery, however, could only get them so close to the walls, and then they'd have to proceed by hand. "Even if we are in a rush, we can't risk accidentally damaging these walls because some operator pressed too hard on the gas pedal," Burke said to mild laughter.

In the back corner of the lab, however, Dr. Papadopoulos did not laugh. Since the start of Burke's presentation, the old professor had appeared stoic, almost indifferent, his lips curved in a frown. Giulio had noticed the change in Papi's demeanor. It was unexpected given the exciting nature of the discovery. The more Giulio had listened to Burke, the more he'd felt his own excitement mount, especially when he imagined himself behind the wheel of a front-end loader.

"What do you think, professor?" Giulio asked. "A Byzantine shrine—isn't it great?"

Papi sniffed. "Perhaps, perhaps. We shall see."

"You don't think it's a shrine? You don't think it could be ... *the one*?"

Papi gripped the top of his cane. "A shrine, a bathhouse, a commoner's home—who can say? It is possible you will dig for a week and find only potsherds." He gestured toward several plastic bags lying on the table. "Not glamorous at all. But still educational for you, of course." The friendly spark in his professor's eyes returned. But only for a moment. Papi looked away—at nothing in particular—and his face resumed its gravity.

Burke was thrusting some papers at his assistant Duffy for general distribution. It was the official schedule for the dig. As Burke explained, the assembled team was to be divided into four groups of 10-12 members each, with each group working in separate 6-hour shifts around the clock. The groups were to be led by Stoltzfus, Calvino, Hromadova, and Foo. Burke and Ayhan would generally oversee.

The group began to talk as each received a copy of the schedule. Giulio found his own name; he was assigned to work with Calvino.

"And I've noted here," Burke projected his voice over the chatter, "that Professor, uh ... Pa-poop-u-los—"

"Papadopoulos," Ayhan corrected with a whisper.

"Er, Papadopoulos, of course, will graciously assist us in the processing lab."

As Burke spoke, he stepped briefly into the line of the projector, and the blue and red image lit up half his face.

Giulio observed it. For a second it appeared to him that Golden Boy Burke had a giant red *X* on his forehead.

Scene 3

# Outlook Not So Good

*Office of Reggie Lovett*

*Midtown Manhattan*

*Tuesday, March 2*

"Man, you did it! What a performance. I got calls from both Miramax and Lionsgate for financing and distribution. The old backers are on board. You've got life, man, life! It'll be like it was before, like nothin' ever happened. No one will even remember Running on Fumes. Oh, man was I sweatin' when Kitty asked you about the Mystic 8 Ball, but Natalie was brilliant. Handled it beautifully. I just knew y'all could pull it off. I sent a thank-you to Kitty. Woman really saved your asses. Mmm-mm, is this tasty. Heaven is shinin' on us now. We are in the mo-ney!"

Reggie's eyes shone as he spoke to Ray. His role as Ray and Natalie's longtime producer meant that money was always the best news. He propped his feet on his desk and sipped a celebratory bourbon. Another glass—untouched—sat on a cocktail table before Ray. He slouched in a leather armchair and fiddled with a

TV remote. Kitty Lightly's heart-shaped face hung suspended on the TV screen like an apple bobbing in water. She was about to introduce Ray and Natalie. Reggie, who'd finagled their appearance on *Entertainment Now*, had recorded the interview.

"That's great news," Ray said. "Natalie will be thrilled." He smiled as he said this, but the enthusiasm in his voice was a mere simulation.

Reggie couldn't detect the difference and went on exuberantly. "Miramax wants to have a working title. Dish Movie doesn't quite cut it. I thought maybe Dishing for History. Talk to Natalie about it. Oh, man, I just knew if you two got back together, you'd work it all out. Everything is going so well. Your contributors are linin' up nicely. I confirmed that Steve Finder is on board, plus the archbishop in Istanbul, the museum curator Ayhan, and that professor at Oxford—Winters. Oh, the other one—Burke—he canceled. Secretary called, said he's goin' on some excavation, will be outta the country. But we can get some other Disher. Ask Natalie what she thinks. And last week, while y'all were filming at the Vatican museums, guess what? I secured your press passes. Won't get you an interview wit' the Pope, but it'll get you inside the ropes." Reggie grinned and swirled his bourbon, waiting for Ray to react to such good news.

But Ray didn't react. He was watching Kitty: "... after your incredible success with The Tent at Ground Zero, the two of you split up. Why stop a good thing? I mean, what happened?" The camera turned to Ray: "It was just creative fatigue, really. You see, after such success, it's not always clear where you wanna go next—creatively and professionally, I mean. And that film was very personal to us, very draining. New York City is our adopted home. We were there during 9/11. And the family at the center of the film—we've known them since our days at NYU (he gestured to Natalie, who nodded). So, emotionally, it was a very difficult documentary to make. And afterwards, we knew we needed time to recharge. Our solo projects provided that."

Ray frowned, irritated at his own lie, that he'd needed to lie at all. What he'd said to Kitty was true enough, but it wasn't the reason he and Natalie had separated. Not even close. The reason wasn't professional. It was personal.

"Hey," Reggie took his feet off his desk. "You hear me?"

"Hmm? Yeah. Miramax. Lionsgate."

Reggie scratched his bald, brown head, then drained the rest of his bourbon. "What's the matter wit' you? I got all this great career news, and you just sittin' there."

"Dude, we just got back from Italy. I'm tired."

Another lie. Ray picked up his untouched glass of bourbon but didn't take a sip. He kept his eyes on Kitty: "... well-known that you took your name 8 Ball Productions from the toy, the Mystic 8 Ball. Like, omigod!" A production assistant lobbed a Mystic 8 Ball to Kitty. She caught it and lifted it over her head in victory. The audience cheered. "Am I the best show host ever?" she giggled, shaking the ball. The Mystic 8 Ball's inner white die floated up through deep blue liquid and pressed one of its twenty faces against the transparent window. "Omigod," Kitty squealed. "It says—As I see it, yes!" The audience roared. Kitty tossed Natalie the ball.

"Wanna play? I thought you'd have your toy with you, and we could play together. Like, where is it?"

Grimacing, Ray set his bourbon back down and stood. He crossed Reggie's midtown Manhattan office and peered out the window onto West 53rd Street. It was early evening, the hour when boundaries fade, turning windows into mirrors. From only three stories up, Ray could see snow swirling and pedestrians scurrying along bundled in hats and scarves. March had come in like a lion. As Ray looked on, his own reflection got in the way. He saw his own chestnut hair, his gray eyes and unshaven face. Across the street at the Sheraton Hotel, a man loaded a suitcase into a taxi.

He hadn't turned off the TV. At his back, he could hear Natalie answering Kitty's question: "... an object so fundamental to us, something that brought us together, well, it's long lost its status as a toy. But we used to play with it a lot. Especially while we were filming Monica's Dress. When things got tense, it always made us laugh. It belongs to Ray, actually. He first suggested using it when we were in film school. We couldn't decide if we should call our first film The Full Chester, which to me sounded like porn, or Milkshake and Sixpence, which I took from the title of a Somerset Maugham novel. The ball chose Ray's title, The Full Chester. It must know what it's doing since we won at Tribeca. Ha-ha. So, now the Mystic 8 Ball is like a sacred relic to us. An object to be guarded. I'd never part with it."

Ray shook his head and thrust his hands in his pockets. He saw his own face again in the window. He disliked how his reflection seemed to drift above the street like a tethered balloon. Over at the Sheraton, the taxi drove away.

Reggie left his desk and turned off the TV. "Don't blame her for lying. What could she do? Like I said, I thought she handled it beautifully. Kitty didn't know it's a sore subject."

Ray said nothing. A shadow of sadness and anger clung to him. For the three years he'd been without Natalie, the shadow had latched itself to his every word or action, sapping his vitality. He couldn't get rid of it. His friendship with Natalie had been the most important of his life; she was the only woman who'd ever taken his ideas seriously. With her, there was more possibility in the world. He'd always sought to prove himself worthy of her admiration. And for one moment, he thought he'd gained it totally. He'd hoped that seeing her again (Reggie had arranged the reunion in December) would dispel the shadow. But it hadn't. His sadness and anger had deepened and thickened like the ink in his lost Mystic 8 Ball. A ball Natalie had lost. Like his heart, she'd thrown it away.

Reggie rubbed his chin, searching for words. He stooped over his desk to retrieve some papers. "Look, uh, these documents here, you'll need 'em to get your press passes. When you get to Istanbul, go to the Church of—"

"Y'know, Regg, right before we went on the show, I complimented her. Said she looked great. But she turned it around on me. Made a joke about my Detroit documentary. Said Kitty's brain needed a fill-up."

Reggie wasn't sure he should laugh, so he didn't. He waited for Ray to go on.

"She has to know Running on Fumes was—well, I don't have to tell you. I remember one critic said it needed fuel. Why do people have to be so clever when they insult you?"

"Maybe you misunderstood her," Reggie said.

Ray scoffed. "No, I know her. Always has to be so smart. Not that her film was any better. I saw it, y'know—Almost a Loneliness. You said it was about us. I still don't see how. All the woman in the film did was throw furniture out of her house, write poems, and ride around on her bike."

Ray's tone was bitter. He glanced at Reggie's reflection in the window. Reggie's bald, brown head was haloed by light from a ceiling fixture. "You told me she said she missed me, that she needs me," Ray said. "That she has deep regrets, that she knows she was wrong. So, why doesn't she say so? She won't talk about what happened. It's been three months. What should I do?"

Reggie puffed out his cheeks in a long exhale.

"I never would've agreed to film the Dish Movie with her if you hadn't convinced me," Ray went on. "Did she *really* tell you she needs me?" There was accusation in his voice.

Reggie threw up his hands. "Man, what can I say? Why would I lie to you? Can you tell me that?"

Ray couldn't think of a reason why Reggie would lie. He'd produced *Monica's Dress* and *The Tent at Ground Zero*, walked across the stage with him and Natalie to accept the Academy Award for Best Documentary Feature, and he was their friend. He knew the reason they'd separated. He wouldn't lie about something so important.

Ray faced Reggie. "Forget I asked."

Reggie joined Ray at the window; it only took him two strides, for he was as wide and as tall as a linebacker. He handed Ray the documents for their press passes. "Look, man, give her time. Y'all can't work everything out at once. Focus on the Dish Movie. It's a film y'all have wanted to make for a long time, isn't it?"

"Since film school," Ray said. "Natalie's crazy roommate was a Disher. We thought she was highly entertaining."

"See? You both are committed to the story. I've always loved the idea. It's got great potential. A familiar subject will help you re-establish a working relationship. That's why I suggested it. You gotta get your careers back on track. After that, the rest will fall into place." He looked at Ray intently. "Plus, she needs to trust you."

Ray snorted, catching Reggie's drift. "Staci wasn't a factor. Believe me. She never meant anything to me."

Reggie pinched his lips together in a show of disbelief.

Ray detected this. "What? You think it was my fault?" He retrieved his coat from a chair and tucked the documents Reggie had given him into an interior pocket. "If it'd been up to me, Natalie would never have married that idiot Peagram. You know that."

Reggie shrugged. "Staci. Peagram. It was a complicated situation. I'm sure Natalie sees it differently."

"Don't I know it. She always tells herself stories. And she sticks to 'em. You can't persuade imagination." Ray crossed to the door. "I gotta go. I'm on the clock. You know how she is with schedules."

Reggie followed him. "Don't go to the studio mad. I just gave you good news. When you tell her, she'll be happy. Make it work for you. 'Cause she needs to feel you want it to work. You blame her, it'll scare her off. Don't do it, man. I got a lot invested in y'all. A lot invested."

"I don't blame her," Ray said. *Not to her face.* He added this last part mentally so as not to feel he was lying. He put his hand on the doorknob.

"Good. Give it time," Reggie said. "Don't press the issue. Let it develop. She divorced Peagram, didn't she? That should tell you something. Now that he's gone, she'll come around. Trust me."

"I do."

Reggie clapped Ray on the shoulder. "You two are good business—together. Take my advice and y'all will have your names in lights again in no time. And I like my name in lights too. Ha-ha. You won't let me down, right?"

Ray swore he wouldn't and tugged open the door. Once he stepped onto the sidewalk of West 53rd Street, large snowflakes coated his hair and eyelashes. He hailed a cab. "One forty-nine 5th Avenue," he told the driver, then settled back into the seat, reaching into his coat to make sure he had the papers Reggie had given him. He did.

One forty-nine 5th Avenue was the location of the Sound Lounge, a studio across the street from the iconic Flatiron Building in the Flatiron District. Natalie had suggested the new location. Formerly, they'd used Midtown Studios, but they couldn't go back there. Not after what had happened.

Ray felt his gut clench, remembering. When he looked at Natalie, it was often all he could think about. He wondered if she felt the same. She didn't seem to. For three months their conversations had been entirely professional and always about the present. *How much time does she need?* Despite Reggie's counsel to wait, Ray was losing patience. He tried to be generous, supposing that if *he* were the one who had to apologize, he might delay his confession too. He was sure when Natalie did apologize, he'd forgive her.

Because of the snow, traffic proceeded tentatively. At the intersection of 7th Avenue and West 45th Street, Ray instinctively looked out the window to his right even though they weren't turning that way. Two blocks in that direction was Midtown Studios. He immediately thought of Natalie, of that fateful night three years before. He saw an image of her in tears and himself helpless to do anything. He'd never seen her cry, never encountered such grief from her or from any woman. Experiencing it had terrified him:

It was a Monday night in August. Their film *The Tent at Ground Zero* was set to premier on September 8th, right before the fifth anniversary of 9/11. Reggie had thrown a party at his place a week before. Ray was at the studio watching the film one last time, not expecting Natalie to show up. He thought the studio a safe place to hide, as he could no longer cloak his frustration over her infatuation with that uptight British egghead, the cultural studies professor, Geoffrey Peagram.

She arrived at the studio anyway, wearing the tight, distressed leather jacket he liked. Her hair was up in a ponytail; when she sat down on the futon, it swished over her shoulder. He loved it when her hair was up; something about the openness of her face made her seem very touchable.

She had news—Geoffrey had proposed over the weekend. She wore a big diamond ring. Ray was invited the next Saturday to an engagement party. He didn't want to go. Natalie pressed him for the reason. He gave excuses. They didn't satisfy her. "You're not happy for me?" she asked. He, at the computer, kept his back to her. They started to argue.

"I'll come to the wedding," he said.

"If you're invited."

"C'mon, Nat, you know I—"

"Don't call me that. Geoffrey doesn't like it."

"Oh, what—I have to watch everything I say now?"

"Not *everything*. Don't blow things out of proportion."

Ray's frustration boiled over. "I'll just start calling you Mrs. *Pea* Gram. He'll like that."

Natalie grabbed her messenger bag and strode toward the door.

"What, so you're leaving now?" he said.

"What does it look like?"

"C'mon, wha'd I say?"

"Look, if I have to tell you—God, Ray, sometimes you're so stupid."

Her words both accused and pleaded; he felt wounded yet ignited. He got up; he didn't want her to leave. Not ever. He'd kept a secret from her, the secret of his love. It was far past time for him to tell her. As Natalie reached the door, he grabbed her just above her elbow. The strap of her bag fell off her shoulder. Her lips were so close; he knew just what he wanted to do with them, what he'd been waiting to do for a long time. She kissed him back passionately and gasped, losing balance. He restored it by pushing her hips against the door. She touched his face eagerly. He shuddered, unable to contain his joy. His breath quickened in bursts, like laughter. When he carried her to the futon, she hugged his neck and whispered, "Don't stop." He didn't.

But then, at the height of their lovemaking, Natalie began to weep as if she'd break apart. Caressing her did nothing to shield her from the shadow of sadness that had descended. What had he done to cause such grief? He'd risked himself, risked *them*. He should've taken the risk long before. Finally, he had—to save her from marrying the wrong man. She'd urged him to hold her. She'd taken the risk with him. But her tears told him she regretted it. Why? Desperately, he sought to fight the shadow swallowing her.

"Nat, please don't cry. Why are you crying?"

Natalie's eyes were shut. She covered her mouth with the back of her hand.

Ray thought if he could get her to speak, then she would accept what they had done—what it meant. "You ... you don't love him. You thought you did, but you don't. That's what I think. That was my theory all along."

"I—I don't—know," she managed to say.

Ray felt a spasm of panic. Maybe he hadn't won her after all. He was still in danger of losing. He couldn't let that happen. He searched for the right words to guide her back to that feeling that had told him *don't stop*. "I think you do know." He smiled, hoping she'd smile back at him.

"No, I don't know."

"Trust me, this proves it. I'm right. You don't really love him. I think I win."

Natalie pinched her brows. She raised up on one elbow and looked him full in the face. "How can you say that?"

"What? Wha'd I say? You don't think this proves it?"

She sat up. "Is this just a game to you? Am I just the ball you slam through the hoop?"

He didn't understand her question, but her tone crushed his confidence. He reached for her. "Weren't you playing along with me?"

She pushed him away. "This is my life, Ray. My *life*." She fled his side and gathered her strewn clothes.

He cursed. The shadow of grief that had enveloped her was winning. How could he beat it? The Mystic 8 Ball! It was a toy, but it'd brought them together. Its answers always made Natalie laugh. Laughter would dispel her grief. His words had failed. He would let the 8 Ball speak.

Ray grabbed the toy from a chair. "Should Nat marry Pea Gram?" He tossed it in the air.

"How dare you ask it such a question."

Ray held his breath. He turned the ball over and gazed at the dark, round window. The white die bubbled up, dispersing the liquid shadows. Outlook not so good, it said.

"See," Ray grinned in relief. "I'm right. Ha! I'm right."

Natalie's eyes were hollow, despondent. She shook her head. "Goodbye, Ray."

Weeks later in September, after the release of their film, Natalie left for London. She was going to marry Geoffrey; they were planning a December wedding. Ray implored her not to go. She couldn't be persuaded. "I don't exist to prove your theories right," she told him. "And you're wrong—I do love him. We have a lot in common.

He's steady and reliable. I trust him. He needs me. All this time you and I have been friends, you never—" she broke off, a quaver in her voice. "You can't expect me to believe you—" she broke off again. "Oh, it should never have happened. My God, that night you made me feel like I'd lost my mind."

When the taxi stopped opposite the Flatiron Building, Ray didn't immediately recall the directions he'd given the driver. "Why are we stopping?" he asked stupidly. The driver gave him a look. Ray pushed open the car door, wishing to leave these thoughts of his night with Natalie behind as he might leave a day-old newspaper on the seat. If only shedding his past with her were so easy.

For three years he'd tried to move on with his life, but he kept circling back. The seeds of his sadness and anger, like magnets, drew him. *Don't stop.* Two little words whispered in his ear. Life-giving words. He'd listened. He hadn't stopped. But *she* had. Her two words had been a promise of more, of a future. But she'd given him nothing.

Such a betrayal, he could never forget.

▂ ▂ ▂ ▂

From her usual spot at the bar table, Natalie sat high up on a perch chair. She flicked her wavy brunette hair off one shoulder and impatiently fiddled with the straw in her water bottle. She re-crossed her legs, reaching for the foot ring of the chair with the toe of her boot. The chair was suited for a taller woman. Natalie was slim and petite. She wore little makeup, nothing to accentuate her intense green eyes. If not for its aura of sadness, it would've been a very pretty face. In her periphery she could see the comfortable leather sofa right next to the bar table. She never sat there. Ray did. That was his spot. Their first day at the Sound Lounge, they'd both made their choices and hadn't deviated since.

Across from Natalie at the soundboard sat Clark Cannon, her and Ray's longtime videographer. His meticulous camerawork on *Monica's Dress* and *The Tent at Ground Zero* had been no small part of the success of 8 Ball Productions. He wore a white t-shirt and camouflage pants. His wavy black hair, the genetic gift of his Samoan mother, was gathered in the back, and about his neck hung a ball chain from which dangled two dog tags that had belonged to his grandfather.

On a large screen before them ran footage they'd filmed days before in Vatican City. They were outside the Pius-Clementine Museum. An elderly woman and her attractive blonde granddaughter waited in line to get in. The women were French tourists from Le Havre. "Why are you here? What have you come to see?" (Ray's voice). "Je suis venu voir le bol du Christ," the elder woman replied. "What does she say?" (Ray's voice again). The granddaughter translated: "She says she's here to see the bowl of Christ." "Why is it so important to see the bowl?" Ray asked. The elder woman answered quickly. "C'est sacré. Le seul objet qu'il a touché." "She says it is sacred," the granddaughter explained. "It is the one object he touched."

"Fast-forward a little," Natalie said, merely to say something, to test her voice. She struggled to concentrate, staring instead at the back of Clark's head. She wanted to ask him a question—a question about Ray—and now was her opportunity before Ray arrived.

Clark clicked a button.

Natalie smoothed an imaginary wrinkle in her skirt, a wildly styled safari print. She was thinking how best to word her question. "That's far enough."

Clark hit *play* and the scene shifted to the interior of the museum, to the Greek-Cross Room where on a marble pedestal under glass sat the Last Supper Dish. A protective barrier kept visitors at a two-meter distance. A placard explained that the bowl was a typical Roman design for festive tableware—terra sigillata, round, on a ring base, its exterior decorated with leaf-scrolls in low-relief. It rotated gently on a trivet beneath soft lights. The elderly French woman and her granddaughter reappeared. When the elderly woman saw the Dish, she crossed herself and genuflected. A lavish mural to the right of the Dish depicted The Last Supper. Unlike the other disciples at the table, the betrayer Judas sat with his back to Jesus. He held an open money bag full of silver coins, the price at which he had valued his master. Next to this mural was another depicting the Garden of Gethsemane. Jesus was about to be arrested. Judas had arrived with armed men. The artist had painted Judas kissing Jesus on the cheek. On a scroll above Jesus' head was his reply: "Judas, are you betraying the Son of Man with a kiss?"

Natalie cleared her throat loudly. "Hey, can you pause it there a minute?"

Clark did so and swiveled in his chair to face her.

Natalie lowered her eyes. Now that she had Clark's attention, she hesitated to follow through. She felt absurd at what she was about to ask, but she just had to know. She wasn't convinced Ray would tell her the truth. "Um, I've wanted to ask you—because you know Ray and I so well. And you worked with Ray on Running on Fumes, but—but now here we all are again, and—" she looked up at him, "well, I've wanted to know if you've seen Staci recently."

Staci. The tall, lithe, platinum blonde fashion model who boasted about her breast implants and dotted the *i* in her name with a big, bulging heart. Natalie hadn't seen the woman since the night Ray had brought her to Reggie's party in celebration of finishing *The Tent at Ground Zero*. Nor did she wish to see her. Kitty Lightly's near resemblance had been painful enough.

Clark smirked. "Not since Running on Fumes."

Natalie's heart beat hard. "She was in Detroit when you were filming?"

"Part of the time. At first. You know how she is. Flies in. Giggles and jiggles. Flies out."

Natalie was too upset by this news to think of a follow-up question.

Clark saw the look in her eyes. He dropped his voice reassuringly: "Look, that was two years ago. She's long gone. She's not coming back. Believe me."

"How do you know?"

Clark shrugged. "You saw the film, didn't you?"

Natalie looked aside. Ray had always wanted to make a documentary about the rise and fall of Detroit's auto industry, but the idea had always struck her as cliché. Ray's attempt to make the film without her had failed miserably. It was just like him—undisciplined. Halfway through watching it, she'd given up counting the number of rabbit trails. The only interesting part had been his recurrent image of the black and gold Pontiac Firebird. Evidently, he'd intended it to be a symbol, though of what, she didn't know. Symbolism had never been Ray's strength.

"You mean Staci left him?" she asked. "Over the film?"

Clark nodded. "Took up with some Italian actor. He'd just won an award. Got her a bit part in some movie. Don't know the details. Don't want to."

Natalie pursed her lips. *Always thought she was after a film career.* She sat back in her chair to process Clark's news. Ever since December when she and Ray had met in Reggie's office for the first time in over two years, she'd been waiting for Ray to apologize to her for his betrayal. Reggie had assured her that Ray took full responsibility for what had happened, that he wanted to make things right. "He's heartsick," Reggie had said. "He's lost without you." Ray? Heartsick? Lost? she'd responded doubtfully. Then why didn't he reach out to her on his own? "Because, uh, he thinks you must despise him. Do you?" No, she'd said, not if he was heartsick. Only Reggie's revelations of Ray's remorse had convinced her to work with Ray again. But now she was losing patience. Why wouldn't Ray apologize?

"So, it isn't Staci," Natalie said under her breath.

"What?" Clark asked.

"Nothing. You can resume the footage."

Clark swiveled his chair to do just that, but then he looked back at Natalie. "Like, I don't wanna get involved and stuff," he glanced at the ceiling, "but, well, I hope this time you guys work it out."

Natalie's arched her eyebrows in curiosity. "Did Ray ever tell you why it didn't work?"

"No," Clark said, "and I didn't ask. It was obvious. He loved you. But you didn't love him. Not enough, I guess."

Natalie blinked in disbelief. "Didn't love him? You—you think it was all my fault?"

Clark shrugged.

"Did Ray ever tell you he loved me?"

"Didn't have to. Guys know when a dude's got it bad."

"But what about Staci?"

Clark snorted, signaling that this was a stupid question.

Natalie felt her face flush. She said nothing.

Clark turned back to the soundboard and resumed the footage of the Vatican museum.

But it was impossible for Natalie to watch anymore. She told Clark she needed a break. With no destination in mind, she left the studio and walked down the hallway toward the elevator. Once there, she took the elevator down to the lobby. Snow was falling hard. She retreated from the building's entrance and sat to one side of the lobby in a chair next to a sickly palm. She massaged her brows with her fingers.

Words and images from her night with Ray at Midtown Studios came back to her—what he'd done, what he'd said. *I win.* Just two little words, but they'd been so destructive. He could've said many things. He could've said that he loved her. But he hadn't.

"You're wrong, Clark. So wrong," she murmured. She sat up and ran her hand through her hair. How many years had she been in love with Ray? Probably since she first saw him at a party when they were in film school. He'd flirted with two tall blondes—Angela and Staci—for most of the night. Natalie hadn't even bothered to introduce herself, quickly surmising that she had no chance. She tried to put him out of her mind. But his boyish physique, his energy, his dramatic storytelling attracted her. She could overhear him telling a funny one: he'd sneaked into a Lollapalooza concert without a ticket and somehow ended up backstage with the Red Hot Chili Peppers before security threw him out. Without him even knowing it, he'd made her laugh.

Just then, as Natalie watched, Ray entered the lobby. She couldn't see his face. He didn't notice her and crossed to the elevator. He stood with his hands in his coat pockets, his hair shimmering with melted snow. *He loved you. But you didn't love him.* The elevator opened. Ray vanished.

*No, Clark, it was the opposite.* She'd loved Ray for years, but at some juncture during the filming of *Monica's Dress*, she'd wearied of hoping. They were friends and filmmaking partners, and that's all they would ever be. Ray was like a child, attracted to shiny objects. Their friendship was solid, real. It didn't dazzle. She couldn't make him love her that way. Sometimes she thought that theirs could've been a great love story. But Ray had never wanted it to be.

And then she'd met Geoffrey.

That night in August, days after Geoffrey had proposed, she'd called Ray several times. But he wouldn't answer or call her back. They had to talk. Geoffrey didn't want to live in the States. She'd have to move to London.

## THE DIE IS CAST

What this would mean for 8 Ball Productions, she wasn't sure. Filming *Tent at Ground Zero* had been such a difficult project. Maybe they needed a break—a long one. She didn't want to tell Ray this over the phone. She'd gone to the studio on a whim to see if he was there.

He was, wearing the dark blue Henley shirt she liked— unbuttoned—it was always that way. He wore the shirt so frequently that it was saturated with his scent. She'd often thought Ray smelled like summer. When she told him the news about her engagement, he couldn't be bothered to attend the party. He had no believable reason. Maybe he didn't like Geoffrey, but couldn't he be happy for her? she asked. They started to argue:

"I'll come to the wedding."

"If you're invited."

"Oh, c'mon, Nat, you know I—"

"Don't call me that. Geoffrey doesn't like it."

"Oh, what—I have to watch everything I say now?"

"Not *everything*. Don't blow things out of proportion."

"I'll just start calling you Mrs. *Pea* Gram. He'll like that."

She was sitting on a futon; she grabbed her messenger bag and headed toward the door. Because she hated how Ray always pronounced Geoffrey's last name as if it were two words. And he knew she hated it. Why did he have to provoke her? She couldn't talk to him like this.

"What, so you're leaving now?" he said.

"What does it look like?"

"C'mon, wha'd I say?"

She was angry. She wanted to wound him for all the years he'd left her hoping. "Look, if I have to tell you— God, Ray, sometimes you're so stupid."

She seized the doorknob. Abruptly, she felt a tug at her shoulder. Ray had grabbed the strap on her bag. She stumbled backwards; the bag fell to the floor. Ray took hold of her arm. He stood there clutching her above the elbow. His eyes sought hers. She was about to form the words, "What are you doing?" when suddenly his lips were on hers and his right arm held her waist. She felt such shock—and such energy—she kissed him back hard. She thought she'd set all her desire for him aside. She'd stopped hoping. But here were his lips, and she couldn't stop kissing them. When he slipped one hand up between her shoulder blades, under her jacket, she drew back, feeling weak and unbalanced. He restored her sense of grounding by pushing her hips against the door. She touched his face, feeling a surge of heat. It swirled up her torso and rose into her throat. The breath between his kisses was like laughter. She felt as if all her emotions were struggling to claim possession of her, each one stretching and gripping her heart.

She'd never felt such passion. She didn't want to lose it, but he could take it all away. Were these kisses real? Did he love her? After all this time? She couldn't form any words. "Don't stop," she managed to whisper.

He had no words either. They made love without speaking. The room was silent; their film which had been running on the computer—Ray had not turned it off—came to an end, and the screen went black. Her heart seemed to fly apart. But it was like an explosion in outer space; there was no sound, just motion. Natalie felt the silence all around her like swiftly moving clouds, billowing and expanding. There were no words to moor her;

she was totally unbound. As Ray held her, she started to cry, weeping into the silence—long, gasping, seizing sobs. She didn't know why. She couldn't control herself. The energy she shared with Ray had taken over. Her mind didn't seem to work.

Ray tried to explain her emotions to her:

"Nat, please don't cry. Why are you crying?"

She tried to focus on his beautiful eyes, but through her tears, his face was a blur. She had no words to answer him.

"You ... you don't love him. That's what I think. You thought you did, but you don't. That was my theory all along."

"I—I don't—know."

"I think you do." He smiled, a teasing, ironic smile it seemed, as if he were withholding the punchline of a joke.

"No, I don't know."

"Believe me, this proves it. I'm right. You don't really love him. I think I win."

Win? What had he won? She could only think of Geoffrey, the man she'd promised to marry just days before. She suddenly felt the weight of her engagement ring. And then, in the very same instant, she thought of Staci. In her stilettos and skin-tight cocktail dress, she'd jiggled her breasts all over Reggie's party. Ray hadn't been able to keep his hands off her. Natalie had even seen them kissing.

"How can you say that?" She swiped her tears off her cheeks and raised up on one elbow. Clarity had returned to her mind. *I'm Staci. Just a prize.*

She fled his side, feeling a piercing betrayal. His kisses had merely been moves in a game. She was the joke. He was laughing at her. Playing was all he was capable of. He tossed the Mystic 8 Ball in the air, asking it a ridiculous question, making a toy of her heart.

Remembering that night with Ray, Natalie trembled, shaken afresh by a conviction that she'd found something hollow in Ray's heart, something insubstantial, a shadow. She'd run from it. She'd married Geoffrey. But it had trailed her. She couldn't quite lose it. Nor fight it off.

But wanting to be rid of it had brought her back.

In sadness she looked up, imagining Ray in the studio with Clark, waiting for her. As she still waited for him. Would he ever make things right with her?

*It could've been a great love story.*

Scene 4

# A Package Examined

*Atlanta, Georgia*

*Monday, March 8*

The Summit Art Museum had just opened for the day when Jane Whitaker zipped her Range Rover into a parking space. Her Rover was white with customized baby-blue racing stripes. From the rearview mirror dangled a locket that Jane often wore; it held a picture of Baby Girl. Jane's Rover had been a high school graduation gift from her father. The locket and its picture, however, shared a different history.

Jane had just come from the airport. Swiftly, she stepped out of the Rover and opened the back-passenger door. She hadn't come to the museum alone; Baby Girl was curled up in a ball against the rear seat. It was the usual defensive posture of the little dog whenever it had to ride in a car. The shock of sudden momentum sent it in search of firmer ground, as it was so easily tossed about. Convertibles were especially an anathema; it instinctively sensed the danger of blowing away and wedged itself on the floor between people's feet. In her Rover, Jane often forgot to defer to Baby Girl's fears and drove with all the windows rolled down.

## A PACKAGE EXAMINED

Before leaving the airport, Baby Girl had suffered an accident of nature. In a restroom, Jane had swapped its soiled blue sweater for a pink one—cashmere, with its name stitched in sea green thread around the throat. In one motion Jane collected the little dog and the brown-paper package that lay on the seat next to it. With these two treasures secured in her Versace jacket, she hurriedly weaved her way through the parking lot.

"Omigod! Not kids!"

Two school buses were parked at the front curb, and a swarm of children buzzed about. If Jane didn't beat them all to the museum doors, then she'd suffer unendurable delay. They were blocking the front walkway, and there was no detour. Jane pushed through them, stepping on small toes. Baby Girl assisted, snapping at stray, poking fingers.

Free of the bevy of tiny feet, Jane broke into a run. The morning clouds appeared stormy; the air was unusually cold for a March day in Atlanta. But momentarily the clouds parted, and a shaft of sunlight fell squarely on the museum's porcelain-enameled exterior, making it gleam bright white. Jane might've interpreted this well-timed light as a heavenly sign if she'd been paying attention. But just at that moment, Baby Girl decided to be squirmy, and Jane had to reach inside her jacket to keep the brown-paper package from falling out. Thus, she didn't notice the shaft of sunlight, nor the silver sedan that had pulled into the lot behind her. Nor did she see the man in dark glasses who'd gotten out of the sedan and stood next to it, watching her.

At last she passed within the shadow of the museum's glass atrium. The doors flashed before her and she burst through them (or tried to—they were revolving) and dashed to the front desk. "Is Dr. Carlisle in? I'm here to see Dr. Carlisle." A tuft of fox fur from her jacket collar stuck to her lip gloss as she spoke, and she brushed it away impatiently. A droopy woman with two chins occupied the front desk. A new employee, Jane surmised. At least, in all her visits to the museum to see Dr. Carlisle, Jane had never encountered her. The woman's face and hair had succumbed to gravity. She peered at Jane vacantly over her glasses.

"I called him this morning," Jane continued quickly, "but he wasn't in. I left a message. Just tell him it's Jane—" she paused, catching herself. She didn't like to use the Whitaker name unless she had to. And she didn't know if she had to in this instance. "It's just ... Jane. Dr. Carlisle knows me."

These details moved the woman not at all; her eyes fell on Baby Girl's head peeking from Jane's jacket. "We don't allow pets," she said by rote.

"Oh, she's not a pet."

The woman lifted her two chins and squinted through her glasses. "Is it stuffed?"

"Ha-ha. No, she's real. See? Baby Girl, wave to the nice woman." Jane gripped one of the dog's forepaws and waved it up and down.

"Our policy is no pets. You'll have to leave it outside." With a flick of her wrist, the woman waved Jane aside.

"I told you—she's not a pet. She's an E-S-A. Here, see?" Jane rolled down the neck of Baby Girl's sweater and pulled out a pink collar with a little silver heart dangling from it.

"So?" The woman's tone belied true curiosity.

## A PACKAGE EXAMINED

"Can't you see it?"

"It's a dog collar."

"Ha-ha. Yes, but see it's stamped right there—E-S-A—which means E-mo-tion-al Sup-port Animal. I have her official certificate and everything." Jane tucked the collar back under Baby Girl's sweater.

The woman looked Jane up and down. "Whatcha need emotional support for? It's just a museum."

"Oh, ha-ha. No, she goes with me everywhere."

"Everywhere?"

"Yep."

For the first time, the woman became faintly animated. The corners of her lips twitched, and she tapped her fingernails on the desk. "Is it trained?" she asked.

Jane rolled her eyes. "Yes, I understand I'm responsible for accidents."

"No, I mean did you have it trained at a school for dogs?"

"Oh, no, nothing like that."

"But you have a certificate. So, it had to pass a test?"

"Not exactly."

"Well, what are its skills?"

"All ya gotta do is fill out a form online and register, and they'll mail the collar to you and stuff. It's super easy. Anyone can do it. Isn't that right, Baby Girl?" Jane kissed the head of the little dog.

"Who's *they*?"

"It cost, like, only seventy bucks or something. Look, can I see Dr. Carlisle? I'm kinda in a hurry."

"No skills at all. For heaven's sake," the woman laughed, her chins jiggling. Without the slightest seriousness, she dialed Carlisle's extension.

# THE DIE IS CAST

Jane pretended not to have heard this remark; she glanced up at the atrium's glass ceiling. Swift gathering clouds had displaced the sun. Everything was gray; it was just like the day she'd gotten off the bus in Göreme, Turkey.

Dr. Carlisle was finishing up a conference call. Would she mind waiting?

Grudgingly, Jane stepped aside. Near an abstract sculpture to her left was a bench, and she perched herself on the edge of it, unzipped her jacket, and set her package and Baby Girl in her lap. The placard next to the sculpture identified its title: *My Mother's Desire*. Jane read the title absently and glanced at the sculpture, though she'd seen it often enough. It was eight feet high, the color of American cheese, and full of holes and dimples like a sponge. Its shape was oval but puckered on one side like a lima bean. At the very top, a protuberance resembling a face without eyes grinned grotesquely. None of this interested Jane.

Instead, she busied herself picturing Dr. Carlisle's face when she showed him what she'd found in Göreme. After years of skepticism, he'd finally be convinced, for to Jane there were only two kinds of people in the world—Dishers (such as herself) and Dish-deniers (such as Dr. Carlisle)—and it was the duty of Dishers not only to find the lost Last Supper Dish but also to convert Dish-deniers to the belief that it was, indeed, possible to find it. Jane had been working on Dr. Carlisle for several years. He was an expert in Middle Eastern antiquities. She knew this time she'd brought him irrefutable evidence.

How long could a conference call be?

## A PACKAGE EXAMINED

Jane tapped her feet impatiently, upsetting Baby Girl. Or perhaps the little dog was upset because the children had arrived. As a rule, Baby Girl disliked the presence of other small things. Through the holes in the sponge-like sculpture, Jane could see the children stepping through the revolving door in pairs. They were all dressed identically in khaki pants and blue polo shirts. Their chatter echoed through the atrium, a sound which reminded Jane of the marketplace in Göreme. It'd always been crowded with Americans. Everywhere she'd gone in Göreme she'd met a fellow Disher from the States. When she'd first arrived in town, she'd found it so overrun with Dishers that it'd taken her a whole afternoon just to find a hotel. And later that night, she'd waited over an hour to get a table at the popular Café Safak. Now, over three weeks later, there was still something vaguely disappointing to her about these facts.

Clearly, she wasn't the only reader of *TrueDishers.net*, a website held by Dishers to be the definitive source for all things Dishing. Jane read the weekly archaeological news feed which reported on excavations, discoveries, and scholarly opinions relevant to the imminent recovery of the Last Supper Dish. And its recovery was always imminent; the website's contributors were quite confident. "The persistent press of truth overthrows even the foulest of lies." So wrote Jimi Bowler, Jane's favorite Disher blogger; he always had such a way of putting things. Readers of the website called him The Disher with the Golden Tongue.

"Ms. Whitaker," a voice said behind her.

Jane secured her package and Baby Girl and jumped up. "Dr. Carlisle!"

"I'm sure I know what this is about, but I'm very busy today, Ms. Whitaker."

Carlisle was a short and jittery man with a high forehead and thinning hair. His face was unremarkable except for his perpetually red nose. And he always wore a tweed jacket and bow tie. The utter predictability of his appearance had early on assured Jane that no matter their disagreements about Dishing, this was a man to be trusted.

"You've heard about the Karanlik Kilise?" Jane exclaimed, her eyes wide.

"Er, uh, no." Carlisle spied the package in her hand. "Brought me another souvenir, I see. What is it this time?"

"Something you must see," Jane squealed, flexing at the knees. Carlisle flinched and braced himself as Jane hopped forward. Experience told him that it was hopeless to follow her wandering narrative for more than a minute. Before she even got started, he'd generally already planned his escape. On this day, however, his thoughts were of a different nature. He glanced past Jane to the museum entrance. There he saw that a man wearing dark glasses had just entered. Over the man's shoulder hung a camera bag.

"... and so, the Karanlik Kilise—y'know, the Dark Church—no one's been able to excavate it for thirty years because of the Turkish government, but now they can. And, like, the church is literally carved right into volcanic rock, and before it was closed off, some said it was a monastery—y'know, because of all the frescoes. I read online that there are a bunch of monasteries in Cappadocia

## A PACKAGE EXAMINED

because Christians hid there from the Romans. They say on TrueDishers that if the Dark Church really is a monastery, then it might be the lost monastery of Saint Nil the monk, one of the Four Keepers, and if that's the case, then it's totally possible that the Last Supper Dish is there too, because, like, where else could he have hidden it before he was killed?"

"Indeed," Carlisle said, momentarily tuning in to Jane's speech. The man in dark glasses spoke to the woman at the front desk; she glanced uncertainly at Carlisle, who nodded back at her with the slightest tilt of his head.

"Can you believe it? It's one of the key theories. Steve Finder just wrote a novel about it," Jane said breathlessly.

"A Steve Finder novel, eh?" Carlisle said. "Well, what more proof do we need?"

Jane didn't detect Carlisle's irony. "Finder does all this research," she said emphatically, "and his stories are just so a-maa-zing. Every one of his books is different but the same, too, y'know? This one is called Bucky Browne and the Templars of Doom. Princess Calixta and Bucky have to find the Map of Fortunatus or else—"

"Or else the world as we know it ceases to be? Amazing how that happens, isn't it?" Carlisle's tone indicated that he'd heard Jane explain Finder's novels to him before. He motioned her toward his office. The door was already half open, and he chose not to close it. He offered Jane a chair, and she sat with her back to the entrance, Baby Girl in her lap. Carlisle took his place behind his desk.

"So, you've come to tell me they've found the Last Supper Dish in this church or what have you." Carlisle waved his hand over his desk as if shooing away a fly.

## THE DIE IS CAST

Jane sighed, all at once deflated. She began to stroke Baby Girl's head. Once she'd arrived in Göreme, reports had begun to circulate that the Dark Church wasn't a church after all; nor was it a monastery. The excavations had revealed something quite different, something so unexpected that Jane still had difficulty taking in the facts. She'd been so sure and had traveled so far—hundreds of Dishers had. The facts, she felt, had an obligation not to disappoint.

"Am I to understand you did not find the Last Supper Dish?" Carlisle hid a smile. He leaned forward and folded his hands on his desk.

"No," Jane said, looking at Baby Girl.

"But what about the, what did you call it—Dark Church?"

"It might not be a church, after all."

"Then it's a monastery?"

"It isn't that either."

"What is it then?"

"Some say an inn, or—" Jane stopped herself, confused. Dishers hadn't been permitted to enter the excavation site, but an American she'd met had sneaked past security and taken pictures of the frescoes. Jane had seen the pictures. The women in them had all been naked. "—or, y'know, something like an inn," she concluded lamely.

"But Finder's novel? You were sure it held the answer."

"But I wasn't wrong. I mean, in his story they do find the lost monastery. So, I mean, if the lost monastery were eventually found ..." her voice trailed off.

Carlisle straightened in his chair; it squeaked. "Ms. Whitaker, might I make an observation?"

## A PACKAGE EXAMINED

Jane glanced up at him.

"You're obviously a young woman of means and, er, intelligence—"

"Thank you."

"—but might I suggest, well, to put it bluntly, that you divert your means and intelligence toward better ends?"

Jane stared at him blankly.

"Surely it has occurred to you that you might be chasing something that doesn't really exist?"

"But it has to. Why else would so many people be looking for it?"

Carlisle sighed. "Oh, for the same reason you are, I suppose. Because they want it to be true. It's a shame—a shame to see people waste their time on a lost cause."

"But it isn't a lost cause. Just because I didn't find the Dish this time doesn't mean I won't. It's out there. You just gotta believe it."

"Ms. Whitaker, your desire for something to be true doesn't mean it is."

"I know you don't believe in the Dish."

"But I do. I believe it's in the Vatican Museum. Most scholars do. There are those on the fringes, academics without any ideas desperately trying to get tenure by publishing something. So, they make extraordinary claims. Most of these sad people are at third-tier institutions."

"Like, just because you all believe it's at the Vatican, doesn't mean it's true," Jane mimed. She began to unwrap the package in her hands.

A shadow in the shape of a man fell across the entrance to Carlisle's office; Carlisle cleared his throat nervously.

Baby Girl yelped and sniffed the air.

"What's the matter, Pookums?"

"Uh, Ms. Whitaker," Carlisle said quickly, fiddling with his bow tie, "the difference between you and me is that I believe what I believe because of the evidence, and you believe what you believe in spite of the evidence."

"Nuh-uh," Jane countered. "There's evidence—plenty." She tried to think of something she'd read on *TrueDishers.net*, but her mind got lost in a blur of assertions.

"How many times have we had a conversation just like this?" Carlisle said. "You come to me with some trinket or other you've found somewhere, hoping I'll validate your belief that it's a link to the Last Supper Dish. Let's see, first there was the Grecian pottery—depicting, predictably enough, Dionysian revelry—obviously pre-Christian." Carlisle looked up at the ceiling and began to count on his fingers. "Then there was that horrible faux Roman glassware—a Victorian reproduction. Then the silver medallion of Syrian origin bearing the likeness of Saint Nicholas, as I recall, not Saint Zoticus, as you supposed. Then the medieval French manuscript about *bouillie*—a suggestive word, I grant you, to someone with no knowledge of French. But perhaps we must blame deficient American education for your mistake here," Carlisle chuckled. "Of course, I need not mention your, uh, regrettable adventure in Moscow—"

"That wasn't my fault," Jane interjected without looking up. "The sign wasn't clear. It should've been in English."

"At any rate, you've been so wide of the mark in every case. I've tried to be patient, and I don't mean to be disparaging, really I don't, and I'm grateful to your family for their financial contributions to—"

"I don't have anything to do with that."

"No, no, I understand, but—"

"Is that the only reason you've been nice to me?"

"What? No, no—" Carlisle protested.

"Not that I care."

"—no, you misunderstand. I appreciate your sincere interest in antiquities, but I must be frank—I think you're wasting your time. You're not an expert in these matters. But even if you were, I doubt you could show me convincing evidence that the real Dish is still out there."

"Oh, is that so? How 'bout this for convincing evidence." Carefully, Jane lifted a small rectangular piece of wood from the folds of brown paper she'd unwrapped and triumphantly turned the face of it toward Carlisle.

"Who's that supposed to be?"

"Saint Nil! A gen-u-ine Nil," Jane enunciated proudly.

"Impossible. No one has ever found a complete one."

"I know."

"There was that fellow—Burke—a couple years ago—"

"But the inscription on that one wasn't intact, and that's the most important part."

"Did they find this icon in the excavation?" Carlisle's voice sounded doubtful.

"I dunno. Like, he didn't say, the man who sold it to me."

"Was this man taking part in the excavation? Because it's illegal for the artifacts to be sold like souvenirs."

"Oh. To be honest, it was all a little confusing to me. He didn't speak English very well."

"Did you get his name?"

"Oh, yes. Babu. He was sort of a quirky guy. He had such a cute shop in town. I went in only because there was, like, this cat in the window, and it didn't have a tail."

Carlisle sat silently for a moment.

"It was destiny," Jane giggled. "Isn't it beautiful?"

Carlisle stood and held out his hand. Anxiously, Jane parted with her treasure. The icon was painted golden all around, and a somber bearded man with bright wide eyes stared out from the center. A halo was about his head, and on his white robe were three gold crosses. In his left hand he held a book, and in the other, a bowl. There were words in Greek on the reverse side. Jane had tried unsuccessfully to decipher them using Google Translator.

Carlisle laid the icon on his desk and pulled a digital camera and a magnifying glass from a drawer. He snapped several pictures and then, leaning over his desk, inspected the icon with the glass. "Ah, encaustic on panel. Very good."

"What does that mean?"

"Encaustic is a painting method—beeswax. Quite common in the East."

Jane held her breath. Her disappointment about the Dark Church had been profound indeed, but on her flight home from Göreme, she'd been unable to shake the notion that Some Great Guiding Power had intervened. This Guiding Power had destined her to find the small piece of wood now lying beneath Dr. Carlisle's examining eyes. It had drawn her to Göreme by means of its own irresistible will and had, without her prior awareness, predestined her every step. It could be no accident

## A PACKAGE EXAMINED

that she'd seen the tailless cat. Finding the Saint Nil icon in Babu's shop had been the Power's objective for her journey all along. And if the icon was a genuine Saint Nil, then she was one step closer to finding the Last Supper Dish after all.

As every Disher knew, the icons of the Four Keepers—Kostas, Zoticus, Panikos, and Nil—were the key to the mystery. All anyone had to do was solve their riddles, and the icons would reveal the hidden location of the true Dish. Any good Disher knew the Saint Kostas riddle by heart:

Latin invaders, remember the words of Kostas:
God still guards the Queen of Cities
And her most precious treasure.
If you dare desire the Dish of Christ,
Go and find my brothers.

Jane repeated Kostas's message to herself, mantra-like: Go and find my brothers, Go and find my brothers, Go and find my brothers ...

Carlisle began to read the icon's inscription. "Hmm, interesting." He straightened for a moment and scratched his chin, searching his memory.

"What's interesting?"

"Let's see." He bent over the icon again. "Speak Memory of the cunning hero, the wanderer ..."

Jane jumped to her feet. "What's that mean?"

"Translating, Ms. Whitaker. This Greek is painted clumsily, I'm afraid."

"But you can read it?" She leaned over the desk.

"Uh—wanderer—yes—blown off course time and again."

Jane's heart leaped. She repeated the words to herself: Speak Memory of the cunning hero, the wanderer, blown off course time and again. What could it mean? Who was the wanderer? Who?

Carlisle chuckled in bemusement. "Fascinating."

"What is it? WHAT?"

"After he plundered Troy's sacred heights."

"Who—who's it talking about?"

Carlisle straightened and set down the magnifying glass. "Odysseus, I believe, if I remember my Homer."

"Who is—?"

"Odysseus—Greek fellow trying to get home after the Trojan War. Takes him ten years, I think. These lines are lifted straight out of Homer's Odyssey."

Jane frowned. She remembered somewhat hazily a professor once mentioning Homer in a college course she'd taken on Western Civilization. She'd never bothered to read the textbook. "But—but why are lines from the Odyssey on an icon of Saint Nil?"

"Because this isn't an icon of Nil. It's what we in the business call an artifake."

"You mean—"

"There are artifacts, and then there are artifakes. An artifact is the real thing. An artifake is made to look like the real thing, but it isn't." Carlisle took the icon in his hands and pointed at the bearded man's robes. "Look here—this can't be Saint Nil because Nil was a monk. But this man is an archbishop. See the three crosses on his vestments? He's wearing what's called an omophorion.

## A PACKAGE EXAMINED

And look closely at the left-hand corner. Icons always indicate the saint's name, generally with initials—a monogram. You can see the original monogram has been painted over—erased."

"But he's holding a bowl," Jane cried forlornly.

"Yes, the cleverest deception. In an icon the saint's right hand is raised in blessing. This man's hand has been altered and the bowl added in. Someone went to a lot of trouble. I'd say this was originally an icon of John Chrysostom, a Greek Orthodox saint. A late example—early nineteenth century."

Jane slumped back into her chair. Her eyes started to sting, and she clutched Baby Girl hard to keep from crying. All thought of the Great Guiding Power fell from her mind, displaced by a thought more material and precise: how could Babu have been a cheat? He had such a cute shop.

"Interesting that whoever did this tried to write in Greek," Carlisle said. "They must not have known that the riddles on the existing icons of the Four Keepers are all written in Latin. Just another sign this is a forgery. I'm sorry, Ms. Whitaker. I hope you didn't have much invested in it. Not that money would be a concern for you, I suppose."

Carlisle handed the icon back to Jane. She rewrapped it in the brown paper much less carefully this time. Babu had sold it to her for the bargain price of only five thousand dollars. Naturally, she'd charged the purchase to her father.

When Jane stood with Baby Girl to leave, Carlisle cleared his throat loudly. Jane mumbled a "thank you for your time" and shuffled out. The hallway was empty. As she re-crossed the museum's atrium and pushed through the revolving door, she felt free to let the stinging in her eyes take its course, and she clutched Baby Girl tightly.

She thought about dropping the icon in a trash receptacle along the walkway, but she couldn't let go of it—not yet. Because she *was* invested in it, but it was an investment of the heart. She'd wandered into a shop in the middle of Turkey and had opened the door to her dreams. The moment she'd seen Saint Nil (or, rather, Saint Chrysostom) she'd felt the axis of the world shift: suddenly, she lived in a world where justice prevailed, and the powerful were thrown down, and the weak and deserving were raised up.

She lived in a world she'd changed. She'd made a difference. And the best part of all had been her knowledge that soon the world would know.

But now her hopes were deferred. She'd failed again. It was the same old world after all. And Dr. Carlisle would probably be a Dish-denier to the end.

▼ ▼ ▼ ▼

Moments after Jane had departed the museum in tears, a man wearing dark glasses and holding a camera with a long-range lens stepped into Dr. Carlisle's office.

"Get what you needed?" Carlisle asked, still seated.

"Too easily," the man said, smirking. "Do you mind?"

"Please." Carlisle motioned to his desktop. With a handkerchief he dabbed tiny beads of sweat from his hairline.

## A PACKAGE EXAMINED

The man set down his camera on the desk and opened his camera bag. He pulled out a digital recorder, tapped a few buttons, and Jane's voice sounded clear and distinct: "*How 'bout this for convincing evidence.*"

"Such a silly girl." Carlisle shook his head sadly.

"Sure you don't mind being quoted?"

"Not at all. That was the deal. It's the correct course. Maybe it will help her—if she can be helped."

"We'll publish the story as an exclusive as was agreed, but it'll reach the broader market for sure. I'll alert my friend at the Times. It's Jane Whitaker, after all."

Carlisle frowned. "Lots of Stuff—Right Here." He leaned backed in his chair. "I always detested that slogan."

"It's inaccurate in her case," the reporter said, tapping the side of his head.

Carlisle laughed. "True enough. I don't know how anyone's brain could be filled with so much nothing. It's a travesty of education."

The reporter smirked. "Maybe this'll give her something to think about."

Scene 5

# Tonight, We Dig

*Istanbul, Turkey*

*Excavation site at the demolished Sirkeci Rail Station*

*Monday, March 8*

Like a conqueror who at last enters the gate of a city that had long shut him out, Adam Burke stood at the gate of the excavation site with a hardhat under his arm, proudly surveying his domain. He lifted his chin to peer through his glasses. To his left beyond the security fence, a cluster of tall buildings formed the end of the city block. To his right sat two bulldozers and a front-end loader. And before him, a path sloped downward to an expanding pit, where even as Burke watched, student-workers pushed wheelbarrows of dirt up to the surface. Earthen mounds dotted the perimeter of the site, steadily spreading like suburban sprawl. Such progress pleased the professor, and he stepped forward, but not before glimpsing above him the giant sign erected at the corner of the site. It was written in Turkish and English: COMING SOON—MARMARA METRO STATION.

All too soon, Burke thought, scowling. He and his team were already two weeks into the dig, one third of the time allotted to them by the Turkish authorities. *Must dig faster.*

Past the bulldozers, a large white tent was being set up to sort recovered artifacts—once some were found. They'd found nothing yet. Duffy, Burke's graduate student, had only just remarked upon this: "I guess dirt doesn't count, huh, sir?" For this impertinence, Burke had sent Duffy to labor with the tent. He spied Duffy now, stubby and wide, squatting near a mass of scattered poles.

Burke continued his forward march. Twilight hastened. High above the pit, towering spotlights shone down like giant surgical lamps, penetrating with their white heat the delicate heart of the ancient edifice. At any moment, the walled-up heart might surrender its secrets, powerless to resist its dissection. The burial shroud was being torn away. What rough form would be resurrected? At the edge of the pit Burke gazed down. He could see two carved-out chambers, the west and the north, both eight meters deep and five meters wide. How much deeper? he wondered. How much wider before they reached the walls of the Byzantine shrine? If it were a Byzantine shrine. They still had no clear confirmation. But it must be, thought Burke. *Must be the one.*

Because this was his domain. His moment. History had called out his name. His alone. As he watched the digging, his lips twisted in a sardonic grin. "Deep and wide enough for you, Winters," he muttered. "I'm gonna bury you."

## THE DIE IS CAST

▼ ▬ ▬ ▬

After two weeks of long work shifts, both mornings and evenings, Giulio Makarios felt the only thing he was learning from his field experience was that digging wasn't much fun. Maybe if he'd been allowed to operate the front-end loader, he would've felt differently. But from the very first day, he'd been thwarted—passed over in favor of Dr. Foo. All the archaeology students had been. None of them were permitted anywhere near the machinery. That was exclusively "for the experts." So said the slave master.

*Slave master* was Giulio's private name for Burke. He disliked how the professor paced the edge of the excavation pit, inspecting the progress and shouting down "encouragement" to the crews, all the while digging very little himself. Giulio stood in the west chamber, digging toward the inner west wall. Behind him, at what would've been the south wall of the structure if the wall had survived, long wooden planks ascended to the surface. Giulio had been up and down the ramp innumerable times pushing a wheelbarrow.

Giulio's mind felt slow and his tongue, thick. When did his shift end? He dropped his spade and massaged his right shoulder, his arms feeling weighted with chains. He undid his bandanna, pushed away his thick, black hair and wiped his forehead. Then he did the unthinkable—he took off his gloves and sat down on a bucket.

"You there—McKenzie—what's going on?"

It was the voice of the slave master.

"Nothing!" Giulio shouted up. "And it's Makarios."

"Well, keep at it!" Burke shouted down. "If the radar images are accurate, we're less than a meter away. Your shift doesn't end for another hour."

Giulio cursed in Greek and put his gloves back on. He stood and stretched his back, then stooped to pick up his spade. He displayed all the signs of resuming his digging, but when Burke stepped out of sight, Giulio sat back down. Just then Dr. Calvino, one of the four lead archaeologists, tramped down the ramp with an empty wheelbarrow.

"A gift for you," Calvino grinned, "courtesy of Burke."

"Thanks," Giulio said cheerily though seething inwardly. When Calvino turned away, Giulio scooted the bucket closer to the wall of dirt and resumed his seat. Of the four lead archaeologists—Stoltzfus, Calvino, Hromadova, and Foo—Giulio disliked Calvino the most. It was rumored among the Greek graduate students that Calvino was from Venice, sprung from that "Latin tribe" that had ransacked Constantinople in 1204. Thus, to the Greek students, Calvino's Disher credentials were in question. I'll dig, Giulio thought, but I won't stand—not for you. Angrily, with atypical force, he jabbed the dirt with his spade.

Thunk.

Just his luck. Another rock. The big ones were hell to dig out. With the side of his spade, Giulio scraped at the rock to gauge its size. When he did so, a large clump of dirt at the height of his eyes fell to his feet.

"Hey!" he called out. Before him, four shiny flat stones glinted like copper in the spotlight. He brushed away more dirt. More small copper stones appeared, all neatly arranged in curving lines. Inside the copper lines were peach stones, like the color of his own flesh. He traced the copper lines with his finger and a shape emerged. It was ... *a hand.*

"Hey," Giulio called out again, leaping up from the bucket. Maybe it was his fatigue, but he could've sworn the stone hand had reached for him. "I got something!"

Instantly, Burke appeared above. "That you, McKenzie?"

"Yes. But it's Makarios."

Burke flicked on a flashlight. "My God! What's that?"

"It's—a hand. A stone hand," Giulio said. He omitted saying the word "just," though he wanted to say it, to assure himself that the hand couldn't have moved.

"Step aside, McKenzie, you're blocking the light."

Giulio obeyed but forgot the bucket was behind him. He tripped and fell flat on his back.

"A hand!" Burke shouted, as though Giulio hadn't just said so. "Duffy, I need a camera."

For a second, Burke disappeared.

Giulio got up and brushed the dirt from his butt.

Burke trotted down the ramp, followed by Calvino.

With a flourish of his hand, Giulio gestured at the stones, imitating one of Burke's poses in *National Geographic*.

Burke grabbed Giulio's spade and thrust the flashlight into his chest. "Hold this."

Quickly, Burke squatted and scraped away more dirt, enlarging the opening made by Giulio. Gold-colored stones appeared above the hand. "The light, McKenzie. Step to it!"

Giulio shone the light over Burke's shoulder.

"Where's Duffy? I need the camera."

"A mosaic," Calvino declared. "Those are tesserae."

"Yes, copper-leaf," Burke murmured to himself.

"I thought that too when I uncovered them," Giulio said.

"Magnifico," Calvino exclaimed. "Then it is a shrine."

Burke leaned in close to the colored stones and puckered his lips as if to kiss them. Instead, he blew some dirt away. The image above the hand almost took shape.

"I dug hard to get to the inner wall," Giulio said to Burke.

"McKenzie, hold the light steady," Burke commanded. "Good God, man! Where's Duffy? Is he here yet?"

"Yes, sir," a voice called behind Giulio. Duffy had been running, for his wheezing breaths were hot on Giulio's neck. He was no athlete—pasty, squishy, and round—just like Burke. It was a toss-up which one Giulio hated more—Burke for being a slave master or Duffy for being a slave.

"I brought the camera." Duffy sidled up to Burke.

"Good, good," Burke said, not bothering to look. "I need a brush. Does anyone have a—"

Calvino pulled one from his utility belt and tapped Burke on the shoulder with it.

"Ah, excellent." Burke grabbed the brush and swept it over the mosaic. "Let's see now, we have a hand ... a hand holding something. Holding what?" Burke dropped to one knee. After several more dramatic sweeps with the brush, he whispered, "A hand holding ...?"

Suddenly, Calvino and Duffy gasped.

Giulio's eyes widened. In his excitement, he accidentally switched off the flashlight.

Burke didn't notice. Slowly, he stood. Throwing his head back and raising both arms in victory, he shouted at the sky, "A DISSHHHH!"

"Are you sure?" Calvino asked, though his eyes flashed affirmatively.

"A Dish!" Burke shouted again. "It must be. I knew it!"

Giulio sucked in his breath, imagining himself on the cover of *National Geographic*. Just then, Burke swung his elbow hard, knocking him out of the way. Giulio stumbled backwards and tripped again over the bucket.

"Duffy—photo!" Burke ordered.

Duffy filled the space vacated by Giulio.

Burke knelt beside the mosaic and rested one hand on his hip. In the other hand he held Giulio's spade. Duffy readied the camera. Giulio raised himself from the dirt just in time to see the flash. "Now, Duffy, take some close-ups of the stones," Burke commanded, standing. He tossed the spade down near Giulio's feet and took back his flashlight. "You really oughta wear a hardhat," Burke said to him before jogging up the ramp. Calvino followed closely after.

Giulio sat rubbing the back of his head. He'd narrowly missed hitting the wheelbarrow.

Once at ground level, Burke shouted, "Listen, people!" He waved his arms theatrically. "I need your attention."

All the crews stopped digging; a crowd formed around Burke. Among them were Stoltzfus and Foo, two of the other archaeologists.

"We've made first contact." Burke pointed his flashlight down at Giulio and Duffy. Everyone gasped and cheered.

"We've exposed a portion of a mosaic."

More cheers.

Burke nodded to the group, savoring the moment. He let them whoop and holler a minute more. "Now, listen, people, this is important. Hear me, please!"

The crowd quieted. All eyes were on him.

"The mosaic is in good condition, and—"

"What's it look like?" Stoltzfus yelled.

As an answer, Burke twirled his flashlight and directed the beam down into the pit. "It looks like—A DISH!"

Upon hearing those two little words, all the archaeology students rushed down the ramp, racing to be the first to see. Giulio scrambled to his feet so as not to be trampled.

"My guess was right," Burke declared to Stoltzfus, Calvino, and Foo. "We're on the verge of unearthing a major, Byzantine shrine. Possibly even *the* shrine—"

Calvino grabbed Burke's arm. "Ah! *The* shrine?"

"That's right," Burke said, lowering his voice, "the Shrine of the Four Keepers." He pronounced the name reverently, relishing both the sound and effect of his words.

"Madre di Dio," Calvino murmured.

"Now listen up, people," Burke yelled down to the students. "Given the nature of our discovery, we must push forward with all possible haste." He twirled his flashlight once more and swung it up over his head like a sword. "So tonight ... WE DIG!"

## THE DIE IS CAST

Many hours later, well after midnight, as Burke hungrily looked on, the burial shroud was at last lifted. Throughout the night, the mosaic hand had grown, becoming an arm, a torso, a neck. And then, under the hot, white spotlights, the curtain of dirt opened upon a face. It was the face of a man—a youth—with ringlets of hair and bright, wide eyes. He held a golden bowl up near his head, lifting it towards heaven.

Burke recognized the face. He didn't need to verify the accuracy of his memory, but he did so anyway, because the sight of the face thrilled him, and because being right thrilled him even more. He pulled out his phone; there was a link to an ancient manuscript on *TrueDishers.net* that he always kept bookmarked:

… and thus did the heart of Emperor Andronicus burn with rage for the Latins, who in their woeful plundering of our wondrous city didst not spare even the most holy of relics, alas. Yet did the Emperor learn the tale of noble Kostas, wizened Zoticus, fair Panikos, and grave Nil, and this didst serve to cheer him, for so these monks didst say to have saved the Last Supper Dish of our Lord, wherein the betrayer Judas didst dip his hand as the Book doth say. Wherefore the four monks kept unto themselves knowledge of the Dish, so that the Latins findeth it not, nor would they tell forth its secret but cast it into the teeth of the Latins until the four were treacherously slain, for shame. And straightaway upon learning the martyrdom of the four, the Emperor didst gather unto himself holy men of likened mind, and together didst they build a sacred shrine, and with such haste that—

Winters, Winters, Winters, Burke thought as he delightedly scrolled through the ancient text. You old Dish-denier. You'll wish you'd taken the Annals of Andronicus seriously now. Mere Byzantine imperial propaganda you always call it. Making a career out of laughing at me. Look who's gonna be laughing now. You think you're so important sitting in your fancy corner office at Oxford!

Burke glanced up again at the mosaic. With inward glee, he clicked off the ancient text and clicked on his camera, adjusting the frame to capture the image of the glittering golden bowl held in the young man's hand. See this, Winters? he thought, snapping several pictures. Get a good look. 'Cause it's coming for you. There's no escape. Go ahead and try to keep your International Archaeology Association's Lifetime Achievement Award—if you can! But it's gonna take it. And it's gonna take your Royal Archaeological Institute's Book of the Year Award too. It'll take everything you think you've got. 'Cause that's the power of the Dish.

Burke opened his email and clicked on Winters's name. He almost decided to send Winters a picture of the bowl when he abandoned the idea. It was enough for him to know that he *could* send the email, that he possessed the power to snuff out his rival's glory with a click of a button.

He enjoyed having this knowledge. He wanted to enjoy it a little longer. "Soon, Winters," he muttered, putting away his phone, "soon."

Scene 6

# A Bridge of Sorts

*The Sound Lounge*

*Flatiron District, Manhattan*

*Monday, March 8*

Bucky Browne ran through the darkness, a darkness pierced only by the pale halo of light projected by his trusty flashlight. The light slid along the powdery, curving surfaces of the rock walls, dancing up to the passage's low ceiling and down to the uneven floor. Bucky's expert eye scanned above them for small holes cut into the rock. He knew the holes might still hold spears that could be triggered to drop and pierce their skulls. These Cappadocian caverns were the ancient strongholds of the first-century Christians; the traps designed to kill Roman soldiers could kill any of them too. Such was the great peril of the Maze of the Martyrs.

"How much further, Bucky?" Princess Calixta asked, a step behind him.

"If I remember the Map of Fortunatus correctly," Bucky said as he slowed to a walk, "the Chamber of the Patriarchs lies just ahead." Suddenly, he stopped. Yes, there it was.

## A BRIDGE OF SORTS

Before them lay a stone bridge spanning a great chasm. Beyond it he could discern a small portal; it was the only distinguishing feature of the sheer wall facing them across the chasm. More lights flashed in the passage. Bucky heard the heavy breathing of Bartholomew and Peter. The two monks had finally caught up. Bucky felt a pang of sympathy. While the pair had been helpful during their quest, they were not used to such exertion.

"Peter, look," Bartholomew pointed. "The gateway!"

"You two ready?" Bucky asked, grinning.

"Our cassocks are dusty, but otherwise, yes," Peter replied, chuckling.

"Stay behind us because we're ... more properly attired." Bucky glanced at Calixta, who quickly checked the belt that held her throwing knives.

"Let's go," Calixta said. "Grimani and his Templars can't be far behind."

Bucky adjusted his holster. "The Dish of Christ awaits us."

Their progress was slow across the narrow bridge. "Don't look down," Bucky warned the monks. They passed through the gateway one by one. The Chamber of the Patriarchs was circular with a vaulted ceiling. Bartholomew held his lantern up to a wall, and painted figures appeared. "The armies of the archangel Michael," he whispered.

"Yes," Bucky said. "They're seraphim assembled to protect the Dish." Ever the archaeologist, he longed to study the details of the ancient frescoes.

"A table," Bartholomew gasped, striding to the Chamber's center. At the head of the table sat a chair—a throne. Both the table and throne were carved from the rock; they rose from the floor. On the table before the throne was an unadorned clay bowl, small enough to be held in one hand.

"The Last Supper Dish," Calixta murmured in awe.

Reverently, Bucky approached the Dish. He recalled the mysteries they'd solved, the dangers they'd braved to reach this moment. Now, with the Dish in their hands, they could expose the Catholic Church's greatest hoax—one perpetrated for centuries—the hoax that the Church possessed the true Dish of Christ, Christendom's holiest relic. The public outcry would topple the Vatican with the strength of an earthquake. The wealth funneled from generations of believers would dry up; they would know at last that every pontiff since Pope Innocent III had harbored in his heart a foul lie.

Bucky reached for the Dish.

"Not so fast, Professor Browne," called a voice all too familiar. "Turn around slowly—with your hands raised."

When Bucky obeyed, he saw the arrogant face of Cardinal Grimani and two cloaked Templars, each with a rifle aimed at his heart. A fourth Templar placed a gun to Bartholomew's head while another restrained a disarmed Calixta, her knife belt fallen to her feet.

"As you see, we have silenced the sharp-witted Calixta," Grimani sneered. "Now back away from the Dish, Professor."

Bucky scanned the room for Peter. Did he escape?

"You search for your friend," Grimani said. "Here he is."

Bucky felt his golden Colt pistol pulled from its holster.

"Thanks, Bucky," Peter said.

Bucky smirked. "Don't mention it."

"The Cardinal promises to spare your lives," Peter said, tucking Bucky's gun into his cassock, "if you don't resist."

"You have betrayed us!" Bartholomew cried in anguish.

"I prefer not to call it *betrayal*," Peter replied. "I simply made a rational calculation. How would we in the Orthodox Church be rewarded for exposing the Pope's lie? What's in it for us—poetic justice?" Peter scoffed. "I prefer a reward a little more *tangible*."

"Judas!" Bartholomew shouted.

"Oh, I got more than thirty pieces of silver," Peter winked.

"And now I grant the first of your rewards," Grimani announced. He gestured toward the Dish with a warm smile. But his eyes were cold.

Peter set down his lantern and lifted the Dish in triumph.

"No!" Bucky yelled. "You read the warning on the map!"

"Fortunatus was a mad, blind fool!" Peter jeered. His eyes shone in the lantern's light. "Look who has the Dish of Christ now!" All at once, his eyes widened in fear. He dropped the Dish with a clatter back onto the table and clutched his right hand. His fingertips were smoking. Suddenly, they burst into flame, each finger a hideous candle. "Help me!" he screamed.

"Fortunatus was right—the curse of Judas!" Grimani cried. He retreated from the table in horror. "It is the true Dish."

As fire consumed him, in madness Peter ran from the Chamber and plunged to his death into the chasm. Distracted by the spectacle, Grimani and his Templars failed to observe Bucky and Calixta exchange glances. In a swift, powerful move, Calixta dropped to one knee and threw the Templar who held her over her shoulder. She grabbed a knife from her belt and with a sinuous twist, stabbed the Templar's leg. Bucky dove for his pistol. It had dropped from Peter's smoldering robe. *I must get the Dish.* The Colt singed his hand, but he fought against the pain and pivoted on his heels.

"Get down, Barth!" he shouted and—

Natalie quickly shut the novel and slid it across the table from her. The Sound Lounge door had opened behind her. Ray and Clark had returned with pizzas. She felt silly for trying to hide the fact that she'd been reading Ray's copy of *Bucky Browne and the Templars of Doom*. It was just that she'd unexpectedly gotten caught up in the story; some part of her resisted the idea of Ray detecting this.

"You finish it?" he asked eagerly, seeing the book.

Natalie waited to reply, wanting her voice to sound matter-of-fact. She swept the book further to the side of the table to make room for the pizza boxes. She was a great reader, just not a great reader of genre fiction, and certainly not action-adventure novels. Stories involving a conspiracy, a secret society, a race against time, a dramatic chase scene, a ninja-warrior princess, and a hero solving impossible clues didn't really move her. Or so she thought.

"Um, almost. They're at the Chamber of the Patriarchs."

"That's a great scene. How far are you? Has Calixta—"

"Don't spoil it for me."

"You like it, don't you? Finder's a great writer."

## A BRIDGE OF SORTS

Natalie didn't quite agree but said nothing. Compared to her usual literary fare, Finder's style was irreparably cliché, hackneyed, and without imagination, like a can of chicken noodle soup. And yet, despite the flaws in his prose, he'd made her care when the betrayer Peter had plunged off the bridge to his death. That shouldn't have been possible.

"You remember Cave of All Fears," Clark said to Ray, "when Lady Xenia fights the samurai assassin?"

Ray grabbed a slice of pizza. "Banzai!" he shouted like a samurai warrior.

Clark assumed a karate stance.

Ray thrust his pizza slice at him as if it were a sword.

The two simulated the movie's famous fight sequence.

Steve Finder, creator of Bucky Browne, Lady Xenia, and Princess Calixta, had written three novels featuring their search for the Last Supper Dish. *Templars of Doom*, which Natalie had been reading, was Finder's latest installment in the indefinite series. His prior two novels, *Bucky Browne and the Midnight Crusade* and *Bucky Browne and the Cave of All Fears*, had both been adapted into films. *Templars* was in pre-production. It'd broken the sales records set by his first novels, solidifying his reputation as the most popular writer of action-adventure thrillers in the last decade. Ray and Natalie were set to interview him the following day for their documentary. As was their custom, they met with Clark the night before to strategize.

Watching Ray and Clark's fake battle from her perch chair, Natalie asked Clark teasingly, "Who are you supposed to be? The assassin or Lady Xenia?"

"Isn't it obvious?" Ray said. "With his long girly hair?"

"C'mon, man." Clark swung his foot at Ray's head.

Natalie laughed. "Look out, Ray!"

"With that hair, you could've been Kimber Grant's stunt double," Ray said, ducking to avoid Clark's mock kick.

"Kimber?" Natalie asked.

"She played Lady Xenia in the movie," Ray said. He pretended to jab his elbow at Clark's ear. "She's new. She was in Girl Fighter. But, uh, you probably didn't see that either."

Natalie hadn't.

But Clark had. "Kimber." He whistled. "Man, her slick, leather bodysuit—so hot."

"That scene with her in the plane," Ray said to Clark.

"So whack! Like, top-five crash sequences of all time."

The two went on discussing *Girl Fighter*—and Kimber—leaving Natalie out.

Natalie didn't need to have seen *The Cave of All Fears* or *Girl Fighter* to imagine Kimber Grant in her slick, leather bodysuit. She frowned and slid *Templars of Doom* back toward her to examine its dust jacket. Bucky, wielding a gold pistol and holding a torch, halted before a chasm. Light from the torch reflected off his Barmah hat and belt buckle bearing his monogram "BB." A step behind him in high-heeled purple boots, Princess Calixta brandished a pair of knives. Her white blouse strained to contain her breasts, and her brown eyes, heavily shadowed in teal, narrowed in defiance of some unseen enemy. "You'll never beat me. This is my story. Why are you even here?" she seemed to say.

Natalie dropped the book into her messenger bag out of sight and pulled out her iPad.

"Guys," she said, "time to get to work."

Clark commandeered one of the pizzas for himself and sat down at the soundboard.

Ray pushed up the sleeves of his Henley shirt—a gray one—and plopped onto the sofa. But he couldn't sit still and jumped up. "Okay, here's what I'm seeing." He spread his hands toward the blank screen on the far wall. "Bucky Browne! Lady Xenia! She's just hidden the codex of Saint Jerome. But now—betrayed and captured. Trapped in the dungeon beneath the Papal Palace of Castel Gandolfo. Awaiting torture at the hands of evil Cardinal Scevola. Can Bucky save her? Then we cut the scene. Transition to, uh, a Finder book signing. Or he's sitting at a coffee shop—"

"Would Finder give us permission to use his film clips?" Natalie interrupted. "Who owns the copyright, I wonder?"

"I'd like his autograph," Clark said. "Think I could get it?"

Ray glanced at Natalie sheepishly, a sign that Clark had just voiced his own private hope.

"Ask him if he knows Kimber Grant," Clark said.

"Course he does," Ray said. "He must've met her at the premiere."

"I mean, like, personally. Do they hang out and stuff?"

"Maybe he knows who's gonna be cast as Calixta."

"Yeah, man. Like, ask him if he has any input. Or certain actors in mind when he writes."

"Maybe he does. He writes the screenplays, doesn't he?"

"Guys," Natalie cut in. She grabbed a pen from the table and rapped it several times against her iPad. "Get serious. We can't go there and ask him fanboy questions. Now, look, Reggie said we don't have that one professor contributing anymore—what's his name—Burke, the Disher Golden Boy." She consulted her notes and continued in a teacherly tone. "So, I've been thinking we should ask Finder the questions we were gonna ask Burke to cover. To fill in the gaps. We wanted to have Burke explain the three theories about where the Four Keepers hid the Dish from the crusaders. Finder could cover that." She pointed her pen at Ray. "Each of his novels explores one of the theories, right?"

Ray nodded. "Uh, right. In Templars, the Dish is hidden in the Cappadocian Mountains. Midnight Crusade, they search in Greece on Mount Athos. In Cave of All Fears, Bucky finds a vault under Hagia Sophia in Istanbul."

Natalie made notes on her iPad. She delighted in graphs and flow charts. Orderliness always reassured her. It proved her theory that the world existed to be managed. Tidy columns acted on her mind as a filing cabinet might, clarifying her thoughts. "Okay, so Dishers believe the riddles on the icons reveal the hidden location of the Dish. Are the icons of the Keepers factors in the plots of Finder's first two novels? I know Bucky finds a Saint Nil icon in Templars."

"They are," Ray said. "Bucky uses the Kostas icon to search on Mount Athos. Panikos leads him to Hagia Sophia."

"What about Zoticus?"

"There's no Zoticus icon in Finder's books. At least, not yet. Maybe that's coming in the sequel to Templars."

"This is all good. We should ask Finder about the riddles. Burke was gonna cover that too."

"You think Finder really believes the Dish is still lost?" Clark asked.

"Do you?" Ray kidded.

"Of course. If the story's got Kimber Grant in it, that's good enough for me."

Natalie rolled her eyes. "Clark, Kimber's an actor playing a fictional character in a novel. None of it is real."

"No, her body is definitely real. That's what's so convincing." Clark looked for Ray to join in his joke.

But Ray peered at the floor.

Natalie noticed this. She observed Ray's face intently, hoping to deduce his thoughts. *You thought Staci's body convincing. But she left you.*

Ray looked up—not at Clark but at Natalie. His eyes appeared pensive. "Think I should ask Finder? Y'know, if he believes his own stories?"

Natalie looked at her iPad. "Well, we're always after the truth, aren't we? But hasn't it already been asked? Thought I read in another interview, he confessed he's a Disher."

"Said he believes in justice. Maybe that's not the same."

"Dishers think he's one of them. Would crown him king if they could," Natalie said. She looked up at Ray flirtatiously and added, "I read that his fans pass out his novels to Dish-deniers. Like to try to convert them."

"What do you mean?"

With a coy smile, Natalie reached into her bag and pulled out Ray's copy of *Templars of Doom*. "Are you converting me?" she laughed, holding it up for him to see.

Ray shrank back defensively. "You trying to be funny? I gave Templars to you as research."

Natalie sighed and lowered the book to the table. She was, in fact, trying to be funny, to speak Ray's language, but she hadn't succeeded. She rarely did. Quickly, to hide her gaffe, she switched back to work mode. She flipped *Templars* over. On the back cover was a big photo of Finder in black and white. He leaned with chin in one hand, staring at nothing, a pose implying that he was a man of sensitivity and introspection, a man bearing the burden of his own penetrating intellect. Below the photo was an endorsement from *Business Weekly*: "Steve Finder is not only a compelling novelist but also a modern prophet in the wilderness sounding the clarion call for justice." Natalie read the endorsement aloud, then stared at the book for a moment.

"What are you thinking?" Ray asked hesitantly.

"Oh, maybe it doesn't matter what Finder believes about the Dish. What matters is what his readers believe about him. This endorsement makes him sound like an activist for social justice. Is that why people read his books? To participate in the cause against the Catholic Church?"

"Reading a book's not doing anything," Clark said. "People are fooling themselves if they think that. Don't people read to escape their lives for a while? Just to have fun?"

Ray stroked his chin. "Why don't we ask him that? Why he thinks his books are so popular?"

"I like that," Natalie said, making a note. "Part of the purpose for our film is to explore the power of stories to shape people's beliefs. Even the stories people tell themselves."

"She likes it." Ray signaled a fist bump with Clark to celebrate Natalie's approval.

"Maybe he's just in it to meet women like Kimber," Clark interjected as he fist-bumped with Ray.

Natalie pretended not to have heard this, but Clark went on: "If he was, if it was just a game to him, and his fans knew, would they, like, still buy his books?"

"I wouldn't," Ray said. "He'd be a total phony."

"It's pointless to ask him," Natalie said impatiently, "he'd never own up to it."

Clark grinned at Ray. "You got tactics. Remember Monica's Dress?"

They all chuckled. During the filming of that documentary, Ray had pretended to end their interview with the dry cleaner, but he secretly signaled to Clark to keep the camera rolling. Trusting that he wasn't being recorded, the man let slip that the semen stain on Monica's dress "was shaped like Florida, the Keys and all."

"Tactics won't work in this case," Natalie said. "Finder's too experienced. He's been interviewed a hundred times. Anyway, I still think such a line of questioning about his personal beliefs would get us off track. Even if he told you he's a diehard Disher, would you believe him?" she asked Clark. "People will lie when money's at stake."

Clark shrugged. "Good point."

"How 'bout this," Ray said, "we ask him what he thinks would happen if the true Dish were ever found. How does he think the world would change? That sorta gets at the issue of what he believes in without asking him directly."

"Tactics," Clark said.

Natalie thought Ray's idea very good and said so. Their strategy session went on for another hour. Ray never sat down but paced about, tossing out ideas to Natalie, the big contours of his vision. She fleshed out the details, shaped and organized them. Several times Ray leaned against the table to look over Natalie's shoulder at the image taking form on her iPad. Whenever he pointed at the screen, she playfully slapped his finger away. By the hour's end, their ideas had become so perfectly melded into one structure, it was impossible to tell who had thought of what.

Natalie leaned back in her chair, stretching her arms over her head, feeling very satisfied. In moments such as these, she remembered how good 8 Ball Productions had been. How good it could be again. She'd loved working with Ray. Loved experiencing their passions for the work align, and their ideas materialize. When they were working, nothing else mattered. It was just them and the world they were making. No one could interfere. She could easily fool herself into believing that he loved her.

*Templars of Doom* still lay on the table. After examining Finder's picture on the back cover, Natalie hadn't returned it to her bag. She picked up the book and flipped it to the front. The bosomy Princess Calixta appeared a bit less haughty than before. For the last hour, neither Clark nor Ray had once mentioned her. And Kimber Grant was quite forgotten. Did Ray love her after all, as Clark had said? Natalie wondered. Or did he only love their work?

Clark gathered his coat to leave.

Ray sank down on the sofa and propped his feet on the coffee table.

Natalie threw away the empty pizza boxes and returned to her perch chair.

Clark left, and suddenly, in a room that minutes before had been complete with conversation, there was silence.

Natalie felt a flutter of nervousness. She bit her lip. If ever there was an opportunity for Ray to talk to her about what had happened between them, then now was the time. She felt sure when he did apologize for what he'd said and done, she'd forgive him. And yet, as the silence lingered, she keenly felt how uncertain the outcome of such a discussion would be. What if it didn't go as she hoped? As Reggie had promised? What if, after all, Ray didn't love her? What would happen to their *Dish Movie*, to 8 Ball Productions, only barely resurrected? She thought of the poor critical reception to her solo project, her screenplay *Almost a Loneliness*. The film had languished with a two-star rating. "Too much symbolism and not enough sizzle," one critic had complained. Her personal relationship with Ray was in great doubt. What she most wanted was a sure thing.

Ray took his feet off the coffee table and leaned forward on his elbows. His shirt was unbuttoned; she had a clear view of his chest. She detected that his Henley shirt was new and wondered if he still had the old blue one she liked. Ray intertwined his fingers and tapped his thumbs. Natalie detected that he didn't know what to do with his hands. Formerly, during such a lull, Ray would've played with his Mystic 8 Ball. But he didn't have the toy anymore.

## THE DIE IS CAST

Natalie lowered her eyes, remembering what she'd said to Ray that September night three years before. She was set to leave for London to marry Geoffrey. She'd hoped to make a clean break, but Ray had shown up at Midtown Studios while she was packing:

"Nat, please, don't go. It will be the end of us, of everything we've built together."

"Built together? You mean 8 Ball Productions? Is that what really matters to you?" she said hotly.

He looked about wildly for his Mystic 8 Ball, realizing it was missing. "Where is it?" he demanded. "Is it in there?" He grabbed the box she was filling. It was cardboard and bent against the pressure. He rummaged through it but didn't find the toy. He cursed. "Tell me where it is."

She didn't look at him but reordered the box, eliminating all traces of the mess he'd made.

He leaned over the desk to bring his face in line with hers. "Please, Nat ... tell me ..."

With some pleasure, she detected the desperate hope in his voice. A grim smirk slowly cut itself across her face.

"I threw it away."

With anxious eyes Natalie looked up at Ray seated on the sofa and still twiddling his thumbs. She didn't want him to speak. The situation between them was too complicated. There was too much to sort out. And there was too much at stake professionally. The *Dish Movie* should be their priority. They should focus on what was working between them—on what had always worked.

"I—I wanted to tell you," she blurted.

Ray jerked his head up, anticipation in his eyes.

"Um, our press passes. The papers you gave me from Reggie. I've looked at them, and there's a problem."

Ray frowned. His shoulders slumped. "Oh."

After their interview with Finder, Ray and Natalie were going to Turkey to film. They'd timed their trip to coincide with the arrival of Pope Boniface, who was to celebrate the Feast of Forgiveness in Istanbul with the titular head of the Orthodox Church, Ecumenical Patriarch Philotheos.

"We're instructed to pick up our passes by 4:00pm the day before the Feast," Natalie said. "At the Church of Saint George. But that's the same day we return to Istanbul from Cappadocia, from our cave tour. What if we're delayed? We need to get them before we go to Cappadocia."

"I'll call Reggie tomorrow." With a wry smile, Ray added, "I'm filming the Pope. I almost feel guilty."

"Why guilty?"

"No reason, just ... well, I was raised Catholic. My grandmother made sure of it. But I haven't been to confession in, oh, twenty years at least."

"I've never been. My parents were Protestants. They don't do confession. You just say a prayer in your heart."

Ray snorted derisively. "Lucky you."

"Is it awful? Confessing? I wouldn't know."

Ray leaned back into the sofa. "The first time is the worst, I guess. Because the priest—well, at my parish it was Father Stanley. He was a meek and cheery guy. Smoked like a chimney. Always went to our little-league games."

"That doesn't sound so bad."

"No, but see in the confessional, it was different—he was different. He sat behind the lattice. You couldn't see all his face. It was just a shadow sorta hovering there like a phantom. I was just a kid. I mean, you imagine things. You knew he was there listening, waiting for you to say something. You rehearse what you're gonna say ahead of time. To prepare. You know what you need to say. There's a formula to it. In the name of the Father, Son, and Holy Spirit—that's how you're supposed to start. But when you get in there—I mean, you fumble around, and it doesn't come out right. You feel like an idiot. Half the things you'd planned to say, you forget. Which is probably a good thing. I mean, you can't take forever. There are people in line behind you." At the end of this speech, Ray looked up at Natalie. His eyes, as before, appeared pensive—sad.

Natalie studied his face, trying to understand. His voice was surprisingly serious. Why was he telling her this? Maybe Reggie was right—Ray was heartsick.

"One time," he said, "I remember, I was so tongue-tied, I couldn't think of anything—what I'd done, what I was supposed to confess. I—I made up something."

"You lied to the priest?"

"Yeah. That was the last time. After that, I never went back." Ray peered down at his hands. He seemed to study them and rubbed his palms together.

Watching him, Natalie could feel her heartbeat. She scarcely wanted to breathe, to disrupt the stillness. Ray sat across from her, but the space between them suddenly didn't seem that far. The silence in the room hovered like a sheltering cloud. It was so intimate. Natalie was acutely aware of her own body, of Ray's presence. He'd shared a secret with her. Maybe something he'd never told anyone else. She felt a responsibility to speak, to assure him that she treasured his secret, that she could be trusted with more. Here at last was a bridge of sorts, and despite her fears and the uncertainty, she wanted to cross it.

"Is—is something wrong?" she quietly asked him.

"Hmm? No, no. It's nothing." He stood up. "We've got a game plan, don't we? The interview questions—they're good. Everything's good. Look, I'll see ya tomorrow, okay?"

Natalie stepped back from the bridge.

"Right. Yes, everything's good."

Scene 7

# Family Secrets

*Grandeur, Georgia*

*Tuesday, March 9*

Max Whitaker wanted to be at Augusta National practicing his swing. The day was sunny but moderate with little to no breeze. Given such optimal golfing conditions, naturally his mother would summon him to Whiningham, the family estate, to lecture him about his daughter Jane.

"Max, I asked you a question."

Reluctantly, Max shifted his gaze from a window to his mother. They sat in the home office that had once belonged to Max's father Everett Maximilian Whitaker. Patricia sat behind a claw-footed desk, her head half-obscured by the wing of a bronze eagle that formed the base of a lamp. When Everett was living, the desk had faced the west window that overlooked the lake. Since his death, Patricia had angled it toward the room's center. But everything else she'd left the same. On the wall behind the desk were mounted two Civil War rifles and a collection of hunting trophies—a buck, a black bear, a wild boar, and most impressively, a lion. Except for the fact that Everett had purchased the trophies on eBay, the office might've belonged to famed author and big game hunter Ernest Hemingway. Everett had been a big fan.

"Max?" Patricia said again. Her eyes were icy blue just like his. And just like him, Patricia was tall and broad shouldered, her face attractively angular. But the similarities ended there—as she often reminded him.

Max sat in a leather armchair. He leaned back, casually resting his head in his hands and stretching out his long, lean legs. Though he was past fifty, his golden hair was free of gray and fell in lazy layers to his shirt collar in a strategic display of youthfulness. He wore a green golf shirt, and his face and arms were tanned, partly from year-round golf and partly from bronzing lotions. His teeth were unnaturally white, his nails manicured. He was, after all, the face of Whitaker Corporation and had to maintain an image. He had no idea what Patricia had asked him. Not that his reply would matter.

Patricia had sleek, silver hair cut to the angle of her jaw. Her hair was immobile in any weather. She swiped at a disobedient strand swaying before her left eye. "Well?"

"Look, Jane is who she is."

"How profound."

"What can I say?"

"Say you'll put a stop to this—this Dishing of hers!" Patricia spat out the word *Dishing* as if she'd swallowed a bug.

"I can't stop her. She's an adult."

"An adult? Please. With that little rat dog of hers?"

"She wouldn't listen to me. She's never listened to me."

"That's just an excuse not to intervene."

Max frowned. "It isn't an excuse. It's a statement of fact."

"You only think so," Patricia countered, narrowing her icy eyes. "When have you ever seriously tried, hmm? Your daughter goes gallivanting around the world—"

"Hmph. You think it's so easy to help someone."

"—making a mess and putting herself in who knows what kind of danger. Max, she went to the middle of Turkey."

Max glanced out the window and said nothing.

"Are you listening to me?" Patricia asked irritably.

"I heard you," Max answered crossly. "You want her grounded? I can tell Flint not to fly her anywhere, but she'll just go to the airport or ask one of her friends."

"*Friends*. Ha! Is that what you call them?"

"Meena's the one who flew her to Moscow—"

"Dilettantes—all of them. It's shameful."

"—and she has her own money. Well, not technically."

"No. Technically it's our money. Hard-earned. Technically she has nothing."

Max studied the ceiling. "So, shall we disinherit her?"

Patricia narrowed her eyes. "Don't tempt me."

"What did she cost me this time? What's my tab?"

"This isn't funny at all."

"Did she buy an island and set up a Disher kingdom?"

"Dammit, Max!" Patricia slapped one hand on the desk.

Max smirked. Few things in his life amused him, but one thing that always did was pushing his mother to the brink. After so many years, he thought for sure he would've gotten tired of provoking her. But he hadn't.

"It's a circus with reporters," Patricia said. "Is that what you want? Another Moscow? The paparazzi camped outside your penthouse? Or chasing you around the golf course?"

"Fine." Max sat upright. "What happened now?"

"Did you even read the article I sent you?"

Max glanced at the floor, a sure indication that he hadn't.

With exaggerated calm, Patricia folded a newspaper in her hands and stood. She walked around the desk and thrust the paper in Max's face. "Front page."

Reluctantly, Max took the paper and propped it on one knee; it was the local *Atlanta Journal-Constitution*. In the bottom right corner below the crease were two color pictures: Jane by her Range Rover holding Baby Girl; and a headshot of a man in a bow tie whose name was Dr. Frank Carlisle. WHITAKER HEIRESS FRAUD EXPOSED BY EXPERT read the headline. Max scanned the story:

Monday, March 8, Atlanta

Officials at the Summit Art Museum announced Friday that they have uncovered a potential forgery scheme involving Ms. Jane Whitaker, granddaughter of the late Mr. Everett Maximilian Whitaker, cofounder of Whitaker Corporation.

Dr. Frank Carlisle, curator of the museum since 2005, said he received information from Whitaker regarding a Byzantine icon purported to depict Saint Nil, a thirteenth-century Orthodox monk. "She made extraordinary claims about the icon's authenticity. But Saint Nils are rare. Only one has ever been found, and it was a partial one at that," said Carlisle.

Saint Nil, one of the legendary Four Keepers of the Last Supper Dish, has long been a person of interest to Dish enthusiasts. "His icon is believed to hold the key to recovering the lost Dish—if you believe it's lost," said Carlisle.

Photos Carlisle obtained from Whitaker provide strong evidence that the Saint Nil icon in question is a sophisticated forgery. "I was immediately suspicious. Clearly, upon inspection, I could see the bowl was superimposed," said Carlisle. "Weeding out counterfeits is part and parcel of my job."

Carlisle denied that the Summit Museum would ever traffic in or profit from the display of inauthentic artifacts, but he confessed that he knew of other institutions that were not so scrupulous. "Dishing is big business, and the antiquities trade is one of the least policed."

Whitaker, whose arrest in Moscow last November drew international attention to—

"That's *your* daughter out there making a fool of herself." Patricia stood over Max with her arms crossed. "Making a fool of *us*," she added.

And that's what really matters, Max thought, folding up the paper. He scowled, having heard this criticism from his mother before, and not just about Jane.

Patricia returned to her desk. "That man Carlisle makes Jane sound like she's the head of a global antiquities cartel. Did you know this story has been picked up by the Times and the Tribune? Listen to these headlines—Dishing on Daddy's Dime—and—Whitaker's Cappadocian Humiliation. It's like a conspiracy. Like they knew she'd run to the museum the second she stepped off the plane. This behavior of hers has escalated far beyond anything I could've imagined. She should've outgrown all this years ago."

"Maybe she still will. Let her be."

"I don't understand it. Do you know what she said to me this morning when I showed her these stories?"

Max raised his eyebrows.

"She said—People talk about me. So what? It just proves I'm special." Patricia shook her head, experiencing the consternation of her granddaughter's reply afresh. "I mean, really! She doesn't care what people say, so long as they're talking. That's what matters. Can you believe?" She let out an exasperated snort and waited for Max's reaction.

Max said nothing. Because in one instant, he saw everything clearly. Ever since he could remember, his mother had used the threat of negative press against him, to keep him obedient. "Whitaker Corporation is a vast empire," she'd often said to him, "but all empires are only as strong as everyone's belief in their strength. Do not be a cause of doubt. Do not be the weak link." And he'd listened to her—mostly. The follies of his youth had long since receded from the public's consciousness, though his mother never let him forget them. Not that he could forget, even without her reminders. Because the product of those follies was Jane. And what of Jane? Max strove to hide a smile as the irony of the situation sank in: *Jane is immune to negative press.*

"I don't understand it." Patricia tapped her fingers on the desk. "Here. Look at this—have you seen this?" She opened her MacBook and pressed a few keys. "Kathleen showed it to me. I'd no idea ..."

Kathleen was Max's older sister. She'd never married nor had any romantic interest as far as Max knew. Not that he wanted to know. She'd been close to their father Everett, though since his death, she'd latched on to Patricia, acting as a liaison for her at Whitaker Corporate Headquarters. Kathleen had none of Max's physical charms but made up for this deficiency by being, as Patricia often remarked, "a steady star in a storm." At the mention of his sister's name, Max stood and flicked the *Atlanta Journal-Constitution* at Patricia's desk. But the newspaper hit the bronze eagle lamp and fluttered to the floor as if the eagle had swatted it out of the air. Max stooped to retrieve the paper, overcome by the feeling that his own escape was similarly doomed.

"Sit down, Max."

Slowly, Max slumped back into the leather chair, pulled down by gravity and by the long-ingrained habit of obedience. After all, it was easier to obey. He could feel the sun setting on his golf game. Long ago it had set on his hopes; long ago he'd believed that if he obeyed his mother enough, some day she would stop demanding it. That day, he knew, would never come.

Patricia pushed her MacBook toward Max. "Jane has a Dishpix account."

"What's that?" he asked indifferently.

"Just look."

Unwillingly, Max took the Mac in his hands. On the screen was a thumbnail image of Jane looking like an elfin princess. Her eyes, wistful and languid, were shadowed in blue, and she wore a shimmery, silver kimono with a matching diamond headband that fell like fringe over her forehead. Her long blonde hair was parted in the center, as were her lips. Next to this image was a heading and a tagline:

### Adventures with Lady Jane
'Cause adventure is my destiny!

Max scrolled down the screen. There were more images of Jane, an endless inventory. "What is this, a blog?"

"A social media site," Patricia said scornfully, "for people as ridiculous as her."

"You mean for Dishers."

"Yes!"

Max scrolled back up to the top. In Jane's latest post, she was posing in a street, wearing a white Barmah hat and holding a brown-paper package. The image appeared to have been taken at noonday—the colors were bright and saturated. Jane's blue eyes appeared violet. Max clicked on the image and it enlarged. There were scores of comments posted beneath it. The first one said: "totally dope hat! where can i get one?" The second one said: "looking good girl! nobody dishes like u!" He quickly gave up trying to read the rest. There were too many emojis.

"Who's taking these pictures?"

"She is."

"What for?"

"Isn't it obvious?" Patricia said sarcastically. "To document her travels."

"Her travels. Right." Max chuckled. "But all the pictures are of her. Oh, wait, here's one of Baby Girl."

Patricia leaned forward and massaged her temples.

Max set the Mac back on the desk.

Patricia sighed and spun it toward her. "Who does she think she is?" she hissed. "Lady Jane—what the hell is that? Is she European royalty? Is she living in a Steve Finder novel? I regret encouraging her to read. Just look at this—she's got eighteen hundred posts and over a hundred thousand followers. Why they're following her and where she's leading them is beyond me. It's the blind leading the blind."

"Probably it shouldn't be taken literally."

"Wait till reporters find this—if they haven't already. The press lives to attack us. They'll exploit any possible advantage. Jane makes it far too easy. She should be ashamed. You know what her problem is?" Patricia snapped her Mac shut. "She assumes everyone loves her. Even worse, she thinks everyone should. It doesn't occur to her to think that some trinket salesman in a shop with a tailless cat in the middle of Turkey might be lying when he says he has a Saint Nil for sale. Everybody lies. Lying is the easiest thing—"

"Tailless cat?"

"Yes, er, um, Kathleen mentioned it."

Patricia kept talking, but more to herself than to Max. As she spoke, she fiddled with the 6.5-carat diamond in her wedding ring. "I don't know when this got so out of hand. I should've kept her close. I should've never let her move with you to Manhattan, I don't care how bored she was of Atlanta. I should've never let her enroll at Harold

More. All those friends she met—a terrible influence. They'll all end up as tabloid trash. I should've insisted she go to the University of Pennsylvania and study business. It's the family tradition for heaven's sake. What's she doing at NYU? Studying forensic science, then fashion design, then criminal justice … you know what she told Kathleen recently? She said she's decided to become an actress. An actress! Oh, what would Everett say? I thought when Gloria left … but maybe some things are just irrevocably in the blood."

Here Patricia's drifting discourse ceased, as if at the mention of the name *Gloria*, it had found its designated port. Max could've predicted the ship's bearing, as his mother often anchored on the subject of his first wife.

Gloria was Jane's mother. And as anyone in the family could plainly see, Jane was just like her.

Max shifted in his chair, pretending to ponder Patricia's speech deeply. It pleased him to see his mother so discomfited over Jane. He liked to imagine Patricia suffering anxiety over the possibility of her legacy being wasted, that when she, Max, and Kathleen followed Everett to their graves, Whitaker Corporation would be deposited into the hands of a fool. Dollar by dollar Jane would squander the Whitaker fortune, bankrupting their 8,500 retail stores by spending the 498 billion dollars in annual sales searching for the Last Supper Dish. If Patricia believed this, if she were afraid for her empire, then Max felt he owed Jane his congratulations, for she'd accomplished the one thing he'd never been able to do: she'd gotten free.

For the first time, it occurred to Max that his mother might've summoned him to Whiningham because she sincerely needed his help. And now that the moment had arrived, he wondered if he would help her after all.

"You, uh, want me to talk to Jane?" he offered casually.

"Would you?" Patricia looked pleadingly at her son; the corners of her mouth twitched in an expression that seemed almost kind. "I pray desperately that you would."

"What should I say? Max stood and tossed the *Atlanta Journal-Constitution* onto Patricia's desk, this time successfully. "What could be said that hasn't been said already?"

"Maybe it'll be enough for her to see that you care." Patricia picked up the paper. "After all, you're her father." She glanced at the picture of Dr. Frank Carlisle. "And she has just suffered a betrayal."

Max imagined Jane up in her room, a tearful mass of grief, and was struck by the futility of his task. Talking Jane out of Dishing would be like asking her to give up Baby Girl. The two simply went together. He put his hands on his hips and looked out the window, searching for inspiration. "Adventures with Lady Jane ..."

"Yes, perhaps you might begin by proposing that she and her followers should disband," Patricia suggested helpfully.

"Mm, yes." Max's tone was noncommittal. Inspiration had struck him, but it was inspiration of a different sort. "Saint Nil. Was that the name? The icon in the article?"

"I believe so."

"Huh. Interesting. Saint Nil. Saint Nothing." His gaze remained fixed on the window. "Say, speaking of prayer, what kind of prayer do you pray to a Saint of Nothing?"

"I wouldn't know, I'm Presbyterian." Patricia glanced at her watch.

Max smirked and turned toward the door. "Could a Saint of Nothing give you something? I mean, if you prayed for it—for something?"

"Please, Max, you know I don't like irony. And don't go far. I may need you at Corporate soon."

Max opened the door but glanced over his shoulder. "It's an interesting speculation, don't you think? Maybe a Saint of Nothing can only give you nothing. But if you prayed to him for nothing instead of something, would that truly be a prayer?" He kept a straight face as he spoke, unable to resist a parting provocation.

Patricia stared her son down, her blue eyes furious. "Someday you'll wish you'd done more to intervene," she said, "But it'll be too late. Jane will be far away. Far beyond your reach. She'll be gone. Just like her mother."

▼ ▼ ▼ ▼

Max shut the door to Patricia's office with more firmness than he'd intended. He was angry that his parting shot had boomeranged. Although he hated to admit it, his mother was good at getting to him. When she reminded him of Jane's mother, she always hit the bull's-eye.

*Gloria.*

*Gloria Kilday.*

Max marched down the hall toward the Great Room at the center of the house. Whiningham was situated on eighty acres near the town of Grandeur, twenty miles southwest of Atlanta. Everett had named his property

Whiningham after vacationing one summer in England. Touring the royal palaces had much impressed him. "Our money's as good as theirs, and even better, 'cause we got more of it." The Whitaker home was classic colonial with six grand columns supporting a covered second-floor balcony. Everett had greatly expanded the original structure, adding the East and West Wings during the economic boom of the 1980s.

As Max entered the Great Room, his eye caught the large gilt frame hanging above the fireplace. Once that frame had held his and Gloria's wedding picture. Now it held a mirror. He opened the front door and went out onto the porch. He leaned against the balustrade and scanned the horizon past the boathouse. There was nothing on the horizon. No matter how many times he studied vistas or skylines or faces in a crowd, there was never any revelation, never a dramatic reappearance. She'd vanished, and she wasn't coming back.

*Where are you, Gloria?*

This question remained a sore knot on his soul; every now and then he felt it ache. It ached more as Jane had gotten older. Because Jane was so much like her mother.

In the weeks before Gloria's disappearance, Max had noticed nothing amiss, nothing but the usual problems—such as Patricia blaming him for being so recklessly "fooled by beauty." His marriage had been the product of an eight-week whirlwind romance, an adventure halfway around the world, culminating in an elopement to Vegas (Gloria's idea) for a wedding witnessed very happily by several Elvis Presleys. Max had never felt so alive.

## FAMILY SECRETS

In retrospect, he'd missed some signs: Gloria's increasing aloofness after Jane's birth, for instance. But then again, Gloria always stood apart from others like "a goat in a world of sheep," as she often said with conviction. His most distinct memory of those final days was of an early evening in March: he and Gloria were walking near the lake at Whiningham and she remarked how free the clouds were, "like fallen leaves" because "both are given over to the wind." Soon after that, one morning after Easter, Max found an envelope on his dresser. Opening it, he read:

> My head is spinnin'
> Seein' visions
> Stars lift me up
> I kiss the moon
> Leave earth below.
> Round 'n round we go.
> Our lines recited
> I do, you do
> The stage is set
> We wear our roles
> This little show.
> Round 'n round we go.
> The curtain drops, I
> wanna hide, stars
> align, they chase
> the sun, earth runs
> away, say yes, say no.
> Round 'n round I go.

## THE DIE IS CAST

> Breaking up
> Breaking out
> Spinning apart
> Round 'n round
> I gotta stop.
> P.S. Please take care of Jane.

Max brushed the balustrade with his hand as if rubbing out a stain. He wandered to the porch's other side, away from the lake. Even after all this time, he still felt cheated that Gloria had plagiarized her goodbye note. Except for the P.S., she'd quoted the lyrics to "Round 'n Round" from The Circling, a one-hit-wonder techno '80s girl band.

As it turned out, her plagiarism had been symptomatic. In Max's mind reverberated the everlasting echo of Patricia's scream: *My jewels!* Evidently, he'd married a criminal. When she could, Patricia still accused him of doing so knowingly, of giving "the noble Whitaker name" to a woman who'd (no doubt) conspired from the very beginning, acting a part, and playing them all for fools. Kathleen didn't quite take her mother's position, pronouncing Gloria's theft "tragic," though to Max it seemed his sister still took delight in declaring "the utter ruination" of his life.

Everett initiated a manhunt that lasted a year. Jane had just turned three. Authorities tracked Gloria into Ecuador, but Patricia insisted her husband call off the dogs. She wanted "the whole ridiculous affair" put to rest because she was tired of the headlines: WHITAKER IN-LAW STILL ON THE RUN; WIFE STEALS 1.3

MILLION IN JEWELS; WHITAKER FAMILY CLAIMS NO KNOWLEDGE OF KILDAY POLICE RECORD. How humiliating, Patricia lamented, to answer the same questions wherever she went: "When did you realize your jewels were missing?" and "When did you suspect your daughter-in-law?" and "What will happen when you find her?" Patricia's answer: "Justice will happen!" As Max well-knew, his mother's position on "that pernicious woman" never wavered.

Max never called Gloria's theft a crime. He believed his wife simply succumbed to her inherent weakness, as anyone would have who'd grown up poor, in and out of foster care, and (as it turned out) with a history of petty theft a hundred yards long. In the early years after Gloria's disappearance, Max pressured his parents to make a public statement absolving Gloria in hopes that his wife might see it. "Maybe if she thought she was forgiven, she'd come back," he argued. But Patricia refused. Her obstinacy remained an infinite rift between mother and son.

To Max's knowledge, ever since her disappearance, Gloria had corresponded with the Whitaker family only once—on Jane's sixteenth birthday. Kathleen brought Jane a package mistakenly already opened. In it was a locket and chain, finely crafted, antique, and 18K gold. The locket was decorated with jewels and with a profile of a woman's face. There was a note in Gloria's characteristic slanted script:

> To my beautiful girl, all grown up, a poem:
> When the wind is rushing by,

## THE DIE IS CAST

> When it roars in the dark
> Like a river just out of sight,
> Threatening with its fury to uproot you,
> Let the wind come and rage,
> Let it tousle your hair
> And lick your cheeks.
> Give yourself to its embrace,
> And what was once a storm
> Will soon become a dance.
> From one who loves you deeply, from a distance

Jane had shrugged and pronounced the locket "pretty." But Patricia declared it "garish" and considered it an act of micro-aggression: "How dare she give jewels as a gift. Flaunting her crimes in my face. That pernicious woman!"

Publicly, Max conceded the irony of Gloria's choice, but privately he hoped for more such gestures for Jane's sake—but also for his own. Because despite his intentions and despite all the women who'd come after her, he still cared for Gloria. And because he wanted to know *why*. Why had she left? It couldn't simply have been for the money.

Soon after Jane's sixteenth birthday, Max hired detectives who traced Gloria's package to Saint Petersburg, Russia. But they failed to trace the sender. And then there were no more packages. No more clues. Just the one shimmering burst of sentiment. Max once searched the internet for Gloria's poem. He found nothing. Evidently, to mark the occasion, she'd blessed Jane with an original composition.

Soon after receiving the locket, Jane bought herself a puppy—Baby Girl.

Max paced on the porch. Jane was upstairs in her room. He looked again toward the lake. Is my mother right that I should intervene? he wondered. His only intervention in Jane's life had been allowing her to move in with him to go to high school in Manhattan. How that had turned out, he couldn't say. Jane had returned to the penthouse one Saturday looking kaleidoscopic, wearing a pink dress, an aqua cashmere cardigan, red tights, a brown felt hat, and blue bumblebee sunglasses. She carried three Chanel shopping bags. "I've been out spending your mo-ney," she giggled. Max had felt blinded by a memory. He saw himself back at the University of Pennsylvania standing in The Quad, waiting to glimpse that imaginative girl in a hat he'd met in Cultural Anthropology.

Jane's resemblance to Gloria was uncanny. Patricia called it "disturbing" and accused Jane of deliberate simulation. "Why would I do that?" Jane countered. "It's stupid. I don't know her." Kathleen believed Jane had repressed a traumatic childhood memory of Gloria. She encouraged Jane to access her unconscious. "Why do you all act like there's something wrong with me?" Jane retorted. "I'm not broken. I don't need fixing." Before his death, Everett predicted Jane would turn criminal like her mother and suggested the military academy as a pre emptive cure. "Just because you don't have a map doesn't mean you're lost," Jane asserted. It was a quote from a Steve Finder novel.

Max turned toward the front door and placed his hand on the knob, fully intending to open it, to hike up the

Grand East Staircase and have it out with Jane. But he didn't.

Once in his life, he'd intervened. He'd given a poor women riches. She was gone now.

Max took his hand off the door and headed toward his car. What did it matter if he put off talking with Jane for one more day? Nothing would change Jane. Patricia would find fault with him regardless of his decision.

Yes, he knew Jane's obsession to find the Last Supper Dish was absurd, but still, he admired her resolve. And yes, her naïveté was aggravating, yet also endearing. And yes, her adventurousness was quixotic, but also exhilarating. Her sanctimoniousness maddening. But her kindness remarkable. She was always beautiful.

She was all the things her mother had been.

And maybe, after all, he didn't want that to change.

Scene 8

# Panikos the Youth

*Istanbul, Turkey*

*Excavation site at the demolished Sirkeci Rail Station*

*Tuesday, March 9*

"Adam, how impressive," Ayhan gasped. She'd just descended the ramp and entered the pit facing the west wall of the shrine. She wore a tailored, red-leather jacket and held a thermos and two paper cups. Her eyes widened as she beheld the bold, bright image of a monk. His beardless face was framed by soft ringlets of hair like a woman's, and dimples on either side of his lips made him appear to be smiling. His eyes twinkled mischievously, or perhaps it was the effect of the morning light. The crisp, white rays of dawn played upon the mosaic, causing the tesserae to sparkle like diamonds. Burke brushed the smooth stones at the monk's shoulders to remove vestiges of dirt.

"Yes, isn't it?" he grinned. He stared at the image like an artist examining a finished portrait.

Ayhan poured him a cup of coffee.

Burke held the paper cup before his eyes as if it were a victory chalice. A vision flashed in his mind, a vision of himself on a throne surrounded by knights and maidens, all chanting, "Hail to Burke, the Scholar King!" Before him stood Winters bound in chains, naturally. What should his sentence be? Banishment from the realm? Or the dungeon?

Ayhan poured a cup of coffee for herself and set down the thermos. "You work alone? Where are the others?"

"Asleep. We spent all night digging out Panikos here. Calvino, Stoltzfus, Foo—everyone. It was quite the undertaking, but with my supervision—"

"Adam, you worked all night? You need to rest."

Burke waved away Ayhan's concern. "I've waited my whole life for this, Zainab. I was going to be here no matter what. And besides, I wanted to be the one to introduce you to our new friend—Panikos the Youth, one of the Four Keepers." Burke gave the monk a playful whisk on the chest with his painter's brush and addressed the mosaic. "Panikos, meet Dr. Zainab Ayhan, curator of the Museum of Ancient History. Here's to the beginning of a beautiful friendship."

Burke raised his cup in the gesture of a toast. Ayhan laughed and tapped her cup to his.

"You are giddy," she teased. "May I?" She lifted the brush from Burke's hand and stepped in front of him. Reaching up, she gently swept the brush across Panikos's halo which dipped inward at intervals like the petals of a giant sunflower. There was a graceful angle to the youth's neck, and his shoulders were thrown back, lifting his chest. She ran the soft bristles along Panikos's side down to his waist. The folds of his robe accentuated the curve of his slim hip.

"I did not expect it to be so very large," she murmured.

With unhurried strokes, she rhythmically caressed the youth's hip, tracing the brush down the line of his leg. "The proportions are excellent. The stonework flawless. Magnificent." She took a step back, her eyes lingering on the golden bowl Panikos held aloft. When she turned to look at Burke, her face was flushed.

Burke stood unblinking, his mouth agape, hypnotized.

"This coffee is too warm, I think," Ayhan said with a nervous laugh. She tried to hand the brush back to Burke.

He gazed at the brush trying to discern its magical properties. Watching Ayhan use it on Panikos had strangely moved him. He felt warm indeed and tried to lift his hand to take the brush from her, but his arm felt weak.

"An extraordinary find," Ayhan said, still holding the brush. "You have ... outdone yourself ... professor." As she spoke, her voice wavered with passion.

Burke shook his head to clear his muddled mind. He felt the full force of Ayhan's beauty, and at the same time, the force of his own physical inadequacies. Did she notice his bald spot? The answer to this question made him nervous. He fled from knowing the answer by using an old trick—he lowered his chin and looked at Ayhan over his glasses in a pose of erudition. Her face at once blurred. He would never see in her eyes the answer to the question. Instantly, his mind cleared. "Er, you were the one who called me. It was you who brought the team together. It couldn't have happened without you." Slowly, he lifted the brush from her hand and slid it into his back pocket.

They each sipped their coffee and stared up at the golden bowl.

Ayhan broke the silence. "You say this is one of the Four Keepers? You believe this is their shrine? The bowl the monk holds is suggestive."

"Yes, uh, the shrine," Burke said, trying to keep his mind working. "I have two things to show you. The first being Panikos, obviously." Burke looked about him for a place to set his coffee. He turned over an empty bucket and set his cup on top. "Our young monk here—a few things about him bear discussing. The Annals of Andronicus describe his complexion as fair. I checked the reference last night."

"The Annals were written by the Emperor's historian."

"Right. Theodore Metochites. But he isn't quite as specific as, uh, excuse me for a second, will you?" Burke trotted over to the ramp and climbed halfway up.

"Hey, Duffy!" he shouted over the lip of the pit.

Duffy was snoring, propped up against a mound of dirt.

"Hey, Duffy, get up and get over here."

A groggy Duffy, his thinning hair matted with dust, staggered to the pit's edge.

"Bring me the photos of the archway," Burke ordered.

Duffy rubbed his eyes. "The what?"

"The archway! The photographs! Now hurry up."

Duffy scuttled away.

Burke rejoined Ayhan, feeling somehow that by commanding someone else, he'd regained command of himself.

"Let's return to our Panikos, shall we?" he said with authority, stepping around her. The sun had come up, and the light about them warmed. Like a potter desiring to keep his hands in the clay, Burke scratched out some imaginary debris in a crevice on Panikos's hip. "There can be no doubt this is the fabled shrine," he said. "I felt it from the first. Call it a hunch. Weeks ago, when you called me, before I even got here—I just knew."

Ayhan smiled wryly. "Women's intuition, perhaps?"

Burke grinned, welcoming the teasing. "To be honest, and this may sound silly, but I've always felt I've had a certain destiny. I can't explain it."

Ayhan studied his face. "Destiny. Another word for desire, is it not?" She paused. "Your desire is very strong."

Burke looked up at Panikos. "It's strange. What I've wanted my whole life ..."

Ayhan looked at Panikos too. "He would be just the first of four mosaics. If it is destiny."

"Yes, I expect to find Kostas or Zoticus right here," Burke pointed to the left of Panikos. "And maybe Nil would be to the right." He gestured to the rough wall at the edge of the chamber on the other side. "I'll be ordering this all be widened. We need to form a trench in that direction," he pointed east. "If this is the west aisle, then—"

"Then that way is the apse," Ayhan interjected.

"Right. And the altar if it survived."

Ayhan shuddered. She sipped her coffee, then set her cup on the bucket next to Burke's.

Burke too felt a tingling pleasure. It was the pleasure he always felt when clues aligned, and he beheld a vision of the truth. He saw the shape of the shrine now, clearer than any radar image. It appeared before his mind's eye like a block of fine marble, and he was the master sculptor.

"Oh, Adam," Ayhan stepped closer to him, "do you think," her voice dropped dramatically, "do you think the Dish is here?"

Burke placed his hand on Panikos's knee. The tesserae pricked his fingertips. "Go ahead, Zainab. Touch him."

"May I?"

"Of course."

Shyly, Ayhan reached out her hand—then pulled it back.

"Go on," Burke coaxed. "Look at him. He wants you to."

Ayhan laughed self-consciously. Gently, she placed her hand on Panikos's foot.

"Can you feel it?" Burke asked.

"Feel it?"

"The truth of history, Zainab."

She ran her fingers up Panikos's leg. "Tell me, Adam, tell me this is really the Shrine of the Four Keepers."

"I don't have to." Burke reached into his pocket for his phone and held it up to her. "Putney can tell you."

She laughed. "Ah, Putney, the famed English pilgrim."

"That's him. Putney. His travelogue is remarkable—the earliest text we have that locates the Shrine of the Four Keepers in Constantinople. He visited the shrine in, oh, 1350, I believe."

"But Putney does not disclose the exact location."

"True enough," Burke chuckled and began hitting buttons on his phone, "but what he lacks by way of direction, he makes up for—"

"Does he describe this mosaic?" Ayhan asked excitedly.

"—in his description of the interior."

Ayhan leaned in to look at Burke's phone.

"In a minute, I'll show you—I have Putney on speed-dial," Burke joked. He moved his index finger up and down the phone's screen, probing the text. It took him longer than he thought to find the exact spot.

Ayhan fidgeted. "Where is it? Do not tease me."

"Sometimes the things we want so badly must come slowly. Ah, here we are." Burke read a section of Putney's travelogue:

And when I entered the hall, lo, the Four Keepers encircled me and filled mine Soul with awe. Kostas standeth tall and stern, his black eyes see the black secrets of mine Heart. He poureth out Judgment with the Dish. Panikos the Youth dances with Joy, for the Dish is his blessing from God. The wise and aged Zoticus peereth into the Dish and seeth there its Divine Mysteries. And grave Nil holdeth the Dish close unto his breast, for he and his brothers are charged to keep the Secrets of Man. These are the words of them that serve the Shrine to teach pilgrims the true Mysteries of the Dish. I record them so all may know.

"He mentions the Last Supper Dish," Ayhan exclaimed.

"He mentions *a* dish. It's a controversial reference," Burke said. "But consider his description of Panikos. He says the monk is dancing. That's an odd pose. In most iconic images, the saint sits or stands and looks right at you."

"I see many in my work. Very straight-forward objects."

"But our monk here," Burke pointed at Panikos's legs, "is a bit more vivacious than the standard saint."

Ayhan nodded. "The curve in the hip gives the impression of motion."

"Has a hint of a smile, doesn't he? Have you seen any mosaics where the saint is smiling?"

"I cannot recall any. Faces of saints are dour and serious—uniformly formal."

"Exactly." Burke leaned in closer to Ayhan so she could follow the line of his arm as he pointed to Panikos. "His left leg. It's lifted slightly off the ground."

Ayhan stepped up to the mosaic and traced the line of the leg with her fingers.

"He is—" she began with a half-smile, then stopped. "No, I want to hear you say it," she implored. "Keep going."

Burke touched Panikos's ankle and traced the line of the foot down to the toes as if he were tickling the youth. "The foot is off the ground, but the toes are pointed down."

Ayhan shuddered, unable to suppress her delight.

Burke's voice rose in crescendo as he quoted Putney: "Panikos the Youth dances with joy, for the Dish is his blessing from God!"

Ayhan held her hands up to Panikos to dance with him herself. "Then it *is* the Shrine of the Keepers."

"Yes, Zainab. YES!" Burke grazed the glassy surface of the tesserae with his fingertips. "This is the very same wall Putney described 700 years ago. I've never seen a mosaic of any saint dancing. I've always thought Putney was being fanciful or poetic. After all, in the icons we have of Panikos, he doesn't appear to be dancing. He doesn't have any feet. The icons only depict him from the waist up. But I guess Putney was right. He describes what he saw literally. This is a one-of-a-kind mosaic, and it matches Putney perfectly."

Ayhan reached for Burke, grabbing his sleeve, her eyes wide. "Adam, we have done it. The long-lost Shrine of the Four Keepers. That means the Dish—"

"Is very close," Burke finished her thought.

Ayhan closed her eyes, overcome with ecstasy. She kept her grip on Burke's arm.

Burke's eyes followed the line of Ayhan's hand up to her elbow, her breasts, her neck. In her tight leather jacket, her body disclosed every curve. Gazing at her face, Burke felt once again entranced. He had no thoughts, only a strong urge to take her in his arms. He wanted her ... not *her* exactly, but a woman like her, a woman like one he'd known long ago, a woman he'd loved. Ayhan reminded him of the original; she was a close copy, the closest he'd ever seen. So much better than Hromadova. After years of getting nowhere close, perhaps his search was over. He'd no longer be alone with his memory, living with his books and his research, while Winters, that academic Don Juan, cavorted about with his cadre of acolytes, capitalizing on both his stellar intellectual reputation and fetching head of hair. Wouldn't Winters seethe to see Burke with a woman like Ayhan on his arm, a woman of superior brains and beauty.

Burke ran his eyes from Ayhan's face down to her hand. Her fingers, creamy and slender, still gripped his arm. Tentatively, he reached to touch them ...

"Umm, sir? I brought the tablet with all the photos."

The high, pinched voice of Duffy, like the sound of an alarm clock, instantly awakened them. Ayhan opened her eyes and let go of Burke's arm. Burke dropped his hand to his side and stared blankly at his bald assistant trying to recall his name.

"Sir? Am I interrupting?"

"Yes! I mean, no!" Burke snatched the tablet from Duffy. "I was, er, merely sharing the more salient features of Panikos here with Dr. Ayhan."

"Okay, sir," Duffy said. His voice betrayed not the slightest embarrassment. This fact irritated Burke more than the fact of Duffy's interruption itself. By God, his assistant should be coated in embarrassment. Briefly, Burke studied him; a bubble of saliva formed between Duffy's lips. Burke waited to see if the bubble would burst. How could Duffy not feel it? Did people without intelligence know what they were missing?

"Er, why don't you go back to sleep," Burke said to him.

Once he and Ayhan were again alone, Burke quickly scrolled through the tablet's photos, hoping to recapture the moment. He tapped on an image of a thick, triangular block of limestone resting on the ground. It was a fragment of a much larger stone. Two of its sides were rough and irregular, but the third side was a smooth half-moon. "Ah yes," he said to Ayhan as though Duffy had never interrupted, "this is the second thing I wanted to show you."

It took Burke a second to realize that Ayhan was no longer standing next to him. She was sitting on the bucket, having removed the coffee cups. She held her cup in her hands, tapping the sides of it with her fingers, evidently deep in thought. His cup she'd set in the dirt.

Burke felt awkward standing over her and wasn't sure if he should kneel. So, he didn't. He held the tablet down in front of her eyes so she could see the photograph.

"What? Oh, yes." Ayhan barely glanced at it.

"Foo uncovered this gem yesterday afternoon. It was on the north side. I didn't have a chance to study it until this morning. Because of all the commotion with our new friend here, obviously." Burke chuckled, but Ayhan didn't.

He gestured for her to take the tablet, which she did. But she gave the photo only a cursory review. "A pendentive? Fallen from beneath the dome? What did Foo think of the inscription?" She handed the tablet back to Burke and looked up at Panikos and at the golden dish he held aloft.

"A pendentive, you think? Supporting the dome? Hmm."

Burke swiped at the screen to show her the next photo, a close-up of the inscription along the bottom edge of the fragment. "It does look like a pendentive except for the curvature. The picture I showed you was upside down—I mean, the stone was. This one is better." He held the tablet down to her, but the tablet's gyroscopic sensors flipped the image on its head. He set the image right-side up and handed the tablet to her again. Same result. Technology's refusal to cooperate flustered him, and he rotated the tablet again only to have the image resolutely correct itself a third time. "Er, anyway, I don't think it's a pendentive. The curvature is convex. A pendentive is typically concave."

Ayhan smiled politely. "Yes. You are right. Of course."

Eagerly, Burke traced the rounded edge of the stone with his finger and rushed on. "This is a section of a tympanum, I believe. This straight edge must be part of the lintel. I think it crowned the shrine's central entrance."

Ayhan cast her eyes about furtively, looking for her thermos. She poured herself another cup of coffee.

"You can really see the inscription in this one," Burke said, trying to show her another photo. "It's written in Latin. Foo's Latin is a bit shaky. He hides it well, but we all know. Don't tell him I mentioned it, it's supposed to be a secret." Burke pinched the photo to zoom in on the words. "Can you read it? It's sorta fuzzy."

"You can read it, I am sure."

"Yes, but I want to see if you recognize it."

"Should I?"

Burke smiled knowingly, and Ayhan reluctantly took the tablet. She squinted at the lettering. "Stipendia—what is that in English? Stipend or—"

"Wages," Burke said.

"Ah. Earnings. Payment. I see."

She read again: "Peccati ... this word is unfamiliar to me." Shaking her head impatiently, she handed the tablet back to Burke. "I—I cannot read further."

"Peccati means *sin*," Burke explained. "Wages of sin. In English this fragment of the inscription says—keep until the wages of sin are paid. Now that should ring a bell." Burke searched Ayhan's face for signs the bell had rung. He himself was buzzing with glee. She took a sip of coffee. There was a pause while Burke waited for the sound of ringing. When no bell rang, he exclaimed: "PUTNEY!"

Ayhan shook her head, nonplussed.

"You don't recognize the passage?" Disappointed, Burke held the tablet toward her and pointed at the inscription. "Putney records these exact words as he enters the shrine. THESE EXACT WORDS! Isn't that tremendous?"

"Putney. Of course. Yes, a tremendous find," Ayhan said, although her utterance lacked the enthusiasm of Burke's. Nevertheless, Burke went on unperturbed.

"Yes, Putney. Give me a second, and I'll show you." Burke again retrieved his phone.

"No, please, no need to look it up for me." Ayhan glanced at her watch. She picked up her thermos and stood to leave.

"Listen to this. Putney again proves to be accurate."

"There is no need. I believe you. I must go—"

"Here it is. I have it, I have it." Burke motioned her to wait, while reading:

I passed beneath the gate and, lo, there above me was written: The Dish of Christ revealeth he that is true and he that betrays. And this Legacy we keep, until the Wages of Sin are paid. And, lo, upon reading such words, mine own Heart quailed within me, till my steps faltered, lest I wouldst approach the Most Holy altar with mine own Soul stained with Sin and—

Ayhan patted Burke's arm to signal she was done listening. "A great moment. I am happy for you. But I must go." She picked her way across the pit to the ramp that led out.

Burke felt a fluttering of panic. Had he said something wrong? The sun was fully up, but the air had become chilly. The sight of Zainab leaving filled him with a vague sense of loss and futility. He decided to follow her.

"Be happy for *us*, Zainab," he blurted before he was aware of forming the words. "Just think—this find changes the entire field of medieval archaeology. Winters will—" Burke stopped himself, aghast. As a rule, he never, ever shared his secret thoughts about his rival. He couldn't believe he'd spoken Winters's name aloud.

But Ayhan was halfway up the ramp and hadn't heard. At the top she looked back. Burke was several paces behind.

"Take a rest, Adam, please. You look—how do you Americans say it?—strung out."

Ayhan quickened her pace, furthering the distance between them. Burke decided not to close it. He saw the sheen of Ayhan's jacket in the sunlight, and then she was gone.

Holding his phone in one hand and the tablet in the other, Burke walked back down the ramp. All at once he felt the full weight of his fatigue. He bent his knees and slowly lowered himself onto the bucket. As he did so, he kicked over his coffee cup by accident. He regretted this, but the coffee had long grown cold anyway. He bent and picked up the cup, looked at it for a moment, then crumpled it in his hand. All the while, the dancing Panikos with the sunflower halo and the golden bowl smiled down at him.

▼ ▼ ▼ ▼

Ayhan navigated the excavation site without another look back. Her thoughts, however, remained behind. As she neared the security fence and the entrance gate, she saw before her eyes only a golden bowl floating in empty space. The bowl was detached, disconnected from person or place. Like a circle, it was perfectly complete. Independent.

Once at the entrance gate, she pulled a white scarf out of her jacket and wrapped it about her dark hair. The security guard opened the gate for her; she ignored him as she stepped past, her mind whirling with possibilities.

I am happy for us, she thought, briefly recalling Burke's last words to her. She put on a pair of sunglasses and strode with purpose towards her car.

*Very happy.*

▼ ▼ ▼ ▼

Back at his apartment, Giulio Makarios was still awake. He lay on his bed, staring at the ceiling. Hours ago, he'd thrown the pillows about the room in anger, knocking over the lamp on his nightstand and breaking the light bulb. This slight destruction hadn't satisfied his wrath, and he lay drumming his fingers on the mattress, plotting greater feats of strength.

*Burke.*

How he hated this name, but he couldn't stop thinking it. He imagined throwing the pompous professor headfirst over the edge of the excavation pit. *Splat*. Maybe Duffy—that idiot—had gone over first, bouncing once or twice on his big, fat belly. The stupid pair could lie there together in the dirt, consoling each other over their broken necks.

Such were Giulio's thoughts as light penetrated the closed curtains at the foot of his bed. Impatient for lack of sleep, he got up and threw the curtains open. But all he saw beyond the window was the image of Burke posing in triumph next to the mosaic, holding a spade that he'd never once used. Damn that Golden Boy for taking credit for the discovery. *His* discovery.

Giulio couldn't get this image of Burke out of his head. He thought of skipping out on his next shift, for how could he bear seeing Burke again?

An hour later after a shower and breakfast, he reconsidered. After all, Dr. Papadopoulos had recommended him for the project above his other students. It was an honor to take part in the excavation; the opportunity shouldn't be wasted.

Thinking of his professor gave Giulio an idea. He sat down on his couch and reached for his phone. If there was one person who could help him right Burke's wrong ...

He emailed Papadopoulos a photo he'd taken on the sly, a photo of the stone hand holding the golden bowl, the only proof Giulio had that he was involved in the discovery. His message said:

"Dear Dr. Papadopoulos, I wanted to let you know what I found last night digging out the west wall. It's a remarkable mosaic. We spent all last night uncovering the rest of it. I don't have a picture of the whole thing since students aren't allowed to take photos. The mosaic is of a young man—a monk. But I have a problem now. Last night, Professor Burke made it look like he had found the mosaic. He pushed me aside, took all his own photos, and I wasn't in any of them. What should I do? I think I should get some credit since I did most of the digging."

An hour later, Giulio's phone buzzed, startling him. He had dozed off on his couch. He reached for his phone. Papi had responded:

"Thank you for sending this to me. Very remarkable. Yes, you should be credited. I will mention the matter to Dr. Ayhan first. Burke is too busy now to talk to an old, lame man. I advise you to take pictures of the entire image today and send them to me. If there are more mosaics, send those too. Be discreet. No one needs to know."

Scene 9

## A Case of Projection

*Upper West Side, Manhattan*

*Tuesday, March 9*

Ray was all smiles. It was just the kind of day he liked. Planning sessions were all well and good—and unavoidable working with Natalie—but in the plan's execution, anything could happen. It's what made filming documentaries such a great adventure. Who would they meet next? How would the story go? What would be the obstacles? How would it end? To him, these were the important questions, the great mysteries to solve.

He turned the SUV onto Amsterdam Avenue. Natalie sat in the front seat trying to finish reading Steve Finder's *Bucky Browne and the Templars of Doom*. Clark sat behind Ray eating a bag of donuts. The morning was bright but cold. Snow from the previous night clung to bare tree branches. Meteorologists hesitated to predict a quick thaw.

Ray hummed the theme music to the film *Bucky Browne and the Cave of All Fears*. He was greatly anticipating meeting Finder, a man of action and adventure. A man just like himself. Like Bucky. He imagined Finder wearing a Barmah hat and collecting Colt pistols.

Suddenly, Natalie snapped shut *Templars of Doom*.

"Where are you in the story now?" Ray asked eagerly.

She puffed her cheeks in a long exhale. "Um, they just left the Chamber of the Patriarchs."

"Then you only have one more chapter."

"Thank God," she said under her breath.

But Ray heard her. "What? What's wrong with it?"

"Oh, nothing. It's fine as far as such stories go. I just have questions about the plot, that's all."

"You don't follow it?" Ray asked. "He twists it a lot."

"It isn't that. Maybe you should ask him—no, never mind. I shouldn't have brought it up. We're almost there."

"Now you got me curious," Ray said.

Natalie flashed her green eyes up at him. "Sure you wanna know?"

Ray hesitated, always fearing Natalie's criticism. "Just tell me," he sighed.

She shifted in her seat to look at him. "Okay, but remember, you asked. So, in my view, the plot is—wait, here, I'll read it to you." She flipped several pages: "To possess the true Dish is to possess a tremendous power. Both sides know this. Believe me, Calixta, the Dish wasn't lost. It was hidden and hidden well. Such a power must be guarded. It must be kept safe. And now—keeping it safe is up to us."

"So?" Ray said.

Natalie became animated. She gestured with the book as she spoke. Her eyes shown with intensity. "Bucky says the Dish is a source of power. So, if the Orthodox Church secretly possesses the true Dish, as Finder writes, then why don't they just say so? Why keep hiding it? Why not reveal it and prove the Catholics are lying? Nobody would hide a source of power. They'd use it."

"But you don't want power in the wrong hands. The Orthodox have to protect the Dish. To keep the Catholics from getting it. Cardinal Grimani is after the Map of Fortunatus."

"But why is a map to the Dish's location even necessary? Think about it. Finder says the Orthodox monks hid the Dish in the Chamber of the Patriarchs. Wouldn't they know where to find it? The fact that they need the Map of Fortunatus to find something they themselves hid doesn't make sense. It's a plot contradiction. Bucky and Calixta's adventure technically isn't necessary. They go all over Europe to get the map. Why don't Peter and Bartholomew just take them to the Chamber to begin with? Don't you see?"

Ray didn't see. Natalie had to be missing something. No writer of any competence or success would make such an elementary mistake. Certainly not a writer Ray liked. To dissuade Natalie from explaining her point again, he pretended to steer the SUV with extra caution around a bank of snow as he turned onto West 84th Street. They passed a row of immaculate brownstones.

"Their adventure's totally necessary," Clark interjected, "if Finder wants to live on the Upper West Side."

"That's the only place they didn't go to look for the map, ha-ha," Natalie said to Ray teasingly. She lightly touched his arm with the book before dropping it into her messenger bag. She then began gathering up her hair. She always put it in a ponytail when they were working.

## A CASE OF PROJECTION

Ray parked in front of Finder's townhouse. Natalie got out and retrieved her audio bag from the back seat. Clark gently lifted out his camera. As Ray raised the back gate to get the lighting equipment, he could feel his mood souring. "Plot contradiction," he mumbled. Was Natalie making fun of him? Or was she trying to be funny? He didn't know, but he regretted sharing his enthusiasm about Finder with her. Equipment bags in hand, he joined Natalie on the sidewalk.

"Did I say something wrong?" she wanted to know.

"Oh, maybe Finder would think so." He tried to laugh.

"You'd tell me, right? If I said something to offend you? I mean, you didn't reply to what I said, so I wondered."

"I was just thinking 'bout the interview. Reviewing the questions. 'Cause it's Steve Finder. Don't wanna mess it up."

Natalie seemed to accept this lie and turned up the sidewalk. Ray and Clark followed. The sidewalk hadn't been cleared from the night's snow. Ray kept stepping in Natalie's footprints. In front of him, her ponytail swished back and forth. Watching it was hypnotic; he often imagined caressing the back of her neck.

It irritated him to feel the familiar ambivalence about Natalie's dazzling mind. He remembered the first time he'd felt it—at a party in film school. For much of the night, she'd sat on a sofa talking with some hipster dude in glasses. Her feet were tucked up under her. She wore a green sweater with a V-neck just low enough for the imagination. Ray thought she was adorable, like a gymnast or a figure skater, a girl he could pick up and lift over his head. He'd come to the party with two other girls,

Angela and Staci, but he worked his way closer to hear Natalie's voice:

"... but how could he?" she was saying. "If he loved her, he wouldn't accuse her of betrayal. It's a case of projection. Same way with Gertrude, his mother."

"Then Ophelia is a victim of his general lack of love for everyone—in your view."

"Specifically for his father, I think. The ghost says—if you love me, avenge me—but Hamlet goes out of his way not to. Not until the end. And then it's practically an accident. I don't think he loves his father at all. He can't deal with it and blames everyone else for *their* lack of love."

Ray had no clue what she was talking about. What did he know about *Hamlet*? Only that in high school, he'd watched the movie instead of reading it. An hour later, Natalie and the hipster dude had transitioned from drama to poetry. He couldn't imagine talking all evening about literature. Was that the way to flirt with a girl like her? Ray knew he was many things, but "poetry guy" wasn't one of them. Yet listening to her talk with passion about stories mesmerized him. Like watching a pitcher on the mound throw a wicked slider, making the batter look like a fool. He didn't want to be that fool. But he also didn't want to stop listening. Could he ever become that kind of guy?

The three of them climbed Finder's stoop. Natalie rang the doorbell. They waited. Ray observed Natalie studying him. What was she thinking? He never knew. Her mind was a mystery he couldn't live with—or without. It was the best and worst thing about her. Best when she applied her mental powers to their work. Worst when she directed her mind toward him. Those intense eyes of hers made him nervous. When they focused on him, he couldn't hide. Nothing about him was lost on her. From their earliest acquaintance, he'd surmised that Natalie was the kind of woman who'd want to know his secrets, analyze the things he liked, and ask probing questions. She always seemed to find the painful spot in him. Her inquisitiveness put him on his guard. And his personal flaws were the secrets he wanted to keep.

Ray felt a rush of nerves and swallowed. He knew more about Finder's books than Natalie. Maybe this was his time to step into the box and take a swing. "There's a secondary purpose for the Map of Fortunatus," he said to her, "for the plot of the story, I mean."

"You think?" She raised her eyebrows in interest.

"Well, uh, yeah. Peter and Bartholomew don't know the riddle, do they? Fortunatus wrote it on the map— The heart knows what the mind never will. Remember? That's why they need it, I think. The riddle gets them—"

Suddenly, they all heard a distinct click, and two sets of solid wood doors swung open as if to usher the three of them before a throne. Later, Natalie would remember how Finder had looked at her with his amazing violet eyes. His skin was smooth like plastic wrap pulled tightly. She'd not noticed his dimpled chin in the dust jacket photo. Based on his picture, she'd half expected him to look black and white. But Finder showed up in full color.

"Sorry," he said, grinning, "my elevator is slow."

Ray reached to shake his hand, but Finder bowed dramatically to escort Natalie in. Would they indulge him if he gave them a tour? With grand gestures, he directed their attention to the gas fireplace and 5-inch wide American oak floors in the front room; the limestone in the bathroom; the mahogany windows in the dining room; the two Sub Zero refrigerators, six burner stove, Bosch dish washer, and Caesar stone countertops in the kitchen. He hoped one day to take an interest in cooking. On the third floor, they entered his office or "holy of holies" as he called it. He pointed out his Bucky Browne movie posters, framed copies of himself on the covers of *Time* and *People*, along with photos of himself hugging Ramsey King and Kimber Grant, the pair who played Bucky and Lady Xenia.

"Beautiful desk," Natalie said, touching its leather top.

"A Louis XVI," Finder said. "An original, not a repro."

"This where the magic happens?" Ray asked.

"Excuse me?"

"Your novels—your writing."

"Oh, that. I do the final edits here. I spend most of my time in the Hamptons. Fewer distractions." Finder smiled at Natalie, then led them to the elevator because there was a "positively amazing" view to be seen from the fifth floor.

"Oh, I don't really like heights," Natalie said.

"Not to fear, I'll protect you," Finder said gallantly.

The elevator was narrow, forcing them all to stand close. A predictable silence ensued. Finder broke it: "Ah, an ARRI Alexa." He nodded at Clark's camera. "Impressive."

"Just came out this year. The Aston Martin of digital cameras," Clark beamed. "It's a new era in filmmaking."

"They'll use those on the set of Templars of Doom."

"Not surprising. It's just as good as 35 mm. It's got wide exposure latitude, optical viewfinder, built in microphone. Plus, it's super lightweight. With this baby, I'm locked and loaded." He patted the camera affectionately.

"Sure are." Finder reached to inspect the camera.

"Ah-ah-ah." Clark shifted the camera away.

"You'll have to excuse Clark," Natalie said. "He's very protective of Sneak Peek."

Finder looked puzzled.

"The camera." Ray pointed. "Sneak Peek."

"You name your camera?" Finder asked Clark.

"Actually, this is Sneak Peek X."

"You name all your cameras Sneak Peek? Why?"

"Because that's their name."

There was silence. Then Ray said, "You're right, Steve, this elevator is slow."

At last, the doors opened. Finder led them out, his arms raised in a sun salute. "This," he said, pirouetting, "is my urban oasis." He led them to a sun-flooded sitting room with a skylight, then slid open the terrace door and motioned them outside. When Natalie hesitated, he took her hand. Patches of snow shimmered from the tops of empty planters. Half of the terrace was in shade.

"Worth the risk, isn't it?" Finder said to Natalie.

"Wonderful." She put her hand to her throat, then lifted the flap of her bag and pulled out a camera.

"You can see where you parked if you forget," Ray said.

Natalie elbowed Ray sharply.

"What? There's our SUV right over there," he said.

## THE DIE IS CAST

"But you're not noticing what matters—the winter sky, the snow, the trees."

"Bare ruined choirs where late the sweet birds sang," Finder murmured pensively.

"Man, that's beautiful," Clark said. "Did you write that?"

"Shakespeare." Finder and Natalie answered in unison. The two of them laughed at the coincidence, then Natalie caught Ray studying her and looked again at the view.

"Why, look at this," Finder said, pleased. He lifted *Bucky Browne and the Templars of Doom* from Natalie's bag.

She blushed. "Oh, yes. I—I was reading it."

He opened the cover. "No autograph. That won't do."

Ray cleared his throat. "Uh, Steve, if you don't mind, I thought we'd start by filming you coming home, walking up the stoop—you know, show you around the neighborhood, living the writer's life in New York City, that sort of thing."

"Hm? Oh. I don't walk around here," Finder said, giving Ray scant attention. "Certainly not without my bodyguard."

"But we need to see you in action in your environment."

"At the corner is a Joe's Coffee," Clark suggested.

"I've never been there. I don't drink coffee," Finder said.

"What if you ordered tea?" Ray asked.

"I don't drink anything caffeinated."

"A bagel then—ordering a bagel."

"It'd have to be gluten free."

"Okay, if they have them, can we film you at Joe's?"

## A CASE OF PROJECTION

Finder eyed Natalie. "Thoughts, Ms. Ashbrook?"

Natalie smiled. "I think this is your environment." She gestured around them.

"So do I. Say, are you getting chilly?" Without another look at Ray, and with Natalie's copy of his book in hand (or Ray's copy, rather), Finder led her off the terrace.

Ray and Clark lingered behind.

"Jackass." Ray's voice was low in restrained fury. "What a total phony. Bet he doesn't even know what a Barmah hat is. Just likes the way the word sounds." Ray's eyes locked on the spot where Natalie had been standing.

Clark noted it. "She's not gonna fall for any of that," he said confidently.

Ray grunted. He would never have thought it from reading Finder's books, but meeting Finder in person reminded him of someone—someone he hated—Natalie's smug and pretentious ex-husband Geoffrey Peagram. Finder's quotation of Shakespeare, for example. Peagram had done the same, bridging the distance to Natalie's heart in a way Ray had never been able to, showing off how easily a guy could cross the bridge if he knew the right words.

"She has before," Ray said to Clark.

"That's why she won't fall for it this time."

"We'll see. Not that I care."

"Dude, don't be stupid. You guys gotta work it out. You'll drive me crazy."

Ray exhaled sharply. *Work it out. But how?* He thought of the first time Natalie had introduced him to Peagram. It was at a Tribeca Film Festival. She'd been dating him long-distance for half a year. He'd come to New York to visit. At the festival, Natalie and Ray were to participate in a panel discussion on independent filmmaking. The day of, Natalie let Peagram tag along. Though a cultural studies professor, he'd suddenly become an expert on documentaries, tossing out titles of obscure foreign films Ray hadn't seen, showing him up on his own turf. Ray had recognized this as a common ploy, but Natalie had been enraptured.

"Total phony," Ray repeated under his breath, but he was thinking of Geoffrey. "If I had any say—" abruptly he stopped. A thought took hold of him, a perfect plan of action. Once he thought of it, he couldn't let it go. He nudged Clark. "Listen, during the interview, I'm gonna try ... well, if I stop the interview suddenly, or whatever happens, you keep the camera rolling, okay? Let Sneak Peek do his thing."

Clark's eyes widened. "Dude, don't do it. Natalie will—"

"Oh, don't worry about her. She'll thank me. Trust me."

Clark wasn't convinced.

"Dude, you said last night I got tactics," Ray went on. "Stupid questions, rabbit trails, forgetfulness, flattery. I'm just gonna use my full arsenal, get him off-balanced, and have him show what a faker he is. He's not writing novels because he cares about the Last Supper Dish. See how he flirts with Natalie? He's doing it to pick up hot chicks. Just like you said last night. So, we'll find out how well he knows Kimber. It'll be hilarious."

"Well, nothing wrong with that, I guess." Clark grinned and shifted his eyes toward Sneak Peek.

## A CASE OF PROJECTION

Ray laughed. "You got all that in there? His jackass home tour? I knew you would."

Clark winked and turned off his camera.

▼ ▼ ▼ ▼

After taking advantage of the angle of the sun to pose Finder in his "urban oasis," Ray, Natalie, and Clark set up for the interview in his office. Finder would sit at his desk. Adjustments had to be made to the room—pulling the drapes to minimize an echo, and rearranging Finder's bookshelf so that his novels appeared in the frame behind him. He owned copies from all over the world; they'd been translated into 52 languages. To make way for them, antiquities were moved: a Byzantine icon, a galloping horse figurine cast in bronze, and a Roman architectural fragment depicting a crouching lion in relief. Finder insisted on handling the latter because the piece was "very rare, one of a kind."

During all this, Finder and Natalie chatted away. He'd seen her film *Almost a Loneliness*, a work, so he said, "of superior beauty and truth." He wanted to know how she'd chosen the title. Natalie explained that she'd taken it from an Emily Dickinson poem, one of her favorites. She lamented that the audience—and critics—hadn't understood her grand vision for the poet in the film. "She's yearning for love and peace," Natalie said. "That's what the dove symbolizes at the end." Finder was very consoling. "That's how it goes with many great works of art," he said, "they're only appreciated years later." Sadly, his hero Bucky Browne, he suspected, would soon be forgotten, precisely because he'd achieved "worldwide popularity." But what could he do? It was the cross he had to bear.

All this gave Ray ample time to perfect his plan to expose Finder's phoniness in front of Natalie. He'd never hated a film contributor. And he'd been so eager to meet Finder. The sweetness of anticipation had, in mere hours, soured. For that, Ray hated him even more. He knelt to secure a cable to the floor with tape, smushing it hard with his palm as if rubbing it in Finder's face. Meanwhile, Natalie tried to clip a lavaliere microphone to Finder's lapel, but she couldn't loop the wire to her satisfaction. "How clumsy," she said, looping it a third time. "Like I've never done this before."

"You haven't done it to me," Finder said to her softly.

Ray heard this. He stood, eyes narrowed, glaring at the back of Finder's head. *Game on.* He sat down next to Clark's camera. "Guys, it's time."

Natalie put on her headset and fiddled with the dials on her sound mixer. During the sound check, Finder said, "This is exciting. Never thought I'd be in an 8 Ball Production. What's the title of this film, anyway?"

"Bucky Browne at the Vatican, the Search is Over," Clark said from behind Sneak Peek.

Finder laughed tensely. "What is it really? Can't be that."

"Why not?" Clark asked.

"I wouldn't let you use Bucky's name," Finder said, "and you wouldn't be able to afford the legal fees when I sue you for copyright infringement." He chuckled good-humoredly, though his face betrayed a latent seriousness.

"Clark's joking," Ray said. "The title's a work in progress. We choose it last. That's how it always goes." Subtly, he signaled to Clark and Natalie to start recording.

Finder didn't notice. He touched the band of his Rolex. "How do you work like that? You don't have a story until you have a title. I choose a title early on."

Ray smiled insincerely. "Oh, really? Do you plan everything in advance? Plot the stories first? Then write 'em?"

"My last two novels were written that way, yes."

"You have people in mind when you write? I mean, do you pattern your characters on, uh, anyone you know?"

Finder chuckled. "No, Bucky's pure fantasy. Well, I did pattern Lady Xenia's castle after Batman's cave."

"Kimber Grant played her in the movie, I think." Get right to the point, Ray thought, see how he reacts.

Finder nodded. "She's great. A beautiful, wonderful actor. I was very pleased with the casting of that film."

"Dishing is fantasy too, I guess. Searching for a supposedly lost relic." Ray smirked as if sharing a private joke with Finder. "Stretches the bounds of belief, don't you think?"

Finder glanced at the camera. "Is that on?"

"Hmm? Oh, no, we're just chatting. Sort of a warm-up. That's how we do things."

"So, that's not a question you want me to answer?"

"Can if you like." Ray pretended to organize his notes. *He's a pro, gonna be work to trip him up.*

Finder relaxed back into his chair. "Well, it is tantalizing to imagine—that the Catholic Church has subjected the world to a delusion. I can tell you Dishers don't think their search is a fantasy. They're true believers. Hardcore conspiracy theorists. I've done a lot of research. You should read Mark Twain's letters. I always thought he was a cynic, but he was passionate about Dishing. It attracts certain kinds of people." Finder counted on his fingers. "Let's see, Isaac Newton, Catherine the Great, Benjamin Franklin, Napoleon Bonaparte, Queen Elizabeth I, Leonardo da Vinci—all of them were Dishers. What do they have in common?"

Ray shrugged. "They rule?"

"All very imaginative—visionaries," Finder said. "That's my theory, anyway. When I wrote my first novel, I was shocked at how many people would tell me they're Dishers. Wherever I go, people confess to me. They come out of the cupboard." He laughed. "But I'm used to it now. Like, Marc Vasquez, the mayor of Los Angeles is a Disher. And Fran North, CEO of Total Tech, and Nikolay Gryzlov, the president of Russia—I met him during the filming of Cave of All Fears. We were on location in Moscow. Of course, actor Ramsey King. He converted when he got the role of Bucky."

"What about Kimber Grant?" Ray asked. "I'm sure you talked to her about Dishing too." *Here's a right hook*.

Finder glanced at Natalie and hesitated. "She's very mysterious. And all business on the set. She once said—"

"Let's start, shall we?" Ray interrupted as if uninterested in Finder's answer. "Ready?" he asked him.

Finder nodded and sat up straight.

Ray pointed at Clark and Natalie to roll camera and sound, even though they already were.

"Let's talk about the Last Supper Dish," Ray said. "The Vatican claims to have it. Dishers think the Vatican is lying. They believe the true Dish has yet to be found. There are three key theories about where the true Dish could be hidden. The theories derive from the riddles on the icons known to exist of the four legendary Keepers of the Last Supper Dish—Kostas, Zoticus, Panikos, and Nil."

"That's true. But no icon of Zoticus has been found. Several Kostas and Panikos icons exist. And a fragment of Nil."

"Right. Dishers believe the riddles on the icons reveal where the Keepers hid the Dish from the crusaders. Can you explain what these riddles are? And how you made use of them in your novels to send Bucky on his adventures?"

Finder smiled confidently. "The riddle on the Kostas icon says—If you dare desire the Dish of Christ, go and find my brothers. Historians have long interpreted that to mean that you must find men like Kostas. He was a Greek monk. Most Greek monks to this day live in monasteries on Mount Athos in Greece. It's an extraordinarily secretive place, wholly closed to the public. They wouldn't even let *me* in. So, in my first novel, Bucky Browne and the Midnight Crusade, Bucky searches for the Dish on Mount Athos. He doesn't find it there, but he does discover a clue—the Panikos icon—that takes him to Istanbul. He goes there in the sequel, Bucky Browne and the Cave of All Fears."

"Why does the Panikos icon direct him to Istanbul?"

"The riddle on the Panikos icon tells supplicants to kneel before Saint Andrew and pray before entering the earth—or something like that. Historians have said these are worship instructions. They imply a church. I proposed in Cave of All Fears that there must've been a mosaic of Saint Andrew in Hagia Sophia, the great Byzantine church in Constantinople. Maybe it was plastered over by the Ottomans when the church was converted into a mosque. Possibly, the mosaic marked the location of a trap door. Really, if we assume the writers of these ancient riddles were directing pilgrims to locations known at the time, then Hagia Sophia is a more likely hiding place for the Dish than Athos. Most of the monasteries on Athos were built long after the time of the Four Keepers."

"You really believe the Dish might be in Hagia Sophia?"

Finder chuckled. "Well, as I always say, if I can't convince myself of what I'm writing, I could never convince anyone else. Actually, while I was writing Templars of Doom, the third installment of Bucky's adventure, I thought the Dish must be hidden in a mountain cave. Bucky uses the Saint Nil icon to search in Cappadocia." Finder became reflective. "Nil is the most mysterious of the Four Keepers."

"Why's that?" Ray asked.

"He was an outsider for one thing. Kostas, Zoticus, and Panikos were all natives of Constantinople. Nil was from Cappadocia—the town of Göreme. And he was singled out in the Emperor's history, the Annals of Andronicus."

"Andronicus—who's he?"

"The Byzantine emperor who came to power—mid-thirteenth century. He reclaimed Constantinople from the crusaders who'd ruled it for fifty years. It was just after Kostas, Zoticus, Panikos, and Nil had been killed for causing an uprising over their claims to have the Dish.

## A CASE OF PROJECTION

Andronicus built a shrine and created an order of monks in their honor—the Order of Andronicus. The history written during his reign—the Annals—describes Nil as one entrusted with the secret things of God. Possibly, this is a reference to the Dish. Some say before the crusaders sacked the city in 1204, Nil had taken the Dish to Cappadocia, to one of the monasteries. It's believed the Order of Andronicus was formed to protect the Dish. Some think the Order still exists, operating in the shadows ... in secret."

"To what end?" Ray asked.

"To continue to protect the true Dish, of course."

"Ah. But why take the Dish to Cappadocia in particular?"

"Because the Dish would've been safe there. Cappadocia was controlled by Muslims. They had no interest in relics."

"Then you believe the Last Supper Dish is hidden in Nil's hometown," Ray said, pretending Finder had said so.

"It's a valid theory, as valid as the previous two. People have overlooked it though. Probably because the Nil icon was discovered only recently. Plus, the wording on it is half-missing—across the sea, sail again, the port—there's nothing definitive in these phrases. But since I published Templars of Doom, Saint Nil has become a household name."

Finder smiled smugly. Relaxed and self-assured, he rested his fingers comfortably on the arms of his chair. He used no supplemental hand gestures as he spoke. There was no need. His voice, resonant and measured, pronounced each word decisively, without the slightest hesitancy. It was a voice convinced of its own power.

Ray appeared to look at his notes. *Very smooth. Let's try a different tactic.* A silence descended.

Finder's smile faded. He puckered his lips, puzzled.

Ray glanced up. "Forgot what I was gonna ask ..."

Finder shifted uneasily in his chair.

"I remember." Ray slapped his knee. "Will Bucky ever find the Dish?"

Finder blinked rapidly, a bit startled. "Er, uh, I do have another adventure planned for him, so we'll see."

"Will Lady Xenia reappear? Kimber reprise her role?"

"Love to have her—" Finder paused with another glance at Natalie. "There are discussions. That's all I can say."

*Damn, almost.* "Fair enough. Let me ask you this—what do you think would happen if the Dish were found?"

"You mean in real life?"

Ray nodded. "How would the world change, you think?"

Finder inhaled. "Fascinating question." He tapped his fingers together, pondering an answer. His eyes scanned the room and lingered on his Bucky Browne movie posters. His face became pensive, appearing like his photograph on the back of his novels. "How would the world change? Hmm. Well, after all my research on the Dish, what I know about the conflict, the great historical injustice perpetrated, um, I can say no one would be happier than me to see justice done. I sincerely hope the Dish is found—someday."

"Let's take a break. That was a lot of information," Ray said. He looked at Clark and Natalie, who from long experience knew to keep recording.

Ray stood and pretended to consult with Clark.

Finder took a sip of water.

"Hey, Steve, Clark wants to ask if you know who's gonna be cast as Princess Calixta," Ray said.

Finder grinned. "Well, my personal choice would be Jennifer Eliot. She's amazing. But I don't have much say."

"Did you have a say with Kimber?" Ray asked. *Surprise! Rabbit punch.*

Finder took another sip of water. "I didn't know her then. She'd only starred in Girl Fighter."

"But you know her now."

"Of course."

Ray raised his eyebrows, waiting for Finder to go on. But Finder didn't.

"You said before she's a Disher, right?" Ray asked.

"Um, I don't think so—"

"You two probably have a lot in common."

Finder shrugged. "We both live in Manhattan."

Ray puffed his cheeks in an exhale. *He's anticipating now, blocking me.* "That's enough chit-chat. Shall we get back to it?" He sat down.

Finder narrowed his eyes, examining Ray.

Ray cleared his throat. "Where were we? Oh, yes—your novels have sold 200 million copies. That's just obscene."

"I don't particularly care for that word," Finder said.

"Why do you think Bucky is so popular? You're a man of theories. Do you have one?" Ray asked.

Finder rested his hands on the arms of his chair. "I do. We're all searching for truth, aren't we? But where do we find it? On main street? At Whitaker's? No, no, in the West we believe truth lies in hidden rooms, forgotten books, narrow paths—forbidden places." Finder raised one eyebrow for effect. "We believe truth resides with the misfits, the underdogs, the rebels. Think Star Wars. What's the message of those films? Empires are bad. Empires lie. Rebels are good. They tell the truth. Rebel truth overthrows empires. Skywalker represents what people want to believe about the world. I tap into that belief, that's all."

"So, in your novels, the Catholic Church is the empire?"

"Of course. It's one of the greatest empires of all time. They have millions of followers, tons of money. They act in secret. The Pope has his own police force—"

"Thus, you make it the villain."

"Not really. It's the nature of the genre. We're talking about why rebels fighting against a greater power excites our imagination. Readers just assume the Church is the enemy from the outset. I think a writer would have to work hard to make readers believe otherwise."

"You just give readers what they want. You're not anti-Catholic on principle." Ray had gotten nowhere with his Kimber questions, but he sensed another opening.

Finder hesitated. "Yes, I give readers ... well, I mean, a more accurate way of putting it would be that I'm an artist in tune with my audience. That's the nature of art, after all. I'm sure as a filmmaker you can understand what I mean."

Ray tapped his leg. He looked down at the floor. In his periphery, he saw Natalie shift in her chair.

"Right? You can understand?" Finder repeated.

"What? That you're anti-Catholic?"

"I didn't say that. I'm not for or against the Church."

Ray waited for Finder to elaborate.

Finder appeared to have nothing else to say. The silence lingered, and then only to dispense with the awkwardness, Finder added: "I *am* against the abuse of power. It's possible to be too big to be accountable to individuals. That kind of power gives people a sense of license which is dangerous. In the political realm it leads to tyranny." At the end of this speech, Finder's eyes lingered on Natalie.

Ray noticed Finder's gaze.

Natalie, busy monitoring the sound quality, did not.

Later, at the end of the interview, when it became necessary for Ray to defend his actions to Natalie, he would neglect to tell her how Finder's gaze had provoked him.

"So, you think you're a big hero? You're Skywalker, is that it?" Ray asked mockingly.

"What does that mean?"

"Maybe Pope Boniface is Darth Vader?"

"Actually, I think the Pope is a fan." Finder smirked. "He sent me a nice letter."

"Is that so?"

"Yes, it's so. Well, it was from his secretary, Santorini. His Holiness wanted to request an autographed copy of *Cave of All Fears.*"

"Did you send one to him?"

"With my warmest regards. Maybe you'd like one too."

Ray returned Finder's smirk. *Knockout, you sucker!* "Who would've figured you and Pope Boniface are best buds," he muttered. "Certainly not all your Disher fans." As soon as Ray said this, he realized he shouldn't have. He should've kept quiet and let Finder go on unknowingly making an ass of himself. *Time to retreat.*

"Wait, what?" Finder said.

"Okay, that's it." Ray stood and pointed. "Clark, Natalie, we can cut it there."

"Now, wait just a minute." Finder jumped up. "I didn't say I was best friends with the Pope."

"You're getting his fan mail."

"But the Pope's letter was just between him and me. It shouldn't be made public. If you're gonna use that information, you gotta give me a chance to explain."

"But we're out of time. Clark, how're we doin' on time?"

Clark's look was noncommittal.

"See?" Ray said to Finder with a shrug of his shoulders.

Swiftly, Finder stepped to Ray's side of the desk. "Look, I dunno want you're up to. You've been tryin' to get me to say things. Why are you so interested in Kimber Grant? What's your game? Or are you just royally incompetent?" He jabbed a finger at Ray's chest. "You don't know how to conduct an interview. I saw Running on Fumes, by the way. Totally appropriate title for a film, because it sure was!"

"I'm incompetent? Well, from what I've heard, you're a total phony. You write these stories, but you don't even believe this Disher stuff." Ray slapped Finder's hand away. "Don't point your finger at me."

"You guys," Natalie pleaded, removing her headset.

Finder raised his finger level with Ray's nose. "I'll point it where I want."

"Then point it at yourself, 'cause you're the one who's incompetent."

Finder scoffed. "Oh, really? How you figure that?"

Ray wasn't sure where he was going with this insult. He was just so angry he'd lashed out, forgetting his retreat. In his periphery he saw Natalie stand, and inspiration struck: "Well, because you don't know how to write a proper story. Templars of Doom is full of holes. There's no point to Bucky and Calixta's adventure at all. It's stupid for the Orthodox monks to have hidden the Dish and then to go look for it with a map like they don't know how to find it. Duh!"

"Ra-ay," Natalie said uneasily, stepping toward him.

Ray looked at her. "What? You said so yourself."

Natalie reddened. "I didn't say it ... quite like that."

"You said if the Orthodox Church had the Dish, then they wouldn't keep it hidden. It's a plot hole, you said."

Finder lowered his finger and put his hands on his hips. "It isn't a plot hole. They have to protect the Dish from falling into the wrong hands."

"That's what I said," Ray blurted. "But if having the Dish is a source of power, wouldn't they use it?"

Finder scratched his head as if opening a tiny fissure for the truth to sink in.

Eagerly, Ray looked at Natalie for confirmation. She was subtly shaking her head *no* and signaling him with her hand to *cut it*. "What? That's what you said," Ray insisted. "You know you said it. You told me to ask him."

Natalie looked at Finder apologetically.

"So, that's what's going on—an ambush interview! You two came here conspiring to make me look like a fool."

Natalie shook her head.

"I'm not a fool," Finder seethed. "I'm *Steve Finder*, you got that? One of the greatest writers in the world! No matter what you all think. You're just a couple of phonies yourself. Has-been filmmakers of documentaries for Christ's sake. Let's face it, a Bucky Browne film makes more money in one opening day than you all could hope to make in your lifetimes." He ripped off the lapel microphone. "Have fun making your film without me—see how well that works. I'm done." He strode to his office door and jerked it open. "Now get out!" Then he was gone. There was silence.

Ray looked at Natalie.

Natalie looked after Finder.

And Clark turned off his camera.

Scene 10

## The Secret Order of Andronicus

*Office of the Patriarchate, annex to the*

*Church of Saint George, Istanbul*

*Wednesday, March 10*

"All rise for the Head of the Secret Order." Around a long conference table, seven bearded men in black clerical robes pushed back their chairs. Gabriel waited until everyone was silent, and anyway, Papadopoulos always needed extra time to stand because of his hip. However, as Gabriel scanned the assembly, he saw that Papi's chair was empty. Where was the old professor?

It was past time to begin. Gabriel pulled open the set of mahogany doors, and His Most Divine All Holiness, the Archbishop of Constantinople and Ecumenical Patriarch of the Eastern Orthodox Church entered his Throne Room.

The Patriarch's black robe and the long veil hanging from his kamilavka rustled as he strode toward the dais which held his throne. He was a tall man but with sloping shoulders, and he leaned forward slightly as if his broad chest were too heavy for him. His cheeks were pale, and his eyes, shadowed but bright. His bearing was at once meek but authoritative. He had a long, white beard, and about his neck hung a gold medallion bearing the Chi-Rho symbol. When he reached his throne and turned to face the assembly, the medallion shone brilliantly.

The men before him bowed in reverence.

Gabriel closed the doors and took his usual place at the table to the right of the throne. The Patriarch, still standing, nodded to him.

"His All Holiness Philotheos will now lead us in the opening ritual," Gabriel intoned.

Philotheos lifted his right hand above his head. With his palm upturned, he spread his fingers wide as if he were holding an object. "Behold, brothers, the Dish of Christ."

"Gone! The heretics claim it," the men replied in unison, gazing at Philotheos's hand.

"Truth has become lies."

"And with lies, we expose the truth."

"This is the Legacy of Emperor Andronicus."

"And this we keep until the wages of sin are paid."

For a moment all were silent. Philotheos slowly lowered his hand and sat down on his throne. "The annual meeting of the Secret Order of Andronicus now begins."

The men about the table took their seats.

This was the seventeenth Secret Order meeting over which Philotheos had presided since becoming the Ecumenical Patriarch sixteen years previously. The Patriarch of the Orthodox Church was always the head of the Secret Order as a matter of course, and the meetings were always held in the Throne Room on the first floor of the Patriarchate, the three-story office building behind the Church of Saint George. The Patriarchate hadn't originally been built for offices, but since its construction in the seventeenth century, the structure had undergone several metamorphoses. The Throne Room wasn't a secret room at all; much church business was conducted there. The men who sat before Philotheos had officially been called to discuss "Intra-Orthodox Affairs," which was more or less true (so Philotheos told himself). The Church of Saint George had been the seat of Orthodox Christianity for hundreds of years, ever since the fall of Constantinople to the Ottomans. It was a modest structure located in the Phanar District, a neighborhood populated by a Greek minority. The Phanar was to the west of all the preferred tourist destinations in Old Town Istanbul, destinations like the glorious Hagia Sophia, which prior to the fall of Constantinople had been the site of the Patriarchal throne.

Pleasant banter filled the room. Most of the men about the table were long-time members of the Order and knew each other well, even though they only met once a year—more if there was an emergency. Only one emergency meeting had ever been called during Philotheos's tenure.

"Well then, let us take attendance," Philotheos said, breaking into the chatter. "Brother Gabriel will distribute the usual sign-in sheet. Please sign next to your name only. Let us avoid the silliness this time of writing messages to other members in the space designated for their signature. Yes, Lerry, I mean you."

A few men chuckled, pointing at the young Archbishop of Italy. Leronymos adamantly disclaimed responsibility.

At the mention of his name, Gabriel, the Patriarch's secretary, stood and opened his portfolio planner. He was never without the planner, and it was always overstuffed. A dog-eared document threatened to fall from it as he rummaged for the attendance sheet.

Philotheos patiently regarded Gabriel's trials for a moment, and then his eyes fell on Papi's empty chair. "Where is Papadopoulos? Does anyone know?"

"Maybe he lost his cane," someone offered from the far end of the table, to mild laughter.

"It is unlike him to miss a meeting, and, er—what has happened to Brother Elias?" Philotheos pointed to the table opposite him. There a computer sat on a mobile workstation wheeled in for the occasion. Three monks in black cassocks fussed over a router, a set of speakers, and a 30-inch monitor. The monitor should've been displaying the red-bearded face of Elias, the Archbishop of Boston. It did not.

"We apologize for the delay, Your All Holiness," said Leo, one of the monks. He drew near the throne and bowed.

"Is there something wrong with the video feed?"

"No. The computer is new. We had to rewire everything and reinstall some software." Leo wrung his hands. "I hope our failure has not marred the opening ritual."

"No, my son," Philotheos said kindly to calm the aggrieved monk. "And Brother Elias will forgive you, I am sure. You have communicated with him, I hope?"

"Yes. By phone."

"Good. But we should wait for him. How much longer?"

"It has been a most tiresome affair," Leo said, "and we would have been finished an hour ago if Brother Theo had not lost the wiring diagrams."

"I heard that," Theo called out from behind the computer. "I didn't lose them. They weren't in the box."

Leo smiled meekly and inclined his head toward Philotheos, satisfied that he had insulated himself from blame. He was the tallest of the three monks—well over six feet—but his perpetually hunched posture made him appear much shorter and accentuated his fawning manner. He had a wiry, fan-shaped gray beard which made him look older than Philotheos, though in actuality he was not. "Again, my apologies, Your All Holiness," he said, making another bow. "It should only be a few more minutes."

Philotheos smiled indulgently at Leo. "Worry not over me. But do assist your brothers."

Leo rejoined his brother monks at the computer. There he found Theo still hunched behind it, frozen on his knees, staring in perplexity at a Medusa's head of wires. "You are testing the Patriarch's patience," he muttered, looking over Theo's shoulder.

"Hmm, where does this go?" Theo held up a speaker wire between his index finger and thumb, determined to tame this wayward strand of hair. His square, reddish beard was immaculately groomed; he stroked it contemplatively.

"It goes above the router," a nasally voice instructed.

"Which wire is the router?" Theo asked.

"The white one."

"But there are two."

"The other is for the mouse. They're side by side aren't they? It doesn't matter."

Theo eyed the space above the two white wires.

"He means here." Leo pointed to a USB port.

"No, how could it?" Theo showed Leo the speaker wire. "Look—it cannot fit."

"Then maybe here." Leo pressed his finger against a small, round hole.

"But here is another one just like it," Theo said.

"Well, try one and see. Try the red one."

"Hey, guys," the nasally voice interrupted.

Leo and Theo looked up.

A face appeared from behind the computer monitor. Winnipeg Joe was the youngest of the three monks, and his face was plump like the rest of him and framed by a bushy, blond beard and a wavy mane of hair that threatened to depose his brimless, black skufia cap. He pressed the bridge of his thick glasses to the top of his nose, but the lenses drooped again immediately.

"It's the green one. I told you already." Winnipeg's voice squeaked in exasperation. "The audio inputs are grouped together. You weren't listening." He jabbed the mouse with his stubby fingers and leaned toward the computer screen, examining it over his rebellious lenses. "Finally! Okay, guys, the software has updated. I'm sending the call to Boston."

Leo went to report to the Patriarch, and the face of Archbishop Elias soon appeared.

In the interim, Gabriel had passed out the minutes of the previous meeting and collected the attendance sheet.

Philotheos addressed the men. "Now that we are all here," he eyed Papi's empty chair again, "almost all here." His lips pinched in concern. "Has no one been in touch with the professor? Brother Diogenes, you are his close friend."

Diogenes, the diminutive abbot of the Monastery of Megisti Lavra on Mount Athos in Greece, adjusted his small, round spectacles. "The last I heard, he said he was keeping tabs on something. Was very mysterious. Gave no details. This was weeks ago. I assumed he would be here to report."

"Oh!" a voice exclaimed.

Everyone looked at Gabriel who had yet to resume his seat. He flushed self-consciously, his cherub cheeks glowing bright red. "Er, oh dear. Yes, I remember now. Papi left me a message several weeks ago. Said he was taking part in some excavation or other. It was here in the city, as I recall." Gabriel lowered his eyes in embarrassment, hating to be caught forgetting details. As the Patriarch's secretary, it was his job to remember such things.

"Ah, very good. Perhaps that explains it." Philotheos relaxed and settled back against his throne. "You have all had a chance to review the minutes—"

There was a murmur from the table.

"What's that? Your copy has a smudge? Will it truly bother you? Very well. Brother Gabriel, give Chrys another copy, a clean one, please. Thank you."

The old and crotchety Archbishop Chrysanthus of Athens was appeased, and Gabriel finally sat down.

"Any emendations to the minutes?" Philotheos asked.

A hand immediately shot up. Philotheos could've predicted this. "Yes, Anthimos, you have the floor."

Anthimos was the Archbishop of Chalcedon, an influential position in the Orthodox Church because

Chalcedon, on the Asiatic side of Istanbul, was an historic region with deep Christian roots. Several martyrs had lost their lives there. Anthimos had thick cheeks and a silver beard with a streak of black down the middle. He sat, as was typical, to the left of Philotheos, between Chrys and Lerry. Due to his status, he was the only member of the Order whose skufia was red rather than black. He adjusted the cap briefly before he spoke. With his other hand he fiddled with a gold pendant that hung about his neck. The pendant bore an ancient image, one that had adorned the crowns of many Byzantine emperors. It depicted a double-headed eagle with outstretched wings. The eagle had rubies for eyes and held a cross and a globe in its claws.

"The minutes say I was absent at the last meeting." Anthimos eyed Gabriel accusingly. "But I was merely late—delayed at the airport upon my return from Crete."

"I remember his presence," Lerry declared.

"Yes, and I arrived despite my difficulties and, I might add, despite the unusual morning hour at which the meeting was held. The adjusted time was never satisfactorily explained to me. We have these meetings in the afternoon because of the time differential for Elias in Boston, and if it were up to me, we would always do so."

"Here, here," Chrys seconded.

Philotheos regarded Anthimos coolly, unmoved by the mild challenge in the archbishop's voice. "We all remember your presence," he said. "You are many things, Anthimos, and one of them is memorable. The minutes will be amended. Are there any other revisions?"

Anthimos smiled at Philotheos, but his smile curled quickly into a sneer. Chrys whispered something to him, and Anthimos laughed. Philotheos suppressed the urge to frown and decided it was best he didn't know what was said.

Elias had discovered typos in the activities report: "It's in the minutes Gabriel mailed to me. Here's the offending sentence—The unkeep of the unchurch has fallen lax, as we devote time to planning the Patriarch's European trip."

"Yes, I see the same sentence," Leo said.

"There are several others," Elias added.

Everyone looked at Gabriel, whose cherub cheeks were still red. "Sorry. I will clean up the mistakes."

"I move that the minutes be accepted—with revisions," Diogenes said.

"Second," uttered several voices.

"All those in favor?" Philotheos asked. There was a murmuring of assent from the voting members. The secretary Gabriel and the monks Leo, Theo, and Winnipeg were mere initiates of the Order and enjoyed no voting rights. "The minutes are accepted. Does the Order need to consider any old business? Yes, Diogenes."

The diminutive abbot stood to distribute some papers.

"This is the projected budget for the coming year. Note that while our expenditures for subsidizing our gatekeepers and for contracting our field agents to commit our nefarious deeds remain unchanged (Diogenes used air quotes for the word *nefarious*), our website outlays have increased. I am happy to report that our new design has increased traffic significantly. Users like the new search function. Our archived articles and blogs are getting a fresh read, plus—"

"Especially Jimi Bowler, the Disher with the Golden Tongue," Winnipeg interrupted, winking at Diogenes.

"Jimi, Jimi, Jimi!" Theo chanted. A few others joined in.

"Please. Please. It is a silly designation. I have had great material to work with this year," Diogenes said, deflecting the praise. "The excavations at the Karanlik Kilise, for instance, and Steve Finder's new Bucky Browne novel—"

"You should write an adventure novel," Theo said.

"That would be so awesome," Winnipeg exclaimed.

"You could call it Jimi Bowler and the Monastery of Mystery," Theo said. He nudged Winnipeg and they laughed.

Diogenes eyed the snickering pair over his round spectacles. "How about The Big Bad Computer and the Three Little Monks."

"Sounds like a comedy," Elias said.

"I reject that title," Winnipeg cried, offended. "It wasn't my fault. No one listens to me."

"May we please let our brother continue with his report?" Philotheos motioned for silence at the table.

"Events this year have caused a buzz among Dishers," Diogenes continued, "and we have capitalized on that. I am confident we will see dividends in the coming years. Thank you, thank you all, for your contributions to the website. Elias and Chrys, especially. Your series of blogs on the Cappadocian monasteries and on the symbolic significance of the Dish have been extremely popular. There may be many imitators, but there is only one TrueDishers.net."

Lerry clapped, trying to start general applause. Philotheos stared him into silence.

"But as I said," Diogenes continued, "these site upgrades have increased our outlays to the tune of $18,000. See page two. Most of this is maintenance costs for the site."

"That is troublesome," Philotheos said.

"Well, the Order insisted on video graphics and larger archives in addition to the search features. Plus, we had to invest in back-up services, software upgrades, and enhanced security. And we did not want to jeopardize our credibility by placing advertisements on the site."

"Yes, and I believe that is still the case?" Philotheos looked about for confirmation, which he received.

"In my opinion, the site's improved functionality only increases our credibility," Diogenes said. "Assuming we continue to generate compelling creative content, I predict both a substantial growth in readership and in donations. The increased profitability should be enough to offset our outlays. *More* than enough."

"I consider this expense a worthwhile investment, Your All Holiness," Elias said. "The Secret Order must continue the work of Andronicus into the twenty-first century."

"I move to accept the budget," Anthimos said.

"Second," Chrys said.

"Very well. All in favor?" Philotheos asked. His lips curled in satisfaction.

The operating budget was approved.

"Any further old business?"

Anthimos immediately cleared his throat: "When will you review my letter recommending the young priest in my diocese?" he asked Philotheos brusquely.

"I also have a recommendation pending," Chrys said. "Two in fact. These need your approval, Your All Holiness."

"We must bring in several more initiates," Anthimos said. "The perpetuation of the Order should always be our priority. As Brother Elias has just said, we must continue the work of Andronicus into the twenty-first century—and beyond. As I recall, Diogenes's recommendations of Theodore and Winnipeg Joe were handled promptly. Why months of delay for ours?" The archbishop's voice fell just short of an accusation, but his eyes narrowed critically.

"And do not forget, Your All Holiness, *we* reviewed *your* recommendation of Leonardo quickly," Chrys added, pointing across the table to Leo.

"Of which I—and Leonardo—are grateful," Philotheos said, glancing at Leo who inclined his head slightly toward the Patriarch.

As they all knew, it was the duty of Order members to scout for priests or monks within their home dioceses—men deemed to possess the spirit of the Order's founder Emperor Andronicus. Prospective men were recommended to the Order, and if approved, were invited to undergo a years-long initiation under the tutelage of the Patriarch. If an initiate proved to be unworthy, then he was taken (the Order called it a "transfer") to a monastery on the secluded Greek peninsula of Mount Athos to pursue a life of spiritual contemplation. But most initiates eventually passed into full membership. Some, due to their newborn name recognition as a close associate of the Patriarch, would even advance in the ranks of the Church and be installed as the next archbishop. In this way, the archbishops in the Secret Order groomed their successors both in the Orthodox Church at large and in the Order specifically. On rare occasions, a lay member of the Church could also be invited to membership if the man's life was judged to be exemplary and befitting of the aims of the Secret Order. As such, Professor Papadopoulos had been invited to join fifteen years previously.

Philotheos knew that Anthimos and Chrys needed to be answered about the new initiates. But he didn't have a ready answer. Discomfited, he shifted in his throne and scratched at his beard. "Er, my apologies, Your Eminences, but the preparations for the papal visit have distracted me." This was true, but only partly. But that part was his own secret. He looked at his secretary: "Gabriel, do remind me to look at these recommendations before the end of the week."

Anthimos and Chrys grunted, willing to be appeased.

"Is there any other old business?" Philotheos asked.

There was a significant pause. The men eyed each other, waiting to see who would venture to bring up the one subject they didn't want to discuss. However, the Patriarch's allusion to the papal visit had made the topic unavoidable. By a consensus of eyes, the duty fell to Elias.

"Er, Your All Holiness, there is the matter of the overtures made by the Vatican."

Philotheos looked up at the ceiling and frowned. This was old business indeed. Very old business.

The men were silent.

"He doesn't really want to give the Dish back ... does he?" Winnipeg asked.

Philotheos drummed his fingers on the arm of his throne. "I do not know, my son. I do not know."

"If he does want to give it back," Anthimos said, leaning forward so all could see him, "we reject his offer. You must reject his offer, Your All Holiness."

Debate ensued.

They'd been debating this question for three years. The trouble had started one winter day when Pope Boniface X had publicly apologized for the Fourth Crusade of 1204 and had invited Philotheos to Rome. As a result, the Secret Order's meeting that year had been particularly animated. Several members, Anthimos among them, had objected to Philotheos accepting the Pope's invitation. "We are Orthodox!" he'd shouted. "They are Catholic! We do not like them. That is what makes us Orthodox!" A compromise had been reached: Philotheos would accept Boniface's invitation, but the Order, through *TrueDishers.net*, would accuse the Vatican of scheming to garner more power at the expense of the Orthodox Church. "It is very convenient to beg forgiveness from a position of strength," Diogenes (as Jimi Bowler) had written. "After centuries of existing in opulence while the Orthodox have suffered in degradation—what do the Catholics lose by apologizing? Nothing."

Upon the Patriarch's arrival in Rome, he'd been astonished to discover that Boniface wished to return to him the relics of Saint Kosmo the Dignified, relics which had been swiped from Hagia Sophia by the crusaders.

"My—my brother," Philotheos had stammered, sincerely touched. "I'm glad to be called so," Boniface had replied, "let us continue these dialogues of love." Later, after a photo op for the press, Boniface had drawn Philotheos aside and said, "There's been conversation among the cardinals concerning the Dish. Significant conversation."

So as not to be outdone, Philotheos had invited Boniface to Istanbul. He was to arrive in two weeks to continue the Dialogues of Love as they'd come to be called in the press. The two were to celebrate the Feast of Forgiveness together at the Church of Saint George. Would the Pope bring the Last Supper Dish with him? That was the question.

Chrys gestured toward Philotheos. "Your All Holiness, shall Lerry and I now give our report from our attendance at Boniface's secret meeting?"

The men about the table buzzed with surprise. Anthimos nearly leapt from his seat. "Secret meeting? *You* attended a secret meeting?" He eyed Lerry with astonishment.

"I did. The Pope's invitation to me was hand-delivered," Lerry said haughtily. "A rich, buff stationary. Personally signed. But it was distasteful to sit so near him, surrounded as he was by his closest advisors. A very exclusive affair."

Chrys guffawed. "So conceited a gang of betrayers I have never seen. But we could not pass up a chance to learn the Yankee Pope's current stratagem."

As the men listened raptly, Chrys went on to relay—with numerous interruptions from Lerry—what had transpired among Boniface and the bishops. "... and you should have seen his face when we spurned his proposal. Ha! I gave a most eloquent speech. I assure you all, Boniface will not return the Dish to us. He has resistance from his own Latin ranks as well. Many have signed a petition urging him to keep the Dish at the Vatican. His hands are tied."

Hearing this, the men congratulated Chrys and Lerry for their good work on behalf of the Order. But Philotheos sat silently. He recalled Boniface's face when he'd handed him the reliquary holding Saint Kosmo's relics. Surrounded by cameras, Boniface's toothy grin had exuded charm. But in his eyes Philotheos had detected some other quality—willpower. *Boniface is up to something. But what?*

"Your Eminences," he said, "while we applaud Chrys and Lerry for their efforts, we must remain cautious with Boniface. He courts my friendship. Why? What is his game? For nearly a decade now, he has patiently maneuvered his church into rapprochement with ours despite resistance from all quarters. Chrys and Lerry's rejection of his offer means little to him. I am convinced they were merely messengers to convey his intention to me to return the Dish." Philotheos gripped the arms of his throne. "I sense he will make me an offer at the Feast. Such a move would—oh, it would ruin us! Destroy what our Order has protected for centuries. I need not tell you."

"Maybe we should prepare for the worst," Elias said.

"The Latin game is always the same domination," Anthimos said. "Fling that worthless dog bowl back in his face, Your All Holiness. We have challenged the authenticity of their cherished prize for hundreds of years. We cannot now accept it as the real Dish of Christ. The Dish is out *there*," he pointed at one of the curtained windows, "not with them. What would the laity in our Church think if you suddenly changed your mind on the issue?"

"But rejecting Boniface's offer would violate the spirit of the Dialogues of Love," Diogenes said to Philotheos.

"Good," Anthimos snorted.

"That would not be good," Philotheos said sternly.

The room grew quiet.

Philotheos stroked his long white beard. "We must face certain realities," he began. "Have you walked the streets of Istanbul? Have you asked yourselves—where are all the Greeks? We face onerous taxes, churches in disrepair, our Halki Seminary forcibly shut. We do not even have enough numbers in this city to merit being called a minority. We are a rarity. Extinction would be the final disgrace. We must prevent that." As he looked from man to man, each looked away. "No, we cannot jeopardize the Dialogues of Love. Politically, we need an alliance with the Catholics."

No one spoke.

After a minute, the young monk Winnipeg said: "I agree with His All Holiness."

"As do I," the elder Leo quickly added.

"What can we do?" Gabriel asked. "We have only two weeks until the Feast." He double-checked his planner.

"We must discourage Boniface from making the offer at all," Elias said.

Philotheos raised his eyebrows. "But how?"

Elias smirked. "By doing what the Order does best."

It took them an hour to flesh out the particulars: Diogenes (as Jimi Bowler) would start a rumor via *TrueDishers.net* that Pope Boniface had sent a secret envoy to a town near Russia to investigate reports that the real Dish of Christ had been found. Of course, the exact town couldn't clearly be identified, and reports varied as to whether the Dish had been discovered in a crypt beneath a church or in a hermit's cave in the Caucasus Mountains ... but what mattered was that the Vatican was intent on suppressing knowledge of the discovery. Elias would, as usual, alert the local news station in Boston which would call the Vatican for an official statement, thus making Boniface aware of the accusation. Assuming the story gained traction among Dishers and even better, with international press outlets, they could likely count on Boniface delaying his offer until the rumors were laid to rest. He would not wish his visit to Istanbul to be marred by controversy.

"It would at least buy us some time," Elias said.

"Just the kind of compelling creative content our site and our readers demand," Diogenes said, chuckling.

"I must reiterate my concerns," Philotheos said. "I cannot have the Dialogues of Love jeopardized. I cannot—will not—ruin this fragile rapport with Boniface. The future of our Church in this city depends on this alliance."

"Put out a statement questioning the rumor," Diogenes suggested. "It would align you with Boniface while at the same time giving our story additional media attention."

"There is the upcoming art exhibition in a few days," Gabriel eagerly reminded the Patriarch, happy to have remembered something. "A Catholic delegation will be present. It might be an opportunity for you to express confidence in the goodwill of our Western friends—"

"Bah! Friends!" Anthimos scoffed, glaring at Gabriel.

"At the same time, Your All Holiness, you should naturally still express grief over past betrayals," Elias added.

"A good idea," Diogenes nodded. "And perhaps also lament the deceitfulness of the human heart—in a general sense. The Orthodox laity will seek some sign that you are not softening your stance toward the Western heretics."

Philotheos stroked his beard, considering the matter. Months previously, he'd been asked by Dr. Zainab Ayhan, curator of the Museum of Ancient History, to open the museum's new exhibition dedicated to Byzantine art. The exhibition was a joint venture undertaken with the Galleria dell'Accademia in Venice and would feature artifacts taken from Constantinople during the Fourth Crusade.

"Yes, it is so easy to craft a speech appropriate for every constituency," Philotheos replied wryly. But he wasn't really addressing Diogenes. His countenance clouded, and his thoughts turned inward. With fondness, he recalled his early years as Head of the Order. How satisfying it had been to him to share in a secret life with other men, a life set apart from their official duties as leaders of the Orthodox Church. In those early years, the Secret Order had been more like a neighborhood boys club where he could joke and laugh and feel released from the pressures of his work as Ecumenical Patriarch. Meetings had been dominated by camaraderie, and each of them had faithfully upheld the Order's mandate by maintaining *TrueDishers.net* and by staging an occasion for one of them to harangue the Vatican.

But then things changed. Philotheos tried to suppress the memory of the Order's one emergency meeting. He could not. After that regrettable incident, how hard he had worked to recreate the bond among the men, only to be frustrated by Boniface's overtures of peace. The Dialogues of Love, while beneficial to the Orthodox Church at large, had proven to be a strain to the Secret Order. Fault lines among the members had noticeably re-appeared, fracturing the fellowship. Fortunately, their shared enjoyment at jabbing Catholics had largely bridged the gaps. Not to mention the shared profits from *TrueDishers.net*.

"Er, Your All Holiness?" Gabriel asked, searching the Patriarch's face. "Shall we vote?"

"Fine, fine," Philotheos replied resignedly. Crafting equivocal speeches was tedious work, but the equanimity it brought to the Order made it worth the trouble.

The motion to initiate Operation Russian Rumor passed unanimously.

"Any new business?" Philotheos asked, relieved the men had surmounted the awkward problem created by Boniface.

At once, Chrys said, "Anthimos is to appear in a film."

Anthimos nodded smugly as Lerry applauded.

"What? You have become a thespian?" Diogenes asked.

"I shall be interviewed for a documentary," Anthimos said, "a film about the search for the Last Supper Dish, in fact. The filmmakers are evidently well-known in America. Cozart and Ashbrook are their names, I believe."

"They have made a wise choice," the monk Leo said.

Anthimos beamed and fiddled with his eagle pendant.

"Cozart and Ashbrook, eh?" Diogenes asked, adjusting his tiny spectacles. "Americans, you say?" He leaned back in his chair and tried unsuccessfully to hide a smirk.

"What?" Anthimos asked. "Do you know them?"

Diogenes laughed. "Not exactly. But there were two people with those names who tried to gain entry to Mount Athos not long ago. Wanted to know what I thought about the theory that the Dish is hidden there. Wondered if they could interview me."

"What? They asked you first?"

"I do not know how they got my name."

"Oh!" Gabriel exclaimed. Everyone looked at him.

"Here we go again," Theo snickered, nudging Winnipeg.

"Oh dear. Cozart and Ashbrook. I remember now. They called our office. Asked to interview His All Holiness after the Feast of Forgiveness—which was out of the question. I gave them your name." He indicated Diogenes.

"Some notice would have been nice."

"I forgot," Gabriel admitted sheepishly.

"Did you expect I would let a film crew poke around the Megisti Lavra, stomp about the sacred grounds with cameras and upset the brothers?"

"Of course not. I gave them your name because I knew nothing would come of it," Gabriel cried in self-defense.

Anthimos sat sour-faced.

"Oh, come, come, my brother," Diogenes said to him. "Though you were the, uh, third choice for their film, I am sure you will not disappoint." A few of the men snickered. Anthimos's scowl deepened.

"Remember," Elias said to Anthimos, "you represent the Orthodox Church in the film, not the Order. We, in the Order, know exactly where the Dish is. However, the official stance of the Orthodox Church is that the Dish is still lost, and our Church urgently searches for it—"

"I know the official talking points," Anthimos snapped.

Just then, the doors to the Throne Room swung open.

All eyes turned. It was Professor Papadopoulos.

"Papi!" several voices cheered. "That hip slow you up, Papi?" one of them teased. But Papi's face was grim. The men noticed it and grew quiet.

Papi limped toward the throne, his cane tapping the floor. He handed Philotheos a large manila envelope.

With a troubled countenance, Philotheos undid the clasp and pulled out two photographs. "What are these?"

"Look closely," Papi said.

Philotheos's eyes widened in recognition. His hand shook. "What does this mean?"

"It means the Shrine of the Four Keepers ... has been found."

Scene 11

## Nature Calls

*Grandeur, Georgia*

*Wednesday, March 10*

Max stood on the porch of Whiningham as he'd done the day before, thinking about Jane. After a night's delay to come up with a plan, he still couldn't discern a clear path forward with his daughter. It was challenging enough to talk to Jane, let alone talk to her about Dishing. It was in her nature to weasel out of conversations she didn't want to have.

Looking out toward the lake, he heard the limousine before he saw it. The long driveway up to Whiningham was lined with live oaks, their twisting branches creating an arched canopy. The chauffeur circled the fountain and parked next to Max's Maserati. Max crossed his arms, awaiting the imminent appearance of his sister Kathleen. The limousine could signal the arrival of no one else, as Kathleen had long ago given up driving. Everyone guessed this was due to her obesity, but official inquiries were never made. Byrd the chauffeur got out to open the door for her. Max nodded at him, and both men waited. No appearance of Kathleen's really could be imminent; she was far too fat to get anywhere quickly.

# THE DIE IS CAST

To Max's surprise, it wasn't Kathleen who stepped out of the limousine—not at first. It was a woman in a blue pencil skirt and white blouse, a woman Max had never seen before. Following her out was, regrettably, someone he did recognize: Toby Milto. Max rolled his eyes. Milto was Patricia's personal assistant and had been for twenty years. He was Max's age but half as tall, a thin little man with a mewing voice. Max hated him. Milto waved, "Hello, there, Mr. Whitaker." Max grunted and didn't wave back. Though the two men had known each other for twenty years, Milto never addressed Max by his first name. Max had long suspected that this exaggerated courtesy was meant sarcastically.

At last Kathleen emerged, her face plump and fleshy, her arms puffy and creased like an infant's. Her lank hair fell over one eye. When she brushed it aside, a ruby bracelet twinkled in the sunlight. She always wore the bracelet; it was embedded in the ocean of her skin like a sunken ship.

The woman in the pencil skirt reached the front steps; she carried a canvas bag. Whatever it was that had brought them all to Whiningham, Max was thankful that it involved an attractive, thirty-something woman with full-bodied brown hair and nice breasts.

"I'm Max," he said, flashing her his uber-white teeth. "Welcome to Whiningham." He shook her hand.

"Nicole Dziedzic. Thank you sooo much for having me."

"Nicole …?"

"Dziedzic. It's Polish. Whiningham is an interesting name."

A string of faux pearls adorned Nicole's blouse. Max tried not to gaze through to her breasts but failed. "Yes, my father much admired the Plantagenets," he said wryly.

"Who?"

"Oh ... never mind."

Milto and Kathleen arrived. Both Max and Milto instinctively averted their eyes as Kathleen struggled up the porch steps. Each knew better than to offer her assistance; they would be severely rebuffed. Kathleen lumbered forward flat-footed as if the arches of her feet had long since surrendered. Swaying from side to side to gain momentum, she huffed and wheezed as though breathing through sandpaper. As usual, without asking or being asked, Milto carried Kathleen's business apparatus: a laptop bag and a briefcase. It went without saying that this was purely professional courtesy and had nothing to do with Kathleen's size.

"Why ... are you ... here?" Kathleen said to Max, pausing at the top step to catch her breath. Her patchy, round face appeared childlike except for her eyes that drilled into Max like two tiny blenders.

"Good to see you too, Leenie," Max said, greeting his sister with a nod. *Leenie* was a nickname he knew she detested, and even more so because in one of his more inspiring moments, it was a name he'd given her.

Milto's face glistened. It was always mildly moist. "Not golfing, Mr. Whitaker?" he asked brightly, squinting into the descending sun. His pea-sized eyes shrunk even more.

"Mother know you're here?" Kathleen eyed Max suspiciously.

"No, but she expects me."

Kathleen cocked her head to one side. "Expects you?"

"That's right. I talked to her yesterday."

"Wha'd she say?"

"Nothing much."

"Hmph. A subject you know so much about."

Kathleen swung her hips to propel herself past Max. Milto followed. With quick chivalry, Max strode forward to hold open the front door—for Ms. Dziedzic.

"I'm so happy to be working with you," Nicole said to him as she stepped past. "What you're doing is wonderful."

Max pinched his brows as he let the door close behind him. "Er, it's nothing."

"Nothing? Hardly!" Nicole said. "Thousands of people will thank you."

"Jane here, I assume?" Kathleen broke in as they entered the vestibule.

"Uh, you assume correctly," Max said, quite confused.

Kathleen looked past Max into the Great Room as though Jane would be waiting there for them. She wasn't.

"Jane is my daughter," Max explained to Nicole.

"I know. I'm sooo happy to be meeting her too."

"You're meeting Jane?"

"We'll meet with Mrs. Whitaker first," Kathleen interjected, speaking to Nicole. Then, eying Max. "You coming to the meeting? You said mother expects you."

Max glanced at Nicole and decided it would be best to pretend to know what was going on. "No, I've already been briefed. I'm here for Jane."

Kathleen and Milto glanced at one another.

Max cleared his throat. "Jane's had an incident," he explained to Nicole. "Nothing serious. Not like Moscow. Maybe you heard about that."

"I did. Your daughter is so interesting. Oh, like, I probably shouldn't say this." Nicole bit her lip and looked from Milto to Kathleen to Max. "After her Moscow incident, I was totally intrigued. I started following her on Dishpix."

Max laughed. "You're a follower."

Kathleen frowned and looked Nicole up and down.

"What you must think of me, ha-ha." Nicole said.

"You look pretty innocent to me." Max winked. "But if Mrs. Whitaker asks, don't admit that you follow Jane."

Nicole blushed and nodded, giving her hair a little toss.

Max noted the mild flirtation. "Jane's latest scandal, if you can call it that, is much ado about Nothing." He grinned at his pun on Saint Nil's name, flashing his teeth again.

"Mother doesn't think it's nothing," Kathleen said.

Milto nodded in eager agreement. "Another crisis."

"Everything is a crisis to you, Milto, that's how you keep your job," Max jeered.

"Negative press for Jane is negative press for Whitaker's," Kathleen intoned as if citing an oft-repeated adage.

"What happened to her?" Nicole ventured inquisitively.

"It's silly." Max crossed his arms. "She wandered into a shop in Turkey because she saw a tailless cat, and the owner conned her into buying a rare icon that wasn't rare at all. I dunno how you call that a scandal but—"

"Tailless cat?" Kathleen scoffed. "Where'd you hear that?"

"From mom."

Kathleen appeared confounded. "What happened to the tail? Was it chopped off?"

"Probably it was one of several species of the breed," Milto offered.

"There are cats born without tails?" Kathleen asked.

"It's true," Nicole confirmed. "My grandmother had a Manx named Stubs."

"Why so surprised?" Max asked Kathleen. "Mom said you told her about the cat."

"No, I never heard anything about a cat."

The two siblings frowned at each other.

"Why would mom say you did if you didn't?" Max asked.

"I dunno. She's misremembering. Jane must've told her."

"Jane wouldn't—" Max stopped himself, again confused.

"Figures Jane would be attracted by something weird," Kathleen said to end the discussion.

As the four of them entered the Great Room, Max's eyes glimpsed the gilt frame above the fireplace and then followed the line of the Grand East Staircase up to the balcony. In the east wing was Jane's room. The strange turns in the conversation with Kathleen, Nicole, and Milto suddenly made Max want to see Jane. Clearly, the presence of these three meant some scheme involving his daughter was afoot. And if there was a scheme, why had his mother summoned him the day before? Was he part of the plan?

Kathleen guided Nicole and Milto toward Patricia's office in the west wing, but Max headed (after one last survey of Ms. Dziedzic) in the opposite direction. *I never heard anything about a cat.* How odd, thought Max as he climbed the stairs. Was his sister lying? Patricia had definitely said that Kathleen had told her about the cat. Jane would never have told Patricia. As a rule, Jane told Patricia nothing.

Reaching the top step, Max decided it was stupid to wonder who told whom about a tailless cat. Yet as he turned toward Jane's room, the image of a cat leapt into his mind, an image as white and crisp as Ms. Dziedzic's faux pearls. With it emerged a determination to discover who was lying to him. It was time to intervene.

▼ ▼ ▼ ▼

Baby Girl lay curled up on a blanket on Jane's bed. Near it were a pile of pillows and Jane's Barmah hat. The bed was the dog's usual nest, as it always slept near Jane. It was undressed (Jane had removed a pink sweater) and thus in a state conducive to sleep. It lay with its nose tucked under its tail, a posture suggesting hope of long-term peace. Jane was unmindful of this sign. Kneeling at the foot of the bed, she rifled through an old steamer trunk, tossing its treasures onto the mattress. As a rule, Baby Girl's nerves were ever-alert. It couldn't help but be sensitive to these disturbances. Every time something landed, it lifted its head to assess the danger. After four or five such interruptions, during which Steve Finder's novel *Bucky Browne and the Cave of All Fears* landed alarmingly close, Baby Girl stretched and jumped off the bed. Its Emotional Support Tag jingled.

"Where you goin', little girl?"

The dog welcomed an ear scratch, then shook itself and nosed about the room. It wandered over to inspect Jane's desk (which was bare) and her bookcase (which, though fashioned for large, weighty volumes was filled with smaller treasures, all found by Jane: sea shells from Fire Island; a pearled button saved from a gutter in Brussels; bird feathers, rocks, marbles, an arrowhead, pressed flowers, torn butterfly wings, stray foreign coins, and a jar of pennies). One shelf held several boxes of Grammy's Teeny Treats, Baby Girl's preferred snack and sold only at Whitaker's. Next to the bookcase was an open window that overlooked the horse barns and the meadow where Jane went riding. Baby Girl sniffed the air, then like a cat jumped up on the sill. When it could, it liked to lay there looking out.

Jane's room had endured many metamorphoses during her twenty-two years. She liked "to keep things fresh" and rarely settled on one arrangement for long. Yet there was one object that had passed every decorative test: the trunk that sat at the foot of the bed. Technically, the trunk wasn't Jane's, it was Gloria's, left behind of necessity during the jewelry heist. It was painted turquoise, but the paint was peeling, and the hardware was tarnished. The leather straps were scuffed and cracked. It'd always looked that way. Jane took good care of it.

A keen observer of Jane's room—Kathleen, for instance, who always barged in without knocking—might've said that Jane's current configuration made the trunk the centerpiece. "It's vaguely Mediterranean," Kathleen had remarked the first time she'd lumbered in after the latest renovation. Jane was lounging in a chaise listening to music. Kathleen had to repeat herself after Jane removed her earbuds. "That's good because that's the look I was going for," Jane said. Around her were lightly textured walls and above her, exposed wooden beams. Motley Turkish rugs covered a hardwood floor, and a zebra striped curtain hung from a wrought-iron canopy bed, against which the turquoise trunk really held its own. "That makes sense," Kathleen said, "because your mother visited Turkey once. She often told me she could live there." Jane re-inserted her earbuds. "My room doesn't have anything to do with her."

Although the turquoise trunk fulfilled a decorative function, it served a more important purpose: it held all of Jane's Dishing things. When Jane had inherited the trunk from her mother, it'd contained several records, three hats, costume jewelry, a pair of high heels, and a pink, spiral-bound notebook. Over time, Jane had discarded all the relics but the notebook. She habitually laid it on top of everything else, so the notebook had been the first missile tossed at Baby Girl.

Everything in the trunk beneath the notebook, Jane stuffed in without any order: maps of Istanbul, Moscow, and Rome; an artistic rendering of the lost Shrine of the Four Keepers; facsimiles of the Kostas and Panikos icons; all of Finder's novels (well-worn) plus the film adaptations on DVD; a set of Bucky Browne action figures; movie posters; and a Lady Xenia backpack. A folder of newspaper articles represented Jane's abandoned efforts at scrapbooking. She now bookmarked articles of interest on her iPad: VATICAN REFUSES CARBON DATING OF LAST

SUPPER DISH; PRESIDENT WELCOMES POPE, DISHER PROTESTER ARRESTED; STEVE FINDER ANSWERS HIS CRITICS; PROFESSOR DISCOVERS FRAGMENT OF SAINT NIL.

Besides Finder's novels, there were other books in the trunk: *Dishers Then and Now*; *An Introduction to Iconography*; *Conspiracy of Relics—One Priest's Look Behind the Lies*; and *Mysteries of the Late Byzantine Empire*. All these had been well-meaning gifts from various acquaintances, and at the time, Jane had received each book eagerly. But all their pages were still white and crisp. She'd never read them.

Yet given recent events, one of these books had acquired fresh significance. When Jane found it, she carried it to her bed and allowed the weight of it to pull her down into her pillows. She situated herself cross-legged and arranged two of the firmer pillows before her. One of them bore the face of Lady Xenia. Jane laid the massive text on top:

Mysteries of the Late Byzantine Empire
Rupert Winters

Second Edition
Revised and Enlarged

Oxford University Press
New York    Oxford

The title page didn't interest Jane at all. But the blank page opposite did. On it, the person who'd given her the book had inscribed a message:

"Dear Jane, you've brought me so many interesting souvenirs, I wanted to give you one in return. I didn't have to travel as far as you to find mine—only to the museum shop—nevertheless, this is given with sincere regard for your enrichment. Winters is highly respected. You might say this book represents the scholarly consensus about the fate of the Last Supper Dish. Don't let that dissuade you from reading it. There's much wisdom here that can speak to your experience if you will let it. Beliefs should always be rooted in firmer ground than one's desires. Sincerely, Dr. Frank Carlisle."

Vaguely, Jane remembered sitting in Carlisle's office listening to him explain to her that because the word *bouillie* in French meant "gruel" not "bowl," the medieval manuscript she'd brought to him was actually a recipe for porridge, not a coded message for finding the Last Supper Dish. Afterwards, he'd given her Winters's book.

Jane read and re-read Carlisle's note. After some minutes, she slapped the book's cover closed, drummed her fingers on top of it, then pushed it aside. She picked up *Bucky Browne and the Cave of All Fears*, resettled into her mound of pillows, and flipped with purpose to the end:

"You vill tell us ze location of ze codex of Saint Jerome," Scevola demanded, thrusting forward the fiery torch.

"Never!" Lady Xenia struggled against the ropes binding her to the chair, but it was no use. *I must give Bucky more time to discover the clues I left him.*

"Then you vill die!" Scevola laughed, his eyes narrowing.

"Kill me and all hope of getting the codex dies with me."

## THE DIE IS CAST

Scevola's left eyebrow quivered as he considered her threat. He jerked away the torch and stepped toward the stone stairwell, leaving her in darkness. "It iz time for my evening prayers. But never fear, I vill return."

"I'm not afraid!" Lady Xenia called after him. He did not reply. Anger surged in her. "How can you do this? We trusted you. Bucky is your friend."

Suddenly, she heard the priest's sneering laughter, and his foul voice whispered in her ear, "Ah, but one haz many friends, no? Some more powerful than others."

"You'll regret this! The Pope's not your friend. He's just using you."

"You speak with such passion. Perhaps it iz you, Lady Xenia, who need a friend?" His eyes lingered over her.

"No, thank you. I have Bucky."

"Ah, my dear, another time, perhaps. You have heard ze tales about ze Pope's ... pet?" Scevola began to stroke her luscious blonde hair.

Lady Xenia shuddered at his touch but couldn't pull away.

"Some people say he iz a beast, but he iz just mizunderstood. Perhaps you vill meet him? Yez, I think he iz in need of a new friend."

"Of course!" Jane shouted. She read to the end of the chapter to confirm her new insight. Then she grabbed her phone. A few seconds later, she was face to face with her best friend, Meena Kim.

"Meena, I've got it—"

"Hey, bitch, you missed my soiree last night."

"—Carlisle was paid off."

"Out saving the world, and what about little ol' me?"

"The Pope got to him, Meena. You know what this means? It means I'm getting closer. I'm a threat."

"Oh, I don't doubt it. You're the best Disher there is."

"It's just like in Cave of All Fears. That's what I've realized. The part where Scevola betrays Lady Xenia. She's trapped in the Pope's dungeon beneath Castel Gandolfo. Because she has the codex. I mean, she's the only one who knows. And the Pope has power. Scevola doesn't. That's why he can be bought off. I bet Carlisle knows people in Turkey. He even said—can you believe this?—he even told me once, I remembered tonight, that he was sincerely interested in my en-*rich*-ment. Literally his exact words. He's always been in it for the money. When I got too close to the truth, you see what happened. It's just freaking amazing."

"Wow." Meena appeared impressed. "Y'know what? Someday people are gonna realize you're the one they've been waiting for, and then you're gonna solve this Dish thing just like that." She snapped her fingers for emphasis.

"He said the riddle was written in Greek. I bet it isn't. I bet it's Latin after all." Jane searched around on her bed for the Saint Nil. She had to lift several pillows to find it.

"Probably. He's just trying to throw you off—"

"I bet Carlisle has ties in Göreme."

"—but he doesn't know who he's dealing with."

"I should probably go back there—to Babu's shop."

"Okay, but be careful, I mean, if they're on to you …"

Meena's face disappeared from camera view. Jane saw someone's shoe, then concrete, then a glass door. "Whatcha doin'? Where are you?"

"You should know, bitch. Didn't Roxy tell you? On our way to Car-ta-gena."

Jane heard her friend Roxy in the background shout: "Colombia, here we come!"

"You guys! You were just in South Beach," Jane said.

Meena giggled. "A vacation after a vacation is a must."

Roxy's face appeared briefly. "Jane, you should come."

"I mean, yeah, it's overwhelming," Meena went on, "but what else can we do? Get jobs and wake up for the morning commute?" She and Roxy laughed.

"So, like, you're not doing the internship?" Jane asked.

"Oh, that. Sorta. I mean, I love my dad, but D.C. is just so serious. And you know what I found? I can't do office work. Like, not at all. I mean, 'cause I dress too well and stuff."

Jane nodded in empathy.

"You know how it is," Meena said. "Like, do you wanna work at Corporate?"

Jane groaned and put her head in her hands.

"See?" Meena's eyes shown with confidence. "The fact is—you and me—we're leaders. And, yeah, it's hard to be so smart and stand apart, but you gotta embrace who you are. You only get one life, and you oughta love it because it's one of the most beautiful gifts you're ever given."

"That's so true!" Jane's eyes welled up. She put one hand over her heart.

Roxy restated her invitation: "Jane, are you coming?"

"Look," Meena said, "we're almost at security. If you wanna come, we'll be at the Hotel Casa—" she looked at Roxy for help.

"San Agustin," Roxy said. "Jane, Dominick's coming."

"San Agustin, right. It's super exclusive," Meena said.

"What about Baby Girl?" Jane asked.

"You can bring the little rag. And Dominick misses you."

"He didn't post on my Dishpix page when I was away," Jane said to Meena. "Not that I care."

"Look, we gotta go. Cute shirt by the way, but your roots are showing. Bye!"

Before Meena disappeared, Jane heard Roxy chant: "RATS forever, RATS forever, RATS forever!"

Jane hugged the pillow of Lady Xenia to her breasts but soon tossed it aside. "Baby Girl," she called, getting off her bed. Baby Girl didn't appear. Jane looked about her room, then spied the open window. "There you are." She lifted the sleeping dog out, sat down on her chaise and stood it on her bare thighs, holding its forepaws so that it awkwardly balanced on its hind legs. "Wanna go to Colombia with Mama?" she asked it. Then she clapped its paws together, squealing, "Yeaahhh!" Baby Girl drowsily submitted to this puppetry. Jane snapped a pink bow in its hair. Carrying it out to the balcony, she posed herself against the setting sun and took several selfies, making sure to capture her lean legs and the lettering on her pink t-shirt: IF NOT FOR MY SPARKLY T-SHIRT, YOUR PARTY WOULD BE TOTALLY DULL. It took her a few tries. Baby Girl kept closing its one blue eye. But afterwards, when she applied the Xanadu filter on Dishpix, her pink shirt really popped. "Me and my best girl off to—who knows???" she wrote under the photo as a caption.

Meena Kim was a couple years older than Jane. Her opinion always mattered. Jane had met her—and all the other RATS—at Harold More High School in Manhattan. The acronym had been Meena's invention. It stood for "Rich And Totally Sexy," and membership in the club depended on these two minimum qualifications. Meena's father had made a fortune in New York City real estate before running for U.S. senator. Roxy Boscana's father had been a famous disc jockey in the 1980s. And Dominick Raintree's father had started Raintree Computing.

Jane frowned, examining herself in her full-length mirror. It was true—her roots were showing. Why couldn't she have been born naturally blonde like her father?

There was a knock on her door.

"I'm busy."

"C'mon, Jane, it's me."

"So?"

"I wanna talk to you."

Jane set Baby Girl down and looked about her room, searching for an escape. She returned to her bed and folded herself among the pillows, but not before putting on her Barmah hat. She pulled the brim of the hat down low.

"Okay, whatever. You can come in," she called.

Max opened the door. He couldn't locate Jane at first. Baby Girl eagerly sniffed Max's shoe.

"How you doin'?" Max asked, studying Jane for symptoms of grief.

"Fi-ine," Jane replied in a sing-song voice. She closed her eyes in a pose of sleep. Something golden lay half-concealed underneath *Mysteries of the Late Byzantine Empire*. Max pulled it free and held it in his hands. It was the faux icon of Saint Nil, the source of Jane's five-grand Cappadocian humiliation. A bearded man in a white robe stared back at Max, his expression at once aloof and beseeching. "Look at me," he seemed to say, holding a bowl aloft in one hand.

"This is it, eh?" Max said.

Jane shrugged.

"I can see why you bought it. It's beautiful and fragile."

"That's not why I bought it."

Max chose not to dispute this; he laid the icon down. "In any case, you've, uh, provoked your Nana again."

Jane kept her eyes closed.

"Did you hear me?"

"The feeling is mutual," Jane sighed.

"She dislikes the bad press. She showed me the stories about Carlisle."

"He's nothing. A mere operative of the enemy."

"Is that your theory?"

"It's not a theory. It's a fact."

"How do you know?"

"I just do. There are signs."

Max hesitated, ascertaining whether to explore these depths. "Let me ask you something," he began, "when you saw Carlisle, did you happen to mention anything to him about a tailless cat? I know this sounds stupid."

Jane blinked several times. She looked at Max for the first time. "Tailless cat?"

"Yeah. Tailless cat. You remember. You went into the shop because of it."

Jane sat up and tilted her hat at a jaunty angle. "So what?"

"So, you told him?"

"May-be ... I mi-ight have."

"Did you tell Nana or Leenie ... or Milto?"

Jane rolled her eyes. She plopped forward on her stomach and laid her head on her hands. Max couldn't see her face. She kicked her feet and a DVD of *Bucky Browne and the Midnight Crusade* slid off the bed.

Max stooped to pick it up.

"Oh, my private things," Jane giggled. She rolled onto her side and reached for it.

"Private?" Max handed it to her. "They only sold 100 million of these."

Jane sat up again to gather all the Disher items on her bed. "Do you want something? I'm busy. I'm making plans."

"How about finishing your semester? Is that on the list?"

"Did Nana tell you to ask?"

"No. But if she had, I'd agree with her."

Silently, Jane stacked all her Disher books and DVDs.

"Look," Max said, "I try to be on your side, but you don't make it easy. I get all the blame, like I'm responsible for your every move or every picture you post, or—"

Jane gasped excitedly. "You've seen my Dishpix page! Do you like it? The headband in the profile is cute don'tcha think? It's vintage YSL."

Despite himself, Max smiled. "But ... Lady Jane? Why call yourself that?"

"Ha-ha. Why not? It just came to me. We can be whatever we want."

Max pointed at her hat. "Is that the same one you had in Turkey?"

"Yep. That picture got, like, a thousand comments. Maybe I'll go viral. Wouldn't that be sooo amazing?"

"Well, take it off, will ya? I can't see your face."

Jane started to obey, then stopped. "Like, why are you here? Did you fly all the way from New York just for little ol' me?" As Jane said this, she patted the sides of her Disher assemblage to even the edges. Gently, she laid Gloria's notebook atop the totem so as not to make it collapse.

"No, I was already in Augusta." Max spied the notebook. "What is that? You still have that? Give it to me." He grabbed it from the pile.

"Stop it—it's not yours—"

Max turned away from Jane and opened it. "My God."

"Give it back," Jane whined. She got up off the bed.

Max read aloud: "Gloria Kilday. Anthropology 492: Field Study. Summer, 1987."

"I said—give it back." Jane tried to grab the notebook out of her father's hands.

He brushed her aside. "Today we arrived in Karaman, Turkey. Tomorrow—" Max scanned the rest of the page. "God, that was ages ago," he said, turning several more pages. "She was excited because she'd never been overseas. That's why she signed up for the class—for the adventure." He thumbed through the rest of the notebook, pausing and smirking several times. Suddenly, he snapped it closed and pointed it at Jane. "Look," he said firmly, "your mother was not a Disher. I've told you before. She had a passing interest in archaeology at best. And it was a college class, Jane. A fun summer study abroad. We did a little digging, a little exploring ... your mother brought back a souvenir. But it was all a whim." He looked from Jane to the notebook. "Six weeks in Turkey, and then it was over. We came back, she said she loved me, we went to Vegas, and you know the rest."

Jane silently plucked the notebook from his hand and turned away.

"Your mother was an intriguing, beautiful woman—"

"That's not what Nana says."

"—but she never knew what she wanted—"

"She says she was thoughtless and silly."

"—and I can tell you this for sure—Jane, look at me."

Jane turned her head slightly toward Max, but her hat hid her eyes.

"I can tell you, staring out the window all day isn't going to bring her back."

"I don't stare out the window," Jane said hotly.

"And wherever you go, you won't find her. She doesn't want to be found."

"But I'm not looking for her," Jane said. She gestured theatrically with the notebook as she spoke. "That's so stupid. I don't care about her. Why should I? Like, I don't even remember her. I don't feel anything. I haven't read this," she waved the notebook at Max, "since literally forever. Like, it's not sacred. It doesn't mean anything to me." She turned and tossed the notebook toward the bed. It hit the floor in front of it and skidded underneath. "There. See?" She lifted her chin defiantly.

"Doesn't mean anything to you? Then why'd ya try to grab it from me?"

At these words, Jane began searching the floor for Baby Girl. "You all think I'm some sort of mental case, like totally batshit or something, which I'm not. I mean, I've studied psychology too, and y'know what? I think what you say about me is pure projection. How d'ya like that? You all talk like Dishing is a disease or something, and I just don't understand that because it's always attracted the brightest minds. To me it's about justice, it's about finding the truth, and y'know what? I'm gonna find it. I won't stop. Like, I can think for myself too no matter what anybody else says."

During this disagreement, Baby Girl had retreated to the ajar bedroom door. It sat with its nose to the crack, sniffing.

"Baby Girl, you need to pee?" Jane asked urgently. She collected the dog in her arms and pulled open the door.

"That's absurd," Max said tensely. "I'm not projecting. I'm not looking for—"

"Sorry! Nature calls!" Jane flashed him a smile and disappeared.

When Jane had gone, Max stood with his hands on his hips trying to figure out what had just happened. So much for intervening, he thought. What had he been going to say? He couldn't remember. He exhaled all the air from his lungs and looked about the room, wondering if he should wait for Jane to come back. He decided he shouldn't. What should he tell Patricia? He'd tell her that he'd tried and that he was going back to Augusta. Going back to golf.

Something in shadows caught Max's eye. He squatted, reached under the bed, and pulled out the pink notebook. He stood looking at it, then once more opened the cover:

## THE DIE IS CAST

Today we arrived in Karaman, Turkey. Tomorrow we drive north to Binbirkilise where the monastery is. I can scarcely wait. To be so close to something so ancient, something that's survived. Maybe some spirit of ages past still haunts the place. Some forlorn maiden, perhaps, weeping for forsaken love.

Gloria's handwriting was neat but slanted. She'd pressed hard with a blue pen, creating Braille-like bumps on the reverse of each page.

*Mark my words. You'll wish you'd done more to intervene.*

Max remembered Patricia's warning. She'd said that if he didn't act to save Jane from Dishing, then it'd soon be too late, that Jane would be far beyond his reach. Was his mother right—was it certain that because Jane was so much like her mother, her story would inevitably end like Gloria's? Or was Patricia exaggerating the consequences of Jane's behavior to achieve some secret end?

Max shut the notebook and ran his finger down its spiral. He had no answer to the first question. But the second question ... if he'd learned anything from talking to Jane, it was that the answer to it might rest entirely upon Dr. Carlisle's knowledge of tailless cats.

If there was any chance he could stick it to his mother, then golf could wait.

Scene 12

## The Prodokleis

*Office of the Patriarchate, annex to the*

*Church of Saint George, Istanbul*

*Wednesday, March 10, moments after Papi's entrance*

"The Shrine of the Four Keepers has been found!" Professor Papadopoulos held up a photograph before the ten men gathered about the table in the Patriarch's Throne Room. Dying sunlight slanted through the room's stately windows and touched some of the bearded faces, all of which were frozen in shocked silence. Papi limped toward the lone empty chair at the table. The circle of the Secret Order of Andronicus was now complete.

The silence held a moment longer.

All eyes turned from Papi to the Patriarch who held a second photograph before his face. "Zoticus!" Philotheos pronounced with all the strength of an oath.

"What's the meaning of this? What's going on?" Anthimos of Chalcedon demanded to know.

"An excavation has been underway in the city," Papi said. "Two days ago, they unearthed the fabled shrine."

"Not possible," Elias exclaimed through the computer speakers. "After all these centuries?"

"You might have said *this* is what you were keeping tabs on," Abbott Diogenes declared.

"Forgive me. I did not know for sure until yesterday. The discovery is not yet public knowledge. My student Giulio alerted me. He took these pictures. This one here I can confirm myself." Papi held up a picture of a rounded stone. "It is a section of an archway. One of the archaeologists—Adam Burke is his name—brought it to the Museum of Ancient History this morning. I am assisting in the processing lab. The inscription is clear—Stipendia Autem Peccati—" Papi paused and looked pointedly at each man.

"I—I cannot believe it," the secretary Gabriel said.

"Believe it, my son." Philotheos handed Gabriel the second photograph.

When Gabriel took the photo, he gasped. Two faces stared back at him: one youthful, the other aged. "P-P-Panikos," he stuttered in awe. He bowed his head in reverence.

"Yes, they found him first." Papi pointed to the photo in Gabriel's hands. "And Zoticus yesterday. They are working on Nil as we speak. The walls on the west side of the shrine still stand. That is where the four mosaics are."

Leo, Theo, and Winnipeg Joe jumped out of their seats and peered at the photo over Gabriel's shoulders.

"Extraordinary," Theo murmured. "That's Panikos and Zoticus for sure. Look at the halos."

Leo pointed to Panikos. "His is shaped like a flower."

"And Zoticus's halo is notched. Like a watch gear," Winnipeg said. "I think you look like him," he said to Leo.

"That is as it should be. He is, after all, Zoticus the Wise," Leo said smugly, resuming his seat.

The men began to talk all at once—all except Anthimos. He sat serenely, arms crossed over his chest. The two photographs were passed about and debated.

Philotheos drummed his fingers on the arm of his throne, his mind troubled. He didn't dare imagine the implications of such a discovery, yet he couldn't help but imagine them. After some time, he motioned for silence. "Is there no possibility they have unearthed a church?" he asked Papi. There was a hint of hope in his voice. "Because there are a few others that contain images of the Keepers. The Church at Boyana, of course, has that fine fresco of Kostas with his burning halo. And the Chapel of Saint Sava—"

"There can be no doubt, Your All Holiness," Diogenes interrupted. He looked up from examining the photograph of the archway. "Papi is right. There it is—keep, until the wages of sin are paid—the inscription reads exactly as Putney the Pilgrim describes." Diogenes frowned, appearing as if he might crumple the photograph in his hands. Instead, he leaned back in his chair, removed his spectacles, and rubbed his eyes. "I have written enough about the famed Putney on our website to know. He recalls the shrine's entrance quite vividly." Diogenes closed his eyes to recite the portion of Putney's travelogue from memory: "I passed beneath the gate and, lo, there above me was written—The dish of Christ revealeth he that is true and he that betrays. And this legacy we keep, until the wages of sin are paid. And, lo, mine own heart quailed within me, till my steps faltered, lest I wouldst approach the most holy altar with mine own soul stained with sin." Diogenes sighed and re-positioned his spectacles.

"The fool," Chrys spat. "He had been at the Emperor's Feast the night before, the city's notorious opium den. No doubt his guilt was inflamed by his own debauchery."

"Does Diogenes have that part memorized too?" Lerry joked.

Philotheos appeared not to have heard the commentary of the two archbishops. He stared ahead absently, focused on nothing. "This is the Legacy of Emperor Andronicus," he said, softly repeating the words from the Order's opening ritual. "And this we keep until ... the wages of sin are paid."

Anthimos uncrossed his arms. For a moment, his fingers clutched the double-headed eagle pendant about his neck. The eagle's ruby eyes winked. Anthimos let out a low, rolling laugh. Its sound was akin to a growl. "Brothers, brothers," he said with disdain, reaching for the photo of Panikos and Zoticus. He scanned it briefly, as if with scant interest, and let it flutter back to the table. "Mosaics. A broken piece of stone. An inscription. Is that all that is found? Nothing more?" He laughed again and looked about him. The men's faces were tense, their lips pinched in anxiety. He alone was at ease, a smile spread across his thick face.

"What are you getting at?" Diogenes asked suspiciously.

Anthimos chuckled. "My brother, I can quote from the ancient sources as well as you. Let us see if you recall this description—Thus was the prodokleis fashioned and carried unto the shrine, according to the will of the Emperor—it is a well-crafted sentence, is it not?"

"Metochites!" Chrys called out. "Only he ever wrote of the *betrayer's key*."

Just then, at the head of the table, Philotheos stood.

The men stared at him in amazement. Only once had the Patriarch gotten up from his throne in the middle of a meeting, and that had been years ago. Winnipeg and Theo leaped up, and one by one the others stood as well. Papi, pushing himself up with his cane, was the last one out of his seat.

The sight of Papi's struggle brought Philotheos back to himself. "Forgive me," he said, gesturing to his old friend. He motioned for all to sit. Instead of returning to his throne, however, he paced back and forth before it. His mind was in turmoil. Never in his life did he imagine that the secrets entrusted to the Order would be exposed. Never did he imagine he would hear that terrible word uttered: *prodokleis*. As he well-knew, the word appeared in only one document, the *Coda*, an appendix to the *Annals of Andronicus*. In the *Coda*, Metochites, the author of the *Annals*, had supplemented his own history with explanatory notes, evidently intending to revise the *Annals* to include them. But those revisions—perhaps due to the Emperor's death—had never been completed, and the *Coda* was lost to history. It wasn't lost, however, to the Order of Andronicus. The only copy—incomplete and damaged—resided in their Secret Archives.

"Is the prodokleis found or no?" Anthimos looked from man to man. "It is the only question that matters. And no one asks it." There was a touch of accusation in his voice. "Tsk, tsk. How far the Order has fallen since the days of—"

"We do not ask because we do not wish it to be found," Diogenes interrupted sharply.

"Why? Why should we not wish it?"

"Because if the truth of the Legacy of Andronicus were ever discovered," Philotheos shook his head mournfully, "I dare not think what would become of us."

"Bah! The Legacy is not to be feared. You instructed us earlier today to face certain realities, and yet you do not want to face this?" Anthimos responded.

"You will not insult His All Holiness," Winnipeg cried, pushing his thick glasses up his nose.

"I am with Anthimos," Chrys said. "The Legacy is our life. Why fear it? Why fear that which gives us strength?"

"Here, Here!" Lerry knocked his knuckles on the table.

The Throne Room erupted.

Philotheos sank down on his throne. "Please, brothers, please." He lifted his hands. "We dare not succumb to anger, a passion that shutters the mind and shades the heart. How certain are its desolations. Swift to its prey, it makes men as cruel as beasts."

"Saint Mark the Ascetic," Leo said, recognizing the Patriarch's quotation of the famous fifth-century monk.

Despite the desperation he felt to unite the Order, Philotheos managed a kindly smile. "Your quick recollection always pleases me, my chosen son. As Saint Mark says—anger's food is pride. Let pride be scarce, and anger is ended. May the Son of God have mercy on us."

"Amen." Leo puffed his chest out, pleased to be acknowledged by the Patriarch.

The men about the table grew quiet.

Philotheos stroked his beard pensively. "I must, much as it troubles me ... I must agree with our brother Anthimos."

There were murmurs of dissent.

Philotheos held up his hands. "Please, my brothers. Let us not deceive ourselves in this. Brother Anthimos is right to draw our attention to certain realities. It is not impossible that the prodokleis will be found."

"But still unlikely," Diogenes said. "Or if it is found, it would be in pieces."

"What makes you think so?" Anthimos challenged him.

"Can we not assume the shrine was pillaged when the Turks—?"

"Pillaged and scorched," Papi confirmed. "The stonework brought to the museum thus far shows traces of it."

"The Sultan's soldiers set the shrine on fire then?"

Papi nodded.

"Well, then." Diogenes leaned back in his chair, took off his spectacles and cleaned them. "It is likely that what is to be found in the shrine has been found already—mosaics."

"You are wrong," Anthimos growled.

"Were there not also icons of the Four Keepers at the shrine?" Elias asked. "If I remember Metochites—"

"He reports the presence of a complete set," Diogenes confirmed. "The fact is well-known. It is in the Annals."

"Have the icons been discovered?" Elias asked.

"No, no," Papi assured him, "my student Giulio would have mentioned it."

"Nor will they be found. The shrine was set ablaze. What could have survived? Nothing."

"You are wrong, Diogenes," Anthimos said again, his growl louder this time.

"Ha! Yes, I know it pleases you to think so."

Anthimos crossed his arms over his chest. "My dear abbot, you exhibit all the courage of a church mouse." He made a show of flicking lint from the sleeve of his black robe.

Diogenes's tight-lipped face grew red. "And you are as pretentious as a king's pet cat."

"Brothers, brothers," Philotheos pleaded.

This time it was Anthimos who stood.

"Listen to me, all of you! Do we seriously fail to consider the character of those who once belonged to the Order?" Anthimos looked first at Diogenes and then at the rest of the men. "Emperor Andronicus hated Catholics. He wiped our city clean of them. When he came to the throne, the Latin dogs were at last driven out. He sought to restore the wealth and power stolen from our Empire. Kostas, Zoticus, Panikos, and Nil were not merely simple monks to him. They were instruments of God. Like the four horsemen of the apocalypse—they were a sign from heaven that judgment was come. They died for justice, and their bodies, defiled by the Latins, were never recovered. Never recovered! They were God's prophets, sent ahead of the Emperor to prepare the way. And Andronicus took the path set before him. He built the kingdom and peopled it with others just like the Four Keepers—men zealous for justice. Men whose devotion to the Legacy would have been total and absolute. That is what the Order was founded on. On justice. You really believe those men, confronting the utter end, would have suddenly abandoned their charge? The Sultan's siege of the city lasted for months. The Order would have had time to prepare. They would have made the preservation of the Legacy the foremost task. They would have devised a means of protecting the icons and the prodokleis. Why not at the shrine?"

"That is pure supposition," Diogenes snapped.

"You would say that. Because you do not share their passion for the Legacy. But imagine the possibilities if it were restored." Anthimos's eyes widened. For a moment he stood unblinking as if beholding a vision. Rousing himself, he added, "Sadly, the Andronicus Order has become little more than a supper club for chattering old women." With exaggerated ease, he gently reset himself in his seat, to a flurry of indignation.

"You go too far, Anthimos." Papi gripped the upside-down church at the top of his cane.

"I'm not a chattering old woman," Winnipeg squeaked. "I've hardly said a word."

"Here, here." Theo slapped Winnipeg on the back.

"Enough!" Philotheos commanded.

Diogenes opened his mouth in protest, and Philotheos held up his hand to forestall him.

"My brother, you object to Anthimos, not because he is wrong, but because you fear he may be right. And it is preposterous to think that the Legacy could be found after so many centuries. We have existed for so long assuming those clues are buried or destroyed, never to trouble us. And that may still be the case, but—" Philotheos paused to address the entire room, "Anthimos is correct about the men of those days. They would have done everything in their power to preserve the Legacy. Therefore, we should proceed assuming they succeeded."

Anthimos grinned, looking very much like the king's cat Diogenes had accused him of being. "Well then, now we are getting somewhere."

Philotheos thought for a moment, then looked at Papi. "Professor, you mentioned someone, an archaeologist."

"Yes, Your All Holiness. Adam Burke is his name."

"What do you know of him?"

Papi frowned and tapped his cane on the floor. "He is an egoist, a showman—a man of narrow interests but excessive passion. A driven man. A firm believer in the Dish. He would stop at nothing to discover it. His knowledge of Disher history is extensive. He is well-read in the Annals and Putney's journal, for instance. Of course, he does not know of the existence of the prodokleis, as that is our secret only. Should he discover it, he would not know what he has found nor what to do with it. Your All Holiness may recall—Burke is famous for discovering the partial icon of Saint Nil in Bulgaria a few years back. Naturally, he believes that the riddles on the icons would lead him to the Dish. He does not understand the other markings, of course. No one does—as they are explained in the Coda only."

"Ah, yes. I thought when you mentioned the name, I had heard of him."

"He has devoted his career to pursuing the Last Supper Dish. I am sure he now believes it is within his grasp."

"And nothing would stop him, you say?"

Papi shook his head.

"Then it seems we must stop him."

"What! Why?" Anthimos pounded his fists on the table.

"The truth of the Legacy cannot be discovered," Philotheos said. "Not now. Not ever. The public outrage—"

"Let it be discovered," Anthimos roared. "Let there be outrage!"

"I understand your feelings, but we cannot—"

Anthimos's voice momentarily overpowered the Patriarch's. "Why should we hide the Legacy? Why should we be ashamed of it? As if *we* were the ones who committed the crime. The crime was against us. And it needs to be righted. Do we no longer have the courage to fulfill the will of Andronicus? The will of God?"

Philotheos raised his voice to meet Anthimos's challenge. "Hear me, brother! It is not a matter of courage. It is a matter of survival. Have you not been listening? Do you not understand the world we now live in? What made the Order powerful in a bygone age makes us vulnerable in the present one. There are things one simply does not do if one wants to exist in the public sphere. It would be politically incorrect. Why, Emperor Andronicus himself is now little more than a Wikipedia entry to those in our ever-shrinking congregations. In this country, we are especially open to attack, as you know. Turkish law requires that the Ecumenical Patriarch be a Turkish citizen by birth. After making such a law, what does the government do? Drive all the Greeks from Turkey, of course. This, our beloved city, was once the seat of Orthodoxy. Now it is the seat of Islam. My brother, there are far greater powers than ours at work in the world. We need the Catholics, Anthimos. Despite how you feel, we need them. If this man Burke pursues the Dish, what he finds will destroy the delicate peace that Boniface and I are fashioning. We cannot have the secret of the Last Supper Dish revealed. In the world we live in now, Andronicus's Legacy would destroy the Orthodox Church itself."

Anthimos's face was hard, but he made no reply.

Philotheos took a deep breath to calm himself. After a long minute of silence, he said, "We need a plan in the event that Burke does discover the icons and the prodokleis."

"But Your All Holiness," Elias said, "even if all four icons are at the shrine, Burke still must solve the riddles. Even we do not know the riddles of Zoticus or Nil—what remains of the Coda does not contain them."

"And he must use the markings to reconstruct the map that leads to the gate," Diogenes added.

"Yes, and I have no doubt he would do both. The Legacy was designed to ensure that seekers could solve the puzzles and enter. And Burke, as Papi has described, is the ultimate seeker. We do not want such a man reaching the gate with the betrayer's key in hand."

"It is odd to plan to prevent something that may not ever happen." Gabriel scribbled in his planner. "How shall I describe this in the minutes?"

"We could initiate a smear campaign on TrueDishers," Diogenes suggested, "perhaps by challenging Burke's character and credentials."

Philotheos shook his head. "No, no, I believe this time our course of action must be more—tangible." He looked at Papi. "Professor, is there any way for someone to enter the excavation site unnoticed?"

"I think not. The site is enclosed by a fence. There are security guards at the gate. Plus, according to my student, digging occurs around the clock. Someone is always there."

Philotheos looked to the side and stroked his beard.

"Are you suggesting ...?" Papi lifted one of his bushy eyebrows.

"What? So maybe I am," Philotheos said defensively.

Papi chuckled and looked about him. "You cannot be serious. With these men?"

"I reject that!" Winnipeg slapped the table and his glasses slid down his nose.

"Quiet, you." Leo elbowed him. "What are you rejecting? You do not even know."

"I do so. We are men, Your All Holiness. Ready and willing!" Winnipeg saluted the Patriarch.

"Must you volunteer us so quickly?" Theo hissed. "Think, man, think."

"Ah, my dear professor," Philotheos looked at Papi, "do you agree then with our brother here?" He indicated Anthimos. "You too believe we are smaller men than those of Andronicus's time?"

Papi inclined his head apologetically. "I did not mean to suggest so, Your All Holiness. Please, forgive me."

"My friend, I do not need to. Because you are right. You are both right. We are smaller. Much smaller." Philotheos sighed, then pushed himself back against his throne, sitting tall. "Nevertheless." He rubbed his hands together and looked at each man. "Brothers," he declared, "it is time to prepare yourselves. It is time for us to plan ... a heist."

Scene 13

## Halo Effect

*Grandeur, Georgia*

*Wednesday, March 10, moments before the arrival of Kathleen, Milto, and Nicole*

The wall clock struck the quarter hour. The meeting should've already begun. But meetings involving her daughter Kathleen always met with a delay of at least fifteen minutes, elevators or escalators notwithstanding. Patricia got up from her desk and opened her office door. She remembered that the previous day Max had slammed the door shut—a vain display of strength. Her son's childish efforts to rile her up amused her, and the fact that he'd failed amused her even more. She never tired of the game they played because she usually won.

She was stronger than Max. And he knew it. He might whine and moan, but in the end he obeyed.

Her granddaughter, however, resisted.

Patricia walked about her office—it was once Everett's. She ran her fingers along the surfaces of the massive desk, the leather chairs, the bookcases. These were once her late husband's things, but she claimed them. This was her domain now. She wandered to the far wall on which were mounted the hunting trophies. She especially liked to look at the face of the lion frozen in mid-roar with its great teeth bared. It was a sign that the world would succumb to the powerful. Everyone around Patricia surrendered to her control, except Jane. *That will change soon. I will make Jane submit to me.* Carefully, Patricia reviewed the details of her plan. She believed she'd accounted for every contingency.

Controlling Jane was, in truth, only a means to an end for Patricia—as satisfying as that achievement would be. Patricia's real concern was protecting her ultimate domain—Whitaker Corporation:

"Truth is—people are tired of Max."

"Tired of Max?"

"Correct."

"According to the research, our commercials no longer resonate, especially with young people."

"I see."

"Perception is we're stuck in the 1990s. It's the same reason McDonald's ditched the clown. We need a fresh face."

This conversation, which had set Patricia's plan into motion, had taken place nine months previously in the exact same room. She'd summoned Kathleen and Toby Milto to report on Corporate's research into why Whitaker's nearest competitor All Sales had succeeded in increasing its market share for the sixth consecutive quarter:

"Max has to go. That's number one," Kathleen explained. "Number two—"

"What about our slogan?" Patricia asked.

Milto squinted at his iPad. "I don't recall much about that in the report, Mrs. Whitaker."

"Still tests well in focus groups," Kathleen said. "Marketing talked of shortening the *of* to *o'* but thought it sounded too Irish. It'll still be Lots of Stuff—Right Here."

"Very good."

"So, okay, number one is Max. Number two is our corporate perception problem." Kathleen paused to gather air.

Milto jumped in with his thin, squeaky voice. "The research from marketing is quite thorough. They've really earned their keep."

"Excellent." Patricia leaned back in her chair. "Give me the highlights."

"Sure thing, Mrs. Whitaker." Milto squinted down at his iPad again and scrolled through several screens. He clicked his tongue while the two women waited. "Well, imagine that," he said as if impressed by what he was reading.

"It's simple," Kathleen said impatiently. She fingered the ruby bracelet on her wrist. "We haven't improved our corporate image. All Sales has. They've come out against bullies and are donating money to raise awareness."

Patricia frowned and rocked in her chair. Slowly, her frown became a smile. "But they're a corporation. Bullying is what we do. It's just life." She laughed. "How does throwing money away help them?"

Kathleen drew in air. She spoke in monotone as if reading from a report. "Because companies that endorse a worthy cause see on average a 2.5% increase in yearly revenue. And companies that support a cause every year see greater annual profits than those companies that never support causes. The phenomenon was first observed by Kent Abrams at Forbes in the case of Precise Electric Power. In 1995 PEP initiated their 3-year Lights Out Campaign to save the sea turtle and went from last to first in their industry. It's now the classic example cited in the literature."

Patricia yawned exaggeratedly. "Have we not yet escaped this eternal Victorian revival? Nothing is more tedious than mixing morality and advertising."

"Doesn't matter. It works," Kathleen said.

"Advertising has only one purpose, and it isn't to make people good," Patricia said.

"But people like to feel that they're good."

Patricia intertwined her fingers as if to pray. "If we must shop to save our souls, then—"

"Save the world!" Milto interjected fervently.

Surprised by Milto's zeal, Patricia jumped in her chair.

"Toby is correct," Kathleen said, breathing hard. "Personal salvation is passé. The salvation of the world, though, is a useful idea. If everything needs to be saved, then think of how much shopping needs to be done."

Patricia's eyelids fluttered, her mind excited by possibilities. "Mm, yes. If we did support a cause, it'd almost oblige people to shop at Whitaker's, wouldn't it?"

"Correct. To make a difference," Kathleen said. "Morally, I guess."

Patricia's lips curled in silent scorn. "I hope for all their efforts, the sea turtle was saved," she said insincerely.

Kathleen chuckled; her cheeks jiggled like an infant's.

Patricia looked away. "So, we need a new face. And a cause. Hmm." She tapped her fingernails on the desk.

"Corporate says we're in the midst of a generational shift," Kathleen explained. She extracted a tissue from her sleeve and dabbed the sweat from her upper lip. "According to Gallup surveys, 88% of 18-30-year-olds want retailers to support causes, and 76% switch brands to those that do. But here's the rub—85% have a better impression of a corporation when it donates to causes. It's called the halo effect in marketing literature."

"Halo effect. Fascinating. We must harness this power." Patricia glanced at Milto, who after his outburst had resumed scrolling on his iPad. Sometimes, Patricia wondered if he was paying attention and tested him. "Um, Toby, do you have anything to add?"

He squinted at the screen. "Why, yes. It says here the sea turtle was saved."

"Not incidentally," Kathleen continued, returning the tissue to her sleeve, "teens are 60% more likely to share their approval of haloed brands and retailers on social media. All Sales has greatly benefited from the free publicity."

Patricia leaned back in her chair, pondering the susceptibility of the young to idealism. "Your presentation is pin-point as usual, Kathleen. All we need now is a way forward."

Kathleen folded her hands in her lap. "Have already thought of that."

"Oh?"

"Yes. Isn't the way forward obvious?"

Of course, it was.

In retrospect, Patricia had always known the path. She'd always known she'd eventually dump Max in favor of Jane as the public face of Whitaker Corporation. Out with the old, in with the forever new. If she were honest, she'd confess to having tired of Max long ago. Max with his golden hair, white teeth, and faux tan—merely another image in a world of images. In his latest 30-second spot, Patricia thought his face had shone with unnatural smoothness like the molded face of a doll. Clearly, he'd had a Botox treatment. After fifteen years as the face of Whitaker's, he too felt his age. It was past time to replace him.

The reason Patricia hadn't already replaced Max became clear to her one day several weeks after her meeting with Kathleen and Milto. She'd gone to headquarters on another matter. Milto peeked into her office with his pea-sized eyes to say that marketing was excited about starring Jane in Whitaker's commercials:

"It's the easiest thing to sell young and beautiful."

"Have they already asked her?" Patricia inquired, surprised at the hope in her voice.

"Nope."

"Ah, well, someone will have to—"

"Aren't you gonna ask her?"

Patricia sat unblinking for two seconds. "Of course," she affirmed heartily. Yet she quickly changed the subject. Later that afternoon, as Byrd the chauffeur drove her home, she sat fiddling with the diamond in her wedding band. It was the one jewel Gloria, that pernicious woman, hadn't stolen. Patricia liked how the diamond reflected light from all angles at once. She often studied it when in need of illumination. It never failed her: *Jane will say no.*

THE DIE IS CAST

Nothing in Patricia's experience with Jane cautioned her to doubt this intuition. Jane's inherent obstinacy was a fact just as Whitaker Corporation's 498 billion dollars in annual sales was a fact. Evidence in support of Jane's obstinacy was all too abundant. Patricia still recalled with horror the day of Everett's funeral. Jane, ten years old at the time, had taken one look at the casket and said, "Can we go now?" Patricia blamed Max for his lax parenting. Somehow Jane had grown up without a sense of duty to her family or respect for the Whitaker name. She had no conviction about upholding the great work of her forbears. "We are all links in a very great chain," Patricia had explained one day to Jane when she was still quite young. "You are a link. I am a link. Your father is a link. And your mother ... well, sometimes links don't do what they were made to do. They get rusty. They break. And the great chain falls apart. But we'll make sure you don't break—won't we, Jane?" Jane had just looked at her grandmother cross-eyed and made a fish face.

Patricia intently scanned her memory for a time—any time—when Jane had cooperated with her. She couldn't find a memory. *Jane will say no.* So deep was Patricia's contemplation of this belief that she didn't perceive Byrd turn the car up the drive to Whiningham. When he parked and opened the door for her, she sat there staring straight ahead.

"Mrs. Whitaker, are you getting out?"

A week later, Patricia had obliquely shared her concern about Jane with Kathleen over lunch:

"Do you think Jane will want to support another cause?"

Kathleen didn't answer right away; her mouth was full.

"You know, because of her Dishing," Patricia continued. "No doubt, she thinks that's the only cause there is—finding that stupid bowl. She won't be interested in promoting whatever we decide to do at Whitaker's."

"I dunno." Kathleen stabbed a slab of salmon. "We all know her Dishing isn't really about finding the bowl."

"No, perhaps not." Patricia picked at her salad. "I regret not removing that woman's things from the house."

"The trunk, you mean."

"Yes."

"You couldn't have known what was in it."

"I didn't even look."

"What would you have thought if you had? The notebook looks innocent. And if it wasn't Dishing, it'd be something else." Kathleen paused, her gray eyes vacant like empty spoons. "That's always the way it is. An absent parent. The child goes in search—"

"But Jane doesn't think that. She doesn't think she's searching for her mother."

"I think she does—deep down."

Patricia finished her salad and irritably pushed her plate to one side. Talk of psychology frustrated her. She didn't like to contemplate the interdependencies of human personality. To do so seemed to implicate oneself in other people's idiotic behavior. In her view, people had an obligation not to be idiots, and if they did behave idiotically, they had a responsibility to *stop it*. She looked away as Kathleen dabbed the corners of her ample mouth with a napkin and quietly belched.

Patricia had disappointments about both her children. Max's faults were many and thus required endless enunciation. Kathleen's fault was more singular, and for that reason, stranger, almost beyond speech. Her fault was that she was far too fat to be a Whitaker. There was no one of her proportions on either side of the family that Patricia could recall. Nor could she recall a time when Kathleen hadn't been fat. The puffy, infant creases on her daughter's arms had never shrunk or smoothed, only grown. Privately, she ranked Kathleen's obesity at the top of her list of life's disappointments. Of course, she'd never have admitted her disappointment openly, partly because she thought that to say Kathleen's appearance was "a big disappointment" was too ironic an expression.

"Has PR enlisted a cause yet?" Patricia asked, changing the subject. She took a lingering sip of wine.

"Working on it." Kathleen reached for the dessert menu. She made a brief report: soil conservation, clean water in Africa, and saving the rain forest had been rejected as cliché. At the same time, it was also felt that the plight of the endangered Alabama cavefish, although of scientific interest—the species had no eyes and survived solely on the feces of the gray bat—would not excite the imagination of the public at large. Green energy and recycling were thought to be very of the moment, though Public Relations was loath to draw further attention to the push to ban plastic shopping bags, given that if such an initiative ever succeeded, Whitaker's would have to revamp all its check-out lines, which would require a tremendous outlay of—

"There must be a way to separate Jane from Dishing," Patricia mused, swirling the wine in her glass. She'd only been half-listening to Kathleen. The cause Whitaker's might take up interested her but little.

The waiter placed before Kathleen a thick slice of strawberry savarin.

"You wanna track down Gloria?" Kathleen asked when the waiter had gone.

"For God's sake," Patricia said a bit too loudly. She set down her wine glass, and it clanked against a knife. "Are we as desperate as that? The idea!"

Kathleen shrugged, half-hiding a smile. She twirled her fork in her fingers before diving into the savarin. She ate it methodically without looking up at her mother. "It would focus Jane's mind on other things."

"That cannot be a serious proposal," Patricia said, observing her daughter's pleasure with mild disgust. "You're not taking this seriously—you sound like Max."

"I am, but we may have to take Jane as she is."

"That's exactly what Max would say. You think she can't be persuaded," Patricia accused Kathleen heatedly, feeling that her daughter meant to question her persuasive powers.

"What do you propose to do?" Kathleen stuck her fork into the last of the savarin and looked at it longingly before placing it in her mouth. She chewed with her eyes closed.

As Patricia observed Kathleen's bliss, she thought of a scheme that was so devious, she was almost surprised at the expansiveness of her own mind. She drained her glass of wine and eagerly leaned forward, elbows on the table. Her icy blue eyes shone. "What if—" she began in a whisper. It took her a minute to explain the plan.

"Brilliant," Kathleen said when Patricia had finished.

Patricia thought so too but liked to hear Kathleen say so. She sat back in her chair and hugged herself. "The key is to find the right person to appeal to Jane. The charity the person represents doesn't matter."

"I suggest a woman close to Jane's age, attractive. She must be able to spout all the platitudes about social justice."

"But she can't be a sincere goody-two-shoes," Patricia said. "They're insufferable people. She must admire profit and wealth and be willing to take orders from me to gain some herself. Can you and Toby find such a candidate?"

"Leave it to us."

Patricia smiled in self-satisfaction. She thought of ordering another glass of wine to propose a toast to philanthropy and all its rewards. Instead, she lifted her empty glass and gave it her best simulation.

Such were the preliminary events which had brought Patricia to the fulfillment of all her plans for Jane. She checked her watch and turned away from the wall of hunting trophies. She sat down at her desk again and tried to appear busy. Briefly, she reviewed the résumé of the woman—what was her name?—Ms. Dziedzic. Kathleen had scrawled, "Underpaid. Promising!" at the top. Patricia set it aside and smoothed the collar of her blouse. She fiddled with her wedding ring and checked her hair in a mirror. Was she nervous? No, she decided. She was preparing herself for the hunt. If this Ms. Dziedzic proved to be the one, Patricia would snap her up. Then Jane would be next.

Suddenly, Kathleen's girth appeared in the doorway. She lumbered in, for she never waited to be invited. When enough space opened, Milto swept past Kathleen into the office and greeted Patricia warmly. Kathleen claimed the armchair Max had been sitting in the previous day. When she lowered herself into it, the leather cushion hissed in pain. She wore a fussy, frilly pink blouse and billowy tan skirt. As she settled in, she pulled her skirt down toward her knees. Its waistline had crept north toward her two enormous breasts.

"Ms. Dziedzic." Patricia stood and greeted Nicole, immediately approving of the woman's appearance, which she deemed sleek, chic, and efficient.

Milto recited Nicole's pedigree: a BS in management from USC, an MBA from Johns Hopkins, internship at PBS, three years as proposal development coordinator for CARE, four years as a procurement assistant for UNICEF, located in Copenhagen, currently assistant director of BOMOF, headquartered in Washington, D.C.

"Er, uh, BOMOF?" Patricia asked. She'd followed all the acronyms until the last.

"It stands for Back On My Own Feet," Nicole said quickly and breathlessly. "We're a homeless advocacy organization. It's such an opportunity to be associated with you. Thank you, Mrs. Whitaker for contacting us. We're sooo honored." She placed a hand on her heart in a show of humility.

Patricia glanced at Kathleen. "It was my daughter who found you." She resumed her seat at her desk.

"Oops! How silly of me! You just asked what our name meant, ha-ha." Nicole slapped her own cheek playfully.

"Forgive me, it's nerves. Anyway, our organization has developed a personal shower kit that can be used by any homeless person, including those with physical disabilities and alternative mentalities. We believe in distributing the wealth of good personal hygiene to the less advantaged."

"Distributing hygiene?" Patricia asked skeptically. *How can this woman pitch this drivel and keep a straight face?*

"We want to get the homeless back on their own feet. To improve their self-worth," Nicole said. "Being shelter-challenged is such a sweaty, grimy lifestyle. We give them a chance to scrub away the social stigmas of dirt and odor. Those of us who are soap-advantaged can hardly imagine how we have sanitation-shamed these poor victims into the shadows. It's heartless." Nicole gave Patricia a perky smile. "Maybe you feel the need that is out there, Mrs. Whitaker. They say cleanliness is next to godliness. And if the homeless need Whitaker's to get clean, that makes your stores the next best thing to heaven."

"Indeed." Patricia raised an eyebrow. She had to admit, Nicole's last rhetorical flourish, aligning Whitaker's with heaven, was clever.

"But how does your personal shower thingy work?" Milto asked.

"What an a-maa-zing question," Nicole said with gusto. She extracted a few shiny, stainless steel rods and other parts from her canvas bag. "May I use this chair, thanks!" Without waiting for permission, she quickly arranged the items around the empty chair next to Kathleen.

"You pull the end of the collapsible pole—like this," Nicole demonstrated. "Then you clamp it to a shopping cart." Nicole attached the shower to the chair's back. "The showerhead at the top is spring-loaded and snaps into place automatically. Then you screw the water bottle into the slot—we recommend a minimum of two liters—and roll down the curtain. Voilà! Your very own private shower anytime, anywhere. In working with the homeless, we find that they greatly value their independence."

"Enough to wanna carry that around?" Patricia asked cynically. Listening to Nicole talk was like listening to Jane.

"It's lightweight, super portable—and many of the homeless already have shopping carts," Nicole explained.

"Yes, stolen from their local Whitaker's."

"Ha-ha, we-ell, you do have a lot of stores. We've focus-group tested these showers with our agency in Manhattan," Nicole reported. "They were a hit. Although one man was arrested for public indecency in Central Park. The shower comes with warnings about discretion—setting up in back alleys or boarded-up buildings and wherever."

"Late at night, I assume," Patricia said with alarm.

"Of course. And the best thing—I'm totally excited about this!" Nicole reached into the bag and pulled out a catalog. She handed it to Milto. "We offer this model of the personal shower in three colors. Steel blue like this one, rich maroon, and garden green. The green is suuper cute and matches a variety of sleeping bags and pup tents. BOMOF offers decal options if you're wondering. Your slogan, Lots of Stuff— Right Here, can be placed on any of these color models."

Patricia eyed Milto and Kathleen from across her desk. "What do you two think?"

Kathleen brushed some fingernail crumbs from her skirt. "If the cause is tangible, the halo effect will be too. It's what the research shows."

"Good," Patricia said. "But do you think she has a chance with Jane?"

Kathleen snorted. "Sounds kinda like her."

"I see why you recommended her," Patricia said.

Milto squeaked with mirth.

"Thoughts, Toby?"

"Garden green is rather fetching."

During this exchange, Nicole appeared puzzled.

"Please take that thing off my chair, Ms. Dziedzic," Patricia said. "Sit down. I want to know more about you. I found your presentation intriguing." She scanned Nicole's résumé. "Impressive. You've just gotten a two-million-dollar grant from the Department of Housing and Urban Development."

"Thank you. You see we are serious about—"

"Then you're already substantially funded," Patricia said, seeming to sour. *No need to sound eager.* After all, if Nicole was to be absorbed into the Whitaker empire, she had first to pass a test.

"It may seem so, Mrs. Whitaker," Nicole began, "but our organization supports offices in forty-seven states, plus agencies in Canada and Latin America—"

"What about Europe?" Patricia asked.

"Yes, I was just about to say we have an established presence in the United Kingdom and France, and we're about to open an office in Copenhagen due to my contacts there."

"That's good to hear, Ms. Dziedzic. You see, Whitaker Corporation is a vast enterprise, with subsidiaries—"

"All over the world, I know." Nicole's eyes widened. "In Latin America, South America, Europe, and the South Pacific. You've just opened your first stores in Turkey and India and are currently listed by the Fortune Global 500 as the fifth most valuable company by market value. You're the largest grocery retailer in the United States and Canada and the largest family-owned business, with 2.4 million employees worldwide. Your vast enterprise is … it's sooo big." She looked up as if beholding a heavenly vision.

Patricia pursed her lips, not daring to look at Kathleen. But she couldn't help nodding approvingly at a woman who'd done her homework. She glanced at Milto, who stood proudly squinting. Kathleen appeared bored.

"BOMOF would be very, very honored to partner with Whitaker's," Nicole continued eagerly. Her eyes gleamed. "We encourage all donations, large or small. Because we want everyone to feel they've made a difference. As of yet, we haven't benefited directly from the recent trend in corporate beneficence. Most of our funding comes through government agencies or small, individual—"

"Beneficence? Is that what you call it?" Patricia asked.

"Er, charity, philanthropy—those are the official terms." Nicole laughed tensely. "Or doing good." With a flick of her fingers, she put "doing good" in quotes and rolled her eyes.

Patricia saw Nicole's self-conscious gesture. The woman gushed Jane's vapid idealism, but maybe she wasn't an idealist. *Time to find out.* "What is your salary, Ms. Dziedzic?"

"Excuse me?"

Patricia inspected her diamond ring, making sure Nicole could see it. "Your salary."

"Mrs. Whitaker, we are a non-profit organization. I assure you, 90% of all our resources are put to work in the field to maximize our charitable footprint."

"Mm, yes. What about your personal aspirations? Surely you don't wish always to be a—what is it?—an assistant director of a homeless organization?"

Nicole rubbed her hands nervously. "I—I—"

"Do you enjoy a husband's income? I don't think you're married. Are you?"

"Mrs. Whitaker," Milto jumped in anxiously, "I don't think that question is allowed."

"Never mind, Toby, don't interrupt me," Patricia said crisply. Then to Nicole: "A trusted source told me that you are undercompensated for someone with such a considerable record. It's obvious that BOMOF would benefit from an alliance with Whitaker's. I want to know if such an alliance would benefit you."

"I—I don't understand." Nicole dropped her eyes. Furtively, she glanced at Kathleen, hoping for help with an answer, but Kathleen chewed her fingernails, oblivious.

"Just be honest with me, Nicole, and I will explain my curiosity about you—because it's *you* that we are interested in, not BOMOF—"

"Me? Why?"

"—so, I want to know, if you acquire our contract, would it advance your career at BOMOF?"

"They'd give me a fancier job title," Nicole said wryly.

"But your salary?" Patricia prompted.

Nicole cleared her throat. She looked squarely at Patricia and said, "It wouldn't go up one penny."

"Oh, how unfair. And after all your hard work securing such a big benefactor." Patricia smiled in simulated pity. "But surely you think you deserve better."

Nicole slowly nodded.

"Given all you have done for BOMOF—not to mention the homeless—will you ever get what you deserve?"

Nicole smirked. "BOMOF constantly demands that all its employees sacrifice—for the cause."

Patricia placed her elbows on her desk and lightly pressed her fingertips together as if to capture a fly. Her diamond flashed in the light. "My dear, what do *you* want?"

Nicole gazed at Patricia's ring as if hypnotized. "I—I'd hoped that landing the support of Whitaker's would be a way out for me." After a pause, she added, "I wanted to network with Whitaker's management team and ... and latch on." She placed her hands over her face. "You don't know what it's like living off the success of others. I can't take it anymore. Somewhere, I lost my way. Maybe I saw a movie when I was at PBS, something about saving the children. I'm so tired of groveling for donations. Omigod, I can't believe I said that."

Patricia clenched her hands together; her lips twitched in delight. "Toby, Kathleen, well done."

"Good gosh, Mrs. Whitaker, what a relief," Milto exhaled. He danced a little two-step.

Kathleen nodded—still chewing.

"Let's get to it then," Patricia said, shuffling some papers.

Nicole held up her hand. "Wait, please, I don't understand. I just said—"

"Exactly the right thing." Patricia smiled.

"But—"

"Look, I dislike pretense. You want my money. And you were willing to say so. If this is the way you feel—then welcome home. If you are interested in earning my money, you can do something for me."

"Anything!"

"Very well." Briefly, Patricia explained her conundrum in getting her granddaughter Jane to take an interest in the family business. If Nicole could interest Jane in Whitaker's charitable cause, then Jane might fully dedicate herself to the business—like the rest of the family. "If you can connect with Jane, then I'll initiate a nationwide ad campaign touting Whitaker's support of BOMOF. We'll produce the commercials through our own studio. Toby, if you please."

Milto opened a file on his iPad; it was a rough draft of the script for the promotional video starring Nicole, Max, and Jane. "We're still tweaking it, but here's the gist." He handed the iPad to Nicole. "The slogan Shower the Homeless is being market tested, with promising results."

"Marketing recommends ending with a close-up of Jane to solidify her in the viewer's mind as the face of the cause," Kathleen explained to Nicole.

"We'll be your biggest account," Patricia said, "and you needn't lift another finger. We'll take care of everything." Patricia picked up Nicole's résumé. "And if you are successful with Jane, I will forward this to our division of human resources—with *my* personal recommendation. I must admit, Jane's mind is a mystery to me. She's making a mess of her life and inviting ridicule of our family name. But she's the future of Whitaker's. So, this is important to me."

"I can't wait to meet her." Nicole flashed Patricia a winning smile. "I'm positive she'll jump at the chance to shower the homeless, ha-ha. Trust me."

And with that, the meeting adjourned. Patricia's confidence surged. As Milto helped Nicole pack up her portable shower, Patricia and Kathleen conferred.

"Think we need more time to prepare Jane?" Kathleen asked her mother.

"No. Remember the other part of my plan. We've already planted the seeds."

"Jane's pretty dry ground."

"Then it's time to water it, isn't it? Time for Jane to help us put a halo on Whitaker's."

Scene 14

## Not Getting Anywhere

*JFK International Airport*

*New York City*

*Wednesday, March 10*

"Dear Steve, I'm so embarrassed. What a fiasco! I'm at a loss to explain what happened. There was no intent to trap you, certainly not on my part. I did mention to Ray that I wasn't sure I followed all the intricacies of Templars, but then I don't follow all the twists in Hamlet either. I never meant to suggest you're not good at what you do. Clearly, Ray didn't understand the nuances of my comments. I only hope you can give us a second chance, because you're quite talented and have incredible insight. Not that you need me to say so. We still want you to be in our film, and I mean that. I was happy to meet you, and I hope we can reestablish a working relationship. Sincerely, Natalie Ashbrook"

"Dear Natalie, I can't tell you how mortified I am by my behavior—especially to you. You're an amazing, talented woman. I don't doubt there's been a misunderstanding, and I regret the role I played in causing it. Dare I ask if you will still accept the autographed copy of my book? It was left behind in my office. And your opinion is important to me. I was happy to meet you as well. I'm willing to reconsider my role in your film. We can discuss my conditions, but with your beautiful mind, you can probably guess my first one. —Steve"

"Thanks for throwing me under the bus." Ray half-tossed, half-handed Natalie's phone back to her after reading her text messages.

"It's called diplomacy, Ray. Do I have to teach you everything?" Natalie said, grabbing her phone.

In disgust, Ray crossed his arms over his chest.

Natalie showed Finder's text to Clark.

"Aw, Natsy got a textie from Sweetie Stevie, swept me off my feetie."

Natalie swatted Clark's shoulder. "You know I hate your baby talk. You should be happy. Sneak Peek's footage won't be wasted. We're lucky he even texted me back."

The three of them sat at the airport terminal waiting to board their flight to Istanbul. Clark sat in the middle.

"We've never lost a contributor to a film before. Not one so important," Natalie said. "I had to do something to try to get him back." She leaned forward to speak to Ray. "All Steve wants is an apology. It's his first condition."

Ray guffawed. "Oh, is that what you think he means."

"You're not gonna apologize?"

"What did I do? Just told him the truth. Guy's a jackass. Couldn't take it." Ray leaned forward to look at Natalie. "You could've asked for my input before you texted him."

"I didn't think you'd want any. Last night you said you were glad he quit. You didn't want him in the film."

"But you made it sound like it was all my fault," Ray said.

Natalie raised her eyebrows in disbelief. "Who did the interview? Who went off script? Who suddenly became obsessed with Kimber Grant?" Her voice was cutting with sarcasm. "Correct me if I'm wrong, but as I recall, I'm a sound technician. I handle microphones and things."

Ray and Natalie's argument about the fallout from their Steve Finder interview was far from settled. Certainly, not in Natalie's view. She'd started the argument—with good cause—seconds after Finder had booted them out. "What the hell were you thinking?" she'd demanded of Ray, slamming her door to the SUV. In her estimation, Ray had yet to give her a satisfactory answer to this simple question.

"Look, I told you yesterday—the Kimber questions were a strategy," Ray said. "It's nothing I haven't done before. Dude was working us over from the minute we got there, isn't that right?" He nudged Clark with his elbow, seeking support. "Was tryin' to make sure he looked good on camera. That we'd be happy with his lame, rehearsed answers. But we're after the truth, aren't we? You yourself said he's experienced, knows how the game is played. He was all up on his game, believe me. I'm surprised you didn't detect it yourself." Ray counted on his fingers. "Tour of his house, autographing his book for you, quoting Shakespeare crap, flattering you out the wazoo—"

"I heard you. But what you're saying makes no sense. You were eager to meet him. You like his books, think he's a great writer. You're a fan of Bucky Browne. Couldn't stop talking about Lady Xenia and Princess Calixta."

"Oh, yeah? And you don't like his books. You think his writing sucks. Why defend him suddenly? Guess all his flirting must've worked." Ray mimicked Finder's voice: "Hey, Ms. Ashbrook, let me show you my bedroom."

"Ra-ay! Your insane behavior lost us a film contributor. Of course, I'm defending him. We need him."

"No, we don't."

"Yes, we do. We had a whole planning session about it. Questions we needed to ask him because we don't have Professor Burke. If we don't have Steve too—"

"We'll get some other writer."

"Oh, really? Who'd you have in mind?"

Ray had no answer.

Natalie shook her head exasperatedly. "I still can't believe what I heard. You start the interview, go off on a tangent with Kimber questions, and then provoke him. Even if you think he's phony, why call him on it? You don't stick it to a film contributor. Reggie will be dumbfounded when I tell him what you did. I mean, what got into you?"

Ray didn't immediately answer. Natalie studied his face intently, for it seemed to her that if anyone had rehearsed an answer, it wasn't Finder, it was Ray. She'd half-convinced herself that his crazy Kimber questions were a sign that he had a woman in his life after all, if not Staci, then a woman just as silly. A woman not even Clark knew about.

## THE DIE IS CAST

Ray averted his eyes. "He just thought he could beat me. Thinks he's so special. Greatest writer in the world. Little Stevie! If he's as big as he thinks he is, he could bear up under criticism, wouldn't get so mad. Who knew he'd take it personally? I mean, why blame me? You said Templars of Doom is full of holes. You wanted me to ask him about it."

"Don't turn this around on me," Natalie hissed, trying to keep her voice down. "I'm not a screen for you to project your failures on."

"Great, you get to psychoanalyze me now. I can't wait."

Just then, Clark stood. Ray and Natalie looked up at him in surprise. "What? I'm goin' to Istanbul," he said. "Where are you two goin'?" He went to get in line. Boarding was in progress. Ray and Natalie hadn't noticed.

Natalie fell in behind Ray. She bit her tongue as they stood in line, though she'd thought of a dozen more things to say to him in her defense. At the top of the list was defending her decision to text Steve without Ray knowing. After all, Ray hadn't consulted her about changing strategies for interviewing Finder. He'd botched it all on his own. And after all her careful planning. She had to get them back on course somehow, didn't she?

As she stepped onto the plane, Natalie felt her heart palpitate. She hated flying, especially the instant when she felt the plane's wheels lift off the runway. The plane seemed to her to hang on a string while some cosmic puppeteer mused over its fate. "Oh, lift me as a wave, a leaf, a cloud! I fall upon the thorns of life! I bleed!" Such had been the prayer of Percy Bysshe Shelley to the wild West Wind. A prayer gone unanswered, evidently, given the poet's early death by drowning. All Natalie's favorite authors had died young.

Clark took the window seat. This was unacceptable.

"You know I need to see out," she complained to him.

"Right. So you can alert the pilot when the wing falls off."

She scowled at this joke, as it was so near the truth.

Clark surrendered the seat to her.

Ray took the aisle seat.

Clark motioned him over. "I ain't sittin' in the middle."

"Oh, c'mon, help me out."

"Dude, no way. It's a 10-hour flight."

With a deep sigh, Ray slid to the seat next to Natalie.

"Don't worry, you'll be asleep soon," she told him with a mixture of scorn and envy. She could never fall asleep on a plane even if she tried. Generally, she busied herself monitoring the flight's progress and watching Ray's head loll about. He always fell asleep. The plane might plunge from 35,000 feet into the ocean or careen into the air-traffic control tower, and he'd never know. She'd suffer the wide-eyed terror of their destruction all by herself. It was very unfair.

Clark put in his earbuds and began to play *Call of Duty: World at War* on his Nintendo.

Normally during takeoff, Natalie lightly touched Ray's arm for reassurance, thinking God might kill her but surely not the two of them at once. But this time, she didn't trust that Ray wouldn't yank his arm away from her, so she asked him to move his elbow off the armrest. She held on to it instead, looking out her window as Earth fearfully fell away. Her mind was chaotic, her thoughts like papers blown off a desk in every direction. Images, feelings, and memories which she'd taken pains to separate into distinct piles suddenly comingled despite her desires.

Ray had defended his behavior towards Finder using words all too familiar. *He just thought he could beat me.* She'd heard him say something like that before.

She'd thought of that night at Midtown Studios a thousand times or more. Quite unexpectedly, Ray had abruptly altered the course of their relationship. Maybe she too had longed for a change of direction with him, but that night, she'd been unprepared. She'd already mapped a course out for herself—she was going to marry Geoffrey. Ray's passionate kisses had almost made her swerve off the path; she was dismayed at how easily she'd yielded to her long-nourished fantasy of triumphing over Staci and winning Ray to herself. That fantasy, assisted by Ray's roving hands, had asserted its power and made her its puppet. She hadn't truly been the object of Ray's passion, only a means. He'd merely been out to prove himself to be a better man than Geoffrey. He'd said so himself: *I win.*

As the plane settled into its cruising altitude, Natalie glanced at Ray out of the corner of her eye. He was intently watching Clark play his video game. *Why do you always have to win?* She recalled an incident between Ray and Geoffrey that had happened while she and Geoffrey were still dating:

Geoffrey came to Midtown Studios one evening because the two of them were going to a theater to see a play adaptation of George Eliot's *Middlemarch*. "George Eliot? Who's he?" Ray asked. Geoffrey smirked. "*He* is a woman. Mary Anne Evans. Famous English novelist of the

Victorian era. Wrote using a pseudonym." The conversation immediately degenerated. Ray learned that Geoffrey was writing a book himself—a history of lawn furniture and its signification as an emblem of class status, a "very under-researched subject in the field of cultural studies." "Hmm. Wonder why that is," Ray said wryly, "I mean, Adirondack chairs, right? Who wouldn't want to study them?" Geoffrey smiled insincerely. "Typical choice for the rural and suburban blue-collar worker. Simple wood plank design. The slanted seat exaggerates a state of repose. Appealing to those who wish to pretend they can join the leisure class." Ray's eyes narrowed. "Ever make one?" he asked. Geoffrey shrugged. "I have no interest in it." "That's a shame," Ray said. "The seat is tricky, but if you know what you're doing, they turn out comfortable enough. I made two for my grandmother. She and my dad worked in the steel mill. That's how we low-class people do things—make stuff for ourselves."

Natalie's analytical mind wondered if Ray suffered from an inferiority complex that always made him want to prove himself. She would never have thought so. Ray was all-confidence with her; at least, he was when they were working.

Recalling Ray's behavior with Geoffrey made Natalie quite sure he'd never apologize to Finder. Without both the contributions of Professor Burke and Finder, the success of their *Dish Movie* was doubtful. To detect such obstinacy in Ray alarmed her, because her reason for working with him again had been her belief that he'd changed. Reggie had practically assured her that he had, telling her Ray knew he was wrong, that he accepted responsibility. Had she merely yielded to another fantasy by believing Reggie?

Natalie's head hurt; she felt like the cursed mariner of Samuel Taylor Coleridge's poem, doomed to drift at sea on a listing, lifeless boat. She had no desire to sail in uncharted waters; now wasn't the time to risk their filmmaking careers. Somehow, she had to right the ship. She weighed the likelihood of Finder agreeing to appear in their film for her sake. After all, the two of them had established a good rapport. Ray was right—Finder had flirted with her from the start. It'd surprised her. She'd assumed a writer of bad prose would be rather prosaic himself, but Finder wasn't that at all. He could quote Shakespeare, and he had beautiful eyes. Nothing about her was lost on him. Maybe she could capitalize on his flirtation if she did some flirting of her own.

"Dammit." Clark dropped his Nintendo on his lap. "Nazi zombie got me."

"Why'd you even go in that direction?" Ray asked Clark.

"I dunno, I got stuck on the map."

"You should've gone toward the lake."

"They ambushed me."

"Right, that's why the lake is safer. They don't like water. Anyway, you're not using the right weapon. A bazooka doesn't work. You need the flamethrower."

"But the bazooka is my favorite."

"Dude, you wanna win? The flamethrower is better for zombies. Trust me."

Ray and Clark's discussion about gameplay went on. Natalie wasn't interested, but she couldn't help but hear. As the sound technician for 8 Ball Productions, her ears were her life. Detecting ambient noise that might interfere with a documentary's production quality was her job. With a deep sigh, she pulled her iPad from her messenger bag to scan their itinerary. The footage they captured the next two weeks in Turkey would constitute the heart of their documentary. Working with Ray, she could never quite prepare for the unexpected. But she wanted to feel that she could.

## 8 BALL PRODUCTIONS
*Dish Movie*
### Production #120

Producer: Reggie Lovett   Sound Technician: Natalie Ashbrook
Director: Ray Cozart   Director of Photography: Clark Cannon

### March Shooting Schedule

| Date | Time | Location | Contributor |
|---|---|---|---|
| 3/9 | 1:00pm | Manhattan, Upper West Side, 47 West 84th St. | Steve Finder, author |
| 3/12 | 9:00am | Museum of Ancient History, Topkapi Grounds, Fatih district, Istanbul | Dr. Zainab Ayhan, museum curator |
| | 3:00pm | Tour of Hagia Sophia | |
| 3/13 | 7:00pm | Museum of Ancient History (Opening ceremony for Byzantine art exhibition) | Dr. Zainab Ayhan |
| 3/14 | 7:00am | Church of St. Euphemia, Kadiköy district, Istanbul | Anthimos of Chalcedon, Orthodox archbishop |
| | 11:00am | Divine Litrugy: Triumph of Orthodoxy | |
| 3/15-23 | 9:00am | Göreme, Cappadocia, Turkey | Ali Ozgümüs, tour guide |
| 3/25 | 8:00am | Church of St. George, Phanar district, Istanbul | Filming Dialogues of Love |
| 3/29 | 2:00pm | The Middle East Centre, St. Antony's College, Univ. of Oxford Oxford, England | Dr. Rupert Winters, distinguished professor of Byzantine studies |

The tidy columns and rows stabilized her mind and allayed her suspicion that they were flying toward their own demise. Her eyes fell on the date of March 12. Their interview with Dr. Zainab Ayhan, the curator of the Museum of Ancient History, seemed to Natalie to be their North Star. Navigating by that, they might chart a new course. Natalie had been looking forward to meeting Ayhan, an unquestionably accomplished woman, an intellectual peer. Could Ayhan keep their film from sinking? They'd have to plan their questions very carefully, make sure to ask her questions to elicit information they'd wanted Burke or Finder to cover. With the stakes raised, Natalie felt an overwhelming desire to convince Ray to let *her* ask Ayhan the questions.

An hour passed. Clark gave up his game and began to listen to music. Natalie was creating a list of questions for Ayhan when suddenly Ray turned to her and said, "Remember Reggie told us we need to pick a working film title."

Natalie squinted up at him. "Do we have to do that now?"

"You're busy?" He tried to see what she was working on.

"As a matter of fact, I am." She tilted the iPad so he couldn't see the screen.

"Whatever. I guess all of Miramax can wait for you." Ray leaned his head back and closed his eyes.

This jab irritated her; seeing Ray ready to fall asleep irritated her even more. "Okay, fine. We can discuss it."

Ray opened his eyes to look at her but said nothing.

The silence lingered. It bothered Natalie. Silence always did. She was a sound technician; silence meant there was nothing for her to do. It felt like death.

"Well, we've called it Dish Movie since film school, so I just don't have any clear ideas," she finally said.

"Neither do I," he said.

"Great. This is going to go somewhere."

Silence again.

The flight attendants distributed beverages. Natalie requested a glass of wine.

"I think we need a title with snap, with spirit," Ray said.

"But serious, like The Tent at Ground Zero. The subject matter demands it," she said.

"But we should be willing to be provocative."

"The controversy over the Dish is provocative enough. Maybe the title should be subtle."

"Let's think of how our story begins. Start from there."

"Maybe we should think about where it's headed."

"Well, what's the heart of the story?"

"Does it have one?" There was a latent complaint in Natalie's voice. The wine made it rise toward the surface.

Ray detected it and exhaled sharply. "Okay, forget it, let's not talk about this now."

"But you wanted to. What did I say?"

"You keep contradicting me."

"I'm not. We're just talking. Just—" she broke off, shaking her head in frustration.

"It's no big deal. We'll decide later."

"Oh, I don't understand you," she said dejectedly. Her thoughts had drifted far from the subject of the film title to subjects yet unspoken. "Why is it so hard for you to admit you're wrong?"

"Look, I'm not apologizing to Finder," Ray said firmly.

"I know. That's just it. You never apologize. I can't think of a time. Not as long as I've known you."

Ray frowned as if searching his mind for examples to counter this charge.

"Like that day when you were so late to an interview, we had to cancel it and reschedule," Natalie said.

"That was years ago! We were filming Monica's Dress."

"I'm just using it as an example, okay? You missed it because you had lunch with our perky intern Jackie. When just the night before, we'd been at the studio planning, and afterward you helped me fix my sound screw-up. I'd deleted three minutes of audio by accident. We had to figure it out. You helped me recreate most of what I'd lost."

Ray's frown softened slightly. "I ran up and down the stairwell so you could record the sound of my feet."

"Right. We had to recreate the dry cleaner's steps. You did it over and over. When we finally got the timing right, you did one of your Happy Dances—"

"You joined in."

"You made me. And it turned out to be a very good night, when at first it didn't seem like it was gonna be, and I dunno, I guess I thought—I thought—" she broke off and looked down at her half-empty glass of wine. She remembered the way Ray had twirled and dipped her as they'd danced. She knew exactly what she'd thought that night. It was the same thing she'd always tricked herself into thinking: that Ray didn't just love their work, he loved *her*.

"What ... did you think?" Ray asked hesitantly.

She swirled the wine in her glass and took a sip. "Oh, just that you were reliable." She hoped she sounded glib. "That after such a night, you couldn't possibly get distracted the next day by Jackie of all people." She rolled her eyes and looked out the window so Ray couldn't see her face. Because at that moment, she wasn't really thinking of Jackie. She was thinking of her true nemesis: Staci. "I know she was blonde and beautiful, but there wasn't ever much there."

"I wasn't distracted. She asked me, so I went."

"Right. Like you two didn't have a thing," Natalie said sarcastically. "She could never talk about anything but you."

"That's funny," Ray said matching her sarcasm, "because when Jackie was with me, she only talked about you. She really admired you. Always said you were so smart. You intimidated her. That day when I was late, she wanted to know about what happened with the sound, how we fixed it. I swear I couldn't get away. She had to know the whole story. I praised you up and down for your creative problem-solving. Like I always have with everybody."

Natalie looked at Ray as if his face were in pieces, a work of abstract art. "I—I didn't know any of that."

"Well, it's because you don't listen. I know what you think, but I wasn't into her. She didn't mean anything to me. I dunno how to convince you. We were making a documentary about Monica Lewinsky, and you think I'm gonna hook up with an intern? Who do you think I am?"

Natalie was silent, so Ray went on: "That's why I always told Jackie to have lunch with you, not me. She could've learned a lot from you, but you didn't give her the time of day. I dunno why. You form impressions about people, and then you stick with 'em. There's no changing your mind. I know half the time you think I'm incompetent."

"I do not. You always exaggerate the truth. I just don't understand you sometimes. Like when you said you knew all about piloting a motorboat because you grew up in Pittsburgh. Said you'd been out on the rivers hundreds of times. Turns out you only ever paddled a kayak."

Ray sighed in exasperation. "That wasn't my fault. You were the one who wanted to film the Clinton Library from the river. I didn't think it was necessary, but you wanted to use the river as a symbol of wandering desire or whatever. Were all up on the adventure, as I recall. I just tried to make it happen for you. I thought you were into it. But once we got out there in the boat, you had a full-fledged panic attack, had to put on a lifejacket, like full body armor. I mean, it's the Arkansas River. Like, there aren't massive waves. You weren't gonna fall out. I had everything under control, but you hyperventilated, screaming about the boat capsizing—"

"Ra-ay, I didn't panic until you confessed you'd never steered a boat. You got mad at me and yanked the thing around without warning, turned us into our own wake—"

"I had to get you back to shore, didn't I?"

"—of course, I'm gonna try to grab onto something. I mean, Clark and I were both standing."

As Natalie said this, she looked furtively at Clark. So did Ray. Clark sat with his arms crossed, scowling mightily at them. He'd been listening.

## NOT GETTING ANYWHERE

Ray and Natalie broke off their argument. Because as they all knew, the regrettable outcome of the *Monica's Dress* "boat incident" was that Clark had lost his camera Sneak Peek VI overboard. When Ray jerked the boat back to shore, Natalie grabbed Clark's arm to steady herself. Unprepared, Clark stumbled; the camera slipped from his hands. He immediately dived into the river after it, but there was no saving it. Sneak Peek VI sank to its grave.

Another hour passed. Beyond Natalie's window, the sky appeared indigo. The sun was setting. She glimpsed Ray in her periphery. He was asleep. She rubbed her arms, feeling cold. She couldn't determine if her disagreements with Ray throughout the day had been a beginning or an end. They didn't seem to get her anywhere.

The window turned gray, then black. Natalie stared at it as if a giant white die might emerge in the darkness, clink against the glass, and answer the question in her mind. What would it say, the Mystic 8 Ball?

She could make no prediction. The window merely reflected her image. What she saw of her own face dissatisfied her, and she pulled down the blind.

Scene 15

## What's on Our Hearts

*Grandeur, Georgia*

*Wednesday, March 10, moments after leaving her bedroom*

"But Nana, Baby Girl needs to pee." Jane stood on the last step of the Grand East Staircase, protectively cuddling her dog in her arms.

Patricia summoned all her powers of forbearance at the sight of the little rat. Even so, her forbearance was but small, and she only managed a grimace, the corners of her mouth curling inward like two small, shriveled leaves.

"Very well," she said, "but don't dawdle. There's someone I want you to meet."

Jane giggled as if *dawdle* were an amusing word. She hopped off the step and lightly pattered her way barefoot toward the kitchen. Before she reached the South Hall, Patricia stopped her.

"Oh, Jane."

Jane glanced over her shoulder.

"Did you see your father?"

"Ye-ess."

"He's concerned about you. I hope you listened."

"I did."

"Oh?"

"Yes." Jane paused. "He didn't like my hat." She flicked the brim of her Barmah hat, grinned at her grandmother, and disappeared down the hall.

Patricia was unsure if she should be encouraged by this remark. She hesitated by the stairs, looking up at the balcony, but there was no sign of Max. Toby, Kathleen, and Nicole waited in the center of the Great Room. Patricia joined them, nodding at Kathleen and motioning Nicole toward the fireplace. The four of them took their seats around it. As if by prior mutual agreement, they reserved the chair nearest the fireplace for Jane. There was no fire, however, and they all stared mutely at the barren grate. Not that a fire would've made such an arrangement cozy—except to Patricia. The presence of two giant stone lions flanking the fireplace represented her decorative preferences. The lions faced forward, their massive manes holding up the mantle shelf, and although their jaws were clamped, their eyes were wide and watchful. The stone creatures inspired silence, and for that reason Patricia often sat people there.

A grandfather clock stood as gatekeeper near the entrance to the South Hall, and for some minutes, the only sound was the rhythmic pulse of its pendulum. Patricia sat facing the hall, anticipating her granddaughter's entrance. She felt it was important that her eyes should be the first that Jane should see. It would set the requisite tone for what followed. Meetings that began with an implicit recognition of her command generally ended with her commands being carried out. This is what years as the head of Whitaker's had taught her. And Nicole, less than an hour before, had proven the rule true. After months of plotting to make Jane the corporation's new face, Patricia wasn't about to be careless now. Details mattered, no matter how small.

She glanced over at the woman who'd just become the linchpin of her vast scheme. Nicole sat staring ahead, absently twirling a lock of her hair. Observing this, suddenly Patricia shuddered. *Good Lord, what have I done? This woman is Jane's clone.* She felt her palms get clammy. Nicole had Jane's mannerisms, Jane's way of speaking. She thought of what Nicole had said to her as they'd marched from her office to the Great Room. To prepare her to meet Jane, Patricia had divulged to her Jane's obsession with Dishing. And Nicole had said: "How a-maa-zing that you picked me! I know all about Dishing. I've watched all the Bucky Browne movies twice. Maybe this is destiny or something? Ha-ha."

Patricia shifted uneasily in her chair as she waited for Jane to return. Would Nicole's knowledge of Dishing be the bridge to Jane's heart? Or would Nicole prove to be as ridiculous as her granddaughter? Nervously, Patricia swiped at one gray hair that disturbed her vision. *No time for doubts. I must trust my instincts. The die is cast.*

Suddenly, there was a yelp. Baby Girl raced into the room. In its eagerness, it cut the corner by the grandfather clock too sharply and nearly lost its balance. A quick sniff of everyone's feet easily identified the newcomer.

"Why, you're no bigger than my grandmother's cat," Nicole said, reaching forward to pet Baby Girl's head. Baby Girl pulled back from Nicole's hand and barked.

Nicole's remark was the first made since they'd all sat down. Everyone looked at her. Including Patricia.

"Most cats are bigger. Baby Girl doesn't like them." It was Jane. She lingered by the clock, her hat pulled down low. She'd raided the cookie jar. "Cats give her the shivers." She laughed with her mouth full.

Patricia was too late. She failed to catch Jane's eye.

Jane moseyed in, leaving a trail of crumbs. Her pink t-shirt sparkled as she plopped down sideways into the empty chair next to Nicole and dangled her legs over the arm. "So, like, hi," Jane said to her. "Sorry to keep you. Like, Baby Girl had to poo."

Everyone stared at the dog. Baby Girl wagged its tail vigorously and continued to bark at Nicole.

"Thank you for that announcement," Patricia said to Jane with a forced smile. She'd lost control of the situation and blamed that little rat. "Toby," she said through clenched teeth. She pointed at Baby Girl. "Take care of that."

"Baby Girl probably wants a Teeny Treat," Jane said. "She expects a reward for pooing."

Patricia snapped her fingers at Toby, who scrambled to the kitchen to fetch a box.

Patricia quickly tried to get the conversation back on track. "Nicole ... my granddaughter, Jane. Jane, this is Nicole Dziedzic. Nicole is—"

"Omigod, that's such a cute hat—very European," Nicole said to Jane. "Like, my grandmother brought some hats over with her from Poland. This was after the war. But she, like, stopped wearing them after a while 'cause she was into American fashion and stuff."

"So, what happened?" Jane bit into her second cookie.

"Like, to the hats?" Nicole asked.

Jane nodded.

"She kept the best. We found them in boxes in her closet after she passed. I guess they were, like, fashion relics from the old country, y'know what I mean? I—I have them now." Nicole's voice waivered, and her eyes grew misty. She swiped at her cheek. "Omigod, am I crying?"

"Oh, my dear," Patricia said, almost genuinely touched, "there's no need to be embarrassed." If she'd been sitting close enough to Nicole, she might've felt it necessary to pat the young woman's arm lightly for comfort. Thank goodness she was sitting too far away, because it really was more affecting for everyone to witness her cry alone. The tender display couldn't have been a more beautiful segue. "Nicole has *such* a good heart," Patricia said to Jane. "We might all well learn from her."

Kathleen reached in her sleeve and gave Nicole a tissue.

Just then Toby returned from the kitchen. Patricia noted with satisfaction that he'd found a box of Teeny Treats. She cleared her throat. "Yes, Nicole has set the example. She has answered the call, a call we all should answer, a call to give back, take a stand, and make a difference in the world." Patricia pronounced this aphorism to the group generally, but as she ended, her eyes fell on Jane. "If only we could all do likewise, set aside our differences and come together, just think of what could be accomplished."

"So, like, what do you do?" Jane asked Nicole.

Nicole had gathered herself sufficiently to set aside Kathleen's tissue unused. "I'm a homeless advocate. It's sooo rewarding."

"Omigod, the homeless," Jane exclaimed. She resituated herself in her chair the right way, with her feet on the floor. "Y'know what? They even take shopping carts from our stores in Moscow. I know. I saw one when I was there."

"A homeless person, you mean?" Nicole asked.

"Like, yeah. He looked at me. When I was arrested, and they took me in, he was sitting right by the police—"

"Oh, my, what a mess that was," Patricia interrupted quickly. "Moscow! You'd think they'd implicated Jane in some espionage ring the way it was reported. We're a bit cautious of the press here at Whitaker's, you understand," she said to Nicole.

Nicole nodded. She turned to Jane. "So, like, did Moscow, like, totally change you? I mean, seeing a homeless man, that must've been so difficult. It's so weird, but sometimes you learn what is true in your heart. Is that what made you want to make a difference in the world?"

Jane had finished her cookies. She licked the crumbs from one corner of her lips and stared at Nicole, puzzled. "We-ell," she began hesitantly. She took off her hat, ran her hands through her hair and replaced it. "I was Dishing, like, way before Moscow." She smiled at Nicole.

Patricia held her breath.

"Omigod, I love Dishing," Nicole gasped in delight. "I've seen, like, every movie about it. Your hat is so totally Bucky Browne. You know who you remind me of? Lady Xenia!"

## THE DIE IS CAST

Jane giggled and tipped her hat to Nicole. The two of them started exchanging famous lines from the movies.

"Omigod, I could go on for hours about Lady Xenia," Nicole said with a laugh, "but, I mean, seriously, with your looks, I know you totally changed that homeless man's life in Moscow. It's literally destiny that he saw you by hanging out at a police station. Plus, he needs safety and stuff. And, like, kids too! Like, 1.5 million are homeless each year in the U.S.—that's like every year in a roo-ow. I dunno what the figures are in Russia. Our agency—Back On My Own Feet—isn't there. Which totally sucks." Nicole gestured toward the group. "But, like, Whitaker's is gonna change that. Which is just so a-maa-zing." She turned back to Jane. "And with your help, especially, Ms. Whitaker—can I call you Jane?—like, so many people will be saved. Y'know, 'cause we can't rest until every person has a home—and a shower and stuff. 'Cause, you see, every person is so deserving. That's one thing I believe in my heart. There really aren't bad people out there, only people who are different. And it just does my heart good to see that you care, Jane. Because tons of people in your position don't. I mean, you have everything. And the fact that you're willing to donate your time—being on camera will be, like, totally natural for you. Oh, and, like, there ma-ay be some guest appearances here and there, like when the showers are delivered to the agencies—we'll work around your schedule. But, y'know, to me, it's just the fact that you're so aware. You'll inspire so many people. The responsibility you're taking on," Nicole seemed overcome, "you're just sooo strong. You're different, Jane. Like, everyone can see that."

At the end of this speech, Nicole blinked her eyes rapidly as if to defer another scene of tears. She clutched Kathleen's tissue and sniffed. "Omigod!" She laid a hand on her heart. "Like, I'm going on and on ... but it must be true 'cause you're all listening."

Everyone chuckled nervously.

Except Jane.

During Nicole's discourse, Patricia had observed Jane. Her granddaughter had leaned forward and propped her chin on one hand. Patricia thought she heard her humming, but she couldn't place the tune. "My dear," she said to Nicole, "you've expressed ... what I think is on all our hearts to say." Her voice was gentle, almost prayerful.

Everyone looked at Jane.

"We-ell," Jane shifted in her seat, "so there'll be, like, cameras and stuff?"

Nicole smiled. "Totally. 'Cause it's TV and stuff."

"Like commercials, you mean?" Jane's eyes widened.

"Yep," Nicole said.

"When will we shoot them?"

"Er, uh," Nicole looked about her for help.

"Whenever you like," Patricia said to Jane, hoping her voice didn't sound too eager.

"We could be ready the day after tomorrow, Mrs. Whitaker," Toby said.

Patricia shrugged indifferently and looked at Jane.

"Like ... okay," Jane said.

"Hot dog!" Toby exclaimed. "I'll call marketing."

Baby Girl, who had nestled into the rug near his feet, jumped up at his voice.

And just like that, everything was settled.

Patricia leaned back in her chair and folded her hands in her lap. She listened—only in intervals—as Toby, Nicole, and Kathleen explained the finer points of Whitaker's Shower the Homeless Campaign to Jane. Mostly, she absorbed the moment, marveling at Nicole. Jane had eagerly consented of her own free will. Patricia had been right to trust her instincts. Nicole had read the situation with Jane brilliantly and had known exactly what to do. Patricia couldn't recall the last time she'd heard a more beautiful piece of persuasion. That speech had been a work of art.

And now, busy with the rush of new commitments (and Patricia would make sure there were many), Jane's ridiculous Dishing would be washed down the gutter out of sight. Whitaker Corporation would reap the financial rewards of Patricia's efforts for years to come.

Nicole seemed to sense Patricia's eyes on her. She gave Patricia a demure smile.

Patricia fiddled with her diamond ring, feeling something she hadn't felt in a long time—something akin to respect for an equal. Perhaps she wouldn't send Nicole's résumé to Human Resources, after all. Perhaps she'd hire Nicole herself. If Nicole could persuade Jane to shower the homeless, then what else was the woman capable of?

▼ ▼ ▼ ▼

Jane was highly entertained when Nicole demonstrated to her the use of the portable shower. She told Toby and her Aunt Leenie it was totally weird, but that the thing might be useful for Baby Girl who was awfully afraid of bathtubs. She begged Nicole to let her keep one.

As the assembled parties dispersed, Jane retreated up the Grand East Staircase to her bedroom. She carried Baby Girl in one arm and a portable shower in the other. Upon nearing the balcony and the shadowy hallway beyond, she began to hum again. It was the theme song to *Bucky Browne and the Cave of All Fears*. She thought of Lady Xenia bound to a chair in the Pope's dungeon. The betrayer, Cardinal Scevola, gone to recite his evening prayers, had left her alone in the dark. Fortunately, he hadn't thought to make a thorough inspection of Lady Xenia's hands, or he might've discovered that the fingernail on her right pinky finger was actually a sheath disguising a Swiss Army Slippery Miss XP4, the smallest steel blade in existence—and the most notorious—the blade of choice of the ruthless *Compagnie des Carabiniers du Prince*, guardians of the Palace of Monaco ...

Reaching the balcony, Jane paused and peered below into the empty Great Room. "Whatcha think, Baby Girl?" she whispered, kissing the dog's head. "You ready? Ready to go viral with Mama?"

Scene 16

## The Blinded Seeker

*Istanbul, Turkey*

*Excavation site at the demolished Sirkeci Rail Station*

*Thursday, March 11*

"What do you mean—wrap it up?" Burke spluttered in outrage. "You—you can't be serious!"

From their first meeting three weeks previously, Burke had decided that he disliked Feredun Pasa, Istanbul's Rail Bureau Chief. He disliked him intensely. Why this was so, he couldn't exactly say. Perhaps it was Pasa's tailored suits, or his jade and silver cuff links, or his polished, burgundy leather shoes. Perhaps it was simply that his teeth were very white, or that he prolonged the final *s* at the end of words.

"You understand me, I am sure." Pasa looked down his long, thin nose at Burke. "I am ending all thisss." He gestured dismissively at the walls of the shrine around them. "I want the excavation finished. Over. Done. You see, I use the simplest of terms for your sake." He smiled insincerely and pivoted to walk up the ramp.

"But this is the Shrine of the Four Keepers!" Burke

cried. "You can't just stop everything now. Just like that!"

Pasa glanced over his shoulder. "I can. I have."

"But you said we had six weeks."

"And now you have three."

"But the three weeks are almost over. That's just three more days." Burke crossed before Pasa to impede his exit.

"Step aside, Professor."

"No! Wait!"

Burke's khakis were coated with mud from the morning's labors and sweat dampened the armpits of his Oxford shirt. He wanted to grab Pasa by the shoulders, but he knew his soiled hands would leave marks. It aggravated him that Pasa seemed immune to dirt. Burke tried not to stare at Pasa's white teeth as he licked the grit from his own.

"But I have been waiting," Pasa said curtly, "waiting for monthsss. You have no idea—all the bureaucratic wrangling." Pasa touched his brow lightly. "There is no other course. The Metro can no longer be delayed."

"But we're making so much progress," Burke fired back. He explained that his crew had just recovered all the larger pieces of the shrine's collapsed dome, and that pilgrims would've gathered there under the watchful eyes of Christ and the Apostles, as the dome's interior was richly painted.

Much to Burke's annoyance, Pasa merely shrugged.

Exasperated, Burke directed Pasa's eyes toward the eastern wing of the shrine, insisting that Pasa should at least have the courage to see firsthand everything he'd be shutting down if he carried out his ultimatum. Pasa rolled his eyes at this but reluctantly let Burke lead him in that direction, though with his long, lean legs, he outpaced Burke, and Burke had to trot to keep up. The two men entered a room perfectly square and noticeably featureless in contrast to the western wing which showcased the mosaics of the Four Keepers. The eastern walls were merely rough walls of yellow brick or gray, cut stone. A dais formed the back part of the room's floor. Both men stepped up to it.

"What about this?" Burke demanded. "Just look at this incredible piece." He pointed to a rectangular stone, two meters long and one meter high. It was smooth on the sides and top and looked like a primitive table rising from the floor. Although the stone was deeply gouged and discolored from scorching, an inscription was visible on its front edge. Burke translated the Latin for Pasa, explaining that they were standing before the shrine's altar in the apse, the inner sanctum: ASK AND IT SHALL BE GIVEN THEE. SEEK AND YE SHALL FIND. The stone symbolized, in Burke's expert opinion, the table of the Last Supper, and it must've been used by the Order of Andronicus—the monks charged with maintaining the shrine—before Constantinople was conquered by the Turks in 1453, which, according to the Annals of Andronicus, the undisputed authority of the era—

"Yes, yesss ..." Pasa waved off the rest of Burke's disquisition. He placed his palms on the altar and leaned forward. "I must be frank. I do not care."

Burke stared open-mouthed at Pasa.

Pasa took the opening left by Burke: "My crews do nothing, the machinery sits idle, yet the expenses for the Ministry of Transportation and our private investors grow by the minute. We were already behind schedule when we demolished the Sirkeci station. We never imagined that thisss," he spread his hands to indicate the entire dig site, "all thisss would be here to create further delay. While my investors appreciate the, uh, limited historical value of what you are doing—"

"Limited historical value?" Burke repeated shrilly. "We're standing in the most significant archaeological find of the past fifty—no, the past one hundred years."

Pasa calmly pushed through Burke's interruption. "We have become apprehensive of our high-cost overruns."

"High-cost overruns?" Burke repeated Pasa's words again. It was the only way he knew to emphasize their absurdity. "Don't you understand? I'm on the verge of finding the Last Supper Dish. THE LAST SUPPER DISH! It's priceless. I'm mere moments away from ending the greatest controversy in Christendom." Burke swallowed hard, awaiting Pasa's reply. Claiming that he was moments from finding the Dish might've been overstating the matter.

"Pricelesss? Come now, Professor Burke," Pasa chuckled. "Priceless to whom? Historians and a few religious fanatics? No, no more of thisss. We cannot wait. We will not wait. Nothing you rummage up could be worth the millions of dollars I am losing every day. Perhaps you would like to reimburse me? You and your professor friends could take up a collection from your puny university salaries."

Burke had no comeback for that.

"You have three days to finish. Three daysss." Pasa held up three fingers before Burke's face. "After that, my crews will wipe out what remains." He straightened and brushed imaginary dirt from his palms, clearly enjoying Burke's fury.

Burke tried to deny him the satisfaction and said nothing.

Pasa slithered away.

"Damn him! Damn!" Burke pounded his fist on the altar. He slumped to the ground with his back against it.

"Adam, what has happened?" It was the voice of Zainab Ayhan. "I saw Feredun Pasa exit the site. Why was he here?"

"To shut down the dig. In three days!" Burke wailed.

"Three days? Are you sure you heard correctly?" Ayhan was dismayed.

"Yes, I'm sure," Burke spat. "He was quite happy about it too, might I add. Sickening!"

"But how will I get the Dish—er, I mean, I am still sure *you* can get it, right? You have made progress, yes?"

Since uncovering the mosaics of Panikos and the other three Keepers, Burke had pushed the excavation east toward the shrine's inner sanctum in hopes of finding the Dish. He hadn't done such considerable shoveling since his graduate school days, as his sore muscles proved. Adrenaline, coffee, and the vision of defeating that damned Winters had driven him. But now, sitting before the altar in the shrine he'd been searching for his entire career, he didn't feel anything but aching fatigue and a rising, desperate uncertainty.

"None, Zainab. None." Despite all his talk of progress with Pasa, he could now admit the truth. He stared at the ground and sighed. "I wonder if my search is over."

"How can that be?" Ayhan sidled up to him and leaned with her elbows on the altar. "Am I to understand that the world's foremost seeker of the Last Supper Dish has stopped seeking?"

Burke frowned and looked up at her.

She batted her eyes playfully.

"If you put it like that," he tried to smile, "then, no, I haven't stopped."

"Perhaps I can help." Ayhan traced an image of a bowl on the altar with her finger. "If you talk it out, the way forward may become apparent."

"What's there to talk out? I don't know."

"What did the crew do this morning?"

Reluctantly, Burke stood. "Oh, we canvassed this area with ground penetrating radar. We sank exploratory holes at regular intervals. I thought for sure we'd find a subterranean vault." Burke spread out his hands to indicate the floor where they stood. "But there was nothing."

"Then the Dish could not be hidden under the floor."

"I don't see how. I thought it might be because of the riddle on the Panikos icons—Present yourselves at the gathering of the Twelve. Kneel before Andrew and pray for your souls, for you will soon enter the earth. So, I thought the gathering of the Twelve might refer to this altar, and that maybe a fresco of Saint Andrew was originally on the wall."

"A gathering of the Twelve," Ayhan repeated thoughtfully. "The Dish surely would have been kept near the altar."

"Right. I thought it might even be under the altar. The inscription on the front is suggestive—Seek and ye shall find. But the radar equipment couldn't give us a conclusive reading yesterday, so we had to send for a member of the Metro crew to operate the crane. The altar weighs a ton. When we lifted it, we searched for a vault, a trap door—anything—but we saw nothing. The inscription is worthless. A lotta wasted effort." Burke kicked the side of the altar.

After a moment's silence, Ayhan said, "Does the Nil icon shed any light at all?"

Burke shook his head. "Not a bit. Nil gives us nothing. What we can read of the riddle refers to a port and sailing around rocks. That'd be great if there were water nearby, but as you can see …" There was sarcasm in his voice, and he spun in a circle, gesturing at the dirt all around.

Ayhan tapped the altar with her fingers and straightened. She paced behind it. "What about the ancient histories? Putney or the Annals of Andronicus? You told me the other day that Putney records the shrine's interior with great care."

"He does," Burke said glumly, "but he only says that the holy relics were kept in a golden reliquary adorned with jewels. The Annals also describe the reliquary and the shrine's size and shape, but we don't need that information now."

"That is something." Ayhan's voice sounded hopeful.

"Not really," Burke said. "The reliquary was likely stolen. It's well-known that thieves targeted reliquaries for their material value and discarded their contents." Burke groaned as if uttering these words drained his last bit of strength.

"Surely Putney or the Annals reveal the presence of the Nil and Zoticus icons." Ayhan's voice sounded less hopeful.

"Putney says he was granted a Panikos for his donation to the shrine, and he took it back to England as a memento. But he says nothing specific about the other three. It's evidence for how the icons were spread throughout the medieval world, but it does us about this much good." Burke pinched his index finger and thumb together.

Ayhan cast her eyes down.

Burke jammed his hands into his pockets and kicked at a stone. "I keep thinking this is another of the challenges set up for me by Emperor Andronicus, but I have no map to lead me forward, no instructions to follow."

"But the Dish has to be here." Ayhan threw up her hands exasperatedly. "You *must* be given more time. I will speak to Ahmet Ötürk. As the director of the Ministry of Tourism, he negotiated with Pasa to grant six weeks for our excavation. He will not be pleased that Pasa wants to renege on their arrangement. Do not be distracted. Ahmet will intervene for you."

"Does Öztürk outrank Pasa?" Burke asked. "Can he prevent the dig from shutting down?"

Ayhan gave Burke a sly grin. "Turkish politics can be rather nasty. Pasa is rumored to be involved in peddling influence and distributing bribes. From his casual remarks, I gather that Ahmet knows even more. He will not be afraid to leverage what he knows to make Pasa relent."

Burke glanced at her. In the sunlight, Ayhan's red-leather jacket glistened like fine silk. The top buttons of her blouse were undone, revealing the skin above her breasts. She was beautiful. Yet Burke detected another quality mixed with that beauty. Sometimes her smile seemed more like a bite. She lacked the bow and arrows, but Burke could imagine her as the formidable Diana, goddess of the hunt.

"Would Öztürk go that far?" Burke asked hopefully.

"I know him well," she said. "He is curious about your quest. And it was only with his assistance that I arranged the press conference for you this afternoon. It is scheduled to air on CNN-Turk. All the major glossies—Unearthed, Afar, and Condé Nast Traveler—are sending reporters. Please tell me you have not forgotten."

"Oh, right. That." Burke scratched his chin. For two days he'd been capering about like a playful puppy at the prospect of being on television. But Pasa had quite deflated him. "Great. I get to go on air and say the Dish is slipping away from me because of a stupid subway tunnel."

"Do not say that," Ayhan shook his arm. "I have worked hard to arrange the presser on short notice. You should credit the museum for its role in the excavation and should mention its upcoming Byzantine art exhibition. I have already phoned key patrons to tell them the museum will be featured on CNN-Turk. Please, do not let Pasa bother you. You have my support and that of Ahmet. He is an ally to you, a strong ally. This is, no doubt, the greatest challenge of your career. We will see to it that you have the opportunity to overcome it."

Just then Ayhan's phone buzzed. She answered it and stepped aside, though still within earshot of Burke. She spoke in English: "Hello? Yes. I was going to call you later today. No, I can confirm nothing at this time. Yes, I am there now, so I will call you soon and we can discuss the situation in greater detail." She hung up and sighed.

Burke was leaning against the front of the altar, his back to her. She touched his arm lightly.

"Adam, I need to go." Ayhan stood so close to Burke, he could smell her perfume. He recalled his excitement the morning they stood before Panikos—when he nearly embraced her. He kept his eyes on the ground.

"Look at me," she said, and he did. "Adam, remember who you are. You are the world's foremost expert in Byzantine history, the greatest seeker of the Last Supper Dish. A real-life Bucky Browne. You are standing in the middle of a shrine long thought to be lost. This is the most significant discovery of the last fifty years, perhaps the past century."

"That's just what I said to Pasa."

"Then tell other people about it too."

As Ayhan strode out of the apse, Burke looked down to where she'd held his arm. He placed his own hand there, trying to hold on to the heat pulsating through him.

▼ ▼ ▼ ▼

Drs. Foo and Hromadova had searched everywhere for Burke. The apse was the last place they looked. There they found him standing behind the altar, staring at the far wall of gray, cut stone. He'd remained in the apse for the entire half hour after Ayhan had swept out.

"Ha! You hide from us?" Foo joked.

Burke felt stung by the joke as it was all too true.

Hromadova approached.

Burke cast his eyes at the wall purely to save his sight. It was unfair, of course, to compare her to Ayhan.

"CNN is here," she said. "Dey are waiting. Hurry."

Burke was already nervous about the presser. Hromadova's excitement only exasperated his unease. "I need to clean up a bit," he said, but not really to her.

Nevertheless, she smiled and brushed his arm lightly. "Dere is no time. And you look well enough."

Burke flinched at her touch. She winked at him. Quickly, he stepped toward Foo and urged him to lead the way, which he did, directing Burke to the west side of the shrine. The presser would be held before the mosaics of the Keepers.

Burke couldn't believe the number of cameras. Seeing them made him instantly sweat. He had only one thought: *what am I going to say?* Of all the questions he'd be asked, there was only one question that mattered. And he couldn't answer it. He couldn't say he'd found the Dish. Where in the shrine had he yet to look? Somehow, he had to explain to the reporters that there was still somewhere to search. There had to be a way that the Dish could still be found.

"Hey, Professor Burke, you look a little dusty," said a chipper voice at his back. It was a CNN production assistant. "But you're an archaeologist, so I suppose it'll heighten the effect for the audience." The voice went on cheerily, but Burke didn't hear. All cameras and eyes were on him, even Duffy's, and that McKenzie fellow. The two were perched with the other students above the pit. Burke allowed himself to be moved this way and that in front of the mosaics as if he were a prop. Vaguely, he heard the production assistant remark about his glasses. Off to his left, Foo waved his hands theatrically, mouthing something to him about a "missing trowel." Burke blinked into the spotlights, feeling exposed. *What am I going to say?*

"Um, your glasses, Professor." The young production assistant smoothly plucked them off Burke's face.

"Hey, what are you doing?"

"Our producer thinks you look better without them." The assistant slipped the glasses into Burke's shirt pocket.

"But I can't see—"

"You don't need to. Just look straight ahead and talk like you're in class. You're a professor, aren't you?" He chuckled. "We'll take care of everything. Don't worry."

As the press conference began, Burke tried to focus, but every question he fielded felt like an unsolvable puzzle, much like the riddles of Kostas, Panikos, and Nil. He didn't need to see the confused faces of the reporters to know that his answers were halting and wandering. This was his chance to make history, but he was blowing it.

"Next question?" asked the CNN producer. He was helping Burke locate raised hands among the press corps. "Is there another question? Anyone?" The reporters' initial eagerness had degenerated into politeness. "Yes, to your right, Professor Burke," the producer said.

Burke went to adjust his glasses only to recall that they were in his shirt pocket. He had allowed the production assistant to strip him of his shield of erudition. He felt all his weakness exposed. Without the ability to look erudite, he wasn't. From somewhere, a voice emerged, inquiring if he could explain how his team of archaeologists had been chosen. Burke talked through his choice of Stoltzfus, Calvino, and Foo, and talked around his choice of Hromadova, as that had been a regrettable whim. He kept thinking how much time he was wasting when there was so little time left to find the Dish thanks to Pasa. And then he thought of Winters. No doubt the old man was enjoying the sight of this public shaming telecast around the world.

"—and so, obviously, I have the greatest possible team, tout court, and I feel very fortunate to be their leader, er, coordinator, a facilitator you might say." Burke had lost the thread again. His mouth hung mute and open; he scanned the sky for his next thought. The silence about him felt like the silence in his classroom when his students were too bored to speak. How Burke hated teaching.

"Professor, uh, this is Michael Mistral of Unearthed."

Burke knew that voice. That name.

"I have a question for you, Professor. Because as I've sat listening to you, I keep thinking, yeah, the four mosaics here, they're impressive, but if this is the Shrine of the Four Keepers as you claim, shouldn't we expect more? Shouldn't the Last Supper Dish be here? What do you say, Professor?"

*Mistral.*

Burke grimaced as he realized the import of Foo's theatrics earlier. Foo hadn't been saying "missing trowel" but "Mistral"—the veteran reporter regarded in archaeological circles as a pretentious prig and shameless sycophant of Rupert Winters.

Burke inhaled deeply to gather himself against this full-frontal assault. Of course, Winters had sent his best attack dog. And, of course, his best attack dog would ask the one question he didn't know how to answer. "Mr. Mistral," he began, clearing his throat, "archaeology is an inexact science. As I've said, medieval descriptions of the shrine—like Putney the Pilgrim's—give us enough detail to identify these mosaics, but we ought not expect—"

"I wonder you rely so much on Putney as a source, Professor. To my knowledge, he says nothing about the Dish."

"That's not true," Burke quickly countered.

"Does he say the Last Supper Dish is here then?"

"Well, understand he didn't write his travelogue assuming the shrine would disappear, and that centuries later people would be searching for it. How could he have known what details to include? What he does write is intriguing—"

"Professor, just answer my simple question—"

"There aren't simple answers in my field, Mr. Mistral."

"—where is the Dish?"

How Burke hated Mistral for trying to expose his ignorance. As if he were just some schlub like Duffy and not the world's foremost expert in Byzantine history.

*World's foremost expert.*

Those had been Ayhan's words. She'd lain her hand on his arm. *Adam, remember who you are.* Suddenly, Burke felt the beat of his pulse in his neck. *You are the greatest seeker of the Last Supper Dish. A real-life Bucky Browne.*

Without another thought, Burke reached into his shirt pocket. When he replaced his shield on the bridge of his nose, his mind and his vision cleared. Immediately, he located Mistral.

"Your attitude, Mr. Mistral, is typical of those who possess a superficial knowledge of the facts. Granted, Putney is a challenging read for a non-expert. But as I was saying, what Putney does record about the shrine is intriguing. Allow me to enlighten you." Burke had already pulled out his phone and tapped to the screen he wanted. "Here's Putney's description of the cleansing ritual," he said, beginning to read:

And lo, the Altar made of stone was the span of a man at rest. And round it did sit earthen cups and bowls, and Twelve in number, in remembrance of the Apostles of old. And amongst these wast set yet another bowl bearing a sack of tokens. And it was taken unto each Supplicant. 'He who possesseth the Dish gaineth command of all. If thou wouldst take unto thyself its glories, then receive these tokens as a deposit. Yet, know well, that thou must pay a heavy toll on thy way. Dost thou desire the Dish of Christ?' So spake the monks to each man, and some answered 'yea' and receiveth unto themselves the tokens. And they that spake 'yea' were taken. But when I beheld the tokens, mine own eyes didst weep for shame, and I was afeared, lest I become like unto Judas the betrayer, who took unto himself the thirty pieces of silver, for so wast the sum for the betrayal of our Lord. Wherefore I spake, 'nay, I desire it not.' And thus didst the monks bade me confess mine Sins, and mine Heart was filled with woe, and so didst I confess even the blackest of acts.

"Now I ask you, Mr. Mistral, is the dish that Putney describes the Last Supper Dish? Or a bowl used for the ritual? You complain that Putney is unreliable and then demand an answer about what he means. Mr. Mistral, what do you think the digging here is all about?"

A few in the press corps chuckled at this.

Inspired by their laughter, Burke ended with a flourish: "We dig to answer your question, Mr. Mistral. And we aren't finished digging. Some people would rather we not dig. They would've preferred this shrine remain buried. And you know why? Because they think they already have the right answers. I think you're well-acquainted with those people. For myself, I believe scholars must keep asking questions. I'm confident by the time we're finished digging, we'll know the truth about the Dish. Next question!"

Burke knew he shouldn't make such predictions, especially when the duration of the dig was now in great doubt. Technically, he only had three days to make history, but the reporters didn't need to know that. He'd put Mistral in his place, and that's what mattered. With some delight, Burke imagined Old Man Winters in that dusty office of his at Oxford, seething in rage at the oblique reference to his name.

As soon as Burke had dispatched Mistral, a dozen hands shot up. Now that there was drama, reporters were eager to play a part. Burke took his time selecting someone. A young woman near the front pleased his eyes.

She wanted to know, *s'il vous plaît*, if he had found—or expected to find—icons of the Four Keepers at the shrine, and if so, would their riddles lead him to the Dish?

"If all the icons are recovered," Burke said, "they'll reveal the location of the Last Supper Dish. That much we know." He went on, enjoying the sound of his own voice now that it was in his command. It was, of course, probably not necessary to remind them that several Kostas and Panikos icons had already been discovered, but (he hastened to add) only *he* had found the partial Nil two years previously in Bulgaria. The discovery had caused a stir internationally. As yet, no one had found a Zoticus. But he wouldn't be surprised to find a Zoticus at this shrine. In fact, he thought it likely due to the nature of the Kostas riddle. The seeker who dares desire the Dish of Christ is challenged to go and find his brothers. Where would his brothers—the other three icons—be if not at the shrine bearing their likenesses on the walls? What is more, the historian Metochites mentioned the icons in the Annals of Andronicus, the famous history, which he, for the reporter's benefit, would read:

And so, by the will of the Emperor were icons fashioned in the likeness of the Four, and being blessed thereof unto God were they kept at the shrine sacred to them, and some also were sent to sundry lands, wherefore that seekers might search out their mysteries, for only at the sacred place might the Four be united, and they that knoweth the Four and desireth by them so to be led, would there be found worthy.

Yes, they heard correctly, that was one impressively long sentence. Those medievalists. Chuckle. But the point obviously—which he would repeat—was that Metochites did place all four icons (Burke spread wide his arms) in the very shrine where they now stood. Perhaps it was Kostas and Panikos which were the two icons sent to sundry lands while Zoticus and Nil were only to be found at the shrine. Quite possibly, Kostas and Panikos set the scavenger hunt into motion while Zoticus and Nil ended it. In his expert opinion.

The second Burke concluded this speech, there was laughter. This time it came from one man alone—Mistral.

"Professor, you can't be serious. That answer has more plot twists than a Bucky Browne novel. But Steve Finder is a better storyteller." Mistral's haughtiness was undisguised.

Many reporters turned to stare at him. The few who didn't lowered their hands and looked at Burke in anticipation of his counterpunch. A collective hush came over all.

Burke clenched his jaw. He knew Mistral was baiting him. He knew he shouldn't allow himself to be dragged into a squabble on international television. But he took the bait.

"Real archaeology, Mr. Mistral, isn't nice and tidy like an adventure novel you read at the beach. So, I understand if you feel confused. Is there something I can clarify for you?"

Mistral pursed his lips. "Yes, there is. At least, you can try." He clicked his pen exaggeratedly as if eager to write down Burke's answer. "Professor, I follow your logic, such as it is. But that's just the point, you see. Let's get to the heart of the matter, shall we? Isn't Dishing at heart very illogical?"

"No, you're wrong. Next question."

"Wait—wrong? Isn't that for you to prove?"

"I have to fact-check you? What an upside-down world. You're the reporter."

Several in the audience snickered.

Irritated by the laughter, Mistral consulted his notes. When he looked up at Burke, he spoke contemptuously.

"If this is the Shrine of the Four Keepers, then we're sitting in a structure built by Emperor Andronicus eighty years after the Fourth Crusade. It was built to honor the monks who'd rebelled at least ten years previously against the Catholic dictatorship. Kostas, Zoticus, Panikos, and Nil incited riots in the city by claiming to possess the Last Supper Dish. They claimed the crusaders had taken a dog dish to Rome. The rebellion they incited led to the overthrow of the Catholics and the restoration of the Byzantine monarchy."

"All this is well-known," Burke said wearily.

"But here's the point," Mistral shook his pen at Burke, "let's assume the monks told the truth about having the Dish. And let's also assume that Andronicus got his hands on it when he came to power. Okay? Can we assume that?"

"Sure. Those are the assumptions I make. Is there a question in there somewhere? Perhaps we might move on?"

"This is my question—if Andronicus did have the Dish, why did he hide it and make people look for it? Why did he build a shrine and distribute icons with riddles on them? Why not just reveal the Dish to the world? He could've done so at any time. It could've been done after his reign by any of the other emperors prior to the Ottoman conquest. But it never was. Why? Why didn't the Byzantines reveal the Dish and put the lie to the Catholics? It's illogical."

Mistral leaned back in his seat, his eyes flashing with the dark satisfaction of diminishing his opponent.

But Burke merely sniffed. His greatest joy as a scholar was to hear someone else's argument and think to himself: *I gotcha now!* "Oh, is that all." He gestured to the producer. "Do we have time to address something so elementary?" The producer gave him a thumbs up.

"Okay, for some of you, my explanation will not be new, so bear with me." He exhaled deeply, pretending to ponder his answer. In truth he did so to conceal his glee. Clearly, Mistral had been taking Winters's dictation for far too long. Such cliché talking points were lifted straight from a dissertation Winters had published in the 1970s. Couldn't one Dish-denier out there come up with a fresh idea?

"There are a number of ways to answer your question. Why didn't Emperor Andronicus reveal the Dish to the world? An obvious answer is that he hid it to keep it safe. After all, his empire wasn't invulnerable. Likely, he feared crusaders would return to reclaim the Dish. But no doubt you've heard this explanation before."

"Many times," Mistral said scornfully. "I ask the question because that answer doesn't satisfy me."

Burke paused so the cameras could catch his confident smile. "Let me give you the answer I prefer. Consider the situation—when Andronicus came to power, his empire was on life support. Its wealth had been channeled to the West. It was vastly reduced in size. The Catholic regime practically depopulated Constantinople. What does an emperor need most?" Burke held up two fingers. "People. And money."

"So?"

"How do you get people to come live under your rule? You gotta give 'em stuff. Andronicus didn't have much, but what he did have, he used. I think the quest he designed for the Dish functioned as a citizen recruitment drive. Why else are the icon riddles written in Latin instead of Greek? He wasn't encouraging his own people to search for the Dish. He was hoping to draw seekers from the West. The icons were advertisements. Think of the riddles as commercial jingles. If he could just get enough buyers interested in his product. No doubt, his quest appealed to the disaffected, the adventurers, the religious fanatics. He wanted people to find the Dish, but ultimately, he wanted people to stay. Even if some seekers like Putney the Pilgrim eventually returned home, they still left behind their money, right? Putney dropped a pretty penny in the city just for his bar tab."

Burke smirked at Mistral, daring him to find fault with such an answer. He knew Mistral couldn't. His argument was both ingenious and irrefutable. Mistral had nothing.

Mistral snapped his notebook closed and stood. "Too bad you won't have a chance to validate your theories, Professor. Since your dig will be shut down in three days."

Murmurings rose from the audience.

"Better get your pictures of the mosaics now," Mistral said to the other reporters.

"Is the dig to be shut down?" a reporter asked Burke.

Burke's face reddened.

"Ask him if he knows Feredun Pasa," Mistral urged.

All eyes turned to Burke. One question about the Rail Bureau Chief quickly bred a dozen more.

Mistral stepped to the end of his row—and walked out.

Burke could hardly grasp what had just happened. How had Mistral known?

*Winters.* Of course! Winters and Pasa were conspiring.

"There are, yes, er, forces—very powerful forces—that want to derail my quest for the Dish," Burke managed to stammer over the volley of questions. "And these forces have footholds—or strongholds, rather—in places both far and near. But I also have allies." He saw in his mind a passing vision of Ayhan. "And I have one thing to say to those who stand against me." His voice rose; he pointed his finger at Mistral's empty chair. "I am Adam Burke. I will never stop seeking. The Last Supper Dish WILL BE FOUND!"

Scene 17

# A Change of Fate

*Istanbul Museum of Ancient History*

*Thursday, March 11*

"Murat," Ayhan called to the young man trailing behind her in the hall, "I will be in my office for the next hour. I shall not be disturbed, understand?" She didn't wait for her assistant's reply, opening and closing her door in one motion.

Once inside, she slipped off her shoes and inspected her leather jacket. The feeling of being coated in dust from the dig site vexed her immensely. Adding to her displeasure was the recollection of Burke's defeatism. She resented weakness in a man. To detect it in one to whom she owed some duty was most provoking. It gave credence to her long-cherished belief that she was a woman fit to rule a kingdom far greater than a museum.

Ayhan reclined in the armchair before her desk and closed her eyes. If Burke embarrassed her at his press conference, then he would have to answer for it. She regretted phoning her big-money patrons. That was jumping the gun, as they said in America. She should have waited until she was sure ... until Burke had found the Dish.

Ahmet Öztürk would be ill-pleased if Burke's presser reflected poorly on the museum. She shuddered, recalling prior episodes of Öztürk's anger. His ire was just like his body—excessive. Rousing it was to be avoided at all costs. Regrettably, she'd have to tell him about Pasa. Probably that would best be handled over the phone …

She opened her eyes. Her cell phone was ringing. She sat up, aware that she couldn't recall the last ten minutes. Her mind had retreated from its own agitated thoughts. She'd been asleep.

Patience, she thought, as she answered the call.

"But I am not bothered," she lied, speaking in English. She stood and slipped her shoes back on. "I did say I would call later. Perhaps you did not hear?" It was difficult for Ayhan to feign pleasantness she didn't feel, and she stepped around her desk and turned on her iPad to distract herself from the voice on the other end. "Ah, no, my apologies if that is what you thought, Ambassador. I was just in the middle of discussing the progress of the dig with Dr. Burke. That is why I hung up so quickly." She touched her hair briefly, thinking of dust. The Ambassador went on for a minute or more. On her iPad were images she'd taken of the shrine. As she listened, she flipped through the pictures one by one.

"Yes, but I think it is unlikely today," she ultimately interrupted, cutting short the Ambassador's monologue. "Er, no, there are no snags. Burke just had to stop for the press conference, that's all. Before I left, he told me that—that the altar will have to be lifted. Yes, a massive undertaking for sure. He believes there is an underground vault." She almost regretted this lie but was sure the Ambassador could never discover it. "You see he pursues every possible course. Yes, is most meticulous. I have complete confidence in him. If the Dish—or, rather—*when* the Dish is discovered, you will be the first to know. Yes, you have my word. You know my word is good. I have never failed you in the past. Never."

Once the Ambassador said goodbye, Ayhan twirled in her desk chair and tapped the arms of it with her fingernails. *When the Dish is discovered.* Would it be? If Öztürk could not intervene to give Burke more time, then her entire plan would be in ruins. She needed to call Öztürk soon, but she was not quite ready to stomach dealing with a possible tantrum. And besides Pasa's deadline, Burke's fruitless search created another potential problem for her—a serious one.

Ayhan stood up and put her hands on her hips; an object on one of her shelves had caught her eye. She went to inspect it more closely. It was a copper bowl, not particularly ancient or rare, a bowl used for divination. It was engraved all around with the signs of the zodiac. Below the rim was a band of magical numbers. In the interior were inscribed verses from the Qur'an as well as prayers of blessing and cursing. The bowl wasn't large; she spun it twice in her palm, clockwise and counterclockwise.

*When the Dish is discovered.*

Would it be?

Slowly, she traced her finger around each zodiac sign, pausing over Leo the Lion. The beast clenched a sword in its teeth, and the sun rose like a crown over its head.

She set the bowl back amongst the other artifacts and sighed, frustrated at the idea of devising a contingency plan in the event of Burke's failure to find the Dish. Need she be implicated in his defeat? She scanned her office as if the solution she sought was to be found in the paintings on the walls or the artifacts lining the shelves. With growing irritation, she sat back down, snatched up her iPad, and tapped on her calendar, thinking of Pasa's looming deadline.

*March 12, 9 am: 8 Ball Productions—interview about the Disher tourist industry in Istanbul and tour of Hagia Sophia.*

I must cancel, Ayhan thought. There was too much to be done. Burke needed her help at the excavation site. She had to solve the Pasa problem. The American film company would have to make their silly movie about the Last Supper Dish without her. She searched amongst her contacts and found Ms. Ashbrook's phone number.

But instead of dialing, Ayhan tapped her chin with her phone. A fresh yet only half-envisioned idea had entered her mind, and as she pondered its dimensions, a grin slid across her face. *Burke need not find the real Dish. Any common clay pot will do.* Her eyes looked from her phone to the copper divination bowl sitting on her shelf—and back again.

*I can supply the bowl myself, and then—and then—*

Eagerly, she stood and paced, hunting down the veiled particulars of her idea, flushing them into the open. The key obstacle to pulling off her scheme would not be in supplying an artifake itself. That would be tricky but not impossible. She'd done so before, though on a smaller scale. Her cut of the profit in that sale had been worth the risk. What she'd make this time ... calculating the sum made her giddy.

No, the difficulty in a high-profile case like the Dish would be to forge the provenance, the official record of a genuine artifact's discovery. Perhaps she could ask Burke's slow-witted assistant Duffy to take a picture of her and Burke together before the altar in the apse, with her holding the artifake. Or even better, if she could somehow place her artifake in Burke's hands... no, that would never work. He *was* besotted with her, and she could easily charm him into performing a small favor, but a mere photograph would never satisfy her rabid clientele. She needed a written, official statement from Burke about finding her bowl at the shrine, and she could not manipulate that from him.

How could she forge Burke's testimony? She squeezed her phone, feeling the solution just at her fingertips. Then, quiver pulled taut, her thoughts hit their mark.

*Of course. 8 Ball Productions.*

So simple. So perfect. The plan could not fail. She smiled and licked her teeth. At last, she could set her fate free from Burke's. She could set it entirely in her own hands.

Ayhan returned to sit at her desk. She did not dial Ms. Ashbrook to cancel. She would make a silly movie after all. Just not Ms. Ashbrook's.

Her phone rang. Glancing at the number on the screen irritated her, for it dispelled the dream that her fate rested entirely in her own hands. It didn't. Not yet.

"Ahmet, I was just about to call," she said in Turkish. But Öztürk was in full form and did not hear her. She pulled her phone away from her ear. "No, I am not at the site. I left before the presser. You watched it? Please—Allah,

Allah, there is no need to shout." She winced as her phone rumbled with another of Öztürk's roars.

"The dig being shut down in three days? Yes, I know already. How did you—ah, I see—a reporter asked Burke about it. Yes, it is Feredun making trouble. Burke told me minutes before the presser. Pasa had been to the site to tell him. Ahmet, please calm down. It is impossible to talk to you like this. What? Of course, I was going to tell you. We *are* partners. I cannot deal with Pasa on my own. Only you have that kind of clout. How can you suggest—? Well, I have been in my office talking with the Krayzels. You know it is essential to keep buyers feeling important. Yes, I am quite sure the directive came from Pasa. Burke was most specific."

A crash from Öztürk's office made Ayhan wince again.

"Hello? Ahmet?" she asked tentatively. She heard curses and mutterings. Footsteps. A filing cabinet drawer open and close. More mutterings. In curiosity, she pressed the phone against her ear. That was a mistake. The lion had returned from its den. Öztürk's loud growl made her ears ring.

"Er, yes, Ahmet, I am still here," she said, holding the phone at a distance. "Absolutely, the excavation must not fail. I assured Burke that you are a fearsome ally. Pasa is a monkey compared to you," she added flatteringly. "Hmm? Information? About Pasa? I know you have disliked him intensely for years. What has he been up to, pray tell? Top secret? I am all curiosity. This must be very juicy, indeed."

Öztürk's chuckle was guttural, a very good sign. If his humor had improved, then it meant he had a plan—and a good one. Ayhan's confidence grew; she pressed Öztürk for details on how he would get Pasa to extend Burke's deadline.

"What? You will not say? No, of—of course I trust you, Ahmet. It is just that, well, I do not like surprises." A needle of panic suddenly deflated her. Öztürk's surprises, as she knew from experience, could backfire—and spectacularly. "Yes, I understand. You need a bit of time to pull your plan together. Very well. I will wait, but you *must* let me know. I—I have a plan of my own, you know," she added quickly, hoping to tempt him into disclosure. "A contingency plan if Burke does not find the Dish. We must anticipate every outcome, otherwise—oh, you want to know, do you? So, you are the only one permitted to play coy?"

She instantly regretted this remark, as Öztürk pounced on it, responding with lewd innuendo. Regrettably, after years of partnership with the fat, squat man, she'd heard every conceivable vulgarity. And though she was not above using her physical charms to her advantage, such dreadful flirtations with the disgusting man made her sick. Quickly, she distracted him by divulging the high points of her plan.

"... so, as you can see, with the footage from these American filmmakers, we could easily piece together what we need Burke to say. I think it would be quite convincing."

She smiled at Öztürk's appreciative chuckle. The man was not all bad. He did greatly admire her mind. And he had made her rich. He could make her richer still.

"Gaining access to their footage? Hmm. A fair objection," she said, thinking through the problem. "Perhaps ...

a permission form from your office, one with very fine print."

They both laughed.

"It will be nothing to persuade them to follow my itinerary," she said breathlessly. "Think about what I am giving them, Ahmet—a chance to make history! They would be fools to refuse. I will give them exclusive access to Burke, the shrine, the museum. It will be exactly what they want." She paused, her eyes seeing dollar signs. "That is what you taught me. To give people what they want. So that we can get what *we* want."

Scene 18

# The Mystic 8 Ball

*Hotel Amir, Old Town Istanbul*

*Thursday, March 11*

"... and we should wait until we're at Hagia Sophia to ask Dr. Ayhan to explain where the Dish could be hidden. We can cover that while she's giving us the tour. Especially important is the theory that the Dish is stashed in a secret chamber beneath the church. We need her to describe the tunnels under Istanbul that the Byzantines left behind. Apparently, many are still unexplored. So, while we're at the museum, I think our focus should be the Disher tourist industry. Over the phone, she told me Istanbul is a premier destination for treasure hunters. She said Dishers are notoriously fond of manholes. City workers rescue some stuck adventurer about once a week."

Ray stifled a yawn as Natalie went on. She'd taken over their strategy session in preparation for interviewing Dr. Zainab Ayhan. Clark appeared to be asleep. The three of them sat in a conference room on the first floor of Hotel Amir, a boutique inn with a rooftop view of the Sea of Marmara. Interviewing Ayhan had been Natalie's idea.

She'd followed up a tip Finder had given them long before their disastrous interview, a tip about a great museum in Istanbul where he'd done research for *Templars of Doom*. "Zainab is a treasure trove of resources," he'd said. Ray had gotten his fill of ancient history when they'd filmed in Vatican City. He wasn't excited to interview a dumpy intellectual with scraggly hair, which is how he imagined Ayhan, a woman very much an ancient artifact herself. But given the subject matter of their film, digging into the past was inevitable.

"Guys, are you with me?" Natalie asked. "This interview is vital. We gotta have a plan. One we can agree to stick to."

Ray knew this jab was meant for him. He fidgeted in his chair and tapped his foot restlessly, remembering the way Finder's arrogant eyes had claimed Natalie. She had to be protected from such a predator. He'd tried to tell her when they'd been at the airport. Then on the plane, he'd defended his own trustworthiness. He'd wanted to prove that he was worthy of her love—more so than Finder, and way more than Geoffrey had ever been. But his lips couldn't quite form the right words. But why should he take the risk? Risking himself before with her had cost him.

"Stop shaking the table," Natalie said to him.

"I'm not." Ray crossed his arms over his chest to give his hands something to do. In the past during such planning sessions, he'd consulted his Mystic 8 Ball. It'd helped him think, kept his body and mind in sync. But Natalie had thrown the toy away. He felt its absence keenly. He felt an inner deprivation, as if a part of himself were absent.

## THE DIE IS CAST

The strategy session petered out. Clark had jet lag; Natalie retreated to her room to work alone. It was hours before dinner. Ray asked the concierge where he could buy cigarettes. He hadn't smoked since filming *The Tent at Ground Zero*; Natalie had urged him to quit. But more and more, he just felt like he wanted to hold onto something.

On his walk to the store, he thought of the first time he and Natalie had used the Mystic 8 Ball to make a decision. They were at his apartment. She'd been there dozens of times, had claimed his big, puffy recliner; she sat in it cross-legged like a yogi. He lay on the sofa with his hands behind his head. They couldn't agree on a title for the documentary they were entering at the Tribeca Film Festival:

"But I think The Full Chester makes it sound like porn," Natalie said. "What's wrong with Milkshake and Sixpence?"

"It's too clever. And Who's Somerset Mo-gam? Does anyone even know?"

Natalie giggled. "Maugham. M-A-W-M. The G is silent."

"Then there shouldn't be a G in it. That's stupid."

"His novel is good—Moon and Sixpence—about a guy who leaves his family to become an artist. Just like Chester."

Ray raised his eyebrows. "Maybe I'll watch the movie."

Silent seconds passed.

"Are you gonna come with me to see the play?" Natalie asked. "I have an extra ticket. A bunch of us are going."

Ray wrinkled his nose. "Your friends hate me. Think I'm too stupid to make films, that I'm way outta my league."

"Who cares what they think? You should come."

# THE MYSTIC 8 BALL

"What's it called again?"

"Arcadia by Tom Stoppard. It's about all the important, serious subjects—time and eternity, order and chaos, life and death, tragedy and comedy. Maybe you could learn something." She paused. "Oh, there's a love story in it too."

Ray glanced at her, then kept looking because her head was turned. She was examining the bookcase that held his comic book collection. For a second, he thought of showing her his prized vintage Spider-Man comic #122. But he didn't. *She already thinks you're an idiot. Don't prove it.* She was so pretty sitting there under the glow of a lamp. Her brunette hair was in a ponytail, and she wore a teal t-shirt just like Lara Croft from *Tomb Raider*, his favorite video game. *Don't mess it up.*

"I have an idea." He bolted from the sofa. His Mystic 8 Ball sat on the bookcase in front of the comic books, along with several other vintage toys. He grabbed it and tossed it in the air. "Let's ask the Mystic 8 Ball."

"If you should come to the play?"

"No, what the title of our film should be."

"What? A toy can't make our creative decisions."

"Yes, it can. It'll be fun."

"But—but it's just chance."

"I know. That's why it's fun."

Natalie shook her head. "I dunno. I don't like the idea."

"Well, what are we gonna do? We have two titles on the table, mine—The Full Chester—and yours, er, uh, Milkshake and Mo-gam or whatever. We can't decide between them. But the Mystic 8 Ball can. It'll break the tie."

Natalie guffawed. "Are you really serious?"

"Let's find out." Ray shook the ball and turned its window up. The inner white die displaced the deep blue liquid. "Is that so?" he said, mockingly contemplating its answer.

"What's it say?" Natalie's eyes shone with curiosity.

"If you must know, it says—As it see it, yes."

Natalie grinned. "It doesn't. You're just making that up."

Ray pretended to be greatly wounded. He doubled over as if punched in the gut. "What an accusation. Nat, the Mystic 8 Ball never lies. That's the first rule. And you gotta ask your question aloud. That's the second. If you don't, it won't tell you the truth. Once you ask, you gotta look."

Natalie giggled at his theatrics. "Oh, really? Is there a third rule?" She held out her hand to receive the toy.

But he only dangled it in front of her. She tried to swipe it from his hand. He pulled it away. She leaped from the chair to wrestle it from him. He held it over his head; she was way too short to reach it. "That's not fair," she whined. Their play went on for another minute. Ray pretended to grow weak but still did not relinquish the toy. "Nat, the third rule is that you can only play with my ball if I let you."

Natalie acted offended; her jaw dropped. "Play with your ball?" She snickered. "C'mon, that's the lamest joke ever."

Ray's face reddened; he'd not intended the pun. *Idiot!*

Natalie laughed herself into tears.

Ray arrived at the store and bought a lighter and cigarettes. Walking back to Hotel Amir, he decided to smoke one. The streets in Old Town Istanbul were narrow. Buildings walled him in; he felt squeezed on both sides as if he were walking in a trench. He flicked his lighter hard.

*How could she have thrown it away?* He'd asked himself this question many times. If she'd only stolen the Mystic 8 Ball from him, maybe he could forgive her. But she'd destroyed it. That was something else. It was cruel. The toy wasn't hers. He'd shared it with her. In fact, until he'd met Natalie, he'd never had much fun with it. All it did was answer questions. It wasn't like Lego blocks, couldn't be built into a castle or a spaceship. Nor could it be posed to run, fight, or shoot a rifle like a G.I. Joe action figure. The Mystic 8 Ball resisted manipulation; it did what it wanted.

But with Natalie, the Mystic 8 Ball finally had possibility. Her curiosity about its inner workings gave the toy new life. Ray consulted it often, always keeping it close at hand. He loved to try to predict the die's answers. Should they film at this location? add music to a segment of film? edit out an interview? Their story could go in any direction, depending on the will of the 8 Ball. Would it answer yes? no? maybe? Ray hardly ever guessed right, but his attempt to do so drew forth his own creative potential. For this reason, it seemed to him that the toy's black plastic shell—tinted to mimic a billiard ball—housed a mysterious power.

What this power was exactly, he couldn't say. Thinking too much about it set his mind spinning. It was the power of destiny perhaps. Like the power at work in the superhero stories he loved. Destiny bit Peter Parker when the radioactive spider landed on his wrist. Destiny struck

Bruce Wayne when he witnessed his parents murdered. Destiny crashed into Hal Jordan when he was chosen to inherit the power of the Green Lantern. Destiny told these men—yes, it must be you—and they accepted their call to action.

Ray arrived back at Hotel Amir; crossing the lobby to the elevator, he saw the same blonde woman at the front desk who'd checked them in. She wore a sleeveless dress to show off her arms. They were almost as nice as Natalie's arms, buffed to perfection by years of holding boom mikes. He'd often wanted to ask the Mystic 8 Ball if Natalie would ever love him. But he'd never been able to force his mouth to speak the words aloud. A spoken question would've forced him to look at the 8 Ball's answer. That was the second rule.

In the elevator, he noticed a button: ROOF. He punched it. *Natalie won't be there. Afraid of heights.* When the elevator doors opened, he stepped into waning sunlight and smelled salty sea air. There were empty tables and chairs. He leaned against the balustrade facing the Sea of Marmara. A ship on the horizon reflected the sun's slanted rays. It shone brilliantly like a genie's lamp. He lit a cigarette.

Not once had he considered replacing his Mystic 8 Ball. He only wanted the one he and Natalie had shared, the one that had inspired the name of their production company. After a time, Ray hadn't let anyone else play with the toy except Natalie. Not even Clark. Nor Staci. "Put it down," he once told her when she was at the studio. She ignored him. "Ooo, look, there's something floating inside!" He tried to take it from her. She resisted. "Put it down," he repeated, "it's not a toy." She thought this funny. "I'm serious," he said, "it doesn't belong to you. It's—it's—" he couldn't think of the right word, "—oh, like something sacred." She rolled her eyes. "Oh, take it. I don't care about it anyway." She purposely tossed it to him in a way that made it hard to catch. Nevertheless, he did. She left the studio soon after, which wasn't unusual. Staci took little interest in the films Ray and Natalie made until it was opening night. Then she wanted to accompany Ray to the premieres. Ray obliged, though during the after-parties, he lost sight of her. Inevitably, she'd be at the center of a group—directors, producers, screenwriters. She was always curious about the people Ray knew.

"She's just using you to try to get into film," Natalie once told him in vexation. "It's so obvious." Ray didn't agree with this and was aggravated that Natalie thought him so stupid. But he was in no position to argue. He'd just returned from a spontaneous two-day trip with Staci to Acapulco, Mexico, having left Natalie and Clark in the lurch with work on *Monica's Dress*. He knew he should've refused yet another of Staci's invitations and stayed focused on the film, but she was so persuasive. She was to appear in a bikini shoot with the famous La Quebrada cliff divers, she'd explained. "So, I'll be topless in a rappelling harness. Like, what is that anyway? I dunno, but they say the ropes will cover my nipples."

Always after such adventures with Staci, Clark probed Ray for the intimate details. "Dude, a bikini shoot! How many girls were there? You're living the dream. What's it like?" Ray couldn't resist a gloat-fest; half the fun of being with a model was feeling the envy of other men. Staci wasn't just beautiful, she was a centerfold. A camera changed everything. She was no mere mortal woman; she'd passed into the realm of myth and fantasy. With her on his arm, he too became legendary. That she even noticed him was a wish come true; Ray couldn't believe his good fortune. Sexy and impulsive, Staci was always game for a new adventure. Her displays of affection, her excessive pleasure with small gifts, and her breathless "please, please, Ray" were a sugar rush of confidence. "She's like what you imagine she'd be," he bragged to Clark. "The dream is real, man."

He neglected to say that after a week with Staci, he'd always start to think about Natalie.

Ray firmly crushed his cigarette butt under his toe as if to bury these memories. The sun had set. The golden ship on the Sea of Marmara appeared tarnished. Thankfully, Clark was merciful enough not to remind Ray of his boasts. The dream of Staci had been real enough. It was Staci herself who wasn't. Natalie had been right about her. Ray didn't know if she'd show as much mercy to him as Clark did. It embarrassed him even to think that Natalie knew why Staci had left him. He remembered that day all too clearly. He'd been waiting for her at the airport in New York City. They were set to fly to Maui. But she was late. He called her. No answer. Minutes later, he got a text message:

"Ray, so, I've been meaning to tell you—when I was in Naples last month, I met someone. An actor. You wouldn't know him, but he's super famous in Italy. Guess what?! He got me a part in his next film!!! It's SUCH an opportunity. Please be happy for me. You know it's long been my one wish. So sorry about Maui, but we've had such good times, right? You were always so much fun. Thanks for the great memories. Good luck on your next solo film. ~ Staci"

He'd sent no reply.

Ray flicked the ashes of his cigarette over the balustrade and watched the wind take them. No, he wasn't as stupid as Natalie supposed. Some part of him had always known that he was Staci's Plan B, that there were other men, and that she only came back to him when one of them hadn't gotten her where she wanted to go. He suspected all this. But he preferred not to think about it. Staci had made it easy; she'd always taken his side against Natalie's realism:

"I'm tired of talking about her," she'd said to him the night of Reggie's party. Ray had confided to her his fear that Natalie was going to marry Geoffrey and move to London.

"Let her," Staci went on petulantly, "you don't need her. She holds you back professionally. You'd do better making films on your own. Like, think of the stories you could do without her. The modelling industry, for example. Lots of ideas to explore there. And I'd help you. I know people."

Ray considered this. "I wanna do a film about Detroit's auto industry. But Natalie says the story's too obvious."

"See? She just undermines your confidence. I think it's a great idea, oh, except," she laughed, "Detroit's so ugly. I'm way prettier. Think of me in front of Sneak Peek." She put her arms about Ray's waist; they were in her apartment. "The world's full of opportunities. You need to dream bigger. We'd have fun filming. You don't have fun with her. With her, you're too serious. Why are you even friends?"

Ray didn't have words. *Because she's Natalie.* He didn't say this. "I love making stories with her," he said instead.

"But those eyes of hers! Like, haven't you ever noticed how she studies people? It totally creeps me out. It's not normal. You know she told me once that I oughta stop playing with you?" She laughed cynically. "I mean, who the hell does she think she is?" She released Ray's waist and lowered the straps of her cocktail dress. "You go on and on about her and Geoffrey. Say it'll be the end of 8 Ball Productions. Good! Let it end. *We* can make stories." She draped her hands about his neck and gave him a lingering kiss. "In fact, we already do." She smirked. "Unzip me."

Ray didn't miss Staci. But he did miss the dream of her. He left the roof. An hour later he and Clark joined Natalie in the hotel café for dinner. Given their lackluster strategy session earlier in the afternoon, Natalie was in a surprisingly good mood. She'd brought her phone. Every so often she received a text. She read them with evident amusement.

"Who are you talking to?" Ray finally asked her.

"Nobody you care about," she said wryly. "Just Steve."

Ray said nothing to this. He observed her with a mixture of sadness and resentment. This smart and talented woman who was so important to his life, gave him so many things—except her love. *Why can't she accept what's right in front of her?* Some part of him wished to punish her. He'd done so before—at Reggie's party—had waited for his moment, had timed it perfectly. He'd wanted Natalie and Peagram to see. And they had. On cue he'd taken Staci in his arms and kissed her with simulated passion, all the while keeping his eyes open to witness Natalie and Peagram leaving the room.

After dinner, hours later in his room with Clark, Ray lay in bed unable to sleep. There were too many pillows; like his exhumed memories, they crowded him. He threw them to the floor. A dainty crimson coverlet draped at the foot of the bed smothered his feet. He kicked at it. "What the hell is this even for?" he asked rhetorically. The coverlet fell, bunching into a contorted mass of folds.

"It's pwetty. To give you sweet dweams," Clark joked. He sat in the other bed drinking and flipping channels.

"Dude, keep it down, will ya?" Ray rolled onto his side and closed his eyes, but the flicker of the television penetrated his eyelids. He thought of the studio lights on the set of *Entertainment Now*, of Kitty Lightly tossing Natalie a Mystic 8 Ball. *The Mystic 8 Ball is like a sacred relic to us. An object to be guarded. I'd never part with it*. Natalie had lied so smoothly to Kitty. How'd she managed it? Seeing Natalie in that moment holding a replica of his toy had dazed him. He'd begun to sweat. Because he'd often imagined that she hadn't really thrown it away. He'd fantasized that one day, she'd return it to him—in tears—just like the tears she'd cried the night she'd left him in the studio. Falling at his feet, she'd hold the Mystic 8 Ball up to him, begging forgiveness. "I'm so sorry, Ray. You were right. Please love me."

Then he'd lift the Mystic 8 Ball in triumphant victory, and wielding it like Green Lantern, recharge his ring of power. The realm of myth and legend would open to him once more. "In losing me, you've been punished enough. Yes, I forgive you," he'd say. Then, lifting her into his arms, he'd carry her across the galaxy, like Flash Gordon, Conqueror of the Universe, to the envy of all men ...

▼ ▼ ▼ ▼

Natalie's solitary strategy session in her hotel room went very well. She soon set aside her notes for interviewing Ayhan and picked up her phone: "Steve, sorry for not getting back to you sooner. We've just arrived in Istanbul. Will be here two weeks filming. I do want the autographed copy of your book. I'll put it on my shelf next to Shakespeare. Hope we can work things out for you to be in our film."

To this text message, she got an immediate reply, which she wasn't expecting. Yet when she received it, she realized that Finder's quick timing was exactly what she'd been hoping for. "Natalie, good to hear from you. I wondered if I'd said something offensive. That wasn't my intent. I truly appreciate your professionalism. Believe me, I know the value of being in an 8 Ball Production. The Tent at Ground Zero is a masterpiece. I never cry at films, but you got to me. Am taking care of your book. Shakespeare? Bucky's no Hamlet, but thanks. Let me know when you return to New York."

No reply could've given Natalie greater confidence that she could still clean up Ray's mess. She thought for several minutes about how best to take her flattery to the next level. "Certainly will let you know when I return.

Wish I had your book with me now. Had only one chapter to go to finish it. So exciting! Never suspected Peter's betrayal. Don't know how you writers manage to deceive us. It's magical and thrilling. I'm in suspense until I finish. Don't spoil it for me."

Finder was very flattered, so much so that their flirtation lasted much of the next hour. Natalie thought she ought to keep their conversation going as long as he showed an interest and took her phone with her to dinner. It pleased her to discover that Finder had an affinity for witty wordplay. "Your name has great literary potential," he wrote to her while she was eating with Ray and Clark. "Bucky needs a new adventuress at his side. How about Lady Ashbrook, daughter of the Duke of Severn? Or maybe the River Wye?" "Neither are brooks," she replied. "How about the River Avon?" "You're quite right," he said. "Brook does suggest a smaller estate. I'll only make her father an earl."

Such pleasing banter stimulated Natalie's imagination; she returned to her hotel room after dinner hopeful Finder would reconsider his role in their film for her sake. He had fires to put out on the set of Templars of Doom, he said, but assured her he'd call her in several days. Closing the door to her room, she felt a rush of girlish exuberance, a feeling not quite foreign to her but still rather rare, at least of late.

She'd last felt it in December, standing outside Reggie's office about to see Ray for the first time in nearly three years. She'd spent hours imagining the moment. Then it happened: she opened the door, and there he stood with his back to her, looking out on the street below, his hands in his pockets. Reggie stupidly introduced them as if they were strangers. She'd decided ahead of time that she'd offer to shake Ray's hand, but when he faced her, he kept his hands in his pockets, and she just stood there mutely. "Hi," he said. Staring at him, she felt a familiar mixture of possibility and disappointment. That's how it always went with Ray.

Natalie had yet to unpack her suitcase; she set about the task, hanging some items in a wardrobe and tucking others into drawers. She thought of the first time Ray had said "hi" to her. After seeing him at a party, she was flustered weeks later to be grouped with him for a class project. He introduced himself; they chatted about the class. But he had little else to say. He'd been to see a movie with friends, a sci-fi adventure thriller. Did she like those kinds of stories? She asked him to tell her what it was about. He struggled to summarize but affirmed that "the fight sequences were totally awesome." Afterwards, she reported to a girlfriend, "Yeah, he's hot, but, my God, what would we talk about?"

Still, the group project went well; they were assigned several others. They began studying together at the library. Then unexpectedly, he invited her to go skiing for a weekend. She didn't know how to ski. "I'll teach you," he said. "It'll be fun." She wanted to know if his friends Angela and Staci were going. They were, he said, and several others. She imagined a weekend of Ray flirting with them and declined.

Two weeks later, Ray invited her to a dance club. Staci would be there, he said, but not Angela. That didn't sweeten the pot. She wasn't really a dancer. But she counteroffered, inviting him to see *Macbeth* with her the next weekend. She promised him there'd be sword fights, witches, ghosts, even a decapitation. He was nearly swayed, but he had plans.

"I dunno," her girlfriend said, "he could be into you."

"I don't see how. We don't share the same interests."

"You both like stories."

"Yeah, but ... not the same kind."

"You said he's very good at film. Has a strong visual sense. An instinct for plot and action."

"That's true, but—but—"

"Why talk yourself out of it? You like him, don't you?"

Natalie nodded. "But I feel like maybe I shouldn't."

"Why the hell not?"

"Because I'd have to teach him so much. I need more than plot and action."

"Well, what do you need?"

Natalie thought for a moment. "Maybe—style?"

Months passed. Ray and Natalie talked daily, worked on their group film projects, and went to pubs with mutual friends. He called her "Nat." She daydreamed about him. He had such energy. He was a mood stone, always changing, just like the color of his eyes. Sometimes she thought they were deep ocean blue, other times, stormy gray. But in certain lights, they were violet-brown, like autumn leaves.

Then one night, studying for an exam in his apartment, Natalie dozed off in his puffy recliner. She awoke with a start. The room was dark; she was covered in a fleece throw, which hadn't been the case when she'd fallen asleep. And she was alone. Where was Ray? She followed a flickering blue light through a doorway. He was at a computer playing a video game. He was barefoot, wore jeans and a tight white undershirt. When he saw her, he stood. "You're awake."

"Yeah, um, thanks for the blanket. That was nice." Looking up at him, she felt warm with desire. He was grinning—a lopsided, boyish grin. She wanted to make out with him. The desire was so strong, she was sure he must be able to see it in her eyes. She lowered them, because she wasn't sure she saw any desire in his. Ray had paused his game. On his computer screen, Natalie saw the adventurer Lara Croft with her wasp waist and impossibly round breasts waiting to be reanimated. The sight embarrassed her. Had she gone mad? Ray had stood over her with a blanket and hadn't thought of making out with her himself. Clearly, she wasn't his dream. *And he's not mine.*

"The exam is early. I—I should go."

"Um, right. Okay."

The next day Natalie told her friend that Ray was "definitely not" into her, and that it was actually a relief. "It'd never work out. We just aren't on the same plain, which even he has the wits to see." She said this with all the punishing conceit of a woman whose pride had been wounded. She didn't see or speak to Ray for weeks afterwards.

But then he called her. Where had she been? He'd been thinking about her. He'd heard of a new film festival in Tribeca. He had his sights set on entering and had a great idea for a story—a guy he knew in Pittsburgh named Chester who owned a McDonald's franchise but gave it up to go to culinary school to become a chef. Was she game?

Natalie finished unpacking her suitcase. One object remained. But it was to be left where it was rolling about in a bottom corner. Before zipping up her suitcase, however, she lifted the object out and turned it over in her hands. *The Mystic 8 Ball is like a sacred relic to us. An object to be guarded. I'd never part with it.* She hadn't lied at all to Kitty Lightly about the fate of the Mystic 8 Ball. She'd lied to Ray. She'd told him the night she left for London to marry Geoffrey that she'd thrown the toy away. But she hadn't.

She traced her fingers around the Mystic 8 Ball's window. The die floated under her thumb. She recalled how they'd used the toy to pick the title for their documentary about Chester, and when they won at Tribeca with Ray's title, she remembered him shouting, "See, Nat, the Mystic 8 Ball knows all things." He hugged her so hard, he lifted her off her feet. Then to her amazement, he dipped her and kissed her hard full on the lips—right in front of Staci. It was a magical moment, as if the door of her prison tower had been thrown open. The grievous curse was healed. Sir Lancelot had come to the Isle of Shalott to save his fair lady.

Natalie shook the 8 ball gently. *Will you always tease me with hope?* She didn't look at its answer. Over the years, the blue liquid inside the toy had discolored the white die, turning it blue too. Its replies were hard to decipher. She'd been distressed to discover this one day—packing the remnants of her marriage to Geoffrey, she'd retrieved the ball from her hope chest. When she turned its window up, at first the die didn't seem to appear. She tapped the glass to rouse it from sleep. "Where are you?" Like a spirit doomed to circle some lonely plot of earth, the die responded to her summons, faintly materializing out of the liquid shadows. Her eyes strained to trace the outline of the little island. "Cannot predict now," it said to her. Seeing the die nearly drowned, she imagined it spoke only by gasping for air. The idea that it might succumb to such a tragic fate moved her to tears.

The toy's white die had always been her obsession. Its answers made her curious; often, they made her laugh. At times when Ray had been busy with some task, she'd studied the toy, wondering how it was made and how to open it. What did a twenty-sided die look like? It dissatisfied her only to be able to see one of its faces at a time. She imagined that the die cried out to be liberated, that it hated being trapped against the glass, confined to its spherical cage like the forsaken Lady of Shalott in Tennyson's poem, cursed to see the world only through a mirror.

*Willows whiten, aspens quiver,*
*Little breezes dusk and shiver*
*Through the wave that runs forever*
*By the island in the river*
    *Flowing down to Camelot.*
*Four gray walls, and four gray towers,*
*Overlook a space of flowers,*
*And the silent isle imbowers*
    *The Lady of Shalott.*

# THE MYSTIC 8 BALL

Natalie dropped the Mystic 8 Ball back into her suitcase and zipped it up, musing over the irony that because of the die's discoloration, it would soon be unusable. Ray would get his toy back. But he wouldn't be able to play with it. She set her suitcase under a window. Before she drew the curtains, she glimpsed across the street a small fenced-in green space with a bench—a public garden?—though by the light of a street lamp, it didn't appear to be in bloom. Tangled bushes and bare-limbed trees strained against an iron fence constricting them to their crowded plot.

She readied herself for bed; the room's crisp white walls and white furnishings calmed her with a pleasing sensation of chicness. The crimson accents and hardwood floor reassured her that good taste could still be found in the world. The intertwining leaves in the vine design on the wall above the bed enfolded her in a solicitous embrace. But as she pulled the crimson coverlet up to her chin, her peace was unsettled. She imagined Ray sleeping across the hall. She thought of him pinning her hips to the door of the studio as he pulled off her leather jacket. The traces of the energy she'd felt that night, like the energy itself, stirred itself whenever it so desired, often in the most awkward and intimate of moments—like when she undressed to shower.

"Why not just tell him you love him?" a friend had once counseled weeks into the filming of *Monica's Dress*. Ray and Natalie had just formed their business partnership, 8 Ball Productions. "I don't make it a habit of falling at a guy's feet," Natalie said. "Ray thinks I'm too serious. That I'm not any fun. All he wants are wild adventures.

## THE DIE IS CAST

Three days after celebrating with me at Tribeca, I called him. Guess where he was—at Daytona Beach with Staci. I mean, I've outgrown that sort of thing. And I'm not sure I do love him. We're friends. We make films. That's what works for some reason. Anything else and I'd feel, oh, like I'd be lowering myself."

An hour passed; Natalie couldn't sleep. She stared at the tray ceiling, embellished in each corner by patterns of stems and leaves. She studied the coiling loops, hoping to trace their points of origin. *You don't love him. You thought you did, but you don't. That's what I think. That was my theory all along.* She'd taken the Mystic 8 Ball from Ray out of spite, to prove its prediction about her marriage to Geoffrey was wrong. *Nat, the Mystic 8 Ball never lies. That's the first rule.* Ray had merely used her that night to prove himself to be a better man than Geoffrey. She wanted to prove he wasn't.

The coiling stems above her seemed to have no origin; her eyes moved vainly in a circle. Something about her efforts made her feel caught. She got out of bed and dressed. She'd go out; she'd take a walk around the hotel. But in the elevator, she changed her mind. She hit the button that said ROOF. *No chance Ray is there. He doesn't appreciate beautiful views.* When the elevator doors opened, she stepped out under a half moon. The air was calm but cold; her breath curled back against her face. She didn't go near the balustrade, as she could too easily imagine herself falling. She sat facing the sea and watched the clouds drift across the moon.

At some point during the filming of *Monica's Dress*, she'd given up hope of Ray. She couldn't say exactly when. It was just a hundred different things—a hundred looks, gestures, and touches never brought to fruition. She blamed herself for having hoped at all; she was better than that. And then she met Geoffrey at a poetry reading in Greenwich Village. He'd come to the States to do research for his book about the socioeconomic significance of lawn furniture. After the poetry reading, they'd spent hours talking in a pub. He'd published an essay on Tom Stoppard's thematic use of gardens in *Arcadia* and could discuss the play brilliantly. She'd gone home in the wee hours, her intellect intoxicated.

"Dude's a talker," Ray had said to her upon first meeting Geoffrey. "So? What's wrong with that?" she said. "He says interesting things. I like to listen to him." Ray shrugged indifferently. She wouldn't allow his opinion to cause her doubts. "You wouldn't understand why that's important to me," she told him. Geoffrey finished his research and returned to London. They corresponded daily. His diction was eloquent, challenging her to keep pace. Matching wits with him thrilled her. Often, she got so caught up listening to his British accent and idioms she didn't hear what he said.

He began to call her his "muse" and probed her repeatedly as to whether she had any "romantic attachment" to Ray. "Oh, no," she assured him, "it's just a business partnership. We don't connect on that level." His book, *Setting Out: The Social Evolution of Lawn Furniture*, was soon published. Reviews in *The Citations of Higher Education* called it "exhaustive" and "a landmark work." She invited him back to New York to celebrate, even though she and Ray were deep into filming *The Tent at Ground Zero*.

"You have such an astute literary mind," he told her one night at dinner. "I wonder that you took up with Cozart. Documentaries are all well and good, but have you never considered that fiction might be your true gift?" "I don't know," she said, "I'm not sure I'd be good at it alone." "Rubbish," he said, "with your knack for words? Cozart is bloody lucky to have you. A bit of a chav, don't you agree?" She asked him what that meant. "A chav," he smirked, "is a man of low tastes. A lout, a braggart. I wonder if he jealously undermines your confidence purposely." "To what end?" she asked him. "To keep you hanging on to him so he can use what's yours. Think about it." She did. Later, he said, "You love the theater. Why not write a screenplay of your own?"

That night, Natalie slept with Geoffrey for the first time. His kisses, like slight but incessant breezes, lifted her high above the ground. She was floating on a wave of perfect prose, peering down at herself from the vantage point of a master narrator. Here was a love story to be believed.

Natalie felt chilled; the clouds completely obscured the moon. She got up and took several turns about the roof. Of course, she'd never told Geoffrey about her night with Ray or why she'd brought the Mystic 8 Ball with her to London. At first, she'd kept it in her home office as a kind of trophy. It sat on a bookcase gathering dust, as did most of her other things. She had a new country to explore, after all, and had immediately set about it, venturing far beyond London. At times she went alone; Geoffrey didn't really like to travel. When he began the sequel to his book, *Gnomenclature: The Social Evolution of*

*Lawn Ornaments*, he took her to Oxford and Cambridge when he did his research.

Six months into her marriage, Natalie began devouring books of poetry. She didn't know why. She also began writing her screenplay, *Almost a Loneliness*. Sometimes, as she read or wrote, she played with the Mystic 8 Ball. She moved it from her bookcase to her desk. Several times Geoffrey picked it up but quickly set it back down as if it were a time bomb. She was glad he took no interest in it.

They saw each other less and less. He sought her out to help him edit his new manuscript; otherwise, he preferred his own study. He sat hunched behind a desk that was itself obscured by teetering stacks of books. Photographs carpeted the floor. Once when she brought him his tea, he abraded her for stepping on a reproduction of a Victorian lithograph. She grew weary of his endless monologues on class status and didn't understand his mania for bird baths and sun dials. She couldn't overcome the irony that they owned no lawn furniture or lawn ornaments of any kind.

She began to carry the Mystic 8 Ball about the house, setting it near her wherever she sat to read or write. Geoffrey took offense at this. "My dear, you said you and Cozart were dissolving 8 Ball Productions." "We are," she said, though she'd not talked with her lawyer about it for months. "Then start," he said, "by getting rid of *that* thing." He pointed at the toy as if it were a dog that had just soiled the carpet. After that day, Natalie hid the Mystic 8 Ball in the hope chest in their bedroom, telling Geoffrey she'd thrown it out.

## THE DIE IS CAST

She thought of Ray more and more; it aggravated her when Geoffrey interrupted her thoughts with his tinny accent. The peculiar idioms that had once charmed her began to irritate. She couldn't bear to hear him say, "It's brass monkeys outside," which made no sense, and God forbid he seduce her with a little "slap and tickle." He had a predictable manner with sex; their "together time," as he called it, was always scheduled. One sleepless night, she tried to read his book about lawn furniture. It lay prominently showcased on their coffee table. The next morning, she awoke feeling cold, sore, and disoriented. She'd fallen asleep on the sofa with Geoffrey's fat book compressing her pelvis.

The day came when she knew she had to end it. Ray had been right—she didn't love Geoffrey like she thought. And his love for her was nothing like she'd imagined. She knocked at the door of his study. "Geoffrey, this isn't working." He didn't look up; his glasses reflected the light from his computer screen. When it was all over, what wounded her most of all was that he'd put up so little fight for her.

Clouds so fully obscured the half-moon that Natalie couldn't recall where it hung in the sky. "I'm half sick of shadows," she murmured, turning toward the elevator. She wouldn't make the same mistake again, wouldn't let her imagination give birth to phantoms. Her mind would be firmly rooted in reality. She'd give the Mystic 8 Ball back to Ray only when she was sure of his love, when he'd made his good confession: "I'm sorry for so long disappointing you with hope. I want to know what love is. Please teach me."

Then and only then, she'd drop the Mystic 8 Ball into his upturned hands (he would be kneeling). Seeing his treasure, he'd weep gratefully, thankful for a second chance to prove himself. "It's only right," he'd say, "for me to now be in hope of you." "Ah, yes, but the time is short," she'd say, pointing out to him the drowning die. In despair, he'd weep again, but his tears would be like fallen stones in a river, and from her lofty island tower, she'd step across ...

Scene 19

# Whitaker One View

*Grandeur, Georgia*

*Friday, March 12*

Max had just shut the door to his Atlanta apartment to run what he considered to be an important errand when he got the call summoning him to Corporate.

"I can't explain everything now," Patricia told him. "Your presence is necessary, that's all. Jane will be there."

"Jane? What's—"

"You think you can manage this one thing for me? Oh, and I've invited Ms. Dziedzic for dinner."

After Patricia hung up, Max didn't return his phone to the inner pocket of his blazer. He dropped it into the outer pocket. It annoyed him that his mother assumed he had nothing to do, even though he usually didn't. She'll just have to wait this time, he thought. He shut the door of his Maserati with firmness and would've hit the gas pedal hard as he pulled onto the street, but there was too much traffic.

It was another bright blue day, a carbon copy of the previous, a great day for golf. Traffic puttered along; Max hit every stoplight. At the last intersection before his turn, he decided that seeing Nicole again would be pleasant. If he did stop in for dinner with his mother, then likely he could secure her phone number.

Arriving at his destination, he parked near the entrance to the porcelain-enameled building, its central glass atrium cheerily reflecting the late morning sun. As he entered the museum, he felt tired and foolish. Tired of his mother's whims. Tired of how she kept Whitaker's under her thumb. Foolish for what had brought him to this place—his obsession over a tailless cat.

"Oh, it's *Mr.* Whitaker."

Max extended his hand. The two men met by what appeared to be a sculpture of a giant block of cheese. Dr. Frank Carlisle looked exactly like the picture Max had seen in the *Atlanta Journal-Constitution*: high forehead, thinning hair, tweed jacket and bow tie. The only difference was that now his face betrayed surprise and confusion.

"You're expecting me, I hope? I know it was short notice," Max said.

Carlisle visibly gulped. He fiddled with his bow tie and averted his eyes. "Er, a slight miscommunication with my assistant." He laughed nervously. "You see, I'm used to meeting with *Ms.* Whitaker."

"Of course. Jane—"

"And about that, Mr. Whitaker—I mean, I can guess why you're here, and all I can say is, that story about your daughter and the Saint Nil, getting the reporter—it wasn't my idea. Not my idea!" Carlisle wrung his hands anxiously.

Max pursed his lips, puzzled by this display.

"Oh, this is difficult. Very difficult. What a pickle!" Carlisle's voice squeaked fearfully. "I don't wanna cause trouble. Please, Mr. Whitaker, we here at the Summit are grateful for your family's financial support."

"Dr. Carlisle, please—what's this about?"

"So very, very grateful. We couldn't survive otherwise. Please, you must understand."

"Understand what?" Max thrust one hand into his pants pocket. He felt the weight of his phone in his blazer. He'd forgotten it was in the outer pocket, and he glanced down.

Carlisle followed Max's eyes. "What's that?" he asked, pointing. His finger shook. "Is that a recorder? It's a recorder! You're recording me. Oh, oh!" His voice reached an unprecedented pitch.

"What? No, it's—"

"I wouldn't have done it, believe me. I wouldn't have if—oh, I mean, without strong encouragement."

"No one is accusing you."

"And I was sworn to secrecy. What could I do? I'm nobody. It wasn't my idea."

Max stepped toward the little man, close enough to tweak his red nose. "Stop it, will ya? Listen to me!"

Carlisle nodded vigorously. "I'm listening, I'm listening. Anything you say, Mr. Whitaker. Anything you say." He dabbed his forehead with a hanky.

"If the story on Jane wasn't your idea...then whose idea was it?" Max pronounced these last words deliberately.

"I can't possibly, no, I've sworn—"

"Tell me."

Carlisle glanced sheepishly up at Max.

Max frowned. Because suddenly, he knew. "Was it—?"

"Yes!" Carlisle cried. "It was *Mrs.* Whitaker!"

At Whiningham, Jane stood in her palatial walk-in closet trying to decide what to pack for her trip to Cartagena, Colombia. She was still dressed in her pajamas, and she held a sleeveless Dolce & Gabbana gown in one hand and her phone in the other. Via video chat, Meena was directing her choices. She and Roxy sat in a cabana on the roof of the Hotel Casa San Agustin getting pedicures.

"No, not that one," Meena said about the gown. "You wore that to Dominick's birthday—"

"But he isn't coming now, you said," Jane countered.

"We-ell, maybe," Meena hedged. Next to her, Roxy whispered something, and the two of them giggled.

"What?" Jane asked. "What's goin' on?"

"Okay, bitch. You caught me. I lied. He is."

"Why'd you say he wasn't?"

"Because we want you to come," Roxy shouted.

"Yeah, we thought you might not—"

"But I don't care, if he doesn't." Jane put the Dolce & Gabbana gown back and pulled out a vintage Chanel cocktail dress. "What about this?"

"Ooo, love, love," Meena cooed. "Blue's your best color."

Jane walked to her bed and laid the dress next to her suitcase. She'd already packed several bikinis, wraps, and hats, numerous pairs of sunglasses and sandals, matching collars and leashes for Baby Girl, plus the portable shower—because Meena thought it had creative potential. There were a couple Finder novels for beach reading.

## THE DIE IS CAST

Jane repositioned the dog collars and looked about her—Baby Girl was sunning itself in the window, asleep. Jane tip-toed back into her closet to retrieve the Comfy-Go Pet Tote she always stashed way, way in the back. As a rule, Baby Girl resisted confinement and ran howling from the sight of the thing.

Meena and Roxy were comparing toenail polish.

"Whatcha guys doin' next?" Jane asked.

"Who knows? When you're Rich And Totally Sexy, you don't need to have any ideas." She and Roxy laughed.

"Hey, Jane—look!" Roxy showed Jane her sparkly sea green toes. "It's literally a party on my feet."

"Get your feet outta my face, bitch!" Meena pushed Roxy's legs away.

"I think ... I'm gonna bring the Saint Nil," Jane mused, opening her trunk at the foot of her bed.

"Hey, Jane," Roxy said, "Meena says you need to look more available."

"I did not."

"Yeah, huh," Roxy giggled.

"Look, Jane," Meena explained, "I only said you always look, like, so confident, y'know? Guys will just assume you already have a boyfriend."

Jane closed the trunk lid and returned to her closet. "I don't need a boyfriend. I'm only twenty-two."

"Okay, but Dominick is, like, totally hot. You guys look awesome together. What happened?"

Jane rummaged among her many shoes, looking for a pair of heels to match her cocktail dress. "I dunno."

"You don't know? Was there just, like, no chemistry? Or was he cheating on you?"

"No."

"Then what?"

Jane found a pair with promise. "What about these?" she asked Meena, holding aloft some lacy pumps.

"Meh," Meena sniffed.

Jane tossed the pumps aside.

"Jane, what about Dominick?" Meena pressed.

"I dunno," Jane said in frustration. "I just stopped liking him. I wanted something different. I can't really explain." She picked up sandals in pink iguana print.

"Omigod, the ankle straps. Love, love!"

"I mean, I feel like right now," Jane gestured with the sandals, "I wanna go wherever the wind takes me."

"I'll find a Latin lover for you, Jane," Roxy shouted. "A beautiful Spanish chico!"

"Quit shouting, bitch!" Meena pushed Roxy away. "Hey, Jane, when you get here, don't tell Dominick I asked, okay?"

Jane promised silence on the subject, and Meena and Roxy soon signed off.

The pink sandals made Jane's suitcase overstuffed. She sat on it to zip it shut. In mid-zip, she decided that sitting on a suitcase should be of public interest and picked up her phone. She unzipped the suitcase and sat on it again, this time pretending she was about to fall off: "What happens when you can't leave behind vintage Chanel!" she wrote as a caption, tagging Meena and Roxy so they'd be sure to see the photo on *Dishpix.com*. These feats accomplished, she sat on her bed for a few minutes studying her own Dishpix profile, not for any reason, but just for the feeling she got looking at herself wearing her silver kimono and diamond headband. *Adventure is my destiny.*

Humming the theme music to *Cave of All Fears,* Jane returned to her closet. The kimono was hanging on the back of the door. Reverently, she lifted it from its hook. The fabric was satiny soft, and she caressed it between her fingers. Nothing else she wore made her feel more enchanted, and she giggled while practicing dramatic poses before her mirror. Afterwards, she sashayed about her room with the kimono in her arms, stopping at her desk to retrieve a key, and curtsying at the foot of her chaise. There she laid the kimono down—gently, as if it were a person. She folded the sleeves in front to keep them off the floor.

With the key she'd taken from her desk, she unlocked a dresser. Opening the top drawer, she extracted the diamond headband. Technically, it was a necklace—vintage Yves Saint Laurent—but she wore it as a headband. There was a single row of white half-carats set in platinum, and from each of these diamonds hung, like icicles, a vertical row of smaller diamonds. As a necklace it was very heavy. As a headband it was even heavier. But Jane felt the weight was worth it because the fringe of diamonds on her forehead sparkled beautifully, like magical strands of hair. She laid the necklace on a pillow next to the kimono.

She waltzed back to her bed, pulled her suitcase off to make way for herself, and collapsed as if exhausted into her mass of pillows. There she lay pouting. Corporate and Nana and That Homeless Woman were an hour away. She rolled over and drew her Finder novels to her, opening *Cave of All Fears* near the middle. She flipped backwards to the beginning, pausing here and there at favorite scenes:

"Wait, Bucky! I'm coming with you."

"No, Lady Xenia, I can't let you. It's too dangerous."

"But Scevola has alerted the authorities. I can get you across the border."

"But your life here. Your family. I can't ask you to make such a sacrifice."

"You don't have to ask. I've already decided."

"But why?"

"For the same reason you have made it—for the truth."

Bucky nodded. He understood.

Shouts echoed in the corridor. "They've come!"

Lady Xenia gasped. "Bucky, we're wasting time."

There was no other way, and Bucky knew it. "What do you propose?"

"Come with me."

They ran to the end of the corridor. Lady Xenia led him down a winding stairwell. At the bottom she removed a stone from the wall and pulled a hidden lever. A portion of the wall gave way before them.

"Hurry!"

Together they raced down the secret passage.

It's a dead end," Bucky said, confused by the brick wall before them.

Lady Xenia only grinned and pressed an intercom.

"Frankie, It's me. How is she? Ready to sail?"

A crackly voice replied, "She sure is, milady."

At once, a secret door opened to Bucky's left.

"After you," Lady Xenia smiled.

"Wow," Bucky said as he entered a high-tech control room. "You'd never know by the look of the place—"

"Yes, this underground inlet has existed for centuries. It's why the castle was built. But these—" she waved at the wall of computers "—are new additions."

"I'll say."

A young man dressed in black sauntered over to them.

"Fully fueled and ready to go," he said to Lady Xenia, dropping a set of keys into her hand.

"Thanks, Frankie."

Bucky followed Lady Xenia to the water's edge. A small helicopter fitted with floats rocked gently in the current.

"I got the impression we were going by boat," Bucky said.

"We are. Sort of. This can do both. After all, in my experience, I've found that sometimes the best runway is a lake."

"In your experience?"

"That's right."

"What do you call this thing?"

"A gyroplane. A Calidus 300X Turbo to be exact. It's a prototype. Only three in existence."

"That's reassuring."

"I thought I was with Bucky Browne, the international man of adventure."

Bucky grinned. "Yes. But I'm used to adventuring alone."

"You'll have to get over that." She winked and tossed her blonde hair. "I'm Lady Xenia. Adventure is my destiny."

Jane let the book fall closed and rolled onto her back. She lay there for a minute with her hands under her head and her feet in the air, wriggling her bare toes. She pretended she was dancing upside down, her toes touching the zebra-striped canopy above her bed. She began to hum again, relishing a feeling of anticipation, a feeling that Lady Jane's next adventure was going to be HUGE.

▼ ▼ ▼ ▼

"Has Jane arrived yet?" Patricia stood with Toby Milto in the hall outside the master control room at Corporate Headquarters consulting with the commercial videographer.

Milto checked his iPad, "Er, no, but Ms. Dziedzic has."

In expectation Patricia looked over Milto's pencil head. "Oh, uh—Kathleen is escorting her up."

"Ah," Patricia said, and both knew nothing could be said more than that.

Milto walked to the studio room, and Patricia followed him after a parting word with the videographer. She took her time, stopping to inspect the make-up and changing rooms, and chatting briefly with various employees, a few of whom she knew by name. Secretly, she enjoyed the surprise and the deference of all to her presence. It was a rare appearance for her, and she heard her name whispered as veterans pointed her out to their younger colleagues who'd never seen her in person. Since Max was the face of the company, this wing of Corporate—the Commercial Production Center—was primarily his domain. Certainly, it wasn't Kathleen's, who could never be the face of anything.

Fifteen minutes had passed. Approaching the studio, Patricia's anticipation increased. She'd been desirous of seeing Nicole all morning. She'd awoken feeling a nervous flutter near her heart, a feeling quite foreign. Perhaps she'd last felt it on her wedding day. She realized such anticipation was silly and had marshaled her reason against it. She told herself that Nicole's opinion of Corporate Headquarters was unimportant. The only opinion that mattered to Patricia was her own, and in her opinion, Headquarters reflected the subtlest facets of her own brilliance. Nevertheless, she'd impulsively chosen to wear a pencil sheath dress in black, a departure from her power suits. The dress was feminine yet simple and subdued. It made her look younger.

"Mrs. Whitaker."

It was Nicole's voice. And upon entering the studio, Nicole's eyes were the first that Patricia saw. The second were Kathleen's, which she caught but briefly, for Kathleen was busy settling the bolts of fabric that had ballooned about her as she sat. It was clear that a suitable chair had been brought for her, as the only other seat in the vicinity belonged to the director. Patricia didn't need to study her daughter long to see that the large-print floral pattern of her dress only accentuated the breadth of her drooping breasts and erased any semblance of a waistline, or that the face planted in the center of this distended garden looked like a big, round, button mushroom with eyes.

"A pleasure to see you again," Nicole said to Patricia. And then, with a subtle, sideways glance at Kathleen, she added with exaggerated innocence, "I never expected this to be so—so *big*."

Patricia blinked several times at the indiscreet reference to size in such a context, and with an involuntary glance at Kathleen hastily replied, "Ah, well, this was many years in the making. Our first headquarters was barely a closet at the back of our five-and-dime. The store was in downtown Grandeur. It was opened by my late husband in—" she hesitated, aware that identifying the date would age her.

"1969!" Milto concluded for her eagerly.

"Yes, of course." Patricia simulated a smile.

"It's like its very own world in here," Nicole marveled.

Patricia agreed with this assessment. "Our Merchandise Design Center generally makes such an impression. You must've seen it on your way up." She said this because she was eager to show Nicole the Design Center herself and knew that Kathleen wouldn't have bothered.

"No, I don't think so."

"Really? Well, then ..."

Patricia motioned for Nicole to follow her, at the same time indicating with her eyes to Kathleen that she need not trouble herself to get up. Nevertheless, Kathleen began the work. Patricia made no pretense of waiting for her. Leaving the studio with Nicole and Milto, she made a right turn, then a left, stopping before a set of glass doors etched with Whitaker's iconic cursive *W*.

"This," Patricia opened the doors grandly, "is Whitaker One View." They stepped onto a balcony that ran adjacent to a conference room with walls made entirely of glass.

Nicole sucked in her breath and peered about.

Far below them were aisles and aisles stretching for indeterminable lengths. Fresh produce, dry goods, and dairy aisles lay to their right. Health and beauty products, kitchen and bath accessories, clothing, toys, and office supplies formed an interlocking puzzle directly before them. To their left were aisles of electronics, appliances, tools, paints, and automotive supplies. And receding further left into the distance were a lawn and garden center, hair salon, pharmacy, and Tip-Top Sub Shop.

"It's ... a store," Nicole said, clearly nonplussed.

Milto pumped his arms. "Lots of stuff you need and lots of stuff you don't, but we carry it all right here!"

"We call this Whitaker One View for obvious reasons," Patricia said. "What you're seeing below is our Merchandise Design Center. It's a store simulation only. A theater of products, if you will."

"Theater?" A question formed itself in Nicole's eyes.

"Yes. Look closely." Patricia gestured below.

Nicole placed one hand on the railing.

"It's—" Milto began to say.

"Don't tell her," Patricia commanded sharply.

Milto put his iPad over his mouth.

At that moment, the balcony doors opened, and Kathleen waddled in. They all took two steps over to make room. Nicole was pushed further to the right. She scanned the nearest aisles below, her eyes locking on the fresh produce displays. Three employees in red polo shirts (company dress) were stacking apples and oranges. One of the oranges fell. It bounced three times like a ping-pong ball.

"It's ... not real," Nicole said in disbelief.

"Plastic," Patricia said.

"But how—?" Nicole examined everything again with fresh eyes. "Nothing here is real," she murmured in wonder.

"The cereal boxes are full of confetti, the candy bars are Styrofoam, and the pickle jars are empty. Ha!" Milto practically shouted now that he was free to speak.

"The lamps," Nicole pointed. "They're cardboard."

"Yes," Patricia said. This was the part she liked best to explain. Product simulation was her brainchild. "We cut a piece to a product's size and shape, then paste on the product image. Simulated clothing is clipped to hangers. Most product images are stood up like paper dolls by being slid into plastic supports along the shelving."

"You create cardboard images of everything you sell?"

"Yes, in the Product Simulation Department. There are exceptions. It's impossible to simulate every nut and bolt. We put a real bin of them here in the tool aisle."

"The lawn and garden center has real artificial plants." The voice was Kathleen's. Her upper lip glistened.

"Um, yes, that's true." Patricia replied to her daughter, then quickly turned to Nicole. "Flowers create the unique problem of—of spacing—and, er—" she paused, feeling a sudden hot flash at the sight in her periphery of Kathleen's floral dress, "and we've found that, uh, two-dimensional displays can't adequately simulate their—their girth."

Milto coughed. Nicole observed the discomfort from the pair with cool eyes and a half-smile.

Just then they heard the echo of a yelp. They all looked down. To the left, Baby Girl had scampered in. There were many feet to sniff, and it was very eager, running from shoe to shoe. Several employees knelt to lure in the little dog, but none of them had a Teeny Treat. Near the faux Tip-Top Sub Shop, Baby Girl stopped to sniff a simulated store greeter. The cardboard man fell over, facedown. Baby Girl's nerves reacted, and it raced off howling.

Patricia signaled with her eyes to Milto that he ought to go fix this.

"I'm on it, Mrs. Whitaker."

"Oh, Toby—when you find Jane, bring her directly to the studio, will you?" Patricia said.

Milto clicked his heels and saluted.

After his departure, Nicole said to Patricia, "I'm not sure I understand." She gestured to the scene below. "This Design Center—why simulate products at all?"

Baby Girl's disturbance had permitted Patricia's temperature to return to normal, and she answered Nicole coolly. "Because the purpose of the Design Center isn't to sell products but to practice selling them. A product that ends up at our Whitaker's stores represents many stages in a process." She counted on her fingers. "It starts with product research, then acquisition approval, then configuration for shelving, then visual assessment next to similar merchandise—"

"To figure out how things look together on the shelves."

"Exactly. There's an art to it, you see. Much has been written on the subject. Should gold and silver items be shelved together or separately? Should plastics be on the top or bottom? Should something red be placed by something blue? A world of decisions must be made. Once we approve product displays here, we implement that design in all our Whitaker's stores uniformly."

As Patricia said this, Milto appeared below. Several employees pointed him in the direction of Baby Girl, and he vanished among the cardboard toys. Moments later, in the distance, a row of simulated bicycles collapsed.

"Like, I'm totally amazed." Nicole shook her head, still taking in all she'd learned.

"Are you?" Patricia was quite pleased to hear this.

"Omigod, yes. Product simulations. What a brilliant strategy." Nicole blinked her eyes at Patricia, who thought she detected admiration in them.

"We've worked hard to perfect it," Patricia beamed, her confidence riding high. She went on exuberantly, "Everything contributes to the bottom line. Optimal product displays increase sales, and since merchandise changes continually, using simulations—"

"Yes," Nicole said with a glance at Kathleen, "I imagine it trims the fat from your operating expenses—or, rather—" she stopped, wide eyed, and placed her fingertips to her lips. "Oops, I to-tally didn't mean that. Ha-ha."

Kathleen glared at her stonily.

Patricia quickly opened the doors to Whitaker One View and ushered Nicole out. The doors closed upon Kathleen before she was able to reach them.

A crash at her back made Kathleen turn around. She heard shouts and looked down. Baby Girl had bounded out of Kitchen & Bath. Milto followed in hot pursuit, along with three soldiers conscripted for the chase.

It was then Kathleen saw—was it an angel? To her left near the door of the faux pharmacy, a young woman stood in a shimmery, silver kimono. It was as if a sunbeam had settled on her, for her appearance was like light. A distinct aura circled her head, like radiant transparent glass, or a heavenly halo glowing luminously.

## THE DIE IS CAST

▼ ▼ ▼ ▼

Max left the Summit Art Museum feeling more educated than he would've preferred. He sat in his Maserati in the parking lot trying to take in his new knowledge. It was much bigger than who told whom about a tailless cat, though that small mystery had been solved as well. Jane *had* mentioned the cat to Carlisle, who in turn had mentioned it to Patricia in one of their (as it turned out) numerous consultations. Did Max know his mother at all? That was the real mystery.

Max traced the steering wheel counterclockwise with his forefinger. He saw his immediate past afresh: Patricia's perplexity at Jane, her summoning him to Whiningham, her desire for his intervention. Carlisle's revelations gave Max an unprecedented view of things. He now held the entire script and was sitting in the director's chair.

He started his car and shifted into reverse. However, he kept his foot on the brake because other thoughts suddenly occurred him: what about his distant past? What he'd learned about Patricia—did it apply there as well? Would many other things in his life need to be ... reinterpreted?

Such thoughts threatened to paralyze him, and he ran his hand through his hair to rouse himself. His immediate concern was Jane. His daughter did need to be saved. Not from Dishing, but from his mother.

▼ ▼ ▼ ▼

Baby Girl had been recaptured and properly leashed. Jane stood in an elevator, the dog sitting at her feet, panting. Next to her, Milto propped himself against the handrail and fanned his face fiercely with his iPad. Since reuniting Jane with her Emotional Support, he could only stare at her, shaking his head and mouthing, "Oh no, oh no."

"Thanks," Jane said when the elevator doors opened. "I don't like going in the Design Center. Even for Baby Girl. It's so creepy."

Jane strode down the hall toward the studio room, Baby Girl pattering next to her. Milto crept after at a distance. Onlookers gathered to peer at Jane, among them Kathleen who met them at the intersection to Whitaker One View.

"Hi, Aunt Leenie!"

Kathleen looked Jane up and down. "Why ... are you wearing that?"

"You like it?" Jane twirled once. But the weight of her diamond headband shifted her center of gravity and she teetered into Milto. He dropped his iPad trying to catch her. Baby Girl jumped out of the way as the device hit the floor.

"Oops," Jane giggled. "Baby Girl, go fetch!"

Baby Girl took cover behind Kathleen.

"Best take it off," Kathleen said.

"Oh, I couldn't. It's vintage YSL." Jane fiddled with it in her hair (it had slid crooked). "And it's just so—so *me*."

As Jane spoke, Kathleen lowered her eyes and fingered her ruby bracelet, the one she always wore.

Jane finished setting her headband aright. "There!"

Eyes still lowered, Kathleen said, "You look like a pixie."

"Ha-ha. Cute, huh?"

Kathleen laughed, but when she looked up, her eyes held tears. "Yes. So cute. Always. So beautiful." She swayed on her feet as if she were a child testing her legs for the first time. "Jane," she said sadly, "do you ever feel regrets about your life? How it might have turned out different if—" her tears fell, and she swiped her cheek. "Because believe me, I know, Jane, I understand. I have so many regrets. But I can't help who I am—it's so unfair. I'm sorry, so sorry for everything. I—I can't stay!" Her tears fell faster, and she stepped past Jane and Milto toward the elevator.

Milto regained his speech. "No! You can't," he pleaded, watching Kathleen go. He reached for her in vain. "Don't leave me with Mrs. Whitaker!"

"Like, what's with her?" Jane asked no one in particular.

Kathleen didn't look back.

"What on earth?" Patricia had stepped into the hall.

Seeing Mrs. Whitaker, Milto's eyes dilated like a deer's pre-collision.

Jane waved. "Hi, Nana!"

Slowly, but without any hesitation, Patricia reached behind her and calmly pulled the door to the studio closed.

"I'm here," Jane said, approaching. "Can I go in?"

Patricia's eyes were bright with suppressed fury. She pretended to ignore the employees who'd stopped to gape. "In a minute, dear. The changing room is down the hall."

"But I have changed."

"Then change back. This is no day to make a fashion statement. Toby, show her where," Patricia directed. Her icy eyes indicated that this was his one chance to redeem himself for having let Jane come so far looking as she did.

Milto nodded vigorously. "This way, Ms. Whitaker."

Jane bent and picked up Baby Girl. "You need a drink, Pookie-pie? Poor Pookums. Let's find you a drink."

"Dear, the changing room first." Patricia strove to smile. She reached to pat Jane's little rat with feigned affection but couldn't bring herself to touch it. She turned to Milto. "Er, where's Kathleen? And have you seen Max?"

Just then the studio door opened. Nicole popped her head out. "Mrs. Whitaker, the portable shower is—" she stopped, her eyes captured by the white light of diamonds. "Omigod—Lady Jane?" Instantly, she put her hand over her mouth and glanced at Patricia.

Patricia's eyes fixed on Nicole suspiciously.

"Ah, my fans," Jane purred, gliding past Patricia.

An argument ensued between Patricia and Milto.

"Like, hi, everybody," Jane called out as if a large studio audience had been waiting for her. "Wave to the nice people, Baby Girl." A couple lighting technicians looked up, and the director turned around.

Nicole stood by in wonder, staring unblinkingly at Jane's head. "Are those, like, real diamonds?" She leaned in as if drawn magnetically.

"Like, yeah. There's three hundred or something, and it's, like, 11.9 carats total. At least, that's what they told me."

"Who's *they*?"

Jane was confused by this question. Before she could reply, a young man tapped her shoulder. He wore company dress, and as he spoke, he adjusted his glasses nervously.

"I saw you come in. You, uh, new here too?"

Jane smiled. "As a matter of fact—I am."

"What d'ya do? I'm the cameraman. Er—the assistant."

"And I'm the star! It's my first role. Make sure you get all of me. I'll shine so bright when I go viral. 'Cause I can't help but sparkle," Jane struck a pose with her face upturned.

The young man grinned. "What's your name?"

Jane peeked at Nicole and giggled. "Lady Jane." She dropped her fingers before him. He hesitated, unsure if he was supposed to kiss them.

"Are you ready for adventure? Ha-ha!"

"Lady Jane, huh? Are you European?" he asked.

Jane giggled again, not noticing the young man had abruptly backed away. Nicole had retreated as well. Patricia like a swooping eagle had scattered the little birds.

"It'd be nice if I could count on you not to be utterly absurd," Patricia hissed in Jane's ear, taking hold of her arm.

"What? I'm not doing anything."

"Lady Jane? What the hell is that?" No smile could hide Patricia's fury now.

"I just told him my name."

"That is *not* your name."

"Yeah, huh. We can be whatever we want."

Patricia let out a tremendous snort. "That's ridiculous. There's only one queen of England, isn't there?"

Jane frowned. "But I don't wanna be queen of England."

"You're wearing a crown, aren't you? Now take it off." Patricia waved at Jane's headband dismissively. "This isn't a costume party. And that kimono doesn't flatter you at all. You are Jane Whitaker, my granddaughter. You're representing Whitaker Corporation. That's a great responsibility, and I'm not going to let you turn it into a Dishing game."

Jane yanked her arm away. "What game? I'm Lady Jane. You wanted me on TV. You're the one playing a game!" She hardly knew what she was saying, she was so angry that Patricia had slandered her kimono. She spun away from her grandmother defiantly—and ran right into her father.

"Max!" Patricia cried, her face exasperated yet relieved.

Max's face was confused and angry. "What's happened?" He looked from Jane to Patricia and back to Jane. Their collision had caused Jane's headband to fall into her eyes, and she blinked at him aggrievedly through her diamonds.

"Nana is sooo mean."

Max glared at his mother. "Yes ... yes, she *is*."

Patricia's mouth fell open. "What? You don't know—"

"I know plenty," Max seethed. "What you've been doing!" He pointed his finger at Patricia accusingly.

Patricia appeared not to hear this. She looked past Max, her eyes indicating that he ought to turn around.

"Excuse me." It was the commercial director.

Max shook the man's hand perfunctorily.

"I don't mean to interrupt," the director said, "but now that we're all assembled, perhaps we could take our places?"

## THE DIE IS CAST

For the first time, Max looked about him. He saw cameras, a lighting crew and sound technicians, plus Toby Milto, Ms. Dziedzic, a Whitaker's shopping cart, a shower curtain, and a filthy man in ragged clothing who may or may not have been homeless.

"Jane, we're leaving," he announced.

"Like, why?" She set Baby Girl down to fix her headband.

"I can't tell you now." He took hold of her elbow.

"Let go," Jane said. "You're just like Nana."

"I am not. You don't understand now, but you will."

"What's this about?" Patricia asked in growing alarm.

"Jane, we're leaving. I'll explain in a minute. Trust me." He guided her, diamonds still askew, toward the door.

"Let go."

"Max, she doesn't want to leave," Patricia said.

"Stay out of this. Come on, Jane."

"No! STOP IT!" Jane jerked her elbow from her father's grip and quickly stooped to pick up Baby Girl. "Listen, people! You all think you can just, like, tell me what to do and what to think. But, like, I'm my own person. I mean, I'm twenty-two. But to you, I'm not. 'Cause you don't even try to understand me. Like, ever! I mean, I may be Jane Whitaker, but I'm also myself. And—and if I can't be myself, then I don't wanna be Jane Whitaker." She began to stroke Baby Girl furiously on its head. "I mean, like, look around you. Life is not a cardboard store display. It's about embracing who you are. Because you only get one life, y'know? And you just, like, oughta embrace who you are. Omigod, I just said that! What I mean is—you oughta love your life because it's one of the most beautiful gifts you're ever given."

Max ran a hand through his hair. "Are you done? Would it kill you to listen to me once? I'm protecting you."

"I don't need your help," Jane countered instinctively. Then, with curiosity: "Like, protect me from what?"

"From her!" Max pointed at Patricia.

"Max! Stop!" Patricia reached out to restrain him.

"And I should have long ago." He turned to Jane. "You know why you were arrested in Moscow?"

Jane thought back. "We-ell, they said I was trespassing."

"No. That's not the reason." He sneered at Patricia. "You were arrested because *she* planned it. It was a phony, trumped up charge, a stupid scheme to create negative press about you. She's been tipping off reporters so they cover you. So they write stories about your Dishing and make you look bad. So you'll give it up. She's been at it for months." Max glared at his mother. "Don't pretend you don't know. I talked to Carlisle. He confessed to more than telling you about the tailless cat. He let the cat out of the bag."

"Oh, Max, don't say any more. You know I don't like irony." Patricia appeared about to collapse and felt about her for a suitable chair. Nicole came to her aid.

Jane stood with her brows pinched and one hand on her hip. Slowly, she pulled off her headband, the diamonds clicking and flashing like shattered glass. Her lips tried to form a word, and she clutched Baby Girl hard.

"So ... like?" she began and stopped. Her lips quivered, and she looked from face to face as though unsure if anybody could see her. She backed away toward the door, shivering and shrinking as she went.

Max reached for her. "Jane. Wait. Please."

She motioned him to stop. The diamonds twinkled in her hand like tears. For a second, they stood face to face.

"Baby Girl ... needs a drink."

With a stifled sob, Jane fled.

Scene 20

## Treasure Hunting

*Hotel Amir, Old Town Istanbul*

*Friday, March 12*

At breakfast in the hotel café with Ray and Clark, Natalie was all smiles. It was just the kind of day she liked, a day perfectly planned—because Ray had taken little interest in weaving the details, and because the woman they were set to interview was herself a professional planner. Not even Ray could mess up a day of filming doubly organized. Dr. Ayhan managed a serious cultural institution, held a degree from Oxford, had published numerous scholarly essays, and had been elected fellow of the Society of Antiquaries of London. She could help make their *Dish Movie* the serious artistic statement Natalie hoped it would be. She gave her iPad to Ray so he could review her questions for Dr. Ayhan and their proper order. Natalie sat primly in a chic chevron skirt, having dressed her professional best. Her hair was up, and she wore more makeup than usual. Dr. Ayhan was a kindred spirit, after all. Natalie hoped to make much of their shared British experience.

"What's this here about Sailing to Byzantium?" Ray asked, scrolling down the screen.

"That's the museum's new Byzantine art exhibition," Natalie said. "We're filming the opening ceremony tomorrow night. Should be interesting. I'm looking forward to it."

Ray wrinkled his nose. He dumped a bag of sugar in his coffee. "Why do they need an opening ceremony? It's not a red-carpet premiere."

"I think it's to recognize all the donors," Natalie said.

"What's By-zan-ti-um?" Clark asked with his mouth full. He and Ray had both ordered stacks of pancakes. Clark had requested extra syrup; his pancakes floated in a river of it.

"An old name for Constantinople," Natalie said, biting into an olive; she'd ordered a Turkish breakfast. "Sailing to Byzantium is a poem by W. B. Yeats. The museum's using his title for their exhibition, I guess. There'll be artifacts on display taken from the Byzantine Empire during the Fourth Crusade. That's what Dr. Ayhan said. Here—she sent me a brochure." She handed it to Clark, but Ray snatched it.

"Stolen treasure! Hot damn!" He opened the brochure SAILING TO BYZANTIUM: THE ARTISTIC LEGACY OF THE BYZANTINE EMPIRE. He scanned two pages. All at once, he snorted and let the brochure flutter to the table.

"What's that for? You hardly looked at it," Natalie said. She didn't appreciate Ray ignoring her instruction.

"Oh, nothing. I got the gist. You can have it back."

Natalie picked up the brochure. "The artifacts are beautiful, aren't they? The Byzantines had such a distinct style."

Ray smirked. "Yes, very difficult to replicate, I'm sure."

"What's so funny?" she asked.

"I wasn't laughing."

"You were smiling." She eyed him suspiciously.

"Who's Yeetz?" Clark asked. "Is he a Turkish poet?"

"Irish," Natalie said, happy to instruct. "It's pronounced YATES," she added for the benefit of both Ray and Clark.

"What's he got to do with Byzantine art?" Clark asked.

"His poem is about Byzantium. Weren't you listening?"

"Is he gonna recite it at the opening ceremony?"

"Ha! If you can conjure his spirit. He lived last century."

"You wanna know what's funny?" Ray asked Natalie.

"I asked, didn't I?" she said.

"Well, sometimes, you don't really wanna know."

"Just tell me already. You got me curious."

"Okay, then look at page two."

Natalie opened the brochure. On page two was a picture of an icon of the Virgin Mary holding the Christ child. The icon was partially damaged; there were scratches scarring the Virgin's cheek. "The lost Theotokos of Sergiyev, by Andrei Rublev," read the fine print. "The work of fifteenth-century Russian icon painter Andrei Rublev is as beautiful and haunting as it is rare. This recently recovered icon was taken from Kiev during the Nazi occupation."

"There's nothing funny here," Natalie said. "It's sad. She looks sorta alone. The way she stares, her eyes so wide and alert, like she's imploring you. The scratches on her cheek make it look like she's crying."

"No, no, it's the description that's funny. I mean, Nazis! C'mon, what a story. They really expect us to believe that? Don't you see?" he asked Natalie earnestly.

Clark perked up. "Dude! What about Nazis?"

"Forgeries, man," Ray said.

"The Nazis forged art? That's awesome."

"No, no, they stole it. Some stuff's still missing. So, counterfeiters know this. They'll forge a Picasso or Rembrandt and say they found the painting, like stashed in their grandmother's attic by Nazis. It's one of the oldest tricks in the art business. I watched a show about it. A reporter went undercover. Museums do it a lot. Half the art out there is fake."

"Wait a sec," Natalie said, "you think this icon by Andrei Rublev is a forgery?" She held up the brochure to page two.

"It's good money if you can get away with it," Ray said.

"But that's ridiculous. They wouldn't put a forgery in an art exhibition," she insisted. "Look, the icon has the tell-tale marks of age. Quite literally. You can see the scratches."

"All the more convincing."

Natalie arched her eyebrows in a show of superciliousness. "Who knew you were such an expert? Look, Ray, Dr. Ayhan is a consummate professional. She's the first woman to be curator of the Ancient History Museum. She wouldn't sully its reputation. You oughta show her more respect."

"Well, I think her story is fishy. You wanted to know."

"Lemme see." Clark reached for the brochure.

Natalie held it out of his reach. "Your hands are sticky."

# TREASURE HUNTING

Clark licked the syrup off his fingers.

"Gross. That doesn't help. Go wash your hands."

"Maybe I'll ask her about it. About the Nazis," Ray said.

"That's absurd. Don't you dare," Natalie warned him.

Clark went to wash his hands.

"Hey, watch this," Ray said. He swiped one of Natalie's olives and hid it in Clark's pancakes. "Buried treasure." He chuckled and gave Natalie a wink.

Natalie rolled her eyes. She leaned back in her chair to signal that she wasn't joining in the joke. Nevertheless, she couldn't help grinning. She collected her iPad. "You're not really gonna ask Dr. Ayhan about the Nazi story, are you?"

Ray sipped his coffee primly. "Yes, as a fellow expert."

"You're just joking, right?" she pressed him. "This is a serious interview. I have it all planned. Can I count on you?"

Ray's lips curled in a half-frown. His eyes were the color of an autumn storm. She saw flecks of brown swirling like leaves in a gray sky. She couldn't tell the direction of the wind. Instinctively, she held her breath.

"I'll stick to the itinerary," he mumbled. "Whatever."

She exhaled, feeling both relief and triumph at having elicited this promise. Clark returned; she handed him the exhibition brochure and tried not to stare at his pancakes.

The Andrei Rublev icon failed to impress him. "Nothing but painted wood. I thought it'd be gold." He tossed the brochure aside and cut into his pancakes. "Y'know what? They say Nazis buried stuff off the coast of Nova Scotia."

"Who's *they*?" Natalie asked skeptically.

"The ManCave Network is doing a series on a treasure hunt at Oak Island. It's called The Perilous Treasure Pit."

"The ManCave Network?" Natalie scoffed. "Now there's a source for valid historical truth."

"Dude, I didn't know you were watching that too," Ray said. "That show is awesome."

"Treasure hunters have been going to Oak Island since the 1800s. Like, even Franklin Roosevelt went up there. The show covered all of that," Clark told Natalie.

"I saw that episode about FDR," Ray said. "He was a big treasure hunter before he became president."

"Yeah, man," Clark went on, "the group doin' the search now found one of Marie Antoinette's rings. Before she was locked up in the tower, she gave all her jewels to her maid who fled France with 'em. The ring's big and purple—they showed a close-up on the show."

Natalie couldn't tell if Clark was joking. "How do they know the ring is hers? Is her name engraved on the band?" she asked with a straight face.

"My question is, why give 'em to your maid? Should've kept the jewels, I think" Clark said. "They could've saved her life. 'Cause she was guillotined, right? So, like, if she'd been wearing a diamond necklace at the time, wouldn't it have stopped the blade? You can't cut through diamonds."

Natalie pursed her lips hard. She felt an onset of giggles.

"Dude, the ring isn't Marie Antoinette's," Ray said. "You gotta watch the new season of the show. They're theorizing now that it belonged to Captain Kidd. He anchored his ship off the coast, the Adventure Galley.

Then he rowed ashore and dug a pit since they were, like, pirates. They found a mine shaft on the island. It's boo-by-trapped, fills with water so far down so you can't get to the treasure."

"No way, man, the ring's Marie Antoinette's. I'm tellin' you, her maid fled to Canada with a chest of jewels."

"Watch the newest episodes! They even found a manuscript they think was Kidd's logbook. He pronounced a curse on the treasure. They say seven people have to die before the treasure is found. Six have already."

"No way I'm searching for cursed treasure," Clark said.

"Even if it was Marie Antoinette's jewels?" Ray asked.

"Not worth risking death. It'd have to be more valuable than jewels ... like plutonium maybe."

"Dude, you can't just find plutonium."

"Y'know what I'd like to find? Kryptonite."

Ray thought that would be awesome and said so. He finished his coffee. "Hey, Nat, what about you? Would you risk death to find treasure? What would be worth it to you?"

Natalie stared at him wordlessly, because he'd just called her "Nat," his old familiar nickname for her, and because she was so giddy from trying to suppress her laughter at his and Clark's conversation, that she couldn't think straight.

Just then Clark stuck his fork in the buried olive. "What the hell? Did you know 'bout this?" he accused Natalie. "I expect better from you." He flung the olive at Ray in mock outrage. It hit his empty mug and ricocheted. Ray flicked it back at him, beginning a game of table hockey. "It's a goal!" Clark cried, claiming victory when the olive fell to the floor. Natalie hid her face in her hands to compose her laughter.

Minutes later, the three of them entered the hotel lobby; Ayhan had sent her assistant Murat to drive them to the museum. He was young and lanky; his shirtsleeves hung an inch short of his wrists. Speaking heavily accented English, he welcomed them to Istanbul. Once their equipment was packed in the van, Natalie took the front seat. Ray slid onto the seat behind her.

As he pulled the van away from the curb, Murat said to Natalie, "You come with news, yes?"

"What? Er, uh, no, I don't have any news."

"But ... you camera. You with news?"

"He wants to know if we're a news crew," Ray said leaning forward. Then to Murat: "No, man, we make films."

Murat looked at Ray in the rearview mirror. "Ah. You film discovery, yes? For news?"

"Er, no, we're not with the news. We're film people. Like Hollywood. You know Hollywood, right?"

Murat's eyes bugged. "You—you like Spielberg? Come to see discovery and film? Make big-time movie?"

"Er, Spielberg, right. Something like that. Close enough." Ray leaned back in his seat.

Natalie urgently tried to turn her thoughts to the serious business at hand. Clark and Ray's goofiness at breakfast had made her far too scatter-brained for meeting a woman of achievement and sophistication like Dr. Ayhan. She took deep breaths to gather herself but could smell Ray's cologne wafting toward her, beckoning like the aroma of a zesty glass of wine. It irritated her to feel the familiar ambivalence about Ray's boyish spirit. His energy was like an ocean breeze caressing her body, warm and cool at once, ticklish and irresistible. Its personal effect on her was like intoxication. Her internal boundaries fell away; she became playful and silly. He always stirred the girlish part of her, the part for which she was half-ashamed.

And yet, Ray's spiritedness was vital to their filmmaking. Counting on him was never as simple as eliciting his agreement. What would he do or say next? She never knew. He was a mystery like the wind, unable to be harnessed. Focused on their work, his spiritedness was ingenious and inventive. To be caught up in his artistic passion was addictive and exhilarating. If only he could stay focused. At its worst, his impetuosity made him reckless, as was the case with his Finder interview. Unfortunately, it wasn't possible for her to tell the difference between ingenuous and reckless until the results were in. It was part of the mystery.

Murat turned the van north toward the grounds of the Topkapi Palace, the home of the sultans for 400 years. A high castle wall with a tower loomed before them. Tourists stepped aside as Murat drove through an arched gate. Bare trees and empty flower beds lined the entrance. March had been unusually cold, suppressing the blossoming of the city's tulip gardens. Natalie lamented this, imagining the flowers in bloom. She thought about Ray calling her "Nat." She didn't realize until he'd said it that she'd missed the nickname. He'd said it so naturally, like he'd never stopped calling her that. But he had because of Geoffrey. She'd only been "Natalie" with Geoffrey; he'd never called her "Nat."

Beyond the trees, they emerged into the courtyard of an L-shaped stone building. A portico supported by four grand columns marked the entrance to the museum. Murat parked the van, and Ray and Clark unpacked. As they carried their equipment bags up the steps, Natalie noticed a row of sarcophagi to her left. The tombs were all purple—carved from porphyry—a stone prized by the Byzantine emperors. She'd seen a similar sarcophagus at the Vatican Museum, the tomb of St. Helena, mother of Constantine the Great. Evidently, here lay members of the imperial family.

*Would you risk death to find treasure? What would be worth it to you?* Natalie hadn't answered Ray's questions. Passing the tombs into the museum, she pondered her reply. The idea that there may be something out there worth risking death to have frightened her. What could be greater than one's own life? Than life itself? She could think of no object, no possession for which she'd throw herself away. But this brought no relief to her mind; admitting that nothing would be worth it felt like an inadequacy, like she'd detected in herself a glaring lack of passion and purpose. Surely, she ought to be capable of taking some great risk.

Murat led them into a vestibule. Its dramatically arched ceiling drew their eyes upward. Slender ribs projected from its flesh-colored surface, straddling the width of the room like giant horseshoes. Rows of marble columns supported the legs of each arch on either side. Sound reverberated throughout, as staffers prepared for the art exhibition's opening ceremony: arranging chairs, constructing a stage, and hanging banners. At the far end of the vestibule, they passed a row of niches displaying marble busts. One of them depicted Constantine the Great.

Clark paused to ready Sneak Peek.

Ray leaned in to read the nameplate, then slipped one hand behind the bust to give Constantine bunny ears. "Say, cheese," he said, posing for Clark.

Natalie exhaled sharply, caught between delight and disapproval. She cleared her throat to suppress the delight. "You're such a dope," she said to Ray. She thought to apologize to Murat for such a display of uncouthness, but Murat was grinning ear to ear. He motioned them down a paneled hallway to Ayhan's office. Her door was closed; he knocked softly. As they waited, Natalie could hear Ray and Clark still snickering about the bunny ears. She gave them a look that warned them not to embarrass her in front of Ayhan.

Murat knocked again. Natalie mentally reviewed the questions she'd written down for Ray to ask: What artifacts were taken from Constantinople during the Fourth Crusade? Describe the tunnel system built by the Byzantines. Could the true Dish of Christ be hidden somewhere beneath Istanbul? A distinct click interrupted her thoughts; the solid wood door slowly swung open. Ayhan stood before them, tall, regal, light crowning her raven hair. She wore a gray pencil skirt and red blouse buttoned loosely at the throat. Later, Ray would recall how Ayhan had looked at him—her eyes smoky and alluring, tinged with a hint of violet.

"I must apologize," she said breathlessly, "I was on the phone. I seem to be much sought after these days."

Natalie reached to shake Ayhan's hand, but Ayhan had already grasped Ray's. She held it longer than necessary and was so tall in her high heels, she could look him in the eyes. Her desk phone rang. "Ah. You see how it is." She smiled demurely. "Excuse me." She released Ray's hand and glided to her desk. He stared at her in wonder. Natalie, Clark, and Murat pushed into the office. When Ayhan answered her phone, she remained standing and spoke in Turkish.

Natalie set down her audio bag and scanned Ayhan's office. It was a little museum all on its own. Shelves lining two walls were jammed with pottery, porcelain, sculptures, and architectural fragments, all labeled with tags. On the wall nearest to her hung a picture of a bearded man in a white turban and red robes seated beneath a golden arch.

"The Conqueror," Murat said, "Fatih Sultan Mehmet."

"I think I've seen this before," Natalie said, examining it. There was writing on the golden arch, but it was in Arabic.

"Is—how you say?—a copy," Murat said. "Real one is in London—at National Gallery."

Ayhan hung up her phone and faced them. "Ah, Ms. Ashbrook, I see my assistant is giving you a tour."

"Yes. I saw this picture in London when I lived—"

"I have such plans for you," Ayhan said, peering at Ray. "How exciting it will be. You shall see." She bent over her desk to retrieve a piece of paper and an iPad. As she did so, her blouse, open at the neck, briefly exposed her cleavage.

"Dude," Clark whispered to Ray, "why didn't you tell me she was hot?"

"I didn't know."

"Like, she could be Kimber Grant's sister."

Natalie heard this. She'd expected Ayhan to be passably pretty based on the headshot of her on the museum website. But the black and white image hadn't done her justice; the full-bodied and full-colored Ayhan was strikingly beautiful. Natalie studied her critically and instantly detected that her eyelashes were false. She wondered if the roundness of her breasts was evidence of implants. Looking her up and down, she couldn't decide, and this irritated her, and the fact that Ayhan's skirt and blouse were undeniably chic.

"What do you mean by *plans*?" Natalie asked her. "We already have an itinerary."

Ayhan thrust a paper at her. "Oh, the interview, the tour of Hagia Sophia—that is all quite irrelevant now. Something astounding has happened. Believe me, this new itinerary will work out to our—er, I mean, to *your* advantage. You see, there has been a discovery. Did my assistant not tell you?"

"Discovery?" Ray practically shouted.

Ayhan handed him the iPad. "Yes. I did not lie when I told you that Istanbul is a treasure hunter's dream."

"You told *me* that," Natalie muttered from behind them.

"This treasure is of immense worth," Ayhan said to Ray. "It is beyond imagination. It is the fulfillment of—" but here her voice broke. She looked down as if all her words lay at her feet. When she looked back up, her eyes flashed with passion. "The fulfillment of many dreams!"

Ray's mouth fell open. He could only stare at her.

"Like, what is it?" Clark asked excitedly. He peered over Ray's shoulder to see the iPad; it displayed photographs.

"A shrine. I should say—*the* shrine," Ayhan answered eagerly. "You have heard of it, no doubt. You must have, given the nature of your film."

"The—the Shrine of the Four Keepers?" Natalie said incredulously, reading from Ayhan's itinerary. "How can this be? When did this happen? How long have you known?"

"My God," Ray exclaimed, flipping through photographs of the excavation site. "I can't believe what I'm seeing. This is freaking awesome!" He lingered over an image depicting the mosaic of Panikos the Youth. "Is he holding ... what I think he is?" Eyes wide, he looked at Ayhan.

She beamed at him and batted her lashes.

Ray blinked back at her; he couldn't speak.

Clark clapped Ray's shoulder. "Dude, the Dish!"

"The Dish?" Natalie spoke up. "It's at the shrine?"

Ayhan briefly cast her eyes down. "We—we are quite sure it is. Burke is sure—Professor Burke. He is leading the excavation. He expects to find it. At any moment—"

"Burke?" Natalie interrupted. "Adam Burke? He's here?"

Ayhan cocked her head. "You know him?"

"Not personally. We were gonna interview him for our film, but he canceled unexpectedly," Natalie said.

Ayhan laughed lightly. "Then you will enjoy your new itinerary, Ms. Ashbrook. I have an interview scheduled for you with the professor." Ayhan inhaled deeply as if gathering strength. "Adam Burke is the world's foremost Disher scholar, has discovered two icons connected to the search for the Dish. But, of course, you must know this already." She paced and gestured grandly as she continued: "And now, he has unearthed the most important archaeological find of the last century. This must be recorded for posterity. You must record it. And you will be able to do it so well, being experts yourselves. What a documentary you shall have! When the Dish is at last lifted from the pit, you shall be there. Only you. To make history with Burke. I am granting you exclusive access—to the excavation site, to the artifacts tent, the museum's processing lab, and of course, to me. In fact, I insist on accompanying you. At the shrine, you will need my expertise to know what is important to film and how to interpret what you see." She cleared her throat. "The altar in the apse, for instance. We might begin there. See page two of the itinerary. I have prepared questions for your interview with Burke. I assure you, these will elicit the most pertinent facts—for posterity. What do you say? Are you prepared for such an adventure?" Ayhan held out her hands toward them. Her smile showed her teeth.

Natalie narrowed her eyes. "What's the catch?"

Ray elbowed Natalie sharply.

"Ow! What? Doesn't it sound too good to be true?"

"That's not what I heard. Weren't you listening? Look!" Ray shoved the iPad under Natalie's nose so she could see the image of Panikos the Youth. "Seeing is believing. That's what I always say." Then to Ayhan: "When do we start?"

Ayhan laughed warmly. "You are all enthusiasm, Mr. Cozart. That is good. So am I. We can start as soon as you like."

Ray grinned. "Please, call me Ray."

Natalie peered but briefly at Panikos. The golden bowl he held aloft glittered and winked. She pushed the iPad aside to scan page two of Ayhan's itinerary. Her eyes fell on the questions Ayhan had prepared for them to ask Professor Burke: 1) Describe the importance of the altar. 2) Describe your plan for lifting the altar. 3) Describe your theory about the Dish being found under the altar ...

"Burke believes the Dish is under the altar?" she asked.

Ayhan blinked rapidly. "It is a mere supposition. But a strong one, nonetheless. The shrine is entirely exposed. It is the likeliest place for the Dish to have been buried."

"So, it isn't certain. He may find nothing," Natalie said. "Is there a timeframe for his search? We can't film forever."

Ayhan momentarily lost her poise. She spun toward the shelves behind her desk, brusquely instructing Murat to retrieve an artifact for her. He grasped a small copper bowl. "Such a skeptic, Ms. Ashbrook. Such questions," Ayhan said heatedly. Then, to disguise her impatience, she sighed. "But of course, I do not blame you. It is only human to suspect a snake lurking in paradise. And only a snake would promise a paradise without one." Murat handed Ayhan the bowl. "If you seek a guarantee that Burke will find the Dish, I cannot give it," she said to Natalie. "I can only give you hope. Have you never experienced a hope fulfilled, Ms. Ashbrook? Something you always desired that was granted unexpectedly? Changes in the world often bring about the very thing we have wanted to receive. Can you not imagine the scene?" She lifted the copper bowl near her head, posing like Panikos the Youth. "Burke triumphant, the Dish in hand at last!"

"I can imagine it," Ray said with a broad grin.

"So can my camera," Clark said.

Ayhan smiled coyly at them; she took Ray's hand and pressed the copper bowl into his palm. Her fingers caressed his as she released it. "Hold onto that. What we can imagine, the heart makes true," she murmured. "The Dish is the truth of history. That is what Professor Burke told me. I believe it. Do you?" She looked from Ray to Natalie.

Ray didn't answer. He was mesmerized.

Natalie's cheeks felt warm. What she believed was that Ayhan was flirting with Ray, and he was enjoying it. Talking with Ayhan over the phone, she'd never thought she'd be meeting a more exotic Staci. But that's who Ayhan was. Her exuberance, her false lashes, her touchy-feely familiarity—Staci had been just like that, activating Ray's desire in a way Natalie had never been able to, flaunting how easily a girl could do it if she used her body to her advantage. *Damn her.*

She resented Ayhan's sudden change of plans. It was just like Staci, slithering in to steal the show. Like the way she'd butted in on an interview at the premier of *Monica's Dress*. Natalie was answering a question about her creative process when Staci sidled up to Ray and put her arms around him. "Oh, who do we have here?" the journalist asked Staci, cutting Natalie off. "You look sorta familiar—have I seen you somewhere?" In reply, Staci giggled. "Possibly. Do you read GQ? I was in an ad—for Gucci's new cologne Eden." "That was you wrapped in the banana leaf?" the journalist gasped. "Yeah, it was, like, so annoying." Staci pouted. "My boobs are so big, they had to tape it on. It kept unwinding!"

"Ms. Ashbrook, what do you say?" Ayhan asked.

Natalie's mind was aflame, as if the heat from her cheeks had risen into her brain. Ayhan had cozied up so close to Ray, her breasts nearly grazed his arm. *What's going on? What's she after?* Natalie didn't know. She only knew that whatever Ayhan wanted, she was working hard to get it. *Ray's gonna fall for her act.*

Natalie had never so despised a film contributor. How idiotic to have imagined the woman to be a kindred spirit. Haughty with beauty, Ayhan just assumed others existed to do her bidding. *You can't have him. This isn't your story. I'm still here.* Later, when Ray demanded to know what the hell had gotten into her, Natalie would neglect to tell him how Ayhan caressing his hand had provoked her.

"Um, may I see the bowl?" she said to Ray with a smirk.

Ray handed it to her though his face betrayed misgiving.

"How interesting," Natalie said insincerely, rotating it in her hands. "What are these engravings?" she asked Ayhan.

"Signs of the zodiac. It is a bowl used for divination."

"Ah. What's this label?" Natalie lifted a loose white tag from the bowl's interior. It was written in Turkish.

"That is a summary of its provenance—a record of where and when it was found. All genuine artifacts have one."

Natalie dropped the tag back into the bowl and thrust it at Ayhan. "Very pretty. I guess this one's real then?"

Ayhan furrowed her brows. "Yes, of course it is." She passed the bowl to Murat to return it to the shelf.

"I'm surprised Ray didn't ask you if it was," Natalie went on. "This morning he told me he thinks museums, uh, make up stories about their artifacts. Pretend that some, oh, icon or something was stolen by Nazis and only just found."

"Now wait just a minute." Ray's eyes bored into Natalie.

"What? You said that's how museums pass fake stuff off as real. Like, oh, like that facsimile of the Sultan over there. You said you think half the artifacts in museums are fake."

"But I didn't mean—I didn't say—"

"Didn't say what?" Natalie arched her eyebrows.

"Whatever it is you're implying!"

"Oh, what? You didn't say you wanted to ask her—"

"No, I didn't," Ray said forcibly to cut Natalie off.

"—about the Andrei Rublev icon?"

Ray glanced at Ayhan guiltily.

Ayhan crossed her arms over her breasts. "Is this what you think of our museum, Mr. Cozart?"

Ray tried to laugh. "I was merely describing some show I'd seen—a late night show." He elbowed Clark, inviting him to corroborate this story. "You don't think I really—"

"I do not know what to think," Ayhan interrupted. Her eyes were darkly fierce. "Have you come here to make accusations? Is this your design? To use your camera to entrap me?" She eyed Sneak Peek suspiciously.

"Not at all! I—I love museums. They're awesome. Especially this one. Really!" Ray pleaded, trying to appease.

His attempt outraged Ayhan even more. "You scoff at this institution? At the work I do? You disparage my reputation? I have not gotten where I am by—by playing games."

"Of course not. No one thinks that. Natalie's just being—I mean, this is all just a misunderstanding."

The cell phone on Ayhan's desk vibrated. She motioned for Murat, who was slinking out of the office. "You! Over here!" Ayhan commanded him.

Murat stepped forward nervously.

"Get these salaklar out of my sight. Let them be fools. Let them make their film without me. Without Professor Burke." She picked up her phone and sat in her desk chair, swiveling it so that her back was to Ray, Natalie, and Clark.

In silence, the three picked up their equipment bags and filed out. Murat ushered them into the hall. As Ayhan's office door shut with a firm click, Natalie looked at Ray, Ray looked back at the door, and Clark turned off the camera.

Scene 21

## Adventure Is My Destiny

*Hartsfield-Jackson International Airport*

*Atlanta, Georgia*

*Friday, March 12, moments after fleeing Corporate*

Upon fleeing Whitaker Corporate Headquarters, Jane drove straight to the airport even though her flight to Colombia wasn't until that evening. After the revelation of her Nana's betrayal, she just couldn't—wouldn't—go back to Whiningham. Ever. Thus, when she parked her Range Rover in the long-term lot, she emptied the contents of the glove box into her carry-on bag, fished under the seats for treasures, and removed the locket containing Baby Girl's picture from the rearview mirror. The keys to the Rover she dropped into a trash bin on her way to the terminal.

At an airport restaurant, the Echo Mediterranean, Jane plopped herself at the bar, ordered an array of cured meats and cheeses, and requested the bartender's choice. "Something tart," she told him, "and a little boozy."

Baby Girl sat whimpering in Jane's lap, having fruitlessly attempted to nuzzle up a nest for itself among the folds of her kimono. Napping was out of the question. Its paws couldn't gain any traction; the shimmery fabric was too slippery. The little dog was agitated. In the airport parking lot, Jane had dropped it into its Comfy-Go Pet Tote like a grapefruit into a sack. At airport baggage check, she'd swung the tote as if the thing were a broom, then tipped Baby Girl out onto its nose at security, and all this in the presence of a K9 police dog, a Dutch Shepherd, a breed sufficiently sized to escape suffering such indignities itself.

From her carry-on, Jane retrieved a box of Teeny Treats. She calmed Baby Girl with a constant stream of them.

The Echo wasn't particularly crowded. An elderly man sat several seats down from Jane at the bar, watching one of two TV screens above. Jane wasn't looking at the TVs or anyone else, but at her phone.

"Like, I just can't believe this. I mean, like, *Jane!*"

"I know, I know!"

"Wait 'til I tell Dominick. He'll be like, wow. I mean, who knew your Nana was secretly working for the Pope?"

"I can't go back, Meena. I can't. They must know all about me, like where I'm gonna be and stuff. I bet my bedroom is bugged, my Rover—everything. I threw the keys away. So they can't trace me."

Since last checking in with Jane, Meena and Roxy had left their hotel, removing to a location neither would disclose, but Meena assured Jane they'd take her there once she arrived with the portable shower. Jane could hear ominous drumbeats. A beaded curtain swung in the background behind Meena's head. Roxy's eyes and lips appeared on screen now and then. She sipped a peach-colored cocktail.

"Omigod, your graduation gift," Meena exclaimed.

"What could I do? If I have to make the sacrifice—"

"You're so strong!" Roxy shouted.

"—then I have to make it. 'Cause the key's where they put tracers. It's literally the easiest thing. Like what happened to Bucky. That's how they found Lady Xenia's castle. I've read enough books to know."

"What about your little ragdoll?" Meena asked. "I mean, if they're listening …"

"Omigod!" Quickly, Jane frisked Baby Girl. "I don't see a bug, unless it's somehow embedded in the collar."

"Just be safe, Jane, and throw it away," Roxy shouted.

"But I need the ESA tag, or she can't go places with me."

The bartender set before Jane her drink and appetizer.

After the bartender had stepped away, Jane groaned, "Like, this is literally so unreal. All this time, my Nana—a closet Catholic. I should probably go back to that place in Moscow. 'Cause if Nana had me arrested, think how close I must've been to finding the Dish. And that whole thing with Dr. Carlisle … it's like this intricately woven web of lies." She tried to lower her voice, glancing furtively at the bartender. "The Catholic Church is, like, everywhere. It makes you wonder who you can trust. Anybody could be a spy."

"You'll be safe here with us, Jane. We're nowhere near a church," Roxy announced.

Jane took a sip of her drink. "Y'know what? If there's one thing I've learned, it's that when you stand up for the truth, you're gonna suffer. Maybe the Rover is just the beginning. Look what they did to Leonardo da Vinci and Benjamin Franklin. Or Steve Finder! You become a target for powerful forces. They try to shut you up, so you'll be, like, too scared to say anything. Which means people just stay deceived because good people do nothing. But I don't care. I'm gonna keep Dishing. It's my cause, and I'm not changing it, even if that means I gotta, y'know, lay low for a while, or maybe—" she hesitated, about to say, *stop being Jane Whitaker*. But she didn't say it.

"We'll miss you, Jane!" Roxy yelled.

Meena pulled Roxy's hair. "Shut it, bitch. That's my ear."

Roxy swayed and hiccoughed.

"You drunk?" Meena flicked Roxy's forehead.

"Ow! Quit it!" Roxy giggled and swiped at Meena's hand.

Meena laughed and shoved Roxy aside. Turning to Jane, however, her voice grew serious. "Look, Jane, I hear you, I do. But, like, think about what you're saying."

"Like, what?"

"Well, like you said, if you've literally become so important to be targeted for what you believe in, then what are they gonna come after next?"

Jane thought for a moment. "Baby Girl?"

"No, bitch. Your money! Who holds your purse strings?"

Jane's eyes widened. "Omigod! Nana!"

"Totally. See? You gotta play this cool, 'cause, like, what about RATS?"

"Like, what?"

"Think about it. If suddenly you don't have money ..."
"Oh. I'm not RATS."
"Exactly."

Jane took another sip of her drink, longer this time. For a second, she contemplated the peculiar tragedy that was her Aunt Leenie, peculiar because of all the rich people Jane knew, her aunt was the only one who was truly ugly. She was far too fat to enjoy being rich at all in Jane's estimation. But did Jane really want the opposite to be true of her? To be totally sexy—but poor? These were deep questions.

In the brief interim of Jane's silent analysis, Meena and Roxy had reconciled. They hung about each other's necks, singing. Meena took the last gulp of Roxy's drink. "Face it, Jane," she said, "RATS is your brand. And it totally kicks ass to live off the success of others. It's not worth the sacrifice."

Jane giggled at the spectacle of her friends and nibbled a piece of cheese. Then something on the TV above her caught her eye. It was a CNN report. There was no sound, only captioning: AND IF IT IS THE LEGENDARY SHRINE OF THE FOUR KEEPERS, THEN YOU CAN BE SURE THE CONTROVERSY HAS ONLY JUST BEGUN.

Jane held her cheese in mid-air.

I'M NEHIR SADIK, REPORTING FROM ISTANBUL.

Jane had only just caught the last lines of captioning when the scene shifted back to the news studio. She waved over the bartender and asked him if he'd seen the report.

He was very sorry. He hadn't. Was she okay? Did she need another drink?

She did. And sparkling water in a bowl. For Baby Girl.

"Jane, like, what's going on?" Meena asked.

"I dunno. Something. I gotta go."

"Hey, like, remember what I said—"

"I will. I gotta go."

"—it's not worth the sacrifice!"

Jane consulted her oracle *TrueDishers.net*. If she had just seen a report about a discovery connected to the Last Supper Dish, then her favorite blogger Jimi Bowler would confirm it. A link at the top of his page made her gasp. It was a story from *Today's Zaman*: BYZANTINE SHRINE DISCOVERY DELAYS METRO PROJECT.

March 11, 2010, Fatih District, Istanbul

City officials confirmed Thursday that work on the Marmara Metro has been suspended due to the discovery of a Byzantine shrine beneath the former Sirkeci Rail Station.

A statement released by Mr. Ahmet Öztürk, director of the Ministry of Culture and Tourism, explains that the Istanbul Museum of Ancient History is overseeing the shrine's excavation. "We are employing the speediest means to preserve our cultural heritage while not neglecting our duty to our future," said Öztürk.

In a telephone interview with Today's Zaman, Dr. Zainab Ayhan, curator of the Museum of Ancient History, stated that preservation of the shrine will require its relocation whole or in part to the museum grounds. "We have called for the assistance of the greater archaeological community to help us make this delicate transition."

Dr. Ayhan also said that the shrine is the most significant artifact unearthed in the city during her seven-year tenure as curator. "The nature of this find will make it of value to all."

Further details about the shrine were not forthcoming, but Dr. Adam Burke, the excavation's principle investigator and professor of archaeology at the University of Pittsburgh in the United States, revealed in a press conference on Thursday that the shrine holds four mosaics in the likenesses of Greek Orthodox saints, Kostas, Zoticus, Panikos, and Nil. Collectively known as the Four Keepers, these saints are believed by many Orthodox to have possessed a Christian holy relic, a supper dish allegedly once belonging to Jesus Christ.

"Without question this is the shrine of the Four Keepers. Its discovery will permanently alter the religious landscape," said Burke. "We must delay construction on the subway until all possible artifacts have been safely recovered."

Not all welcome the Metro Project's delay. Istanbul's Rail Bureau Chief Mr. Feredun Pasa confirmed that construction of the subway is four years behind schedule and 6.5 billion dollars over budget. Further delay could cost the city millions. "It's Istanbul. You dig a hole in the ground, and this is what happens," said Pasa. "If we had to suspend work for every clay pot found, nothing would get built in this city."

As Jane read, she kept mouthing "omigod, omigod." Her second time through the story, she squealed and jumped up from the stool, catching Baby Girl in her arms. "The Dish, Pookums!" Baby Girl hung in the air awkwardly, its hind legs dangling. The over-fed dog appeared ready to barf. Hurriedly, Jane collected her carry-on bag and Baby Girl's tote. But after rushing toward the door, she stopped and returned to her seat at the bar.

The bartender stared at her, mystified.

Jane unzipped her carry-on. Slowly, she lifted out something cold and weighty. It was a bit tangled. When she'd left Corporate with it in her hand, she'd tossed it onto the passenger seat of her Rover to hasten her escape. But now, she methodically smoothed the rows of dangling diamonds, and with a sly grin, set the band on her head.

The bartender stood by, studying her curiously. "What's your final destination?"

Jane beamed, forgetting her former caution about Catholic spies. "Istanbul!"

"Ah. Have you ever been?"

"No, it's my first time."

"It'll be a great adventure, I'm sure. There's nothing like it—Istanbul, I mean. A fabulous city. A city of dreams. You'll uh, you'll fit right in."

Jane giggled and tossed her hair over her shoulder. "Oh, I know I will. I'm Lady Jane. Adventure is my destiny."

After Jane and Baby Girl had gone, the elderly man who'd been sitting at the bar several seats down from her motioned to the bartender. "Was she drunk?" He jerked his thumb toward where Jane had been sitting.

The bartender laughed. "I don't think so."

"You mean that was just ...?" He threw up his hands, not knowing how to classify everything he'd just heard.

"Just who she is, I guess," the bartender replied, catching the man's drift.

"Hmph," the man grunted, "that's a shame."

Scene 22

# Scruuuum!

*Hotel Amir, Old Town Istanbul*

*Saturday, March 13*

"Dear Dr. Ayhan, please don't be upset I got your private cell number. I can't rest until I make things right. I'd never think of offending you, and certainly wouldn't make accusations. I don't know what happened. I did tell Natalie about a show where a reporter exposed a fraud at some third-rate museum. I'm sure it was in South America. Something to do with the Incas. Not icons! Natalie must've misheard me. You're a consummate professional and a true pioneer for women being the first female curator of the Ancient History Museum. Believe me, you have my utmost respect. Your passion for your work is obvious, and I feel privileged that you shared the news of Burke's discovery with us. Your trust in us to film a true historical event is very humbling. I hope I can earn your trust again. Sincerely, Ray Cozart"

"Mr. Cozart, thank you for reaching out to me. I regret our misunderstanding. Perhaps I was hasty in my judgment. The stress lately has made me sensitive to criticism. I can tell you it is possible to earn my trust. It is very simple. Follow my itinerary. Can you do that? If not, then even though I require expert filmmaking to document this discovery, I shall have to look elsewhere. Sincerely, Zainab"

"Zainab, very happy to hear from you. Yes, if that's what it takes, we'll follow your itinerary. You have my word. We could begin tonight. Is it too late for us to film the opening ceremony for the new exhibition?"

"Mr. Cozart, no, it is not too late. It is on my itinerary, so you ought to be here. Burke will be giving a speech. I shall introduce you. Oh, and I do have a favor to ask. We can discuss the matter when you arrive. It is a very small thing. I am sending Murat for you at this moment."

Natalie slammed Ray's cell phone onto the countertop. The two of them sat on stools at the Hotel Amir bar. Ray had searched the hotel to find her. Clark was off gathering their equipment. The bar was crowded. It was Happy Hour. But Natalie sipped only seltzer water.
"You make such a promise without asking for my input, and you expect me to be happy," she said angrily.
"That's right," Ray said. "And you know why? 'Cause that was a masterful piece of work I had to fix. When you wanna blow up something, you really blow it up. Like, to smithereens! I had to use tactics. Getting her cell number was Clark's idea. Murat gave it to us." Ray rubbed his chin. "We'll, uh, have to put him in the film. No biggie."

## SCRUUUUM!

"What? How're we gonna do that? What's he gonna contribute to the story exactly?"

"Well, the story's changed, hasn't it? Look, we can always edit him out in postproduction. He just wants to see himself on camera, pretend he's a movie star. Clark will film him. That was the deal. It was the only way."

The bartender interrupted. Could he get the gentleman a beer? An Efes Blonde, perhaps? Or did he prefer Dark?

Ray waved him off.

"I'm not subjecting myself to that woman's itinerary," Natalie spat when the bartender had gone. "She has no idea how to make a film."

"We don't have a choice. It's her plan or nothing. It'll be an adventure. Mostly, we'll be at the excavation site—"

"Do you realize you've just sacrificed our creative control? That woman has an agenda. I don't trust her at all. And what's this favor? That could be anything."

Ray smirked. "Probably she wants you to apologize."

Natalie scoffed at that. "No way. She can be mad at me forever. I don't care."

"But it's for the film. You wanna save it don't you?"

"Did you tell Reggie about our sudden change of plans?"

"Yeah, he said it sounded like material for a blockbuster. Urged me to go for it. Couldn't believe Burke is in Istanbul. Said that was huge. He assumed you saw the potential."

"So, I'm the only one not consulted, I guess."

Ray cocked his head. "Look, what do you want me to say? I'm tired of defending myself. I shouldn't have to.

You can't turn this around on me. I didn't make her mad. You did that. It wasn't my fault. I had to say whatever was necessary to get us back in the game. You should thank me for my diplomatic efforts." His voice was sharp with sarcasm. "I still can't believe what happened. You plan all the interview questions for Zainab yourself—"

"You're on a first-name basis with her now, I see."

"—demand I follow your script, and then we get in there, and you suddenly go off about Nazis and forgeries, the very subjects you didn't want me to bring up." He stared at her wide-eyed, waiting for an explanation. When none was offered, he added: "Why'd you have to provoke her?"

Natalie rolled her eyes. "I told you yesterday. I was trying to get to the truth of things. They were fair questions. Who knew she'd take 'em so personally? The woman is a total diva. She overreacted."

"But you were so eager to meet her."

"And you weren't. She practically pawed you the whole time we were in her office. Guess she changed your mind."

"That's absurd. She was excited about the discovery. It's like you didn't even hear what she was saying. Don't you realize she handed us the filmmaking chance of a lifetime? Dropped it right in our laps. Dish Movie! My God, up until now, we've been filming ancient history. Dead and buried. We can't even think of a new title for it. But now? Now we can film the very second the Dish is lifted from the shrine. We can make history. Things were just starting to get exciting. Is it so much to ask for you to be happy about that?"

"I am, okay?"

"Well, you could've fooled me. This saves us. It's everything we need. A dream come true. It's the Dish! Professor Burke, the Golden Boy himself! You know how important he is. You said so yourself. But then you go and sabotage the whole thing. I mean, what the hell got into you?" Ray leaned forward and eyed Natalie's face intently, for though he'd asked her this question several times since they were booted from Ayhan's office, he had yet to hear an answer from her that satisfied him.

Natalie set her jaw and averted her eyes.

"You're not gonna tell me?" he pressed.

"I already did," she said crisply. "I sensed the woman was up to something, okay? I see things about people. It's an intuition. I can't help it."

Ray snorted in exasperation. He grabbed his phone and jammed it into his jacket pocket. "Right. I forgot. You're so smart. You know everybody's secrets. And I'm an idiot." He stood. Clark was at the bar entrance, waving them toward the lobby. Murat had arrived. Ray made a show of politely waiting for Natalie to step around the tables ahead of him, and then he fell in behind. She was wearing a skirt and high-heeled boots. Her hair was up, and her soft sweater moved in seamless coordination with her shoulder blades. For a second Ray regretted their argument, for he might've been able to tell her how pretty she looked.

When they reached Clark and Murat, Natalie didn't speak. Ray could've predicted this. Natalie always clammed up when she lost an argument. She was wrong about Zainab Ayhan. Zainab was a woman of spirit and passion, a great visionary, just like himself. She was the kind of woman destiny plucked from the myriad of the hopeful, crowning them with that uncommon charisma which is the mark of all true greatness. Of this, he was sure.

Murat greeted Ray with a fist bump like they were best buds. Imagining himself on the verge of stardom had made him cocky. He winked at Natalie. "You mess up, but I score big." He directed Ray to sit in the front seat of the van. They were going to take "a little tour" through his neighborhood. He'd already texted all his friends about appearing in a big Hollywood movie. He wanted Ray to smile and wave.

"Edit him out, eh? Good luck with that," Natalie hissed in Ray's ear. She'd leaned forward in her seat; Ray could smell her perfume, sweet but muted, like flowers and ashes. He didn't have to turn his head to know her green eyes were boring into his brain. Her voice cut into him as if it came from on high, a divine decree. It angered him to know she was judging him, the whole situation, and finding fault. *Why can't she just be happy I fixed it? It was her mess. Why does she always have to find something wrong?*

As Murat weaved through his narrow neighborhood streets, Ray felt the houses closing in on him. The front seat of the van felt as constricted as the four corners of a confessional. He couldn't escape Natalie's gaze; he was stuck. Her eyes were like Father Stanley's from behind the lattice—near and far at once, intense but distant. They probed his secrets, even ones he didn't know he had. But they shared none. He'd never quite understood her. He asked Murat if he could smoke a cigarette.

"Ra-ay, I thought you gave that up," Natalie complained.
"Yeah, I did ... for a while."
"Well, crack open the window, would ya?"
"I am, I am. I'm not an idiot."

The cigarette acted as in instant barrier. It gave his hands something to do, his eyes a place to focus. He'd never liked to look in Natalie's eyes. Lovely as they were, looking at them too long had always pained him. He didn't know if the pain was in him or in her. But her eyes activated it.

He thought of a day when he'd not felt the pain—back in film school. Natalie had come to his apartment to study for an exam and had fallen asleep in his puffy recliner: "Nat, are you awake?" he whispered from the sofa. He could hear her breathing. Long inhales, slow exhales, not fast and short like his own breaths. He thought something might be wrong with her and tiptoed over to see. But there wasn't anything wrong. She was just curled up asleep like a little girl, her hair in a ponytail and her book fallen closed on her fingers. He'd never seen her look that way. Asleep, she was unlike herself—simple and vulnerable, the epitome of trust.

For minutes Ray didn't move. No girl had ever fallen asleep in his presence. He was witnessing a little miracle. Without his knowing exactly when or how, something between him and Natalie had changed. What did it mean? He listened to her breathe, tried to pace his breath with hers. Couldn't do it. Got lightheaded. He wanted to kiss her. He'd have to bend down—no, the way she was curled, he could easily lift her, hold her close to his chest. That'd be better.

But he didn't kiss her. Didn't even touch her. He just stood above her, taking her all in. For the first time since he'd met her, he felt totally free and at ease in her presence. *She can't see into me.* In that moment, whatever was painful between them suddenly didn't exist. Because her eyes were closed, the shadow that always lurked near couldn't invade their space; it had no windows by which to enter.

Ray shut the door on the shadow even more—to preserve the peace, protect it. He covered Natalie with a blanket. *Now I can't see her. That's fair.* An hour later when she appeared at the door of his bedroom, he was sincerely flummoxed. He'd almost forgotten she was there. Putting the blanket over her had snuffed her out; in his mind, she was already gone. Yet here she was at his threshold, taking it all in. His bedroom was dark, but her eyes were like stadium lights, illuminating the whole playing field. He felt self-conscious, tongue-tied. The peace fled. He didn't like her looking over his shoulder at his Lara Croft video game. He stood and put his hands on his hips to obscure her view.

When she said goodbye soon after, he felt a mixture of relief and regret at being left alone. He reanimated his video game but couldn't regain the same pleasure. He shut it off.

Murat's "little tour" turned into a forty-five-minute delay. By the time he parked the van at the Museum of Ancient History, guests for the opening ceremony were already arriving. Ray threw open his door and jumped out. Natalie hurriedly gathered her audio equipment, and Clark carried Sneak Peek. Because they'd be filming a crowd,

Ray took a second camera. As they climbed the front steps, Clark said to Ray, "Dude's gonna be a pain in the ass." He flicked his eyes in the direction of Murat. "Cause he knows we owe him." This observation irritated Ray. *You know who owes me? Natalie.* He didn't say this, however, but replied, "Yeah, well, I said he could be in the film, I didn't say he could stay in. Maybe I'll have a talk with him about the power of the delete key." Clark arched an eyebrow. "Right. That'll teach him. You have such a way with words." Ray's eyes narrowed; he didn't like Clark's irony.

The museum vestibule was crowded. Ayhan was nowhere to be seen. Two hundred folding chairs were set up, a hundred to a side with an aisle in the middle. Orthodox clergymen filled the left front rows. Clark stationed himself with Sneak Peek centerstage next to a TV crew from CNN-Turk. Dignitaries would speak during the ceremony, among them the Director of the Ministry of Culture and Tourism Ahmet Öztürk, as well as the Ecumenical Patriarch, His All Holiness Philotheos. Ray set up his camera stage right to film the audience. As he looked through the lens, he saw Catholic priests file into the front seats near him, their voices resonating. He peered up at the arched ceiling and asked Natalie if she'd be able to compensate for the echo.

But that wasn't what he really wanted to ask her. He had something to say. He couldn't quite find the words. His history with Natalie, their recent conversations, and the circumstances with Zainab Ayhan had coalesced to form a powerful impression in his mind. But it was more of an overwhelming feeling than a thought, what Natalie might call an intuition. *She's hiding something from me.*

Natalie went to get a chair. Ray studied her closely, searching for evidence to substantiate his new belief. He thought again of her asleep in his apartment. Where had she gone after she'd left that night? She'd vanished from campus for two weeks. It was unlike her to miss class. He'd started to worry. Had he said something wrong? Unexpectedly, this woman who was fast becoming his best friend couldn't be found. Why had she disappeared? He'd never gotten an explanation. In fact, she denied that she'd been gone at all. "Oh, don't be stupid. I've been around. You just didn't see me." Ray's head hurt. Natalie's denial couldn't have been true. He would've seen her on campus if she'd been there; he'd been looking for her. His intuition sharpened. *She's been hiding things from me for years.*

Natalie returned with a chair; she unfolded it near Ray's camera and sat down. Watching her, Ray felt he'd suddenly gained Superman's power of X-ray vision. He saw into her eyes like they were all pupils, just gaping holes. What he saw in her was a dark void, like a part of her was dimly lit.

Natalie felt his hovering stare and looked up. "What?"

"Nothing," he mumbled on instinct.

Natalie shrugged and reached to put on her headset.

Ray touched her arm. "Wait."

She flinched and leaned away. "Ra-ay, it's about to start."

"I know."

She lowered her headset and looked up at him, a question in her eyes. He steadily held her gaze. She looked away.

Ray swallowed hard. His throat was very dry. He tried to find words to speak his intuition. "Look, uh, did Zainab tell you something over the phone? Y'know, something that made you skeptical of her from the start?"

"Huh? No, she—"

"Did she say anything you're not telling me?"

"No, I told you everything. I mean, everything she said. What I could remember. Why do you—"

"Nat, listen," he dropped his voice, "is—is there something you're not telling me?"

Natalie didn't look up at him. She bit her lower lip.

Ray observed this. Her hesitation made him both nervous and eager. It proved his intuition; he wanted to be right. *What's her secret?* As soon as he thought this, he perceived that he already knew. Reggie had told him: *She misses you. She needs you. She knows she was wrong.* Ray's lips curled in satisfaction. The scene before him was almost how he'd imagined it'd be—Natalie at his feet begging to be loved. And how much the better that they weren't alone, that so many people would witness his triumph. He tapped his camera, thought of angling it toward her but didn't. His eyes narrowed, focusing on the top of her head.

*Time to rip the cover off.*

"Hey, listen," he said, trying to sound sympathetic, "you don't need to say anything. I get it. I mean, you're right, in a way. Zainab was flirting with me. Pawing me, you said. And you didn't like it. You, uh, you were jealous. Because, y'know, when you left, all this time, you've missed me." At the end of this speech, he worked hard not to smile.

Natalie jerked her head up, her eyes flashing. "Just like you were jealous of Steve showing me his bedroom, I guess. Because without me, you've been so lost and heartsick."

Ray's jaw tightened. He felt his X-ray vision get fuzzy, as if Natalie's eyes were lead. He couldn't see through them, must've imagined the darkness. Her eyes were green like they always were and peering up at him fiercely. He felt trapped, tricked. Natalie's retort had exposed the hole in his strategy. He lashed out. "Don't play tit-for-tat."

"Don't say stupid things." She lifted her headset.

He held it down. "It wasn't stupid. You always use that word about me."

"Lower your voice. People can hear you."

"*You* don't."

"Look, obviously you have something you need to say to me," she huffed. "So, go ahead and say it. I'm listening."

Ray exhaled sharply, angry and confounded. "How the hell do you—? Why do you do that? Turn things around on me? Think you know so much. You got everybody figured out. Can tell people what's wrong with 'em, and if you can't find anything wrong, you'll use your imagination. But you never look in the mirror. You know what I think? I think you can't bear the idea of being happy. Nothing is ever good enough for you. Who the hell can win with you? You like everything to be wrong—and me most of all."

Natalie bristled. "Oh, you know how to win. I've experienced you winning before. You're a very good player. Quite skilled. From all your rehearsals with Staci, I guess. A riveting performance, truly. You almost had me convinced."

Just then Ayhan emerged from the hall that led to her office. She wore a trim gray skirt and jacket with a red and white scarf strategically draped about her shoulders, partially obscuring what would've been a plunging neckline. Several dignitaries accompanied her down the center aisle.

Natalie put on her headset.

Ray fumbled with his camera to film the procession. In his haste, he zoomed in too far on Ayhan's breasts. And then to spite Natalie, he zoomed in further as Ayhan climbed the stage and took the podium. *She'll love this footage. Take that!*

"Distinguished guests," Ayhan began. Her voice made Ray's ears throb, as if he'd just picked up the tune again to a long-cherished song. His thoughts were all jumbled. He saw images of himself with Staci at the beach, and then Natalie in his arms at the studio. *You almost had me convinced.* What did she mean? He felt exposed, unprotected. Why did Natalie have to mention Staci? Staci had nothing to do with it.

Ayhan was nearly through her opening remarks. She spoke with such energy. Listening to her, Ray felt his hands get clammy. Somehow, her voice soothed and reassured him. He thought of them standing close together by her desk scanning the photos of the mosaic of Panikos the Youth. Her eyes had winked at him like the bits of broken glass, as if his dreams of adventure occupied a special place in her mind. Thinking of how Natalie had almost cut him off from having his dreams fulfilled refueled his anger. *She was jealous. I know she was. I'll make sure she stays jealous too.*

▼ ▼ ▼ ▼

Anthimos, Archbishop of Chalcedon and member of the Secret Order of Andronicus, sat amid his Orthodox brethren. Next to him were other members of the Secret Order—Leronymos, Archbishop of Italy, on his left, and Gabriel, the Patriarch's secretary, on his right. In the row directly in front of Anthimos sat Professor Papadopoulos, leaning forward with both hands on his cane. All during Ayhan's opening remarks, Anthimos sat with his arms crossed. He fiddled with his double-headed eagle pendant, the eagle's ruby eyes winking up at him.

Earlier with unconcealed disdain, he'd watched representatives of the Catholic Church file into the row across the aisle. Among them he recognized the Director of the Holy See Press Office, the young and charismatic Frederico D'Angelo, as well as Bishop Louis Fortier, Apostolic Vicariate of Istanbul and quintessential French snob. Another man, quite elderly and a cardinal given the scarlet piping on his robes, Anthimos didn't know. Nor did he wish to. But Lerry had leaned over and whispered, "That's Eduardo Donizetti, President of the Pontifical Council for Promoting Christian Unity. He was at Boniface's secret meeting. So was Fortier and D'Angelo. What are they all doing here?"

Anthimos had sat silently pondering the answer to this question. "Christian unity. Bah! This exhibition ought to be called Stealing From Byzantium," he said to Gabriel in Greek, loud enough for a few other of his brethren to hear.

"Your Eminence," Gabriel whispered, "if I may be so bold to say—although some people here may not understand your Greek, your scowl speaks in all languages."

Ayhan finished introducing Philotheos. Anthimos didn't applaud with everyone else when Philotheos in his black robe and kamilavka stepped toward the podium. About his neck, his golden Chi-Rho medallion flashed in the spotlight. Anthimos looked for Adam Burke.

"Which one is our man?" he asked Gabriel.

"The one on the far right—that is the professor."

Anthimos nudged Lerry and gestured at Burke.

Lerry raised his eyebrows and nodded.

In front of them, Papi shifted his cane in his hands.

None of the members of the Secret Order had planned to attend the ceremony except for Gabriel, who went everywhere Philotheos did. Public gestures of unity between East and West could be sabotaged from afar as they always were; the Order excelled at it. But the discovery of the Shrine of the Four Keepers had upset their usual strategies. Philotheos had urged the Order to select members who would attend, insisting that relying on Papi's student Giulio for the information they needed was far too risky given what was now at stake. They needed to know if Burke had found the prodokleis—from Burke himself.

"It is a foolhardy plan," Anthimos said to Gabriel.

"Now is not the time, Your Eminence."

"But you must admit—a heist? Bah! The three monks could hardly get a computer to work, and yet we expect—"

## THE DIE IS CAST

"It is the will of the Order."

"The vote was not convincing."

"Nevertheless, the measure passed."

"I know you cannot openly oppose the Patriarch. But tell me, privately—"

"My private thoughts could be of no interest to you. Let us look to our own work and let the monks do theirs. We are here to make artful inquiries as the Patriarch has instructed." Before Anthimos could reply, Gabriel cut in. "Please, Your Eminence, His All Holiness is about to speak."

"Thank you, Dr. Ayhan, for that kind introduction," Philotheos began. "Distinguished guests, I cannot tell you what a joy it is to be invited to open this exhibition celebrating the abiding influence of Byzantine culture. I want to welcome from Venice Cardinal Eduardo Donizetti. Dr. Ayhan has informed me that this exhibition would not have been possible without the generous contributions of the Galleria dell'Accademia." Philotheos gestured toward Eduardo. "My brother, you represent many who have pursued unity between East and West. Your presence underscores how momentous this exhibition is for Orthodox and Catholics alike. It reminds us that the spiritual unity we seek has already been achieved materially through our art and our sacred objects. In these things East and West already agree." Philotheos touched the medallion about his neck. "We pray nothing will hinder our further agreement."

At these words, Anthimos almost leaped out of his seat. "Outrageous," he hissed to Gabriel. "He prostrates himself before a mere cardinal from Venice. The very city that plundered our great Empire."

## SCRUUUUM!

"Your Eminence," Gabriel whispered, "we must trust that in his pleas for peace and understanding, His All Holiness has at heart the best interests of all Orthodox."

"You say that only because you wrote that drivel for him," Anthimos said. He could hardly endure to hear Philotheos continue.

"... and the exhibition's title is quite apt, for it bears a dual meaning. On one hand Sailing to Byzantium is a poem by the Irishman W.B. Yeats, and it illustrates the legacy that the exhibition celebrates. The directionality implied is from East to West. A searching, gray-haired poet in twentieth-century Dublin is inspired by an idea of spiritual renewal. His inspiration is from the East. Constantinople, that shining city, has come to him. But Sailing to Byzantium also indicates the reverse direction—West to East. And in the history of our city this directionality has been just as essential. As Yeats writes— And therefore I have sailed the seas and come to the holy city of Byzantium. Indeed, all Europe came. Why did they come?"

"They were jealous," Anthimos declared, nudging Lerry.

"Did they come because of our literature, our learning, our government? Or did they come because of our religion? Hear this famous description of Hagia Sophia, Church of the Holy Wisdom—Although the sun shines upon her, the radiant glow within her is her own. Yes, I tell you, they came from the West because in an age of darkness, Constantinople was a city of Light."

"Only darkness arises from the West. It was true then and is still true." Anthimos pronounced this aphorism to no one in particular. "Does the Order have no veto power over these speeches? It is embarrassing—all this conciliatory, bipartisan rhetoric and whitewashing of the past."

"Perhaps next meeting we ought to bring the matter to a vote," Lerry said.

They were hushed by Papi. "Quiet, you two," he said, turning his head, "His All Holiness quotes from Procopius, the great historian, from the Buildings of Justinian."

Anthimos leaned forward and nudged the white-haired professor. "I know you, Papi," he whispered, "I know you want to restore the Legacy as much as I do. You cannot sit here pretending to be grateful to these Latin hypocrites."

"Restore the Legacy?" Papi smiled wryly. "I have sworn to protect it—as have you."

"And what about him?" Anthimos pointed at Philotheos. "Has he not also sworn? And yet he talks more and more as if he would betray the Legacy, do you not think so?"

Papi weighed his words carefully. He was used to Anthimos's provocations and as an academic had long ago learned that the safest course of action was to recognize the merits of all opinions. Since becoming a member of the Secret Order, his academic training had served him well. "We must allow that each man has his own means of oath-keeping."

"Bah!" Anthimos, fuming, leaned back in his seat and ran his hand over his silver and black beard to calm himself.

Philotheos was wrapping up his speech: "Tonight we rejoice that the Light still shines. It has drawn us to the shores of Byzantium once more, and we behold its glory.

It gives me great pleasure to declare the Istanbul Museum of Ancient History's exhibition Sailing to Byzantium now open."

During the applause, Anthimos hissed in Papi's ear, "Listen, old man, do you want to make history with me, or do you merely want to study history?"

Papi rolled his eyes, but when he turned his head away from Anthimos, he frowned thoughtfully and spun his cane in his fingers, studying its sculpted ivory top.

▼ ▼ ▼ ▼

Adam Burke hadn't heard most of the Patriarch's speech. His mind rushed ahead to the day when a certain pompous Oxford professor would pick up the latest issue of *Afar*. How Winters would rage with jealousy upon seeing Burke's smiling face on the cover—and the centerfold. He'd just gotten an email from the reporter *Afar* had sent to his presser. The magazine would print full-color pictures of the shrine (and maps and graphs) in a special fold-out section.

Being on the cusp of rendering Winters's scholarly opus irrelevant filled Burke with glee. For twenty years he'd endured that man's pontificating. Soon no academic would think to consult Winters's worthless tome, *Mysteries of the Late Byzantine Empire*. Because the greatest mystery of the Empire would be solved. The Vatican would be brought to its knees. Dishers the world over would be vindicated.

Regrettably, Burke couldn't fully give himself over to these imaginings. As soon as he tried to do so, brute reality clawed at them, shredding his hopes of his rival's humiliation. For though he'd found the Shrine of the Four Keepers, digging it out of the earth with his own hands, the ultimate prize remained elusive. He hadn't found the Last Supper Dish. And worse, he only had one more day to do so. All day at the shrine he hadn't once seen Ayhan. Had Öztürk intervened with Feredun Pasa? Burke had to find out.

Suddenly, he felt a chill in his limbs as if he were feverish. To steady himself, he looked down at his hands. His knuckles were cracked. There was dirt under his left thumb nail. These hands, so close to grasping his dream, couldn't dispel the doubts in his mind. *What if the Dish isn't there?*

The Dish had to be there. It *had* to be. He closed his eyes, remembering the moment he'd shared with Ayhan before Panikos the Youth. Together, the two of them had touched the throbbing truth of history. What had he missed? Mentally, he traced the contours of the mosaics, hoping to will the monks to confess their secret. But their faces remained expressionless, as blank as the blank wall of the apse.

*The blank wall of the apse.* Burke opened his eyes. *Nothing on the wall, the wall of ... ashlar stone.* He held his breath.

All at once, he realized the audience had grown quiet. Had he missed his cue? But glancing at the podium, he saw that Ayhan was about to speak, and the Patriarch was just returning to his seat. Burke watched as Philotheos, dignified and unhurried, sat down next to Ahmet Öztürk. Though he'd scarcely heard a word Philotheos had said,

Burke felt certain that the Patriarch had tried to upstage him, and he eyed him suspiciously. Burke always held that the Orthodox preference for long, flowing beards was an affectation.

"... and now, here to make a special announcement, please welcome from the University of Pittsburgh in the United States of America—Professor Adam Burke."

Burke stepped toward the podium, his mind still mulling the significance of his new insight about the apse's bare wall of ashlar stone—a wall that shouldn't be ashlar stone at all. He almost felt his confidence renewed, but his fingers were cold when he shook Ayhan's hand.

"The world is about to change, Adam," she said softly.

Nervously, he took the podium and slid his glasses lower on his nose in a pose of erudition. "Thank you for—"

There was commotion in the audience. Someone—a man seated stage left—shouted, "Where is it?"

Burke instantly thought of Michael Mistral and pushed his glasses back up his nose to search the audience for the reporter's unpleasant face.

An Orthodox priest jumped up. "Where is the Dish of Christ?" he shouted. "We have seen the report. We know you have found the Shrine of the Four Keepers."

There were murmurings in the audience.

Burke's mind went blank. In his head he heard the slippery voice of Feredun Pasa saying, "Wrap it up!" It did feel right to capitalize on the audience's eagerness by skipping to the end of his speech. With a triumphant wave of his hand, he declared, "It is true, my friends. As reported on CNN-Turk, we have found the Shrine of the Four Keepers!"

The audience gasped. Some exclaimed, "No, it can't be!"

Burke stood relishing the effect of his words.

The aged Cardinal Eduardo stood. He was shaky on his feet, but his voice was strong. "How do you know it is the so-called Shrine of the Keepers?"

"Ladies and Gentlemen, there will be time for questions at the end of my remarks," Burke said. Then he cringed, realizing that he'd already come to the end of his remarks.

The guests began to mutter. There was obvious confusion. Cardinal Eduardo still stood, waiting to be answered.

Burke pursed his lips as he tried to reorganize his speech.

"Professor, this is a most extraordinary claim," someone else interjected. It was the young voice of Frederico D'Angelo, Director of the Holy See Press Office. He stood up beside Cardinal Eduardo, gently holding the elderly man's elbow to support him. "You must forgive my incredulity, but you know, as do most people here, that such a discovery would have tremendous ramifications. What is your evidence that it is indeed the lost shrine?"

Burke shifted into academic mode. "This is the most important question," he began pedantically. "I addressed this in my press conference. We've uncovered four mosaics, and given the designs of the halos and the fact that each figure holds a bowl, the images unquestionably depict Kostas, Zoticus, Panikos, and Nil. I've prepared some slides of Panikos the Youth for your—"

There was a shout from the other side of the aisle. "The Dish belongs to us!"

# SCRUUUUM!

"Excuse me, I must explain," Burke said, trying to reassert his authority. "The shrine has been discovered, but—"

Another Orthodox priest leaped to his feet. "Give us the Dish. Where is the Dish?" Other insistent voices echoed his.

"Please," Burke said plaintively, trying to keep order. He could feel sweat in his armpits. "The shrine's apse remains to be explored, and I'm, uh, confident that once we do—"

"He will not find the Dish, you jealous fools," said a high nasal voice. Burke watched as Bishop Louis Fortier slowly stood. He was a thin man with a pinched nose. He lifted his chin haughtily and leered at the Orthodox seated across the aisle. "Nobody could possibly find the Dish," he sneered, "because it already has been found. *We* have it."

Hearing these words, some shouted, "Liar!" and others, "Judas!" The Orthodox jumped up as one and pushed into the center aisle. The Catholics met them there.

"Scruuuum!" someone in the audience shouted.

There was much finger pointing and chest bumping. Before it ended, two robes were ripped, three noses tweaked, and several beards pulled.

Papadopoulos's cane was knocked from his hand.

Cardinal Eduardo collapsed in his chair.

Scene 23

## Intrigues

*Istanbul Museum of Ancient History*

*Saturday, March 13, moments after the scrum*

There was an adage of the Desert Fathers, one Philotheos recited cheerily when his secretary Gabriel couldn't get the printer to work or when the copy machine jammed. The adage was, "An angry man abandons his dignity."

As the fight broke out between the Orthodox and Catholics, this adage popped into Philotheos's head. Surveying the pit of fury from his seat on stage, he felt his own anger stewing. There could be no doubt who had incited the violence. *Anthimos. That agitator!* Philotheos chided himself for having trusted the Order to choose the best men to attend the ceremony. He never should've put the matter to a vote; he should've exercised his executive privilege. If he had, he would've chosen anyone but Anthimos.

"Stop this. Stop this I say!" Philotheos shouted heatedly, pushing his way into the maelstrom to restore order. An elbow to his jaw knocked his kamilavka askew. "Stop!" No one heeded him. Shouts shocked his ears like thunderclaps. To his right, Frederico D'Angelo cried for medical attention for the collapsed Cardinal Eduardo. To his left, through a colorful cloud of robes and beards, he glimpsed Anthimos standing apart from the mob, fiddling with his eagle pendant and slyly grinning. Someone pushed Philotheos; he stumbled into Gabriel. "There!" Gabriel hollered, pointing at the floor. Philotheos spied a confused heap. It was Leronymos and Bishop Louis tangled in several folding chairs.

Philotheos grabbed fistfuls of Lerry's robe in both hands and yanked hard, stepping back with his right foot for leverage. His foot, however, fell on something round and hard, and as it rolled out from under his heel, he lost his balance and toppled backwards, pulling Lerry down on top of him. Lerry squawked and kicked his legs in the air; Bishop Louis squirmed away. The commotion of the Patriarch's fall effectually ended the battle. All eyes beheld the two fallen men of God, and all the cameras too. Then museum security came and restored order. But not peace. An ambulance arrived for Cardinal Eduardo, and Philotheos was, with a great deal of embarrassment, helped to his feet.

"Your hat, sir." Someone nudged his arm. It was Murat, Dr. Ayhan's young assistant. Philotheos exhaled crossly and grabbed his kamilavka, resisting the urge to explain that it wasn't a "hat" but an emblem of honor dating back to the Byzantine emperors. "Thank you," he said instead. The kamilavka was dented and branded by dusty shoeprints. Philotheos thrust it at Gabriel, who knowing better than to ask, began to expunge these marks of degradation.

Professor Papadopoulos limped forward stiffly and bent to retrieve his cane. Given its role in the affair, it was remarkably undamaged, even the carved ivory top. Papi inspected the inverted church carefully and was satisfied.

"What a kerfuffle! And in front of all the world," Philotheos lamented. "Could you not control those nimrods over there?" He gestured in the direction of Anthimos. After escaping the Patriarch's grip, Lerry had rejoined his co-agitator; the two stood at a distance whispering.

Papi's shoulders slumped, and Philotheos knew he'd been unfairly harsh. "Forgive me, but what happened?"

"Anthimos," Papi sighed, confirming what Philotheos already suspected. "He encouraged Lerry to interrupt Burke. To ask about the Dish. Gabriel can tell you."

"He's right," Gabriel said breathlessly. The excitement of the fight had enflamed his cherub cheeks. "Anthimos said if Burke acknowledged the discovery of a, er, unique-looking bowl, we would know that he has found the *prodokleis*." Gabriel mouthed this last word but did not say it.

Philotheos smoothed his beard. "That is not what I meant at all by making an artful inquiry."

"Nonetheless, Burke confirmed finding only mosaics," Gabriel said. "He mentioned no objects. Not even icons."

"Indeed." Philotheos kept stroking his beard. Anthimos had in one sense done the will of the Order. He'd gotten the information it needed to initiate its scheme properly. On the other hand, he'd incited a fight with the Catholics over the Dish, thereby ruining the evening and perhaps more. Philotheos looked for Anthimos, but he didn't see him. He grew worried. A thought latent for years bared itself in his mind. Its exposure was unpleasant to behold; it saddened him. He didn't wish to think of Anthimos as his enemy. But would Anthimos dare reveal the Order's secrets to Burke?

"Find him," he instructed Gabriel and Papi. "He must not come near the professor."

Papi set off at once. Gabriel, however, lingered; he still held the Patriarch's kamilavka.

Philotheos eyed it. Somehow Gabriel had managed to buff it masterfully.

"Shall I?" Gabriel offered to place it on his head.

"Very well, my son."

▼ ▼ ▼ ▼

Anthimos was giddy. The fighting between his Orthodox brethren and the Catholics felt like a foretaste of the Day of Judgment. How he longed for a final reckoning with the Latins. He sought to exact further justice and began to calculate the obstacles. Philotheos, for one. The Patriarch would issue a statement condemning the violence to minimize damage to Orthodox-Catholic relations ahead of Pope Boniface's visit. Thus, the statement would likely de-emphasize the significance of the shrine's discovery and ignore the controversy of the Dish entirely. Such a course of action opposed Anthimos's own wishes. He conceived a new scheme.

"Did you see me take down Fortier?" Lerry boasted. "I gave his pointed nose a tweak or two."

"And the world applauds," Anthimos said, eyeing the news cameras. He pulled Lerry closer. "Listen, it is within our power to act. We must while Professor Burke is here."

"We have acted. We did the will of the Order."

"But there is more to be done." The pair stepped through the crowd, avoiding medics attending to Cardinal Eduardo.

"He did this," Frederico D'Angelo cried as they passed. He pointed angrily at Leronymos. "God sees all things!"

Anthimos took Lerry's arm and quickly escorted him from the vestibule to an adjoining gallery.

"He's just mad they lost," Lerry said when they were out of earshot. He didn't like Anthimos pulling at his arm. "Let go of me. What's this about?"

"For the moment, young man, keeping you out of jail."

"Cowards. If they dare press charges. Fortier started it."

They'd entered a gallery of reliquaries and icons taken from Constantinople during the Fourth Crusade. Lerry was impressed and inspected the display cases.

Anthimos stood at his shoulder. "Never mind that—"

"But it is our history. Look there—the Vicenza Reliquary of the True Cross." He let out a low whistle.

"Yes, but what of our future?" Anthimos insisted. "Listen, I think we can force Philotheos to restore the Legacy."

"Restore it? How? We are charged to protect it."

Anthimos lowered his voice. "By making sure Burke knows what he has found when he finds the prodokleis."

INTRIGUES

Lerry's eyes widened, then narrowed. "He may not find it. Philotheos has already set a plan in motion if he does."

"Bah! Plan. A desperate scheme of desperate men—"

"The three monks are preparing at this very moment."

"—men without imagination."

Lerry glanced curiously at Anthimos. "There were, uh, no other plans put forward."

"So, you put your faith in Leo, Theo, and Winnipeg?"

"My faith is in God. As is yours, I hope."

Anthimos frowned and stroked his beard. For a minute he said nothing but fiddled with his eagle pendant.

"What do you propose?" Lerry asked. "What if Burke does find the prodokleis? Will you say to him—Professor, you have the key that opens the final secret of—"

"Exactly."

Lerry sucked in his breath. "No, no, you cannot do it."

"Why not?"

Lerry backed away, appearing to examine a display.

"Why not?" Anthimos repeated, following him closely.

"Philotheos would not approve. Remember he said we do not want a man like Burke opening the Red Gate."

"Bah! That is all?"

"That is everything. We have taken an oath."

"And so has he," Anthimos replied vehemently. "Yet what does he do but shamelessly flirt with the Latin hypocrites? I suspect him. I think he keeps the Legacy according to the letter of the law only, but not according to its spirit."

Lerry said nothing.

Anthimos felt he'd gained the advantage and pressed it. "After all these centuries, the Shrine of the Four Keepers has been found. Do you not feel the significance,

## THE DIE IS CAST

the weight of responsibility entrusted to us? It is a sign that the spirit of Andronicus lives. This is our moment. Do you want the moment to be lost because of one man's misguided dalliance with the West? No! We must act now."

As he spoke, Burke entered the gallery in evident search for someone. Anthimos ducked behind a bust of Pope Innocent III. There he waited to make his move. Lerry stood by biting his nails. Anthimos eyed him disapprovingly.

"We will be thrown out of the Order," Lerry whimpered.

"We will not be thrown out."

A few seconds passed.

"What if ...?" Lerry began hesitantly.

"What now?"

"Well, what if the Legacy *were* restored?"

"That is our daily prayer, is it not?"

"Yes, but if it were, and it was proven we knew everything from the first, and yet we still—" he glanced at Burke.

"Yes? So?"

"Would we not be held culpable?"

Anthimos said nothing. He kept his eyes on Burke.

"Someone would be culpable," Lerry said reflectively.

Anthimos cleared his throat. "Remember the Desert Fathers. St. Symeon the New Theologian once said—The one who fears God does not fear evil men, even when assailed from all sides. The schemes of dogs and foxes cannot ensnare him, for he stands firm in the wisdom of the Lord, cutting through their nets as with a sword. It is the wise man who arouses dread in his enemies. They take flight before him, like monkeys fleeing a roaring lion." Anthimos gave Lerry a significant look. "Are you a lion or a monkey?"

Lerry squinted sulkily but said nothing.

A few more seconds passed.

"I do not like his face," Lerry said.

"Nor do I. It is peevish and weak. It disguises a deep self-loathing."

"No, not Burke," Lerry said. "I mean *him*." He pointed at the bust of Pope Innocent III.

"Oh. Him. Coward. He could not decide whether to condemn the crusaders. Vile oath-breakers, all of them—the crusaders for attacking fellow Christians against their word and this Pope for his feeble punishment."

"Like all Latins, I suppose."

"Yes, tempted at last by the spoils of victory. Ah! Look, Burke nears. Now is the time."

Anthimos emerged from behind the bust. Lerry trailed several steps behind. All at once, something blocked their way, something round and hard. It was Papi's cane.

"Step aside, old man," Anthimos growled.

"Culpability is a dangerous thing," Papi said sternly. "You should listen to your brother." He glanced at Lerry and pressed his cane firmly into Anthimos's thigh.

Lerry looked aside guiltily.

"Bah! The same way you listen to that fool Philotheos?" Anthimos spat. "I assume you have your instructions."

"That fool," Papi said, "has protected the Legacy. He has not abandoned his post. Not like you are about to do."

"I do no such thing. The Order has abandoned itself. We have lost our way, and you know why?"

Papi narrowed his eyes; he clutched his cane tightly.

"We have abandoned our true leader," Anthimos said.

Papi smirked. "And I suppose you mean yourself?"

Anthimos pushed the cane aside and stepped closer to Papi. They were eye to eye. "No. I mean Andronicus!"

Papi's eyes widened. He swayed and clutched the top of his cane with both hands.

Anthimos's unblinking gaze bore into Papi; he gripped the old professor by the arm. "Listen, Papi—join me!"

▼ ▼ ▼ ▼

"Wow! That fight was awesome," Ray said to Clark.

"You see that dude crash through the chairs?" Clark said.

"Did I? Guy took out the bishop. I got it all on film."

"You guys! Fighting isn't right," Natalie said. She stood winding up a power cord. The three of them were packing up their equipment, having been warned by museum security that there was to be no more filming.

Ray ignored Natalie. He patted his camera. "Imagine that as our opening sequence," he said to Clark.

"Dude, that'd be awesome. Men in capes mixin' it up—just like ninja assassins. Or—or the Justice League."

"Ha! But where's our Wonder Woman? We gotta have a babe if it's to be the total entertainment package," Ray said.

Before either Clark or Natalie could reply to this, Ray took three steps back. Finally, after a half hour of trying, he'd caught Zainab Ayhan's eye. She'd been attending to Cardinal Eduardo—and to a host of other upset guests—but at last she stood alone near the hallway to her office. She stared unblinking at Ray as if she possessed telepathic powers. Her look was a summons. Not that he needed one.

"Here, hold this," Ray said to Clark, handing him his camera, and then with a glance at Natalie, he was off.

"You want me to film?" Clark called after him.

"You can't. Just hold onto it, will ya? For safekeeping."

Ray fought the urge to look back to see Natalie's jealous glare. Believing in her jealousy propelled him urgently toward his target. As he neared Ayhan, he thought of how to make his flirtation evident from a distance. Ayhan extended her hand to greet him, and he held it longer than necessary.

Ayhan was flustered, her manner brusque. "Mr. Cozart, please accept my apologies on behalf of the museum. Such an unpleasant incident. It shames me. I said I required expert filmmaking, but not to film rubbish."

"You mean that wasn't on your itinerary?" Ray said, risking a joke. "If that's a taste of what we're in for, we're gonna have one helluva film."

Ayhan didn't share his humor. She spun away from him, her eyes full of wrath. "Fools. The ceremony ruined. After months of preparation. When I think of all the time and all the donors—all the money!" She put a hand to her forehead as if in pain. "Oh, I should have anticipated a confrontation. I should not have let Burke speak. All it took was one little word—*Dish*—and the evening was turned upside down. The world could use much less fanaticism, do you not agree?"

Ray sighed. "Maybe. In Hollywood we rely on it. Where I come from, if no one is fanatical about you, then you don't exist. Creating fans is a business necessity."

"You make fun. That is not fanaticism at all," Ayhan said.

"You've never seen a red-carpet premiere."

"Fanatics want to own the world at any cost. What these fanatics may have cost me—oh, I cannot begin to calculate."

Ray stepped nearer. "No one will blame you. What could you do? It was that priest who jumped up shouting. I got it on film. I was getting shots of the audience when—"

"Your cameraman," Ayhan interrupted. "I do not recall his name. He was not given any trouble?" She looked past him in the direction of Clark. "CNN-Turk was quite uncooperative with our request to suspend filming. Ugliness is so entertaining to air. But the negative press for our institution—" she broke off, shaking her head bitterly. Then she looked up, "You will not use the footage, will you?"

For a second Ray couldn't quite think. Ayhan's violet-tinged eyes had lost their ire and become pleading. With her long lashes like veils, she was at once both shy and alluring.

"Er, well, I can't promise—"

"But you have, Mr. Cozart. You have promised." She batted her eyelashes and smiled. Her voice became low and warm. "You promised to follow my itinerary. I know it is a great favor to ask, and, oh, about that—the favor I mentioned—you see, when any work undertaken for our institution bears on its public image, we reserve the right to render our approval of the finished product, which in this case simply means that to make the necessary adjudications, I require access to your footage." Her lips parted slightly, and her smile showed her teeth. "It is a formality, I assure you. Merely a matter of bureaucratic protocol."

Ray frowned. Ayhan's change of mood and manner had muddled his mind. By some mysterious means, she'd made the word "bureaucratic" sound sexy. Some part of him registered this to be a danger. He shook his head. "No, you, uh, you can't have our footage. No way. Natalie wouldn't—"

"Oh, it entails but a cursory review. Look—here is someone who can explain to you."

Ayhan beckoned toward a short, fat man who'd just emerged from a cluster of aggrieved guests. He didn't quite reach Ayhan's height, and his face was unpleasant, pinched and round at once, like a squirrel with its cheeks full. Ray recognized him—he'd been seated on stage next to Professor Burke but had never had a chance to speak.

"Ahmet, allow me to introduce Mr. Cozart, our American filmmaker," Ayhan said with slight nod. "Mr. Cozart, this is Ahmet Öztürk, director of the Ministry of Culture and Tourism. Among his many significant governmental duties is overseeing institutions such as this museum."

Öztürk gave Ray's hand a fleeting shake and directed his beady eyes at Ayhan. He gestured toward the guests he'd just left and spoke to her gruffly in Turkish. Ray could make nothing of it, only that Ayhan seemed to be mortified. As Öztürk went on and on, wagging his pudgy finger under her nose, she glanced at Ray apologetically.

Ray felt divided; half his brain warned him that his flirtation with Ayhan hadn't quite gone as planned and that he ought to retreat, while the other half plotted how he might have another go at it with a fat man in the way. Just then he felt a nudge at his back. It was Natalie.

"What's going on?" she whispered.

"What are you—? Where's Clark?"

"Keeping your camera safe," Natalie answered wryly, jerking her thumb behind her.

Irritably, Ray looked past her. Clark had given his camera to Murat and was showing him how to work it.

"The Ambassador?" Ayhan spoke abruptly to Öztürk in English. "Yes, I will speak to him. But here is Mr. Cozart, *our* filmmaker. Remember, I told you I had procured the services of an American." Ayhan's voice reached the heights of extreme courtesy. "Mr. Cozart and I were just discussing the terms of our agreement. Perhaps, you can confirm to him the fine details, the, er, requisite records for your office?" Suddenly, Ayhan saw Natalie. "Oh, and here is Ms. Ashbrook," she added perfunctorily. Her eyes grew cold.

Öztürk blinked his beady eyes. He looked Ray and Natalie up and down. "You are 8 Ball Productions? I confess I do not play at billiards. But I understand you film the game in your country? Zainab tells me you have won filmmaking awards. That is useful. We require credibility. Allow me to express my appreciation for your efforts on our behalf."

"Er, no, we don't film pool games," Ray said.

Öztürk appeared confused.

Ayhan jumped in, "Er, the form you mentioned to me, Ahmet. From your office. Can you explain to Mr. Cozart?"

Öztürk adjusted the tie about his thick neck. "Government regulations. To film any of the city's historical sites for commercial purposes, you must sign—"

Öztürk was cut off by a woman's screech.

They all looked about to locate the source. At once Natalie felt her hand clasped by a woman as short as herself. The woman had unnaturally yellow hair, and her skin was tan, bordering on orange, giving her a youthful glow. But she wasn't young. She wore a leopard-printed shawl pinned with a pink diamond brooch. There was a man with her.

"What a thrill and a delight," the woman squealed. "I said to my husband—That has *got* to be Natalie Ashbrook. And here you are. Imagine! Gordon and I adored your film Almost a Loneliness." She laid a hand on her heart. "So sad, so moving. We love beautiful things—isn't that right, dear?"

Her husband nodded. He was tall and pale, his black hair combed forward. "Gordon Krayzel," he said solemnly, extending his hand. Natalie felt the weight of a large gold ring.

During this scene, Ray whispered to Ayhan, "Fanatics."

Ayhan arched her eyebrows, then to Ray's surprise, she said, "Ambassador Krayzel, so glad you have joined us. Ahmet was just telling me that you and Sylvia have purchased a villa in Greece. Does this mean your wanderings are at an end? Will we no longer enjoy your presence in Istanbul?"

"Retired ambassador," Gordon said to Ray and Natalie.

"Don't be modest, dear," his wife Sylvia said. "My husband has been all over Europe and the Middle East," she explained to Ray and Natalie. "How many countries, dear? Thirty? He's fluent in six languages—a bona fide polyglot."

"You're Americans?" Natalie asked.

"Correct," Gordon said. "I was the American ambassador to Turkey some years ago. Back when Ahmet here was still staffing the mayor of Istanbul's mailroom." He chuckled.

Öztürk scowled and crossed his arms over his belly.

"But we haven't lived in the States for years," Sylvia declared. "I forget where I'm from anymore. Imagine that. We love the Mediterranean. Our villa faces the sea. So lovely when the sun rises over the island. Gordon has fine taste." She clutched her pink diamond brooch. "This rarity was his first gift. But what brings you to Istanbul, Ms. Ashbrook?"

"Um, I'm—er, I mean *we* (she indicated Ray) are working on a film about the search for the Last Supper Dish."

A strange look passed between the Krayzels and Ayhan.

"Imagine that," Sylvia said at last, her eyes shining.

"The Krayzels are long-time patrons of this institution," Ayhan said hastily to Ray and Natalie. "They have a deep appreciation for ancient cultures and for the work undertaken to preserve the past. No doubt, they will be great fans of a film on the subject." She smiled amusedly at Ray. "Perhaps they will attend your red-carpet premiere."

"Indeed. If you will have us," Sylvia said to Natalie, cozily clutching her arm. "You might call us history's greatest fans. Antiquities are our passion. We're always on the lookout. I never tire of it—hearing of discoveries, I mean. Such a thrill! Poking about in dusty corners of the world—who knows what might turn up." She beamed up at her husband. "Perhaps the greatest of all treasures." Then to Ayhan, "Oh, Zainab, after what we heard tonight about the shrine, do you think we might meet Professor Burke?"

Before Ayhan could reply, Öztürk said, "Remarkable opportunity for you, Ambassador." His lips curled in a half sneer. "Your patience is rewarded it seems. But villas fetch exorbitant sums. Perhaps you have little left to decorate it?"

Sylvia started at these words, but Gordon answered Öztürk coolly, "We've been fortunate. It's best to seize rewarding opportunities when they arise. Regret is a terrible thing. I'm sure you can agree. That reminds me, have you read the latest report of the Turkish Antiquities Trade Commission? About the crackdown on illegal traffickers? Some significant arrests have been made. I hope they make an example of these people. Looters are getting far too creative. It would be a valuable deterrent."

Öztürk's half sneer became a full one.

"Ah, look, dear, there is the Professor," Sylvia pointed.

Burke appeared in the vestibule near the stage; he was elbowing his way toward them. "No, I don't have the Dish. I told you. Now let me pass!" he could be heard bellowing.

Ayhan made a move to intercept him, but it was too late.

"Zainab, there you are," he hollered when he saw her. He rushed over. "Was it really necessary to suspend the filming? CNN-Turk is requesting a post-speech interview."

"The decision was not mine. It was Ahmet's."

Burke repeated his plea to Öztürk.

"No. No interviews," Öztürk said curtly, waving Burke away. "As it happened, you did not even give a speech."

Ayhan attempted to introduce Burke to Ray and Natalie.

Burke cut her off. "But I've found a clue," he declared to her and Öztürk. "An important clue. It's worth airing."

"A clue to finding the Dish?" Sylvia gasped.

"What is it?" Ray asked excitedly.

Burke suddenly realized he was standing in a group and gestured grandly to everyone. "It's the far wall of the apse in the shrine—it's ashlar stone!"

His words made no impression.

Ayhan squinted, puzzled. "What does that mean?"

"Don't you see? The rest of the walls in the shrine are made of yellow brick. The wall in the apse is the only one that isn't. I should've noted the difference before. I thought of it just now while I was up on stage."

Ayhan tapped her chin. "Cut stone. Hmm. Builders sometimes mixed materials to fulfill an aesthetic purpose."

"There's nothing aesthetic about the wall. It's bare! It shouldn't be. The apse is the sacred place where the altar is. The wall should be slathered with frescoes or mosaics. I assumed the Ottomans defaced the wall, but the mosaics of the Keepers in the west aisle are intact. If the Ottomans had defaced one wall, wouldn't they have defaced them all? No, the apse was left undecorated. But why? Something else is going on. I gotta go have a look." Burke peered beseechingly from Ayhan to Öztürk and added: "Say I'll get more time to investigate. I'm on the verge of breaking this open, I can feel it. Have you convinced Pasa not to shut down the dig?"

Ayhan looked furtively at Öztürk.

Sylvia, who'd been listening raptly, gasped, "What? Shut down the dig?" She looked in shock at her husband. "But—but dear, you told me there were no snags." Then to Ayhan: "No snags! He was set to lift the altar. That's what you said."

Gordon took hold of his wife's arm and escorted her out of earshot of Ray and Natalie. With a glare at Ayhan, Öztürk followed the Ambassador, and the group broke up.

"Wait," Burke called to Öztürk. "What about Pasa? Will I get more time? Zainab, what's going on?"

"You must excuse me," Ayhan said to him tersely. "Our guests are very upset." She marched past Burke.

"Yeah? Well, so am I. What about me?"

Ayhan did not reply.

Burke made a move to follow her, but Natalie stopped him. "Wait, who's shutting down the dig?" she asked.

"Oh, the Rail Bureau Chief Pasa. It's just stupid bureaucratic wrangling. Between the lot of 'em, they can't figure out who's in charge." Burke made another move to leave.

"Wait, Professor," Ray said, "CNN-Turk can't interview you, but *we* can." He gestured at himself and Natalie.

"How so? Who are you with? Archaeology Today? Antiquities Quarterly? Near East Times?" Burke asked eagerly.

"None of those. We're 8 Ball Productions." Ray grinned.

Burke appeared unimpressed. "Oh. Er, well, maybe I'll make my assistant Duffy available to—"

"When will the dig be shut down?" Natalie interrupted. "How long have you known?"

"Two days ago, that snake Pasa told me I only have three more days to dig, so you do the math," Burke said acidly.

"Does Dr. Ayhan know about this?" Natalie probed.

"Of course. I told her about it the same day I heard of it. She came to the excavation site. The crew had just lifted the altar with a crane. Took them all morning, and—"

"The altar in the shrine? You lifted it already?"

"Yeah, two days ago, like I said—"

"Well, was there ... anything under it?"

"Yeah, a lot of dirt," Burke thundered. He strode off toward Ayhan and Öztürk despite pleas from Ray to wait.

When Burke had gone, Ray glared at Natalie. "What is it with you lately making people mad?"

"He was already mad. Didn't you hear him?" She put her hands on her hips. "He's got just one more day to find the Dish. And Dr. Ayhan knows all about it. I told you she was up to something."

Ray mimicked Natalie's posture. "How you figure that?"

"Because when we met her in her office yesterday, she already knew about this guy Pasa, but she didn't once mention that Burke was up against the clock."

"So what? Maybe she doesn't think it's a big problem. That it'll get fixed. Just stupid red tape like Burke said."

"Then why didn't she tell him so just now? And why did she act like Burke believed the Dish was under the altar? You remember her theatrics when we were in her office, holding up the bowl? She wants us to interview Burke about his plans to lift the altar. But he'd already lifted it the day before and found nothing. And she knew he had."

"So what? She was just showing us how great the story can be. Like lifting the altar must've been a big deal. But we missed it, so maybe she just wants some of the story recreated. Nothing wrong with that. We've done reenactments."

Natalie huffed. "Don't be deliberately obtuse. All signs say that woman's keeping secrets. What did you two talk about? Did she tell you her great favor?" Natalie fluttered her eyelashes in scornful imitation of Ayhan.

That was all the sign Ray needed. *It worked!* Mentally, he congratulated himself for successfully executing his flirtation scheme, quite overlooking its finer details. He didn't exactly recall the fact that Ayhan had claimed the right to their film footage. In fact, he was sure he misheard her. "I'm right." He smiled blandly. "You are jealous."

Natalie guffawed. "Please. Of her? Why should I be?"

Ray crossed his arms over his chest. "You tell me."

Natalie mimed Ray's posture. "Look, this really isn't the time or place, but clearly, you have a theory you're eager to share. You're very good at theories. Why don't you tell me your theory, and we'll see how that turns out?"

Ray's jaw tightened; he could feel his pulse in his neck. "You think you're so smart. But I wasn't wrong then, and

## THE DIE IS CAST

I'm not wrong now. You didn't really love Peagram. You only thought you did. But you couldn't admit it. The evidence was right in front of you, but you didn't wanna see."

Natalie inhaled sharply; her eyes narrowed coldly. "Oh, I see. You—you think it was all my fault we fell apart."

"I dunno why you won't admit it. Reggie told me everything. That you said you miss me, that you knew you were wrong and have deep regrets. I mean, it isn't a secret."

At these words, Natalie face contorted. She took several steps back and put a hand over her lips. "Oh. My. God. Reggie! He—he couldn't have!"

Ray was both pleased and confused by her reaction. Her horrified look was a sign his words had hit their mark. But maybe there was a bit too much horror. "Well, maybe those weren't his exact words," he said, pretending to lessen the blow now that his triumph was assured. "I'm sure he didn't mean to break a confidence. He was only trying to help."

Natalie shook her head. Then to Ray's amazement, she laughed—but it was a grim, hollow sound. "I didn't know Reggie was such a storyteller," she said icily. "He should write a screenplay."

Ray felt a spasm of pain in his neck. "What do you—"

"Oh, I said no such thing to Reggie. He lied to you!"

▼ ▼ ▼ ▼

Anthimos lurked at the gallery entrance that joined the vestibule. He watched as Burke gesticulated to the museum curator and a short, fat man. Anthimos couldn't remember their names. Behind Anthimos paced Lerry biting his nails, and at his shoulder Papi anxiously tapped his cane, freshly converted to the cause of revealing one of the Order's greatest secrets to the strident American professor.

Papi's conversion Anthimos ranked as his greatest triumph. "Our founder Emperor Andronicus wanted seekers of the Dish. That is the whole point," he'd told the old man. "Let us assist Burke in his search by telling him about the prodokleis. It is the Order's ancient mandate. You cannot deny it." Papi had not denied it nor offered any refutation. "Perhaps it is the proper course," he'd said. "For so long, a true search has not been possible. I—I will corroborate your story to Burke, but that is all. Do not ask more of me."

Anthimos stroked his gray and black beard agitatedly, eager for his moment. Suddenly, the fat man shooed Burke off; the professor was left standing alone near the stage.

"Now is the time," Anthimos urged Lerry and Papi. "Follow my lead." Without a look back, he glided toward Burke.

Burke, seeing himself accosted, eyed Anthimos apprehensively at first, but then his face relaxed in recognition. "Ah, er, Professor Pa-poop-u-los, is it?"

"Papadopoulos," Papi corrected him. Even with his sore hip, he'd been but a step behind Anthimos.

"You're assisting in the processing lab, I think," Burke said, shaking Papi's hand. "My assistant Duffy says you're quite a storyteller. You keep the students entertained."

"Merely repeating what I hear," Papi said modestly.

Lerry sidled up to Anthimos, his face at last visible to Burke. He held his hands inside the sleeves of his robe as if he were concealing a weapon.

Burke jabbed a finger at him. "You! I know you. You started the fight. I'll have you know you cost me an interview with CNN-Turk."

Lerry was offended. "Me? How dare you. It was that French rat Fortier."

"But you're the one who interrupted my speech. Jumped up shouting about the Dish. If you would've just waited, I was about to explain that I hadn't found it—not yet."

Lerry looked guilty; he glanced at Anthimos.

Anthimos took charge. "Professor, my friends here," he gestured at Papi and Lerry, "we have long sought the Dish of Christ ourselves. Surely, you can understand our amazement at your discovery. You must forgive our exuberance."

Burke stiffened as if facing competitors. "Yes, well, I get it. Having the Dish—it would change the world. I'm getting closer," he bragged. "Have a new lead, in fact." He looked at Papi. "You're an expert on Byzantine culture. Do you know why builders constructing a shrine of yellow brick would suddenly erect a wall of cut stone?"

Papi furrowed his bushy white brows. "I—I could not say. Because they ran out of brick?" He grinned sheepishly.

Burke frowned at the joke. "It's in the apse behind the altar. It should be decorated with frescoes, but it isn't. Don't know why. Byzantines took great care adorning interiors. It's unusual to leave a wall bare, especially in a holy site."

Anthimos licked his lips, savoring these juicy bits about the excavated shrine. His hunger for justice needed no further fuel. He imagined the Shrine of the Four Keepers in all its former glory and pictured the poor monks who centuries before had been the last to minister at its altar. With the Ottomans besieging the city, the monks would've expended every effort to preserve the Legacy of Andronicus. They would've anticipated the destruction of the shrine and thus employed their efforts elsewhere. They would've sought to preserve the shrine's heart. Such thoughts made Anthimos's own heart race, and he blurted, "Have you searched beneath the wall, professor? Byzantine artwork in a holy site always tells a story. A blank wall may mean that is where the story came to an end. Look to it, and you will see."

Burke seemed intrigued by this idea, and Anthimos, detecting his curiosity, lured him further on: "We have long studied the legend of the Four Keepers. If you have found their mosaics on the walls of the shrine, you most certainly will uncover their icons. Byzantine architecture follows the rule of correlation. The form of a structure must be identical to its function and furnishings. A basilica in the shape of a cross would not be used as a marketplace, for example. It would be sacrilege. Thus, the builders of the shrine—"

"The mosaics of the Keepers show them all holding a Dish," Burke jumped in. "If we follow your rule, the Byzantine rule, then the Dish *has* to be at the shrine too. By rule!"

Papi, Lerry, and Anthimos exchanged looks.

"You think I will find it," Burke said excitedly.

For a moment, Anthimos said nothing. His eyes, dark and shadowed, held Burke's, searching. He stepped forward and leaned in to whisper, his gray and black beard close to Burke's cheek. "If you desire the truth, you will surely find it. But you must not stray from the path, no matter how dark it becomes." His tone was passionless but threatening beneath the surface, like a frozen sea.

Burke's face grew uneasy. "What do you mean?"

Anthimos licked his lips again. "We believe," he whispered, "you will find along with icons of the Keepers ... a key."

"A key?"

Anthimos nodded. "A key."

"A key to the Dish?"

"A key to something ... far greater."

Suddenly, Papi chuckled. He tapped his cane on the floor several times and nudged Lerry as if to share in the joke.

"What's so funny?" Burke asked. "What's going on? What could possibly be greater than the Dish?"

Papi eyed Anthimos. "Greater? Do you truly believe so?"

Anthimos scowled. "Far greater. Yes. So I said."

"That is a bit dramatic. Melodramatic, I should say."

Anthimos's eyes narrowed upon Papi.

Lerry shifted nervously. "What is the difference?"

Papi looked to Burke for help with an answer. But Burke had put his hands in his pockets and was looking at his feet.

"It does not matter," Anthimos said to Lerry.

"Melodrama is added, extra drama," Papi said. "Over and above. Like metaphysics."

"Then why not call it metadrama instead?" Lerry asked.

"No, metadrama is a play within a play," Papi said. "The classic case is the mousetrap play in Shakespeare's Hamlet."

"It does not matter," Anthimos insisted petulantly.

"It does," Papi said to Anthimos, "because with your mysterious talk of keys, you would elevate us to being heroes in some third-rate adventure story. But we are merely ourselves, standing in a first-rate museum in Is-tan-bul. Melodramatic is the right word for that."

"Bah! It should be Constantinople," Anthimos grumbled. Papi's enunciation of the city's name had touched a nerve.

"Nevertheless, it is Is-tan-bul. And you are out of your mind. Far greater than the Dish? You speak nonsense."

Anthimos's face grew dark with suspicion. He plucked at the pendant about his neck. Suddenly, as with eagle eyes, he saw everything clearly. "Why you—you deceitful old man!" He pointed an accusing finger in Papi's face.

"Is the Legacy greater than the Dish?" Lerry asked sincerely. "What is the official stance of the Order—"

"Shut up, you," Anthimos commanded.

"Ah, look." Papi reached out a welcoming hand. Gabriel had found them. "Perhaps our brother knows the answer."

"Answer to what? What is going on?" Gabriel asked.

Papi's eyes gleamed mischievously. "Lerry wants to

## THE DIE IS CAST

know if the Order considers the Legacy of Andronicus to be far greater than the Dish of Christ itself."

Gabriel nearly fainted. "Good God! Be quiet!"

"You will regret this, Papi," Anthimos raged. "You and your tricks. You planned to undermine me all along. But Burke will know the truth, and I will tell him." He looked about him, suddenly realizing what the others had already discerned—that Burke had long since slinked away. Humiliated, Anthimos lashed out again at Papi. "I should not have trusted you. You chose your side long ago. You will go to your grave like all your kind—safe and comfortable and cowardly. But I am on the side of history. And so is Burke. Nothing will stop us. Nothing!"

With a swish of his robe, Anthimos stormed off. After a second's hesitation, Lerry followed. Watching Lerry, Papi said sadly, "So, you too have chosen sides, young man."

"What is going on?" Gabriel demanded. "Did Anthimos reveal any secrets to Burke? What should I tell Philotheos?"

Papi looked down at his cane. "Tell him ... tell him ... oh, how has this happened, my brother?"

"What has happened?"

"A schism in the Order!"

▼ ▼ ▼ ▼

Cardinal Eduardo was wheeled on a gurney through the vestibule to an awaiting ambulance. Father Frederico and Bishop Louis walked along on one side of the gurney. Louis, muttering to himself in pain, pressed an ice pack against a swollen, red welt under his right eye. Philotheos walked along on the opposite side, his hands clasped and his head bowed prayerfully. But he was not in prayer.

*I must discover Boniface's scheme. Why did he send these men to Istanbul?* Philotheos didn't doubt that their presence attested to some scheme. As reported by Chrys and Lerry, all three men had attended Boniface's secret meeting. Had Boniface sent them as spies? Or to deliver a message? Philotheos mulled the possibilities. Maybe Boniface had learned about Burke's discovery of the shrine and had sent his agents to investigate. Or maybe Boniface wanted to restate his offer to return the Vatican's Dish at the Feast of Forgiveness despite Chrys and Lerry's refusals. Whatever the case, it was certain the evening's commotion had upset Boniface's plan. Philotheos wavered between hope and fear—hope that Boniface might give up his game for good and fear of what might be Boniface's next move.

At the set of glass doors that led out of the museum, the procession halted while the medics cleared a path down the steps to the ambulance. Eduardo gestured weakly for Philotheos to lean in close. "Can there ever be peace?" he whispered hoarsely in Philotheos's ear.

"God knows. Do not trouble yourself," Philotheos said.

Eduardo shook his head sadly. "I have failed. We have—all of us have failed. We shall all be ashamed before Him."

The medics opened the doors and wheeled Eduardo out.

Frederico spoke pointedly to Philotheos. "All this rancor over the Dish. Is it worth the lives of men?"

"In all things, we seek the truth, and that is of immeasurable worth," Philotheos said.

Frederico smirked cynically. "Truth! Would you know it if you found it? I do not think so. You prefer the endless search. The truth is Eduardo is a good man. He isn't your enemy. Nor is Boniface."

Philotheos eyed Louis, and his lips twitched in disdain. "And what about him? Is he my enemy?"

Louis clenched his ice pack as if it were a rock. "I have no love of fools," he sneered.

"Nor I," Philotheos said.

Louis scoffed and said to Frederico, "It is pointless to reason with him. It is like talking to a child. He says *no* and thinks he has won an argument."

Frederico sighed and addressed Philotheos. "The Holy Father seeks peace. He desires to give you the Dish. Some of your party who claim to speak for you say you will not receive it. Are they to be believed? Is this true?"

Philotheos stroked his beard. *So, these men were sent to convey a message*. Mentally, he crafted a politic answer, recalling the scheme the Order had just devised to discourage the Pope's offer. He cleared his throat. "Well, that depends. I mean, er, would not such an offer be precipitous? We have heard a report—that Boniface has sent an envoy to a town in Russia, er, to a monastery in the Caucasus Mountains. Apparently, a hermit has claimed to have found the true Dish of Christ. I am surprised you did not mention it. Is, er, this newly discovered Dish the one Boniface wishes to offer me? Or does he offer the so-called Dish on display at the Vatican?" Philotheos blinked innocently. "Many suspect it is merely a dog bowl. I do not say so myself, of course. Truly, I wish we could know for certain one way or the other."

"I told you it was pointless," Louis scoffed. "And it is just as well. The Holy Father sent us on a fool's errand, and everyone knows it is foolish except for the Holy Father. Maybe our first-hand report about this institution's lack of sufficient security will be convincing." He pointed at the bruise on his cheek. "I shall be happy to frustrate his hope in humanity when I make my report about the gross inhospitality we have suffered."

Frederico rubbed his forehead. "There is no envoy being sent to Russia," he said to Philotheos.

"Perhaps Boniface does not share all his secrets with the director of his press office," Philotheos said.

Frederico rolled his eyes. "The rumor is absurd."

Philotheos went on. "Much as I covet Boniface's friendship, I am afraid the story fills me with great doubts about his intentions. And then, what do I hear tonight but that the Shrine of the Four Keepers has been found? Some thought the shrine only legendary, yet here it is. What other legends about it will prove to be true ... who can say? Surely, His Holiness will understand that the situation is, er, explosive." He glanced at Louis's welt. "As we have witnessed tonight."

"It is a new factor, to be sure," Frederico said. "The Holy Father will take much interest in the discovery. Perhaps it will finally break the centuries of stalemate."

"It is my daily prayer," Philotheos said almost sincerely. "As our Lord said—There is nothing hidden that will not be revealed, and nothing secret that will not be made known."

Louis snorted at this speech. "You fool Dishers. I am glad of this discovery. You will finally see for yourselves that there is nothing to find." He laughed deprecatingly. "The professor's search will end in vain. Because there is no secret. The Dish of Christ is at the Vatican." With these words he pushed through the glass doors. Before they closed behind him, he looked back and said, "No secret!"

Frederico exhaled resignedly and followed Louis out.

Philotheos returned to the vestibule, his thin lips pursed in the firm arrogance of one who has just savored his rival's disgrace. *No secret. Ha! How wrong you are. The secret is everything.* It might have pleased Philotheos to say this to Fortier's face, except he would've had to sacrifice his pleasure in the secret itself. And this he would never do. Because the pleasure of the secret was far greater than any other.

He took his time retracing his steps to the vestibule. The guests had all but departed. The chairs were being put away. In the air was the usual tinge of loss and regret when a show has ended. He lifted his eyes to the arched and ribbed ceiling, imagining a great curtain being drawn. What a Legacy you have left, Andronicus, he thought, a Legacy in word and deed and in spirit. He prayed the Emperor's spirit would not rouse itself further. It must never take center stage.

But if it tried, if Burke succeeding in poking the sleeping beast, then the Order would sweep in, thieves in the night. The heist couldn't fail. Papi was planted under Burke's nose. The three monks would know when to strike. They'd gather all traces of the ancient puzzle.

There would be no clues left for Burke to solve. His search would end. He'd get nowhere near the Red Gate. Thus, the Legacy would be protected. The secret would be left hidden exactly where it was. And the Order would go on as it always did, treasuring it.

So high were Philotheos's hopes for the future that he almost shook free of his one mooring doubt. But then he caught sight of Papi and Gabriel walking toward him, and he wondered what news they brought him ... of Anthimos.

Scene 24

## Confessions

*Hotel Amir, Old Town Istanbul*

*Saturday, March 13, hours after the scrum*

"Look, for the umpteenth time, I didn't tell Reggie what he told you I said. And he lied to me about you. Told me you were—oh, hell, it doesn't matter now. He conned us both, don't you get it?" In her anger, Natalie fumbled with the key card to her hotel room. It fell to the carpet. She was carrying her messenger bag, a bag of audio equipment, and a sack of Chinese take-out.

Ray, across the hall with Clark, observed her struggle but offered no help, holding equipment bags in both hands and a sack of food under one arm. "I heard you the first time, okay? But Reggie wouldn't lie to us," he insisted.

"Whatever. So, I'm the liar, I guess," Natalie muttered. She put down the take-out sack to pick up her key card.

"What's goin' on?" Clark asked uncertainly. He cradled Sneak Peek under one arm as he unlocked the door to the room he shared with Ray.

Ray and Natalie exchanged angry looks.

Clark rolled his eyes. "Why can't you guys work it out? You drive me crazy." He filched the sack of food from Ray. "I'm hungry." He disappeared into the room. The door clicked behind him.

"Hey, don't eat it all," Ray hollered to the closed door. Then to Natalie: "I didn't say you're lying. There could be another explanation. Like, maybe you misunderstood him. You always imagine the worst-case scenario."

"I'm not an idiot. I didn't misunderstand," Natalie said, kicking the door to her room open. She caught it with her shoulder as it closed on her and backed into her room.

"Oh, okay, so I'm the idiot."

"I didn't say that."

"You always think the worst of people," Ray said. "Regg is our friend. Can't you give him the benefit of the doubt?"

"I did that already. That's how I ended up in freaking Istanbul with you. Why don't you call him and ask? Ask him what he told me about you. Really, I insist that you call him."

"Maybe I will!"

"Good! I dare you! The truth will be a great adventure." Natalie let the door swing closed, then leaned against it, dissatisfied with her last retort. She wasn't sure why she'd said that. Briefly, she tried to think of something much cleverer.

But the lights in her room were low, and the bed sheets were turned down invitingly. She let all her bags fall near the door and sank onto the bed wearily, her thoughts taking a different path: *Ray thinks I told Reggie*

*I was wrong. Is that why Ray agreed to film with me again?* The possibility made her throat constrict in despair. If it were true, then Ray was only filming the Dish Movie with her because he believed he'd won. He was just waiting for her to admit it. He didn't care for her at all, not in the way she hoped. The movie was just his victory lap.

She massaged the back of her neck and looked up at the ceiling. Its decorative pattern of coiling stems and leaves, formerly so pleasing to her, now seemed only tacky and unnecessarily fussy. Their lattice-like loops made the room feel smaller. As she'd done on that first night in the hotel, she traced the painted vines with her eyes, searching for a point of origin. But the vines forever looped in a dead-end circuit. They were a mere simulation of life.

*You think you're so smart. But I wasn't wrong then, and I'm not wrong now. You didn't really love Peagram. You only thought you did. But you couldn't admit it. The evidence was right in front of you, but you didn't wanna see. I dunno why you won't admit it. Reggie said you knew you were wrong and have deep regrets.* Ray's words to her at the museum, like the dead vines above her, cut off any hope she had of new life. They may have momentarily resurrected 8 Ball Productions, but their relationship could not be revived. In truth, it had scarcely had any life to begin with. The energy they shared had flamed only for a night. Then it was gone, used up. Like a seed fallen on rocky soil, unable to take root, it had withered in the blazing sun. Thinking all this made her feel dead.

*He blames me for it dying.*

Her head ached; her feet hurt. She wanted the day to end, but staring at her bed, she didn't know how she would ever sleep. Reggie had lied to her, but because she'd believed him, she was stuck filming a movie with a man who did not nor could ever love her. She thought of Ray flirting with that woman Ayhan at the museum, a woman whose script they now had to follow. At least, Natalie thought Ray might have been flirting. She wasn't quite sure. With a deep despairing sigh, she reached to unzip her boots. But a knock at her door made her hesitate. She raised her eyes.

"Nat, open up."

She bit her lower lip. She didn't want to see Ray, to detect the blame on his face. She wanted to imagine for just a while longer that there was hope.

He knocked again.

Resignedly, she crossed to the door, already planning her exit. If she made a witty remark, then he would want to leave quickly. She tried to think of something, but when she opened the door, she only said, "What?"

Ray had dispensed with the two equipment bags and stood holding her sack of Chinese take-out.

"You left this in the hall," he said, handing it to her.

"Oh. Um. Thanks."

She took the food, then stood with her foot against the door, propping it open, trying to think of something clever to say, and trying not to scrutinize Ray's face. But her mind seemed to have downshifted. She didn't have any words. And despite the pain it often caused her, examining Ray's eyes was always what she wanted to do. She risked a quick glance, all at once becoming acutely aware of his body, that she could've touched his hand just now, and that she could invite him into her room. A ceiling fixture in the hallway cast a shadow over his brow, making his eyes dark and unsearchable. She would've had to use telepathy to know what he was thinking, but she had no such powers. His shadowed eyes made him seem far away and gave his face a mournful cast she thought very reminiscent to his appearance the night they'd been at the Sound Lounge with Clark prepping for their interview with Steve Finder. For some reason, Ray had told her about his boyhood experience of lying to Father Stanley in the confessional.

"Is ... that all?" she asked him. Her tone fell just short of a sincere invitation.

Ray looked down; he rubbed the back of his neck. "Well. No. I wanna know some things. I wanna know what Reggie said to you about me."

"Oh, just call him," she said irritably. "He'll tell you."

"I will, I will, but I wanna know—from you."

"What for? I practically told you already."

Ray looked up. "Just tell me. He—he said something that made you want to come back, didn't he? What was it?"

Natalie turned her face away. She had no words, only an image—the image Reggie had planted in her mind of a penitent Ray sitting on a bar stool, swirling bourbon in a glass, pouring his tears into it. Such an image had been sweetly irresistible, and she had gulped it down like a glutton. The dream of Ray's remorse was her choicest meal, one her mind fed on daily in its most secret depths. Such a privately savored feast was not so easily shared— nor sacrificed.

"Did he say I missed you?" Ray guessed.

"No. It wasn't that."

"Did he—did he tell you I was sorry?" he guessed again.

Natalie's jaw clenched. She said nothing, though she suddenly felt wobbly in her high-heeled boots and slumped against the door frame for support. Her eyes darted about searching for an escape. The escape would be her answer. She chose her words carefully, because words, she knew by experience, had a way of destroying dreams.

Ray shifted impatiently on his feet. "C'mon, I don't wanna play twenty questions," he muttered.

"Sorry? Hmm. Not in so many words," she said vaguely.

Ray snorted. "What does that—? No, never mind." He backed away and strode toward his room.

Natalie watched him until his door closed. Then she let hers shut. Alone again, she set the take-out on a table and collapsed into the chair next to it as if Ray had taken all her energy with him. She managed to remove her boots and let down her ponytail. Then she leaned with her elbows on the table and ran her hands through her hair. She needed to eat, but food wasn't what she wanted.

Ray had gone to call Reggie. There could be no doubt of that. She regretted having dared him to discover the truth. She might've been able to feast on her hope of his remorse for one more night. For one more night she could've imagined him tearfully on his knees, saying, "I was so wrong. I played games with your heart and didn't love you as you deserve. You aren't just another prize like Staci. You're the greatest treasure there is, one worth every sacrifice to attain. And now, with your help, I will make the sacrifice. I will become worthy of the attainment." But she had dared him to call Reggie, for she'd wanted him to feel as wounded as she did herself by Reggie's betrayal. And she wanted him to know that his hopes of an apology from *her* were vain. Reggie had lied. She wasn't sorry at all. Not one bit.

*It wasn't my fault.*

Natalie took the cartons out of the sack and let them fall onto the table in little separate islands, angry with herself for having believed Reggie, though maybe, she told herself, the truth of what had brought her back to Ray would sound better coming from him. There'd be less heat to Reggie's confession, less spice, and so, maybe it couldn't consume the entirety of her desire for Ray's apology. Surely, a leftover of her dream would remain, a tender morsel to be stored away. Maybe, after talking with Reggie, Ray would even realize that sorry is exactly what he should be.

Housekeeping had not adequately drawn the curtains for the night. When Natalie observed this, she got up and stepped around the bed to close them herself. Then she saw the reason they weren't closed—one curtain had caught on the corner of her empty suitcase. She knelt to free it, lifting her suitcase slightly. She heard the Mystic 8 Ball, lodged in one corner of it, roll to the other side.

She walked away, sat back down. But her thoughts were of the window, and of the dark, secret kernel concealed beneath it. It was idiotic, but she imagined the Mystic 8 Ball called to her. From the heart of its liquid shadow, the white die spoke her name. *Nat, the Mystic 8 Ball never lies. That's the first rule.* She glanced over her shoulder to satisfy herself that her door was locked. Then she got up and retrieved the toy from her suitcase.

She returned with it to the table and set it down, staring at it as she ate. The number 8 was tipped on its side, looking very much like a puckered mouth. But it did not speak. She spun the toy for no reason other than to watch it spin itself out. The sight of it coming to a stop depressed her. She felt the utter futility of having the toy in her possession. She should've known all along that Reggie hadn't been Ray's confessor. No, by his own admission, Ray wasn't the confessing kind. *I haven't been to confession in, oh, twenty years at least.* She'd planned to give the toy back to Ray once she was sure of his love. But now? She picked up the ball, shook it, turned it over to see its inner die, but grew irritated at the effort to decipher its message through the murky window.

*Just like Ray.*

She sighed mournfully and set the toy back down, carelessly near the table's edge. Hope, creeping in its endless, predictable circuit, had thoroughly exhausted her. Perhaps, it would be better to know once and for all if Ray loved her.

*He loved you. Guys know when a dude's got it bad.*

"Really?" Natalie spoke sarcastically as if Clark were sitting there with her. Remembering what he'd said to her in the Sound Lounge ten days prior had given her a crazy idea. Not once in all the years that she'd had the opportunity had she ever asked the Mystic 8 Ball if Ray returned her love. She'd not had the courage. Maybe it was time.

"Guys know when a dude's in love, huh?" she said in a tone of disbelief. "Do they teach you the secret codes on the ManCave Network?" Her mockery was a means of goading herself to act. She might be able to ask the 8 Ball what she needed to know if she thought she'd done so on a dare.

She closed her eyes and exhaled. The question immediately formed itself in her mind: *Does Ray love me? Does Ray love me? Does Ray love me?* But as she well-knew, silent queries weren't good enough for the 8 Ball. She'd have to ask the question aloud if she were to know the truth. That was the second rule. She willed her lips to form the four simple words. Failed. Tried again.

On the fourth try she blurted, "Dammit, this is ridiculous. Does—does Ray Cozart love me?"

Just then there was a knock on her door. Startled, Natalie spun in her chair, knocking the 8 Ball off the table with her forearm. It bounced twice on the hardwood floor and rolled under the bed.

"Hey Nat, it's me."

Hearing Ray's voice, instantly Natalie dropped to her knees to retrieve the 8 Ball. But the toy had rolled too far. She could trace its outline dimly in the shadows just beyond her reach. She tried to squeeze under the bed, but it was too low to crawl under.

"Oh, shit."

"Nat, did you hear me?"

She hurried to the near side of the bed to see if she could reach the 8 Ball from there. She couldn't.

Frantically, she looked for something to knock it towards her. She grabbed her chopsticks off the table. She slid on her stomach and tried to pinch the toy between them as if it were a giant pea, but she only succeeded in poking it further away.

"C'mon, Nat, open up. Reggie wants to talk."

She smacked the floor once with her open palm, blaming herself for having taken the toy out of her suitcase. It was such a stupid, needless risk. Trying to gather her composure, she took several steps back from the bed and studied the floor beneath it intently to satisfy herself that Ray could not see the Mystic 8 Ball from the door.

Only then did she, with great trepidation, open it.

To her surprise, Ray stepped across the threshold. She released the door handle to let him enter. Then the door closed behind him and there he stood. Instinctively, she put her hands on her hips, trying to make herself wider. At least, she hoped her elbows would obscure his view.

"You left me in the hall long enough," he said irritably.

"I—I was trying to eat," she lied. She didn't like how his eyes scanned her room, for she imagined that he did so critically, hoping to discover how to gain an advantage in their argument. She willed her eyes away from the bed so as not to give away the presence of his cherished toy.

"It's dark in here," he observed.

"Well, it is night," she said tartly.

"So, why don't you turn on the lights?"

"Because I like them low. It's soothing."

He reached for the light switch.

"Don't do that. It's my room."

"But I can't see you."

"Use your imagination."

The lights came on.

Natalie squinted into the glare, anxiously hoping the 8 Ball remained invisible. She didn't dare turn to look. She could feel Ray staring at her. She'd lost three inches taking off her boots and was thus even more diminutive than usual. Her eyes were barely level with his pecs. Beneath his gaze, she was painfully aware of her stunted stature and felt the familiar chagrin over a facet of her body she could do nothing about. It'd always annoyed her that Ray forever looked down at her, even when they were seated.

"What are you staring at? What do you want?" she asked sharply. "Is this about Reggie?"

"You look different. Your hair is down," he said.

"Yes, that is its natural state."

She looked aside as she said this, feeling an unexpected flutter near her heart. From its secret, vibrant source, the energy stirred itself again. She saw an image of Ray pinning her to the door of Midtown Studio and kissing her throat. She'd arrived with her hair up. But after caressing every inch of her neck and shoulders, he'd taken her hair down and without warning, had lifted her off her feet, bringing her face level with his. She'd clasped his neck, peering straight into his eyes, and for one fleeting second, even though he carried her, she'd felt a mysterious symmetry.

"Reggie wants to talk—to both of us," Ray said. "We're supposed to video chat in like five minutes."

Natalie fidgeted but said nothing.

"You wanna settle this, don't you?" he asked.

Natalie bit her lip. The energy she felt dimmed, then vanished altogether, melted away by a grim recollection of something Staci had told her back when she and Ray had been filming *Monica's Dress*. Natalie could not forget. She could still see Staci's simpering face as she sprawled her long legs out on the futon and twirled a lock of hair in her fingers. She'd shown up at the studio unannounced as she always did, but Ray wasn't there. He had just stepped out on some brief errand. So, Staci had waited for him.

"Poor Nat," she'd said, "I can see it in your eyes, you know. The way you look at Ray. Don't deny it. He's, like, totally oblivious, but you can't hide it from me. Women know these things (giggle). I don't mind, by the way. I'd almost feel sorry for you if you weren't so damn conceited. I wouldn't hold out for him if I were you. He'd only pity you if he knew. I mean, I'm sure he'd try to be nice about it. But let's be honest, okay? Like, he'd be totally bored with you. Ray needs, well, (smirk) a girl with a wild streak."

Natalie glanced up at Ray, imagining seeing pity in his eyes instead of blame. She wondered which would be worse to see. She couldn't decide, but she also didn't want to be always left alone, wondering. She felt some unaccountable doom in the very nature of her choices, as if she had been cursed long ago and unawares. *I am half sick of shadows.*

"Yes," she finally said, trying to keep her voice firm, "of course, yes, I want it settled."

"Good."

Ray's tone revealed nothing. His gray eyes were steely, and his lips were pressed in a tight line.

She knew that look well.
It was his game face.

▼ ▼ ▼ ▼

Ray strode down the hall to the Hotel Amir conference room with Clark's MacBook under his arm. From the moment at the museum when Natalie had accused Reggie of lying to them, Ray had been singularly focused on one mission—proving Natalie wrong. She had to be. Reggie was an ally, a time-tested and trusted team member just like Clark. He wouldn't lie. If he said that Natalie had confessed to him her deep regrets about breaking up the team by marrying that idiot Peagram, then it had to be true. Simple as that.

Ray set up the MacBook on the conference table, adjusted the chandelier to maximum brightness, and sat down to dial Reggie. Likely, the two of them could sort it all out before Natalie even arrived. He leaned forward in his seat eagerly, elbows on the table, hands balled into fists. His palms were sweaty. He knew he was eager precisely to dispel a doubt, a small one, a doubt he himself had recently voiced to Reggie: *You told me she said she missed me, that she needs me, that she knows she was wrong. So, why doesn't she say so? Did she really tell you that?* Ray desperately wanted Reggie's story about Natalie to be true. And he wanted it to be true for them both. He just assumed Reggie had told Natalie that he would accept her apology for breaking up 8 Ball Productions, would be totally forgiving and take her back.

*What if Reggie told Natalie a different story about me?*

Thinking this made Ray ball his fists even tighter.

Natalie arrived. She'd changed into a casual sweater and jeans. She immediately dimmed the chandelier.

"Wha'd you do that for? Turn it back up," Ray said.

"It hurts my eyes."

Reggie's face appeared onscreen.

Natalie sat down next to Ray. The lights remained low.

"Okay, what's gone wrong, you two?" Reggie asked. His scalp was brightly haloed by the light of his desk lamp, and his eyes were very round and unblinking. "You wouldn't be askin' for no video chat unless there's another problem. Someone else bail on you like Finder? Don't tell me you messed it up with that curator. She's our ticket to Burke."

Ray looked over to Natalie, offering her the chance to speak. She sat leaning back, appearing very uninvolved, her head resting against the office chair. She declined Ray's invitation with a shrug and a smirk.

"Dr. Ayhan isn't the problem," Ray said to Reggie, jutting his chin forward. "Right now, *you* are."

"Huh? What you mean?"

"We wanna know the truth. 'Cause you been telling stories, Regg. To each of us. Natalie says you lied to her."

"Wha—? Lied?"

"Yeah. So, I—I wanna know if—well, I wanna know if you lied to me too."

Reggie pinched his eyes into a squint as if he had trouble seeing Ray. "Lyin' to you? To Natalie? You makin' no sense."

Ray looked to Natalie again. "Kindly repeat the story Mr. Lovett told you about me, hmm?"

Natalie rolled her eyes as if the whole proceeding was beneath her dignity. "Oh, just ask him," she said to Ray.

"Tell us the story," Ray pressed her.

"Regg—tell him what you told me," Natalie pleaded.

"What story?" Reggie asked, still squinting.

"Don't pretend you can't remember," Natalie said hotly.

"Why won't you say—?" Ray eyed Natalie and shook his head. "Look, I get it. It's hard to admit you're wrong. Nobody wants to lose. Let me help you out. I mean, I bet I know what Regg said—that, y'know, even though you're to blame for everything, marrying Peagram and breaking up our team and stuff, I'd still be totally gracious and be willing to give you a second chance and—"

"What!" Natalie fumed, sitting upright. "That's not the story. Regg told me that *you* were to blame. That you were heartsick that you lost me and took full responsibility. That you were desperate to apologize and beg *my* forgiveness."

"What? But that's not true. Regg!" Ray turned to the webcam pleadingly.

Reggie pursed his lips and cast his eyes down. "Well, I don't recall sayin' it exactly like that."

Observing Reggie's discomfiture, Ray felt a muscle in his chest clench. The lingering doubt about Reggie's honesty now gripped him hard. Reggie had told Natalie a story about him that wasn't true. Did that mean that what Reggie had told him about Natalie was also a lie? *Natalie can't be right. She can't be.* "So, is Nat making all that up?" Ray asked Reggie in a dying burst of hope. "If she is, tell her. To her face."

Reggie rubbed his suddenly damp forehead. He stared down at his desk. His head winked in and out of the light.

Ray grew infuriated by Reggie's silence. It confirmed the lie. Reggie had blamed him to Natalie, told her the break-up of 8 Ball Productions was his fault. That wasn't the right story. There weren't multiple versions of the past. How dare Reggie even think of a story like that. He should've told Natalie *she* was at fault and the Dish Movie was her last chance to fix the mess she'd made of his life.

"I never told you I wanted to beg Natalie's forgiveness," Ray said to Reggie through clench teeth.

"Maybe I got a bit dramatic," Reggie said.

"I said nothing even close to that," Ray seethed.

"I told you," Natalie said to Ray in a superior tone. She leaned back in her chair and crossed her arms. "I told you he lied to both of us."

Natalie's tone pushed Ray to the brink. He couldn't bear to hear her openly claim victory. He sought a victory of his own and turned the full force of his ire on Reggie. If Reggie had lied, making a fool of him, then Ray wanted him to admit it, and when Reggie did confess, Ray wanted to make him pay. He kicked back angrily, the chair rolling him away from the table. "You swore to me in your office that you'd never lie about something so—so painful to me," he yelled at Reggie. "Remember that? 'Cause I sure do, you big phony! Two-faced, lying, sonofa—"

"You damn right, I lied," Reggie yelled back. "Lied to both of you damn fools."

"Ah-ha, you admit it!" Ray declared triumphantly.

## THE DIE IS CAST

"I lied. And I would do it again." The tip of Reggie's thick index finger filled the camera lens. "You *needed* me to lie. Both of ya!"

"What the hell does that mean?" Ray blurted.

Natalie briefly lost her look of disinterest and put her elbows on the table. "How you figure that?" she asked Reggie.

"Well, can't you two see what a mess you've made? When you were together, 8 Ball Productions was as big as Kendra Furns. Getting into Michael Shoore territory. I mean, Kendra Furns practically owns PBS. That could've been you. Your films had style, pace. High drama. You made people excited about documentaries. Documentaries, for Christ's sake! Monica's Dress felt like a mystery thriller, even though we already knew the president lied. Tent at Ground Zero was a grand tragedy right outta Shakespeare. You two wit' Clark, you magic. I dunno what went down wit' both of ya, but whoeva messed it up—Messed. It. Up!"

"Wait a sec," Ray jumped in. "Who you blaming?"

"You want truth?" Reggie's booming voice preemptively silenced any reply. He shook his finger at both. "You and you—had everything. Then you ruined yo-selves."

"Regg, how can you say—" Natalie tried to object.

"I don't wanna hear it from you, Little Miss Sad-Artist," Reggie cut in. "You had a great thing with Ray, but you wrecked it. Just like your sad-ass film about that stupid bike—right in the ditch. And you don't even want the new bike. What the hell were you doin' wit' Professor Bird-Bath? Even I knew you were goin' nowhere wit' him."

"But Almost a Loneliness wasn't about *me*," Natalie declared defensively. "It's about all women who dream of—"

"I'm the broken bike?" Ray asked Natalie. "It's pink with a fruit basket on it."

"Ra-ay, it's a symbol—"

"And don't get me started on your movie, Mr. Hot-Rod Ray," Reggie plunged on. "You let Natalie walk out the door, while you spendin' all your time chasin' that floozy, blonde model. We all know she usin' you. That's why your movie has you drivin' that stupid Firebird in circles."

"The car was a symbol of Staci?" Natalie asked Ray.

"I don't do symbols," Ray asserted flatly. "The film was about the auto industry."

"The point is—no one cared about your solo films," Reggie declared. "They both rotten tomatoes. Bad reviews and empty seats don't pay the bills. That's why I had to get you two back together—by any means."

Listening to Reggie, Ray felt all his angers merge—anger at Natalie leaving him for Peagram, anger at his film *Running on Fumes* failing, anger at Staci using him, and anger at Reggie's manipulation. How easily Natalie had cast him off, just when he'd thought he'd won her heart. Making a film without her had been an act of defiance, but its failure only reinforced how much he needed her. Reggie shouldn't have taken advantage of his wounded state. He should've helped him win again by any means—except deception. Team members had to trust each other.

"I'm not gonna sit here and take this," Ray yelled at Reggie. "Who do you think you are? We're not puppets.

## THE DIE IS CAST

And we're not your cash cows. You lied to me—to *Natalie*—just to make money? You—you can't toy with people like that." Ray pounded the arm of his chair.

"Now, listen—"

Ray stood. "I—I quit!"

"You can't quit," Reggie roared. "I got us back together. Don't blow it up again."

Ray felt the pressure of his pulse in his neck. His ears felt about to burst. In all his years of filmmaking with Natalie, he'd never given up on a story. But he was giving up on this one. The Dish Movie could go on without him. His pronouncement made him dizzy. It felt unreal, but at the same time, he knew those two small words expressed his deepest yearning for all the pain he had suffered with Natalie to end.

He looked down at her. She was staring up at him wide-eyed. Her hair was swept to one shoulder, every brown strand perfectly arranged. He wanted to touch her hair, not to muss it, but just to feel it in his fingers, to reach her somehow. Filmmaking with her had always been his bridge of choice, but it wasn't enough. It had never been enough. He'd relied on that bridge since the day he'd met her. It was old and rickety by now. Looking at her, he wondered if he'd quit partly because of her, to protect her from more pain, to forge a different path with her, build a different bridge.

Ray tried to work his lips to speak something of this to Natalie, but nothing came.

"Let's all calm down," Reggie urged in a cooler tone. "Don't make hasty decisions, Ray. Hear me out first. You listening, Ray? Sit down. Wait 'til you hear me out."

Ray slowly sank back down.

"There's no gettin' around the facts," Reggie said hurriedly. "You and Natalie are at a crossroads. Tent at Ground Zero was an amazin' success—for a docu. You know the stats. Grossed like 40 million in the U.S., add 15 for international. Not quite Mike Shoore, but still top 10 all-time for a docu. The distributer, Miramax, got their standard 45% cut of the box office and video revenue and paid us out of that. After our expenses, we made 1.3 million. We divided up, and each of us got ourselves some nice coin. People remember Tent—and Monica's Dress—so, 8 Ball still has some cachet. But it's been awhile, and your solo films tanked. Do I need to remind you how little you made going solo?"

Ray frowned and scratched his chin. Natalie sighed.

"That's right. And I lost my wallet producing both of your films. My take was so small, I needed loans to cover the overhead. Another big bust an' I'm done. Bankrupt."

Ray looked up quickly. "You lyin' again?"

Reggie shook his head. "I wish. Why do you think I went to extremes to get 8 Ball back to work? When I said I got a lot invested in you—I meant it. Literally. Could either of you survive another bad solo film?" Reggie flashed a grin and went on quickly. "Didn't think so. But it ain't all bad news. While you been in Istanbul, I've been in talks with both Miramax and Lionsgate. Guess what I learned? Disney is building a Bucky Browne theme park. Gonna break ground this year. I mean, Dishing ain't goin' away any time soon. Mira and Lions both want in on some Disher action. When I learned that you two were in tight with this museum curator *and* you found Professor

## THE DIE IS CAST

Burke who is digging up the top-secret shrine of the Dish—I told Mira and Lions. You wanna know what they said?"

Ray nodded eagerly. Natalie did not.

"With Oscar-winning filmmakers covering the *real* excavation of the *real* Dish, they anticipate a gross around 90 million, maybe 100. That's Shoore's neighborhood. I mean, Dishers are worldwide. You'll have international appeal for sure. And what's more, Mira thinks it can negotiate with cinema operators, maybe get a 60% revenue cut. So, our cut will be proportionally higher too." Reggie's grin got wider. "Folks, that's called *winning*. Think about it."

After some rapid mental calculations, Ray whistled.

"Not sure you know this, but Burke gave a presser couple days ago at the shrine," Reggie said. "Aired on CNN-Turk. The discovery is starting to be reported in the news here. You should watch the presser. Man, oh, man! His shouting match with the media practically advertises the Dish Movie for us." Reggie's head and shoulders started to bob as if he were jamming to music. "Now, if you two don't mess it up again, we be rollin' to the bank. You hear me? I hope so. 'Cause the Dish Movie could be so much bigger than just another film. It could be the next phenomenon."

This time as he listened to Reggie, Ray felt the weight of his anger ebb away. Finally, he had what he needed—a plan to win. The failures, the sorrows of the past, even Reggie's lies—all that could be swept aside if only 8 Ball Productions could win big. All the pieces were in place. He and Natalie just had to create a great story. Like Reggie said, the Dish Movie was so much more than a film, so working with Natalie on it wouldn't be a return to the same rickety strategies he'd always relied on to build a bridge to her. The Dish Movie was a magic bridge that only they could cross together. And once they did (and how could she not agree?), they'd be bigger than Kendra Furns and Michael Shoore. The epic success of 8 Ball Productions would be like the marriage of Kendra and Michael, sealed with Ray's own sweet kiss of forgiveness. All Natalie had to do was ask. Ray licked his lips, imagining his name immortalized in the annals of fame—Ray Cozart, a winner forever.

"All right, Regg," he said with a nod. "I'm back in."

Reggie applauded Ray for his good sense. The two men discussed the changes necessary to the movie's shooting schedule in order to film Professor Burke—canceling an interview with Archbishop Anthimos and a cave tour in Cappadocia—and then Reggie signed off.

Natalie, who'd barely said two words as Reggie and Ray dismantled the old itinerary, immediately stood.

"You leaving?" Ray asked in a tone of surprise. He assumed now would be her moment to say she was sorry.

"Yes!"

Natalie strode toward the door of the conference room.

Ray felt a pang of alarm at the vehemence in her voice. He reached for her. "Wait."

"What for?" She turned on him angrily. "You don't need me. You and Regg got it all figured out. I'm sure that woman Ayhan can help you make the film of your dreams."

## THE DIE IS CAST

"Wait? What? You mean, you're quitting?" Ray asked, his voice rising several notches.

"Well, what if I want to? You guys don't care what I think about things. What am I supposed to do—just forget all the past, all the hurt and—and betrayal—and just go on like nothing ever happened with us? Is that what you guys want? I just sweep it all away for you? Just so you can win?"

"But—but we're all on the same team. You're gonna win too. Don't you see—Nat, this Dish Move will save us."

"Right, just like Monica's Dress or Tent at Ground Zero."

"But this one is different."

"How? How is it different? How is there anything different between us?"

Natalie's tone of voice made a muscle spasm in Ray's neck. Her voice was so sad, so despairing, but also so full of hope—and unmistakable longing. He marveled at how much she could communicate at once. Her voice had such energy; it'd always been that way. Her words were woven with emotions. But the weaving unsettled him, because she sparked emotions in him that he didn't know how to speak.

"Nat," he said quietly, trying to grasp at one thread, "do you ... want to be with me? Not ... 8 Ball Productions. I don't mean that. But I mean, just ... *me*?"

Natalie was standing near the door. At these words, she swayed, seeming to lose her balance. She put a hand to her forehead and looked down. When she looked back up again, her eyes were liquid with tears—but there was a fierceness in them too, as if she were trying to cut off the flow of them.

"Always," she said.

Ray blinked several times, trying to comprehend the enormity of that word. "You—you—?"

"Yes, *always*. From the very first. The moment I met you. There, are you happy I said it?"

"Why are you so angry?"

"Because! You're so stupid you have to ask! After all this time. Like, you can't figure it out. Why do you have to humiliate me?" She clenched her fists in front of her. "I wanted to be with you all this time, but you didn't want me. You only wanted my work, what I could bring to the team. You only ever showed an interest in me when we were working. You teased me and made me hope. But you never followed through. You were always such a goddamn flirt! I thought maybe after we won at Tribeca, there was something deeper between us. But no, you were off to Daytona Beach with Staci the next day. I—I gave up on you. You enjoyed distracting yourself so much with her, you weren't willing to risk anything with me. She only ever used you to try to launch a film career. I heard she left you for an Italian actor who got her a part in a movie. Maybe that's some sort of justice. You'd rather be with a girl who uses you than with me. How do you think that makes me feel? And you wonder why I left. What was I supposed to think? You had your tongue down her throat right in front of me at Reggie's party, and then I'm supposed to believe that what happened between us at Midtown Studios was special? You were just trying to keep 8 Ball Productions together, and you're such a boy, that's the only way you knew how to do it. You just used me to spite Geoffrey. You were so jealous that you didn't have the guts to make a commitment to me yourself, you had to try to ruin a commitment I had made. My chance for love! And I guess you did ruin it, so you can be happy you won. And now what do I hear today but that you have the audacity to think breaking up 8 Ball was all my fault."

By the time she was finished with this speech, Natalie was shaking all over. She appeared small and fragile but ferociously defiant. Surrendering the precious treasure of her resentment had taken an enormous act of her will. And she'd done it without shedding one tear. She wouldn't surrender them. Those she kept to herself.

Ray fired back at her as soon as she was through.

"You think you're so smart! That was always the problem. Maybe I did wanna be with you too, but you always thought you were too good for me. What, am I gonna come begging for your love just so you can find fault with me? At least Staci didn't judge everything I do. You only want perfection, but even that's not good enough. For Christ's sake—we won an Academy Award and still you walk away. You don't wanna be happy with anything. And how was I supposed to know you cared? You never wanted to do anything I liked outside of filming. I had to work damn hard just to get a laugh or a touch out of you. I mean, every guy looks for signs. And I risked way more than you ever did, tried to protect you from marrying Peagram—he was only using you for his stupid books, thought you were a great wordsmith or something, but you didn't wanna see that. Hell, I even made love to you, and what did you do? Started to cry like it was some great tragedy. And that was after you told me not to stop, so I didn't. You think none of that was real? That I didn't mean it? What more could I do? Nothing's gonna convince you if you don't wanna believe. I don't have anything to be sorry for. You can't make me be sorry. It wasn't my fault. You're the one who left, so maybe you should show some gratitude that I agreed to take you back."

Ray broke off though he still had something to say. Natalie's accusations had unsealed the well of his anger, but deeper in the well, much further down below all the vehemence, were silent, murky waters of inexpressible sadness. His voice broke as he entered those depths, and he sought her eyes as if searching for aid to speak such grief.

"And—and—you didn't have to be so cruel and throw away the Mystic 8 Ball," he said. "Why? Why did you do it? Y'know, I was always gonna give it to you 'cause next to you, it was the most important thing to me—it was *us*. I wanted you to stay, even if you did marry Peagram, but it's like you had to stick it to me to prove a point. Being without you was the worst thing that ever happened to me. I—I—"

Ray broke off again and looked down at the floor.

Natalie slowly lowered her fists.

"I don't wanna go through that again," he said. "Please. Don't leave."

▼ ▼ ▼ ▼

Natalie shut the door to her room, sank into the chair by the table, laid her head in her arms and cried and cried.

Her grief was a total fusion of feelings. She cried for all her years of hope and longing and for so much barren effort. She cried for time that was irrecoverable and for choices never made. She cried for what might have been and for what could be. She cried for saying exactly what she wanted to say and for hearing many things she didn't want to hear. She cried out of relief and out of regret, because she had won—and lost. She cried out of love and out of fear. And because she had lied to Ray about the Mystic 8 Ball.

*The 8 Ball.*

It was still lodged where it had hidden itself—in the shadows under her bed.

She wiped her eyes and looked about again for some object to help her free it. The stretchable boom pole from her audio bag would work. She knelt beside the bed and extended the device. The 8 Ball rolled toward her easily. She grabbed it off the floor, careful to keep its window down.

But she'd have to risk it. She'd have to look at its answer. There was no getting around it. She'd asked it a question— the most important question. Did Ray love her? What would the Mystic 8 Ball say?

Her pulse throbbed painfully. She told herself fear was ridiculous. It was just a toy. It didn't matter what it said.

But it *did* matter.

*Next to you, it was the most important thing to me—it was us.*

She stood and turned on her bedside lamp so she would be sure to see. She sat on her bed and shook the toy gently. And shook it. Then closed her eyes and slowly turned the window face up. She held it under the light and looked down, hoping, praying—

"Outlook Good," the die said.

Scene 25
―――――――――――――――――――――――――――――――

## The Whitakerware Crusade

*Vatican City*

*Sunday, March 14*

Father Victor Santorini, the personal secretary to Pope Boniface X, rushed into the papal apartments overlooking Saint Peter's Square. He entered the Pope's studio office out of breath and without knocking. Boniface, seated at his small, austere desk, looked up from a memo he was reading. Classical music played lightly from a stereo system.

"Vic, what's going on?" Boniface asked in his baritone voice. Because of his stature, he sat sideways at his desk to keep from bumping his knees.

"Your Holiness," Victor began, struggling between breaths, "thank goodness—thank goodness I caught you before—before Holy Mass."

Boniface laid down the memo. "What's happened?"

"There's—there's a new—a new—"

Boniface held up a hand to stop him. "Sit down and gather yourself. You look harassed by Satan himself." He gestured toward a simple black-walnut chair that matched his desk and the volume-lined shelves that surrounded him. He turned off the music.

## THE DIE IS CAST

Victor sank into the chair gratefully, feeling a twinge of distress at the undeniable evidence of his poor physical conditioning. He imagined himself quite fit, as he was only in his early forties and rather thin. As he took several deep breaths, he wiped his damp neck with a handkerchief.

"Your Holiness, I have just come from the church. There's another protest forming."

Boniface leaned back in his chair, relieved. "But that's not new. You worried me. Why so distressed? Those Dishers make a spectacle of themselves far too often."

"Yes, I know. They've been quiet for months, but it was just the calm before the storm, as they say. What they're doing now—they're taking their protest to new heights."

"Really?" Boniface leaned forward, his blue eyes focused on Victor. "In what way?"

Victor studied the Pope's warm, smooth face. He'd been Boniface's secretary for ten years, ever since Boniface's arrival in Rome from his native New York City—then as the charismatic Archbishop Gerald Whitman. He'd witnessed Boniface's meteoric rise to the highest office of the Roman Catholic Church. Victor had learned over the years that the Yankee Pope gave the impression to the media of being impetuous. Boniface's rapid-fire flashes of feeling would burst from his lips, burning hot with indignation in one moment and with joy in the next. With his candor and easy, informal manner, Boniface had quickly won the confidence of his peers and the devotion of Catholics the world over.

However, Victor knew that much of Boniface's touchy-feely openness was a performance. Behind it existed a mind constantly strategizing. Boniface always knew what would benefit not only the Catholic Church but also his own fortunes. For instance, upon reflection, it seemed quite likely to Victor that Boniface already knew about the latest Disher protest and that the concern on his face (perhaps a bit too concerned) was but the evidence of a pre-conceived plan. Nevertheless, Victor plunged on. "Your Holiness, the protesters have gone beyond carrying signs and yelling about the crusades. Now they're attacking the laypeople."

"Attacking them? How so?"

Victor paused, feeling absurd at what he was about to say. "They're throwing plastic bowls at them."

Boniface raised an eyebrow. "Is that so?"

"Yes, Your Holiness."

"Hurling Whitakerware ... my, my."

Boniface opened a lower desk drawer and lifted out a clear, plastic bowl, the kind used for food storage. The bowl was dirty and scratched. On the sides in bright red marker, someone had scrawled the words, FAKER! LIAR!

"Do they look like this?" Boniface handed it to Victor.

The secretary examined the container. "So, you knew."

Boniface smiled wryly. "Useless without the lid."

Victor exhaled and set the bowl on the desk.

"Come," Boniface said. He stood and waved Victor toward a curtained window.

When they drew back the curtains and cracked open the window, the feeble light of the misty morning touched their faces, and the entire length of Saint Peter's

Square lined by marble colonnades lay before them. In the dim sunlight, the pink granite of Saint Peter's Obelisk appeared brown. To the far right stood the magnificent Basilica. And in the middle, a group of Dishers, about a hundred strong, jumped about chanting. Some were dressed as medieval warriors, a few even decked out in plate armor and plumed helmets. Several others were wearing dog ears and tails; one person was in full dog costume, looking very much like a university mascot. Instead of swords, however, the legion waved ladles and spatulas and plastic dog bones in the air. A few heaved crockpots and Dutch ovens at a police barricade. Several of the police officers' uniforms were soiled with tomato soup. At least, Victor hoped it was just soup.

"Like some Renaissance Festival gone wrong," Boniface mused.

"What is it they're chanting?"

"I asked about that." Boniface retrieved a note from his desk. "Hey hey, ho ho, your bowl was used to feed Fi-do."

"My goodness."

"Catchy, isn't it?"

"What in the world is that?" Victor asked, pointing out the window.

Boniface rejoined him and peered over his shoulder.

The Dishers had marched toward Saint Peter's Obelisk and formed a circle. In the circle they'd set into place a machine which looked very odd, like a large camera tripod but fitted with a motor. Above the motor, two white tires were mounted at an upward angle. Several Dishers were busy adjusting the mounting to widen the space between the tires. Then they tilted the motor back and started it; the tires began to spin rapidly.

"That," Boniface said, "is an ATM."

"ATM?"

"Automatic Throwing Machine."

"Never heard of such a thing."

"They're popular in America. Sports teams use them to practice. You can set them up to throw soccer balls, footballs, volleyballs ..."

Victor frowned, unimpressed. He'd spent most of his youth in libraries.

As they watched, a Disher manning the machine held a large, dented stockpot just behind the two spinning tires.

"There's no way that's going to work," Boniface said.

"Fire the catapult!" the Dishers shouted in unison. The stockpot was thrust between the spinning tires. Instantly, the tires shot it fifteen feet into the air. The police ducked as the pot landed with a dull clatter on the cobblestones behind them.

"Hmm. It did work," Boniface said, tapping his chin.

The Dishers cheered and swung their ladles, spatulas, and dog bones in triumph. The police pushed forward to reach the ATM before another missile could be launched. At the open end of the square, more Vatican City police, over thirty, rushed into the fray.

"The cavalry," Boniface remarked drolly. He shut the curtains and returned to his desk.

Victor sat down heavily in the seat he'd occupied earlier. "The whole thing is outrageous. Imagine! Shopping in the kitchen aisle of the nearest Whitaker's for weaponry.

What if some misguided soul decides to hide a steak knife amid the soup spoons? Someone will be seriously injured or worse. You know the media would make meat out of that, er, I mean ..." Victor grimaced, not intending the pun.

"You're right. No matter what someone else does, it is our fault. Because we don't capitulate to their demands."

"Their demands," Victor spat in disgust. "Accusing us of deliberately displaying a fake bowl for our own profit. What do they expect us to do? Throw up our hands and say—okay, you're right, we're frauds. Who does that? No one. The media is all too happy to give Dishers a voice, fomenting the controversy, and for what? For *their* profit. Always referring to it as the 'alleged' Last Supper Dish." Victor made scare quotes as he spoke. "Such hypocrisy. They only encourage Dishers into more extreme protests. Which in turn gives the media an excuse to criticize us and generate sensational news. If there ever is a steak knife amid the spoons, I will certainly know who is to blame for it."

Boniface breathed in deeply, eyeing the memo he'd been reading when Victor interrupted. "I've found it remarkably interesting being thrust into a controversy that predates me by, oh, eight hundred years. I often wonder, what does this have to do with me?" He shifted two hardbound books aside and laid the memo on a third book which lay open. The book was spiral bound; it appeared to be a collection of photocopies. Victor didn't recognize it but supposed it to be a reproduction of a medieval manuscript from the Vatican Library's vast collection. Digital copies were often made so that scholars could study the ancient texts without harming the originals. The two hardbound books, however, Victor knew, as he himself had retrieved them from the library at Boniface's request three years previously—just before Philotheos had been invited to Rome. They were *The Annals of Andronicus* and *The Travels of Putney the Pilgrim*. Boniface consulted them often; both were stuffed with book markers and notes annotated in his florid script.

"You're the Holy Father," Victor said. "There's no escaping the symbolic significance of your office. It is the way of the world." Victor observed again the battered Whitakerware bowl on Boniface's desk. It was turned so that the word LIAR displayed prominently. "You know what riled up these Dishers this time?" he asked. "It isn't peak season. Hasn't Steve Finder's new novel been out for some time?"

"This did." Boniface handed Victor an article. "It's the lead story on their website."

"TrueDishers again? What are they insinuating now?" Victor casually scanned the pages in his hands. What he read startled him, however. "The Shrine of the Four Keepers has been found?" He laughed incredulously. "These agitators. They can't be serious. Why make up such a story? One so easily discredited?"

Boniface pressed his lips together and said nothing.

"It has been discredited, hasn't it?" Victor asked.

Boniface handed Victor the memo he'd been reading when Victor had burst in. It was from Frederico D'Angelo. "The discovery was announced at the opening of the Byzantine art exhibition."

## THE DIE IS CAST

Victor read quickly. "So, Frederico agrees with Bishop Louis's assessment that the Istanbul Museum of Ancient History would not be suitable to house the Dish." He looked up. "Did not Cardinal Eduardo offer an opinion?"

Boniface pointed to the memo's second page. "You need to keep reading. Apparently, Eduardo couldn't offer his opinion. He was taken ill and in the hospital when Frederico sent this. There was an incident."

Victor read from the memo. "A number of the Orthodox guests disrupted the ceremony, shouting for the Dish, and with no provocation, attacked Bishop Louis and his Most Reverend Eminence, who was taken by ambulance to—" Victor stopped and addressed Boniface: "Good heavens, is Eduardo in danger?"

"It appears it was a case of mere fatigue. Possibly a plate of bad oysters."

Victor sighed in relief. "Still, if even the mere mention of the shrine is enough to start a fight over the Dish, then this museum cannot be a consideration. Displaying the Dish requires optimal security, which this institution lacks. It is too much to ask of them. This confirms my opinion that moving the Dish to Istanbul is unwise."

"Maybe," Boniface grunted, "maybe."

Victor's eyes wandered back to the memo, and he read the final paragraph. "Ah, I see the real reason you sent those three to the exhibition. Because Ecumenical Patriarch Philotheos was there to give a speech. Frederico confirms that Philotheos has no interest in your returning the Dish." He handed the memo back to Boniface.

"I wanted to know if the two guests at my secret meeting last month were accurately representing Philotheos."

"It seems they were."

"Perhaps." Boniface stared glumly at the memo.

"Perhaps? What is there to doubt? They said no to your face, and Philotheos said no to Frederico."

"It's about attitude, Vic. Chrysanthus and Leronymos were defiant, they were eager to say no. Philotheos is a different man. We had a great rapport when he was here. When I told him that I was having significant conversations with the College of Cardinals about the Dish, he seemed ... contemplative. As if he were envisioning the possibilities of what it would mean to Christianity if he accepted my offer."

"Did you add that most of the significant conversations involved the Cardinals yelling?"

Boniface pursed his lips sheepishly.

"Honestly, how else could Philotheos have responded to you when he was here?" Victor went on. "The press was panting for signs of conflict so they could transform the event into a circus. Even if he did seem to consider it then, that was three years ago. A man can change his mind."

"I think the change was the shrine's discovery. Frederico said it was among Philotheos's reasons. Maybe he was interested in my offer up to that moment." Boniface tossed the memo; it fluttered to the floor. "From nowhere that shrine steps between us. How could he accept our Dish now?"

Victor shook his head sympathetically. "He can't. The shrine Emperor Andronicus built has long been held to be the key to finding the true Dish. Most Orthodox faithful believe this. Philotheos must think their dreams are coming true at last. After all these centuries. The shrine will be unearthed, its clues will be deciphered, and they will finally find the lost Dish."

"Exactly. Emperor Andronicus bequeathed hope to the world that the true Dish can still be found—anywhere but here." Boniface gestured toward the window to indicate the Vatican Museums. "Such hope is akin to desire and is thus very resilient. Even if Philotheos is personally amenable to receiving the Dish from us, he wouldn't crush the hopes of his flock. Why, they must think they now have evidence to support their centuries claim that our Dish is fake. It would be an insult to even offer it to them now. They'd throw it right back in our face."

Victor eyed the plastic Whitakerware bowl. "It would be like offering *that* to them."

Boniface exhaled in exasperation. He pushed himself out of his chair and paced, his hands clasped behind his back. "This shrine!" he exclaimed in characteristic emotive fashion. "Why now? What a most inconvenient resurrection. I thought returning Kosmo's relics helped me establish a foundation with Philotheos. Something to be built up."

Victor looked down at his empty hands resting in his lap. "Perhaps this reconciliation is simply not meant to be. Jesus himself said that he came to divide, father against son, mother against daughter. Why should it not be so between Catholics and Orthodox?"

"You can't seriously mean that," Boniface muttered. "We all believe in Jesus." Then he added in a lower tone, "We all share in the sin."

"Sometimes you puzzle me," Victor said. "Weren't you pondering a moment ago why you've been dropped into this ancient game between our churches? So many previous popes have simply permitted the game to go on. Why can't you? We've been good custodians of the Dish—and it's clear the Orthodox cannot be so. They don't even want it back. They deny the bowl we have is even the true Dish of Christ. Why do you care so much about ending the game?"

Boniface resumed his seat and gazed at the books and manuscripts piled on his desk. "A small, still voice." He smiled wryly and tapped his ear.

Victor snorted. "So, you're now the prophet Elijah, hearing the voice of God?"

Boniface laughed. "God showed Elijah tornados, earthquakes, and fire. I think we're getting into that now." He waggled the Whitakerware bowl in front of Victor. "Elijah paid attention to none of these but listened to the small, still voice. I pray that Philotheos is listening as well."

The two men lapsed into a long silence.

"What happens now?" Victor prompted. He assumed Boniface's silence meant that he'd conceived a new stratagem to overcome the debacle at the museum and was only waiting for the right moment to reveal it. Victor had come to rely on Boniface's unwavering determination.

Boniface sighed pensively. "For now, more of *this*." He gestured toward the curtained window, indicating the mock siege occurring in the square. "And more of *that*." He nodded at the article on his desk from *TrueDishers.net*. His face sobered, and he added: "Somewhere in between, there is a narrow path, but only a few find it. We must pray that we can amid the coming storm."

Victor, expecting to hear a strategy from a resolute Boniface, was troubled by these words. "Of course, that is fine on the spiritual side of things, but surely we must release an official statement—about the protests, the discovery—to the effect that we have the true Dish, have had it for centuries. We believe there's nothing to be found at the shrine. Of course, I would word it more artfully than that."

Boniface glanced at the open, spiral-bound book on his desk and frowned bitterly. With dispirited eyes, he faced his secretary and said, "There will be no official statement."

Victor's mouth gaped.

"You see, Vic, I think there *is* something to be found at this shrine. I think this discovery will lead to the resurrection of ... many truths. Truths that, much as we might wish otherwise, can no longer remain buried."

Scene 26

## A Persian Sword

*Istanbul, Turkey*

*Excavation site at the demolished Sirkeci Rail Station*

*Sunday, March 14*

The sky was hazy and the air stagnant. The sign at the corner of the construction site beyond the security fence bore a thick layer of dust. COMING SOON: MARMARA METRO STATION it promised in Turkish and English. The old Sirkeci Rail Station, long since swept away, had left a void in the cityscape, half a block on Halah Street returned to nature, stripped to bare earth. But despite the promise of renewal, bulldozers sat idle, and a crane did nothing but cast a pale shadow. Construction workers were absent. If not for several spotlights blazing down on the pit at the heart of the site, the half-block would've appeared to be a dead zone.

"Adam, please, describing how it was lifted will take but a moment," Ayhan said to Burke as they stood before the altar in the shrine's inner sanctum. "All this," she gestured around them to indicate the shrine generally, "is of tremendous historical significance. All our—I mean, *your* progress should be recorded for posterity. I regret that I did not think to procure a professional film crew before now. I assure you, Mr. Cozart and Ms. Ashbrook are the best."

Burke appeared poised for demolition. He stood opposite the altar with a chisel in hand, having already dislodged crumbling mortar from the apse's notably barren wall. His shirt sleeves were rolled past his elbows, and his khakis were muddy. There was a streak of dust on his cheek. To one side of him stood his pudgy assistant Duffy holding a rock pick and looking very uneasy in the presence of the camera. Clark had Sneak Peek aimed right at them. To the other side of Burke stood Natalie holding high a boom mike.

"Progress!" Burke spoke sarcastically, recoiling at the word. "Look what's in my way." He jabbed at the wall with the chisel. Loose bits of stone fell away.

Ayhan couldn't quite recall why the apse's barren wall was important to Burke. Something about its composition—cut stone rather than yellow brick. That's what Burke had been ranting about at the museum the prior evening. But the wall's material structure made not a fig's difference to her. It could've been made of figs for all she cared. She hadn't brought 8 Ball Productions to the site to film a wall. She'd brought them there to get Burke on camera saying things about the Dish. Things she could use. Profitable things ...

"But think of the difficulties you have surmounted already," Ayhan said, employing a different tactic. "Imagine if Mr. Cozart and Ms. Ashbrook had been here to capture the dramatic unearthing of Panikos the Youth. Or the mosaics of Kostas, Zoticus, and Nil. Imagine if they had been here when you discovered the archway, the one with the conclusive Latin inscription identifying this as the Shrine of the Four Keepers—"

"That was found by Dr. Foo," Burke corrected her.

"And then you dug out this apse and found this extraordinary altar," Ayhan went on undeterred. "You have defied all the odds. I can only think of one other man in your position who has." She smiled coyly and brushed her fingertips gently over the altar's surface as if caressing skin. She had Burke's full attention. "Surely, you have not forgotten?"

Burke scratched his bald spot, leaving behind a dirt mark. "Er, well," he muttered crossly, "Winters won the Royal Archaeological Institute's Book of the Year Award, but that was only because his sycophants at the—"

Ayhan's melodic laughter cut him off. "No, no, you are not using your imagination at all. You, dear professor, are a real-life Bucky Browne. Why, you have practically been starring in an adventure film already." She batted her lashes at Burke. "I think it is about time we made it official, do you not agree? Mr. Cozart and Ms. Ashbrook simply need to get a bit up to date. So, could you not briefly explain for their benefit how you lifted the altar in search of the Dish?"

Ayhan's words broke through. Burke glanced up at Natalie's dangling microphone, suddenly very aware that his words were being recorded.

"Is that thing on?" he asked her.

She nodded.

Burke licked his lips and eyed Clark's camera. Then he deliberately turned his back on it and dropped his chisel.

"Is there any dirt on my face?" he whispered to Duffy.

"Um. Yeah. A smudge. I wouldn't worry about it, sir. It's very small," he lied. "Hardly noticeable."

"A small smudge. I didn't ask for your opinion. Now give me a clean hanky."

"I don't have one, sir."

"Well, where is it?"

"I dunno. Probably in one of the vans."

"No, I mean the smudge."

"Are you asking for my opinion?"

"The facts. Facts! Right or left?"

"Oh. On your left cheek. No, wait, that's my left. Ha-ha. I mean, your right cheek."

Burke wiped his cheek with his forearm. The results were poor, but Duffy assured him he looked much better. Afterwards, facing the camera again, Burke cleared his throat and shifted his glasses down his nose.

"Er, um, okay, for all of you watching this at home, the first thing you gotta understand is that Bucky Browne—well, I mean, that Finder guy doesn't know anything. I did some consulting work for him for Cave of All Fears. The screenplay sucked as far as I'm concerned. For starters, Bucky just falls into a hole in the ground and there the treasure sits. I mean, that's like Alice in Wonderland. A child's fantasy. That's not real archaeology. Real archaeology is a painstaking search for the truth of history and—"

"Adam," Ayhan interrupted before his rant could gain traction, "perhaps we might cover that topic another time. Tell us about the altar." She patted the top of it. "I mean, since the camera is here."

"Right. So, where Mr. Mozart is standing is where visitors to the shrine—"

"It's Cozart," Ray corrected.

"—pilgrims like Putney, for instance, would come and kneel, and then the monks—they would've been part of the Order of Andronicus. He was the emperor who built the shrine. Well, anyway, they'd place a bowl—maybe the Dish—on the altar for a cleansing ritual. Have you heard of Putney from England? He visited the shrine in 1350. His description of the ritual is stark and, frankly, a bit disturbing."

"Oh? How so?" Ray asked.

"Putney says the monks tempted pilgrims to take the Dish for themselves and thus gain command of all. I've always understood Putney to mean that pilgrims had to prove themselves worthy to venerate the Dish. Putney says he—"

"What about this Latin inscription on the altar's front edge?" Ayhan interrupted again. "Ask and it shall be given thee. Seek and ye shall find. Do those words not suggest the Dish was kept by the monks right here in this inner sanctum? Perhaps, in the final hours, even hidden under the altar?" She smiled at Burke—a bite-smile.

"Yes, it's possible," Burke said to her, "but you know it wasn't there. We lifted the altar and found nothing. Look, the altar doesn't matter now." He adjusted his glasses, spun back toward the wall, and picked up his dropped chisel. "This wall is what matters. I told you at the museum it was different from the others in the shrine. Now I think I know why. Look around you. This room is perfectly square. But it shouldn't be. This barren wall should be semicircular, like—like," he looked at the camera, "well, for you watching at home, imagine a bay window on a house, and you'll know what I mean. I think this wall shouldn't actually be here. I think it was a late addition, and if we break it down—"

"Adam!" Ayhan exclaimed. "You think the Dish is behind this wall?" She'd gotten nowhere with her questions about the altar, but she sensed an even better prospect of getting what she was after.

"YEEESSS!" Burke bellowed. "Now, if you'll just let me get at it. We're running out of time." Burke eyed the rock pick in Duffy's hand and snatched it. "That's for me. Here, you can handle this little thing." He thrust his chisel at Duffy. "And go find me a crack hammer and a pickax. And I'm gonna need some muscle. Get that McKenzie fellow."

"My God, is it possible? Is the Dish really here?" Ray murmured in amazement. "This film is gonna be lights out."

"Why would the wall have been added?" Ayhan asked.

"Well, think about it," Burke said. "Sultan Mehmet didn't spring a sneak attack in the middle of the night. He laid siege to Constantinople for months. He'd been positioning his forces along the isthmus long before that. Everybody knew what was coming. Citizens fortified the city's walls in preparation. I think the Order of Andronicus fortified a wall of their own, maybe at the direction of the emperor himself. There was no way they could take the Dish out of the city. They would've walked smack dab into the Sultan's janissaries. I'm betting they hid the Dish in the shrine, right in the apse—buried behind this wall. They anticipated the Sultan's men looting the shrine for treasure. This wall gives the impression there's nothing in the shrine to take."

Burke had been shouting and gesturing wildly as he spoke. Then he noticed Duffy was still standing there.

"Why are you still here?" he demanded to know.

"Um, sir, who is McKenzie?" Duffy asked.

"Y'know—McKenzie."

Duffy puffed out his cheeks, indicating he didn't know. "Uh, sir, if you like, I can go get Stoltzfus. Or Hromadova."

"No, not her! I want McKenzie. The guy with the shaggy black hair." Burke scratched his bald spot as he said this.

"You mean Makarios? Giulio Makarios?"

"Yes, that's what I said, didn't I?"

"Okay, I'll get him." Duffy turned to leave.

"Bring the crack hammer too," Burke called after him.

"How long will it take to get through the wall?" Ayhan asked, her eyes shining. She stepped near Burke and with her fingers, traced the outline of one of the stones. But she was seeing far bigger things, things far beyond the present.

"Depends how thick the stones are," Burke said. Randomly, he tapped joints of mortar with his rock pick as if to test their thickness. Bits of it fell away. "But it doesn't matter, I guess, because we've only got one more day. Nobody in the crew will sleep tonight. We'll blow the wall up if we have to. Pasa will have to drag me away himself before I leave. This is history in the making. It's why we're all here, isn't it? To witness the truth of history?"

"That's why the camera is here," Ray said with a big grin.

Ayhan averted her eyes. "I—I must inform Ahmet of your theory about the wall. He is working with Pasa to give you more time. This development will infuse his efforts with even greater urgency."

Just then Duffy returned with Giulio. The shaggy-haired youth looked dusty and disgruntled. He wore a bandana tied about his throat and carried a crack hammer.

"Finally, McKenzie," Burke said. "At last, we can begin. Give me that big boy." He grabbed the crack hammer from Giulio and thrust the smaller rock pick at him. Then he swung the hammer above his head as if wielding a scepter, forgetting the presence of Natalie's microphone. The hammer clanked against it noisily.

"Er, you're gonna have to stand aside," Burke said to her. "This is a great moment. I need room. Room!"

"My name is Makarios, not McKenzie," Giulio said to Burke irritably. He stood near enough to the stone wall that his body cast a shadow on it.

"McKenzie, you're blocking my light. Step aside," Burke said. "You and Duffy work over there on that end."

Clark adjusted Sneak Peek to zoom in on Burke.

Burke poised himself to swing his hammer at the wall.

"Okay, people," he said. "Get ready. It's time! This is history in the making. And I have a hunch we will make it. I have a hunch this shrine has one secret left to tell us."

▼ ▼ ▼ ▼

An hour later, after Burke, Duffy, and Giulio had only managed to remove five stones from the wall and had called for the aid of Drs. Stoltzfus and Foo, Ray felt Ayhan lay a hand on his arm to suggest that the film crew take a break.

"Gladly," Ray said. "I didn't know archaeology could be so loud. My head's ringing."

"It is a shame they cannot use a wrecking ball," Ayhan said, indicating the frenzied hammering.

"No, I don't mean that," Ray said. "I meant—"

"Dammit, Duffy! This isn't a tea party. Get back to it. Faster, faster!" Burke shouted at his assistant.

Ray and Ayhan exchanged amused looks.

"I trust my itinerary has not disappointed you?" Ayhan asked, but her smug expression left no doubt as to the answer to her question.

Ray smiled and waved to Clark and Natalie. "Okay, guys, cut it there. Let's regroup."

Ayhan led them up the wooden ramp out of the pit and directed them toward the artifacts tent which had been erected near the perimeter fence. The bare ground sloped steeply, and they stepped aside twice to let workers going down with wheelbarrows pass by.

"Dude," Clark whispered to Ray as they walked several paces behind Ayhan, "you want me to get her on camera?" He patted Sneak Peek to indicate the camera's readiness.

"Not sure she wants to be interviewed," Ray whispered back. "She hasn't said."

"This would be a good angle," Clark said, snickering.

Ray chuckled. Ayhan was wearing tight gray slacks and a red-leather jacket. Her lustrous black hair was twisted up and clipped at the back of her head. Ray's eyes roved from her legs to her neck and lingered there.

"Dude, ask her. You gotta get her on camera," Clark said. "I love her accent. And she's so hot. Like exotic hot. That's the best kind of hot, don't you think?"

"Yeah," Ray said to Clark automatically, but the enthusiasm in his voice was restrained. He was thinking of Natalie.

Out of deep, mutual embarrassment over the previous evening's revelations, he and Natalie had hardly made eye contact. That morning both had eagerly and silently thrown themselves into their filming. Natalie's accusations had washed over Ray like a wave, but not a cleansing one. The debris of her words clung to him. His mind felt coated and thick with them, and there was a bad taste in his mouth. But even in the surge of her wrath, she had thrown him a life preserver. *Always. I always wanted to be with you.* He clung to these words. In all the ugliness about him, they were so beautiful, but they also deepened the mystery of her. Because without knowing how, he had won her so many years ago, and without knowing how, he had also lost her.

Natalie, a few steps behind, caught up to him and Clark. Her hand gripped the strap on the audio bag slung over her shoulder, and her face was averted. Clearly, she was lost in thought. Ray peered down at the top of her head; her ponytail swung gently. In his mind, he could still see her standing near the conference room door with her fists raised. And then, when he'd pleaded with her not to leave him again, she'd slowly lowered them and quietly said, "Okay."

That was it. Then they'd stood in silence for a minute. Ray didn't know what to do. He wanted to touch her but was far too amazed that, somehow, his words already had. Maybe for the first time ever. Such wizardry needed to be further examined. Future favorable results would depend on his ability to reproduce the spell. What had he said right this time?

Natalie's foot caught on a rock, and she stumbled.

"Watch it," Ray said, reaching out his hand. "Want me to carry that bag?"

"What? No. I'm fine. I got it," she said, but her words sounded far away, as if she spoke by rote.

Ray shrugged. They continued up the slope. Some part of him mused that maybe, after all, there was no mystery to solve about what had gone wrong with Natalie. Despite her accusations, losing her hadn't been his fault. She'd simply messed up what could've been a great love story all on her own. Perhaps, even now, she was mere moments away from admitting it. He would wait and see.

Once inside the artifacts tent, Ayhan's command was immediately felt. She gave orders to several students to label containers for transport to the museum and enlisted others to carry heavy boxes of artifacts to awaiting vans. She requested an update from the archaeologists Calvino and Hromadova as to the preparedness of two large architectural pieces slated to be moved, and demanded a report from Murat about how much packing material remained at the museum lab. During much of this, Ayhan spoke in Turkish, and Ray, Clark, and Natalie were left alone to loiter about the tables. But

# THE DIE IS CAST

Clark couldn't take his eyes off Ayhan. Every now and then, he gave Ray an imploring look.

There were rows and rows of tables in the tent, most of them crammed with architectural fragments, but others held remnants of Ottoman conquest: broken swords, spear heads, and battered helmets shaped like miniature domes. The Shrine of the Four Keepers was a graveyard of war.

Clark rested Sneak Peek on a table and picked up a battered scabbard. "Dude, look at this awesome carving," he whispered to Ray. "Why don't you ask Ayhan about it?"

"She's busy."

"But if you did ... y'know, we could get her on camera."

"What are you guys whispering about?" Natalie asked.

Ray scratched the back of his head. "Oh, nothing. We're just wondering if we should interview Ayhan, that's all."

"Is it on her itinerary?" Natalie asked sarcastically.

"It'd be good if it was," Ray said defensively. "Burke gave us great material, don't you think? And all this stuff here is interesting." He gestured at the tables. "If she agreed, would you be all right if I asked her some questions?"

Natalie rolled her eyes. "Fine."

It took nothing for Ray to convince Ayhan to appear on camera. She accepted his "small favor" eagerly and promised not to shout. They shared a good laugh about that.

Natalie did not understand the inside joke.

"Oh, it's nothing," Ray said to her as they decided how best to position Ayhan before the tables. "Just something we were talking about before. Look, I'm gonna ask her basic stuff about these artifacts. Shouldn't take too long."

To position Ayhan, Ray nudged her elbows, turning her left and right. She melted into giggles, submitting to his touch freely. In her heeled boots, she could look Ray right in the eyes. Finally, the two of them settled on a dramatic, half-turned pose that faced Natalie.

While Ray consulted with Clark about camera angles, Ayhan eyed Natalie haughtily. "How do I look, Ms. Ashbrook?" she asked with exaggerated primness, patently pleased to witness Natalie's grim demeanor.

"Fantastic," Ray exclaimed, overhearing her question. Clark agreed.

After Natalie's sound check, they were set to go. Murat stood by watching, his lips pressed in apparent envy.

"Roll camera, roll sound," Ray said to Clark and Natalie.

"Ah, well, I guess there is no turning back now, is there Mr. Cozart?" Ayhan said to him with a flutter of her eyes.

"Damn," Clark whispered to Ray. "Just keep her talking. Doesn't matter what."

Ray smiled smugly, already feeling victorious by getting Ayhan on camera as Clark desired. Feeling Clark's gratitude only sweetened the victory.

"Let's start with the obvious," Ray said to Ayhan. "You've been digging up a religious site, the Shrine of the Four Keepers. Why are you finding all these weapons?"

"I cannot say. Truly, it is unexpected. Dr. Foo has a theory. He is one of our archaeologists. Constantinople was a city built on seven hills, just like Rome. The shrine sits in a valley near the first hill. As such, the Ottomans may have used it as a garbage dump. Instead of destroying the shrine, they simply buried it little by little."

"So, you are uncovering centuries of garbage."

"It appears so. These conically shaped helmets date from the sixteenth century." She eyed Ray as she picked up one and held it level with her breasts. "Helmets were fashioned out of two steel pieces joined together. This slot here would have held a nose guard, now lost. The bead at the apex of the cone is also missing. See these rivets?" She tilted the cone so that its tip faced Ray. "This helmet at one time had cheek guards—here and here." Slowly, she slid her finger around the helmet, pausing at each rivet. Then she leaned toward Ray, offering the helmet to him. Her finger traced gentle circles around its tip. "Would you like to touch it? It's very smooth—and firm."

With a chuckle, Ray reached out and stroked the helmet. *Why not?* he asked himself. *This is gonna be great.*

Ayhan seemed to shudder. With a sigh, she returned the helmet to the table. "Most of these swords, however, date from the fifteenth century—around the time of Sultan Mehmet's conquest of the city. This kilij, for instance." She held up a broken scimitar. "The kabza and the balçak are exquisitely crafted. The Sultan demanded nothing less."

"Excuse me? What did you say? The kilij—?"

"Ah, my apologies. I forget my English. I must give you a Turkish lesson." She laughed lightly. "Kilij comes from the root verb kır, meaning to kill. This type of curved, single-edged sword is regarded as a symbol of Turkish power. Seljuk rulers even named themselves Kilij Arslan, meaning sword-lion. Of course, this kilij is broken." With her fingers, Ayhan incessantly plucked at the broken tip. "The namlu—the blade—obviously would have been much longer."

"Oh?" Ray asked, cocking one eyebrow. "How much?"

"The blade unsheathed and at full length? At least 80 centimeters," Ayhan said without batting an eye. "Including the kabza and the balçak," she pointed to the hilt and the hand guard, "approximately 94 centimeters or roughly 37 inches." She dropped her voice slightly and gazed at Ray. "An impressive size, is it not?" Her fingertips caressed the blade's broad side. "Especially when held erect."

Ray raised both his eyebrows. "Well, it's your opinion that matters." He heard Clark—usually silent—snicker.

Ayhan's lips twitched slightly in delight—and cruelty. With the faintest of glances at Natalie who stood near holding the mike, she picked up another piece of broken sword. "This is the point of a kilij, the flaring tip, called the yalman. Notice that it is double-edged. Turkish swords are designed for maximum penetration with minimal effort. One thrust with this—" she jabbed it at the camera "—and you can well-imagine the results. I trust this Turkish lesson is instructive for your audience. But what about you, Mr. Cozart? Do you find it intriguing? Surely, you would tell me if it was merely tiresome." She fluttered her eyelashes at Ray shamelessly.

"Oh, I'm quite intrigued," Ray said, trying hard not to laugh. "Please, go on."

"I can speed up the lesson if you like," she said. "I know we have little time. There is so much yet to be done today. I have not even yet shown you the mosaics in the shrine."

"We can see them after. Take your time." He winked at her, goading her on. "I'm enjoying every moment."

"The four are all covered in cloth. To protect them from the elements. But I will unveil them for you."

"I'm looking forward to it. Now, about the swords—"

"Yes? What else would you like me to explain?" Ayhan's face simulated innocence, except for her eyes.

Ray hesitated, his mind ambivalent. Some part of his brain warned him that, much like his flirtation with Ayhan at the museum, this interview wasn't going as planned, and he ought to retreat. To proceed with this line of questioning would be a step too far. But the larger part of his brain felt thoroughly muddled. Ayhan possessed a mysterious power over his thoughts. The force of her beauty lay heavy on his will, imposing a debilitating inertia. But the inertia was also sweet and familiar to him. Flirting with her was like lazily basking in the sun and feeling men envy the leisure he attained with so little effort. How he missed that feeling. He glanced at Clark. His friend's eyes were hidden by Sneak Peek, but Ray could feel waves of anticipation emanating from him. *Just to enjoy a gloat-fest one more time.*

"You could explain that scabbard over there," Ray said in mock seriousness. "The one with the two balls attached."

"Balls? Er, oh, I see. I think you mean these gold loops." She held up the scabbard. "They enable the sword to be secured at the hip. Like this." She swung her hip toward the camera to demonstrate the placement of the sword.

# A PERSIAN SWORD

"Would you say these swords are fine specimens? Museum worthy pieces?" Ray asked, his adrenaline pumping.

"Very fine. Very worthy indeed. Turkish sword makers were gifted, well-endowed artisans. Sword making was regarded as an art form. Exquisite examples of the craft are highly sought after today. Authentic blades such as these—especially full ones—fetch respectable sums. Quality craftsmanship," she held up an intricately wrought hand guard, "is so rare anymore and difficult to replicate."

"Replicate how? You replicate this stuff?" Ray asked.

With a flick of her hand, Ayhan brushed an imaginary hair from her face. "Hmm? Oh. No. I mean it is easy to distinguish a modern reproduction from an authentic piece. I come across them from time to time."

"Forgeries, you mean?"

"Yes."

Ray laughed. "So, I was right. Nazis and counterfeiters."

Ayhan smiled. "Yes, Mr. Cozart, you were right—and wrong. The Nazi story is but one of many ways to fabricate an artifact's provenance. But experienced counterfeiters I know are true artists, and they are more creative than that."

"Oh? How so?"

Ayhan cocked her head and put her hands on her hips, an action which stretched the leather of her jacket across her breasts. "My, so inquisitive."

"Well, this is an interview," Ray said, not failing to notice her breasts.

"Is it? I wonder if you are planning some counterfeit of your own. I begin to doubt your intentions."

"My intentions? No, how could I fake something?"

Ayhan laughed out loud. "Come, come, Mr. Cozart. Do not play innocent now. Not after we have both come so far. Do I need to remind you that you are a professional liar? A skilled teller of tales? We all know that documentaries are well-disguised fictions, but fictions nonetheless."

Just then, Hromadova, the Russian archaeologist, tentatively stepped forward. She was sorry to interrupt, but the preservation specialists Ayhan had telephoned had just arrived from Rome. They desired to get to work immediately. Moving the Keeper mosaics to the museum would be such an undertaking. Should she take them down to the pit at once or would Ayhan rather accompany them herself?

"Take them at once," Ayhan instructed her. "I will join you all there shortly." Then, with a bite-smile at Ray: "Forgive me, Mr. Cozart. Where were we?"

"Maybe we should stop," Ray said to her with sudden seriousness. Hromadova's interruption, like an alarm waking him from sleep, had made him keenly aware of his surroundings—the white canopy of the tent overhead, the strong smell of dirt, and the hollow look in Natalie's eyes.

"Stop? No, let me satisfy your curiosity first," Ayhan insisted. "We were discussing counterfeiters."

"I'm more than willing to stop," Ray said. "We can resume later, er, well ..." his voice trailed off. Seeing Natalie's expression, he felt an urgent need to backtrack. He tried to change the subject. "Let's talk about finding the Dish," he said to Ayhan. "Burke thinks the Dish is hidden behind a wall in the shrine. He just needs to break down the wall—"

"After witnessing his first attempt, I would say the wall refuses to yield." Ayhan puckered her lips in a faux kiss and gazed at Ray in expectancy.

*Damn, she won't let it go.* Ray rubbed the back of his neck. "Er, right, but what do you think?"

"About the wall?"

"No, the Dish. Is the Dish behind it?"

Ayhan smiled coyly. "He will have to overwhelm it to find out. I think he will." She pressed her palms together. "He will spread wide the blocks with his pick. Slowly, it will surrender." She opened her hands, palms facing Ray. "Then with great force, he will push himself in ..."

Ray's mouth felt very dry. He licked his lips. "And?"

"And touch the innermost secrets of the shrine."

"You mean, you—you think he will find the Dish?"

Ayhan hesitated, her eyes scanning the swords before her. She seemed to choose her words with special care. "I believe the outlook is very good."

"On what basis?"

"His urgent passion, for one. Mr. Cozart, have you ever wanted something so desperately that it drives you mad with desire?" She arched an eyebrow as she spoke, and her violet-tinged eyes were searing.

Ray gulped. That was not a question he could answer—not in front of Natalie. He had willingly participated in this game with Ayhan, and now that he wanted out, she refused to give it up. Even worse, she was winning.

"But—but he may be wrong about the Dish's location—I mean, er, well you know what I mean," he said awkwardly.

"He bases his belief on the ancient witnesses," Ayhan said smoothly. "On Putney, for one. He described a bowl used for cleansing. As Burke explained, the monks tested him to see if he would be found worthy of the Dish. He was given a choice—either take the Dish or confess his sins. It would not be a temptation if the bowl the monks set on the altar was not the real Dish. It had to have been the real one."

"What ... did Putney choose?" Ray asked weakly.

"I—I do not quite recall," Ayhan answered insincerely.

"Did he pass the test?" Ray asked, his voice firmer this time. "Was he found worthy?" He glanced up at Natalie's boom mike and suddenly felt he had to know the answer.

Ayhan smirked, detecting his need. "All men fail one way or another."

"Did he resist the temptation to take the Dish or not?"

"Perhaps I am not the one who can answer such a question, Mr. Cozart. Truly, it has been a great pleasure talking with you. I trust our conversation will enhance your film."

The interview broke up. Ayhan invited them all to join her back down at the excavation pit to view the mosaics of the Four Keepers. Then she excused herself, motioning to her assistant Murat for a consultation.

Ray and Clark quietly discussed a strategy for filming the mosaics, and Natalie, with great precision, packed up her audio equipment. As she did so, her cell phone rang. When she saw the number, she answered eagerly and purposely faced Ray as she spoke, her green eyes wide open.

"Why hello, Steve, so good to hear from you," she said loudly, staring Ray down. "Yes, it's a perfect time to talk. Your timing is impeccable. And, oh, I have so much to tell you. I mean, I've just been about ready to burst. You can't believe where I am and what has happened. Can you handle it?" Natalie gathered her audio bag and backed her way to the tent entrance, keeping her fierce eyes fixed on Ray.

Ray didn't dare meet Natalie's eyes. He pretended not to notice her glare, but he'd heard what she'd said to Steve. He and Clark followed her to the exit, keeping a safe distance.

Once outside, Clark stepped toward the slope that led down to the pit, but Ray lingered, anxious to leave yet curious to eavesdrop on Natalie's conversation. *Little Stevie Finder. Why is she so excited to talk to him?*

"Steve! Ha-ha! You don't believe me?" Natalie was saying breathlessly. "Would I lie to you? Yes, the shrine has been discovered. I'm staring at it right now. Oh, I wish you were here with me to see it." As she said this, she narrowed her eyes at Ray, then abruptly spun away from him, her ponytail snapping like a whip.

"What you waitin' for?" Clark said to Ray.

Reluctantly, Ray joined him, and the two walked down the dirt slope.

As soon as they were out of earshot of Natalie, Clark whacked Ray on the shoulder, "Dude! That was freaking unbelievable!" He shook his head in amazement.

Ray chuckled. "You're welcome."

"Ayhan's dirty talk. You totally egged her on. She knew what she was doing. I couldn't stop laughing. My God! You and hot chicks. Like, how do you do it?"

Ray shrugged in false humility. "What can I say? It's a gift, dude. A gift."

"She was like, wow—but—but—" Clark exhaled sharply, "I don't think Natalie liked it," he finished quickly.

"Oh, well, that was just tactics, right? We were getting such good material. I mean, that was all just in fun, so I went with it. Didn't mean anything to me. Nat will understand it was for the film. It's nothing I haven't done before."

Ray said this, but he still felt like a failure somehow. He glanced back to locate Natalie. She remained near the tent but had seated herself on an overturned bucket. Evidently, her conversation with Steve was only just beginning.

All at once, Ray felt a bit chilled, but there was no breeze. *How? How is it different? How is there anything different between us?* He recalled Natalie's questions, so mournful, so pleading, and his throat tightened. He ran a hand through his hair, remembering something else, something Geoffrey had once told him. Ray, Staci, Natalie, and Geoffrey were all at Reggie's party. Geoffrey had cornered him:

"Does Natalie know how you feel about her?"

Ray had stared back at Geoffrey in perplexity.

"Don't pretend you can't understand," Geoffrey said. "I see the way you look at her. Does she know how you feel?"

Ray sighed heavily. "No."

"Good. I'd appreciate if you left it that way. She could not reciprocate. Not fully. But I expect you know that. She might try her best, as she does with everything, but you two would run out of conversation in short order.

Natalie has a brilliant mind. She needs room to explore, to satisfy her curiosity. She needs a man whose mind would not hem her in. That man is not you. We all lose some. Nothing personal about it. I'm doing you a favor."

Ray felt an urgent need to look back and find Natalie again. But he resisted. He didn't want to know if she still sat talking with Steve. An awful sense of dread had seized him.

"What time is it?" he asked Clark irritably. "This day's been like forever."

"It'll be over soon," Clark said.

Then they reached the wooden ramp and descended into the pit.

▼ ▼ ▼ ▼

Ayhan smiled in secret pleasure as she exited the artifacts tent. Student workers were loading two museum vans with boxes, and she sent Murat to supervise. She needed to be alone, for she had a phone call to make, and it was crucial that it be a private conversation. She headed toward her car parked by the entrance gate.

"Ahmet," she said after closing the door. She placed one hand on the steering wheel.

"Yes, Zainab. News?" Öztürk asked.

"Burke has made a breakthrough. He has discovered a false wall in the shrine."

"Oh? Does he have the Dish?"

"I think it will not be long now."

"Excellent. We may not need to use an artifake after all."

"It would be best if we did not need to, of course. But if it comes to that, the American filmmakers did capture quite useful footage of Burke today."

"Very good. Did you receive the permission form I sent to your office?" Öztürk asked.

Ayhan traced the steering wheel with her fingers. "Yes. You did not need to write the fine print in Turkish. One signature will suffice, and the American man will do whatever I ask. I only need to get him alone. That will be easy. His partner—the suspicious woman—I have directed her suspicions elsewhere." She felt a tinge of regret as she spoke. She need not have toyed with Mr. Cozart's desire, but soon such games would no longer be necessary. She would be free.

Öztürk chuckled. "Dare I inquire into your methods?"

"Dare you become jealous?" Ayhan teased. She disliked bantering with Öztürk, but this also would end soon.

Öztürk's chuckled deepened. "My dear, you are a Persian sword."

"There is still the matter of Pasa," Ayhan reminded him.

"Is he not irrelevant now that the find is imminent?"

"We should prepare for contingencies. If Burke is correct about the wall, then the remainder of the apse is behind it. Digging out the apse will cause delay. It would still be preferable to have more time."

"Very well. We will proceed as planned."

"Tonight then?"

"Yes. At The Padishah. I will take care of Pasa."

"Oh, Ahmet," Ayhan said hurriedly before he could hang up. "I wanted to ask you—" she hesitated. A doubt about their scheme had crept through her brain all day, but Öztürk never liked her to express doubt. It was a sign of weakness.

"Yes?"

"Er, well, I wanted to ask you about the Krayzels—Ambassador Krayzel. Surely, you recall his conversation with you last night. He made a point of mentioning the report of the Turkish Antiquities Trade Commission—the recent arrest of illegal traffickers. It was a threat, was it not? He and Sylvia do know a great deal about us. We could sell the Dish to them outright."

Öztürk scoffed. "An idle threat. Do not let it distract you. He would not report me to the Commission because I could also report him. And what evidence does the Ambassador truly have? Only items from Sylvia's grand collection, but he would not risk losing them. Imagine!"

Ayhan tried to laugh at Öztürk's imitation of the American woman. But the creeping doubt remained.

Moments later, exiting her car, she spied Dr. Calvino. He and four students were struggling to load a large stone fragment into a third museum van. Murat stood by watching.

"Which piece is it?" she asked him. Before Murat could answer, she did herself. "Ah, a section of the central dome."

"Largest section still intact," Calvino said to her, straining against the stone's weight.

The stone was half in, half out. Ayhan inspected the fragment more closely. There was an image painted on it—the shoulders of a man. Where the head should've been, the stone was broken off.

"An image of one of the Keepers?" she asked Calvino.

"No. The Christ. The robe is the characteristic color—"

"Ah, indigo," she said, reaching to swipe at a piece of dirt. At once, she jerked her hand back. The dirt had moved.

Her action momentarily confused the loading, and the stone tipped to one side. Murat rushed to steady it.

"It was a spider," she declared, looking at her hand.

One more push and the stone was secure. Calvino dusted off his hands. "No, it is too cold yet for spiders."

"But it jumped," Ayhan insisted. "I am sure of it." Anxiously, she examined the sleeve of her jacket. "It was black and red, like a drop of blood. Oh, how I hate them!"

"Maybe we disturbed its habitat."

"Yes, perhaps. It is said the frailest house is the house of a spider." She simulated a little laugh, carefully examining the front of her jacket.

"Well, it has a new home now." Calvino grinned and shut the van doors. He walked back to the tent.

Ayhan didn't care for his remark, imagining that she felt something tickle the back of her neck.

Murat opened the driver-side door.

"Wait," she said before he climbed in. "What were Dr. Calvino's instructions?"

"To take this to Girard Lab."

"Right." Ayhan's mind raced ahead, imagining scenarios, calculating the steps. Her scheme with Öztürk must not fall apart. He would take care of Pasa. That meant she would have to take care of Burke. Poor man. She felt sorry that their fortunes could not align. It was just the way of the world. Someone had to lose. And it must not be her.

"Take it to Erdem Lab instead," she instructed Murat.

"But you closed it for the new tile to be laid."

"Oh, that. Never mind that. If anyone asks, tell them I have said we are distinguishing exceptional pieces. They are to be put in Erdem Lab, not Girard. Anything else that Burke finds should be taken to Erdem, too. Even if I am not here to give instructions. You have the code to unlock it?"

Murat nodded and climbed into the van.

Ayhan started to walk away, then stopped. A red and black speck near her boot heel caught her eye. The spider crept cautiously atop the tiny, loose pebbles. Suddenly, Ayhan's shadow fell upon it. To save itself, it darted toward a crevice. But its cruel huntress was quicker.

Scene 27

# No Answer

*Istanbul, Turkey*

*Excavation site at the demolished Sirkeci Rail Station*

*Sunday, March 14, moments after Steve Finder's phone call*

"Yes, Steve, the shrine has been discovered. I'm staring at it right now. Oh, I wish you were here with me to see it." As she spoke, Natalie glared at Ray and gripped her phone away from her ear as if about to hurl a hand grenade. She refused to be humiliated any longer by Ray's outrageous flirtation with Ayhan. Steve Finder's phone call had given her back her pride—and given her a weapon.

"I've been thinking of you so much," she lied to Finder, hoping Ray could hear her. She desired above all else to wound him with a retaliatory flirtation, but his proximity wounded her more. She spun away from him, spied an overturned bucket, and sat down. There was no way she could accompany Ray and Clark down to the pit, and she wanted to be anywhere but near Zainab Ayhan. "The past couple days, it's like I've been living in one of your adventure stories," she said to Finder. "All that's been missing is you."

"I dunno what to say," Finder replied. "This is unbelievable. My God! The shrine? Buried under an old rail station, you say? Of course, I'd love to be there to see it—er, with you—be there with you," he added quickly.

As Natalie watched, Ray shuffled off toward Clark, and the two of them descended the slope. They were obviously laughing. She thought Ray looked back for her once, but she might've only imagined it. Ray shrank before her eyes as if he were melting away, returning to the dust from which all men came. She watched him until he disappeared beneath the earth, swallowed by the deep shadows of the pit.

She accelerated her flirtation. "You *can* be here with me. Why not come to Istanbul?" she suggested to Finder.

"Maybe I will—if you really want me."

"Of course. I dunno when I'm gonna return to New York. Not with all these developments. You really oughta see the shrine for yourself. I mean, what great book material, right? Y'know, Burke is digging through a wall. Thinks the Dish might be hidden behind it. He could find it at any moment."

"What! Find the Dish?" Finder shouted.

Natalie smirked, savoring the effect of her words. Ayhan wasn't the only woman who could provoke a man's desire.

"You can't be serious," Finder went on heatedly. "Burke can't find the Dish. Not yet! Er, I mean—I mean, of course I want the real Dish to be found," he stammered. "Don't get me wrong, it's my dearest wish, but—well, it's just the craziest coincidence. For the new adventure I'm writing for Bucky, I've made the lost Shrine of the Four Keepers a major plot point. How ironic is that? Like, how can Bucky find a shrine in fiction that's just been discovered in real life? I can't write that. Readers will think I've lost my creative edge. And if Burke does find the Dish—" he laughed cynically. "What a nightmare—er, I mean, a dream. The craziest dream!" His voice squeaked. "This discovery is earthshattering stuff. You aren't messing with me, are you? You should never mess with a novelist. You might find yourself the villain of their next book. Ha-ha. How'd you like it if I made Lady Ashbrook a femme fatale? I could, you know. Use her to tempt Bucky. Er, hello? Natalie? Are you there?"

Natalie blinked her eyes rapidly as if Finder's voice had roused her from sleep. "I assure you it's no dream. It's all too real," she said, but she was thinking of Ray. Her throat tightened, and she clenched her phone, fighting against a groundswell of despair. She looked up at the hazy sky. The day was fading fast. Her audio bag lay at her feet, but she still clutched the strap in her hand. She released it and stood to pace behind the bucket. Students carrying boxes passed by on their way to and from the vans, but they paid no attention to her, as though she were an island to herself.

"I dunno what to do," Finder said. "Y'know, I had a title picked out for my novel and everything. I was gonna call it Bucky Browne and the Mirror of Fate. Prescient, huh?"

The groundswell of despair threatened to pull Natalie under; to compensate for it, she laughed shrilly and spoke with exaggerated enthusiasm. "That's too ironic. You gotta be making that up. Did you? Just now?"

"No, that's really the title. I picked it out months ago."

"Oh, I don't believe you. You're so clever. I always enjoy our conversations. You have such a way with words."

"I hope so. I'm a writer."

"See? Ha-ha. You're so good at what you do. No matter what happens, I wouldn't worry about losing your creative edge. If you came to Istanbul, who knows, you might even get inspired." She hesitated, then added, "Maybe—*I* could inspire you. Help you flesh out Lady Ashbrook. If you're gonna make her a femme fatale, shouldn't you, y'know, do some first-hand research?" She laughed girlishly.

There was a pause on the other end of the line.

Natalie held her breath. Part of her mind warned her that her flirtation had crossed a boundary. Initially, she'd only flirted with Finder to lure him back into the Dish Movie, but now her strategic dalliance was in danger of morphing into a real entanglement. But she just didn't care. She was far too committed to spiting Ray to backtrack. If Ray didn't want her, then she didn't want him. She could easily find someone else—someone better. All in a flash, she imagined life without Ray. She imagined herself as the muse of a famous novelist who could quote Shakespeare, had great hair, and lived in a five-story brownstone on the Upper West Side.

"You're amazing," Finder said, his tone quite changed. It was intimate and inviting. "I love talking with you too. Your conversation is a gift anyone should cherish. I told

# THE DIE IS CAST

you Almost a Loneliness is a masterpiece. Your talent for writing is immense. Your style is subtle and intricate, like a beautiful tapestry. It's a perfect image of you. You're everything I imagined you'd be after seeing your film. I must confess, since you entered my world, everything has been turned upside down. And I don't just mean Burke and the shrine. The truth is, Natalie—I—I can't stop thinking about you. I wanted to tell you but didn't want to come on too strong, and I thought you had other commitments—I mean, er, 8 Ball Productions and everything that goes with that—"

"Ray and I aren't together. It's a business partnership," she said without thinking. The words came automatically.

"Oh, really? Well, that changes everything, doesn't it?" He laughed warmly. "I guess I wondered from the first, because I thought you and me—we just clicked, y'know?"

"I thought so too." As she said this, Natalie stopped pacing. Finder's confession both thrilled and troubled her. She stood gazing in the direction Ray had gone. Slowly, she sat back down on the overturned bucket.

"And you're obviously not the kind of woman who plays games," Finder went on. "But then that interview went so awry, I thought I'd ruined it with you. Oh, and about that footage—I know you have the right to do with it what you will, but I'd really like to see it and correct the record."

Natalie replied at once. "Of course," she promised. "We can watch the footage together and figure something out." *Why not? It's Ayhan's film now. Ray gave it away.*

"Oh, oh, that's so good of you," Finder said gratefully. "I can't tell you what a relief that is. God, I'd love to make that happen soon—er, with you. Make it happen with you."

Their conversation lasted another half hour. Natalie kept Finder talking. He had all the right words. His voice seemed to dwell in her own mind as if the two of them shared the very same language. Listening to him appeared to be the antidote for her disappointment with Ray, and remembering his violet eyes evoked in her a sense of possibility that she had not felt for a long time. She greatly desired to be someone's eagerly sought treasure, and though she was sure she didn't love Finder, she was also sure that if he told her a great love story, she'd believe him.

But after Finder said goodbye and the sound of his voice faded from her mind, Natalie sat brooding over her phone, wondering what had just happened. *Did he seduce me or was it the other way around? Surely, I didn't just invite him to Istanbul, did I?* She sighed in deep regret and leaned forward on her elbows to massage her forehead. The memory of Ray's flirtation with Ayhan assaulted her afresh. She urgently needed to end her suffering, and though throwing herself at Steve Finder had felt right at first, it hadn't been the right answer.

She slung her audio bag over her shoulder and peered down the dirt slope, looking for Ray. But he didn't appear. Unsure what to do, she wandered into the artifacts tent, but the sight of the helmets and swords made her so angry. She crossed her arms over her breasts and clutched her elbows in an instinctual but useless gesture of self-protection.

*Damn that woman.* She thought of Ray stroking the tip

of the helmet Ayhan had offered to him and cursed again. Bright lights shining from interior tent poles hurt her eyes. *I knew it. I knew he'd fall for her act.* The white tent canopy seemed to press down on her. She felt trapped and suffocated and retreated from the tent, gasping for air.

She returned to the overturned bucket, set her bag on it, and rifled through its pockets for her iPad. She felt a desperate need to see the old shooting schedule, the one she and Ray had planned together. Surely, a part of it remained. She opened the file and sighed mournfully at the sight of the itinerary all in tatters. Ray had deleted whole columns and crossed out row after row, writing over them with Ayhan's name. Natalie's eyes started to sting. She'd wanted there to be something left, a lifeline to hold on to. But as she scrolled down the screen, she saw there was nothing.

A van pulled through the entrance gate. Natalie glanced up just in time to register that the driver was Ayhan's assistant Murat. He parked by the other vans and got out.

On the second page of the old itinerary, Natalie saw a marginal note: "Rescheduled press pass pick-up. Church of St. George. Sunday, March 14."

"My God, that's today," she said aloud, and her heart leaped at the discovery. Here was a remainder—a vital one. How could they have forgotten? They were set to film Pope Boniface's arrival in Istanbul, but they needed the passes to film within the security barrier. Reggie had rescheduled their appointment to pick up the passes around their (now canceled) Cappadocian cave tour.

Natalie's fevered mind raced ahead, imagining scenarios and her desired outcomes. All at once, she knew what she needed to do. She had a mission. She'd go get the passes herself, and then she'd surprise Ray with them, and he'd be so appreciative of her because she'd saved them from making a horrible mistake, and he'd owe her one because she'd single-handedly fixed everything that was wrong, and then—

Ayhan's assistant Murat walked by.

"Wait," Natalie called to him. Quickly, she checked the time. "Can you drive me on an errand?"

"Err-and," he said in heavily accented English. "I do not know this word."

"Oh, um, an errand is like a little journey. A trip. To go somewhere. Somewhere else. Or, an errand is a little task, a job, like the kind you do for Dr. Ayhan."

Murat nodded in understanding. "You go to museum?"

"Er, well—"

"I take you. I ask Dr. Ayhan." Murat turned to walk down the dirt slope toward the pit. After two steps, he motioned for Natalie to follow him.

"Oh, no, I'd rather stay right here," she said. "I'll wait."

He appeared confused. "You not go?"

"No, I definitely wanna be ... someplace else."

"Okay. You come. I ask Dr. Ayhan. She believe you, see?"

"Ah, you want me to corroborate your story."

"What is corrobo—"

"Oh, never mind."

Reluctantly, Natalie picked up her bag and walked with Murat to the pit. A third of the way down, she noticed footprints in the dirt. She could easily imagine they were Ray's. Twice she purposely stepped in them, matching her gait to his. But she soon tired of the effort and shifted her eyes to the sky. Her feet wanted to follow Ray, to take her back to him, but her mind wanted something else. *This isn't right.*

She remembered the first time she'd gone back to Ray: they'd still been in film school, and she'd been alarmed to realize that she was falling in love. Her symptoms had manifested subtly—a slight nervous tension in Ray's presence, a desire to wear her hair in a ponytail because he liked to see it bounce, and an inability to finish reading any books of poetry for lack of concentration. Ray wasn't the kind of man she'd ever imagined herself loving. He had no interest in poetry, for starters. And worse—he wasn't in love with her.

The night she fell asleep in his apartment confirmed all her fears. Ray had covered her with a blanket and gone to play a video game. These were not the acts of a man in love. In contrast, she'd wanted to curl up under the blanket with him and stay the night. The gap between their feelings embarrassed her; there didn't seem to be any way to bridge it. She was going to have to get a hold of herself and let him go.

Two days later, she packed a suitcase, told her roommate she needed "a break," got in her car, and started to drive. She ended up in Cleveland, Ohio. The next day, she went further north, to the Upper Peninsula of Michigan, to a small lake-front cabin owned by her family. It was November; the cabin, a summer home in her childhood, was shut up for the winter. She spent a week there wholly alone, lying for hours by the fireplace, taking melancholy walks around the lake, and sitting on the pier in the evenings to watch the sun set.

And all the while she pondered the conundrum of Ray. She discarded the obvious options—transferring to a different school or confessing her love to him. Both choices risked their deepening friendship and their potential for creative collaboration. She couldn't decide what would be worse—to go on without Ray in her life at all, or to keep his friendship and sacrifice her love.

After five days at the cabin, she settled on a third option—she'd use filmmaking as a bridge to Ray. He'd already expressed an interest in making a film with her. Perhaps she should take him up on it. Wouldn't a collaboration be the perfect means of influencing him, of planting seeds of affection? Surely, in time, his artistic appreciation for her would bloom and flower. He would grow to love her by experiencing her tender, nurturing tutelage. She'd inspire his desire by sharing with him the immense resources of her mind. He would learn poetry—and many other necessary things. After perfecting him, she'd pluck the tender fruit of her labors.

Natalie and Murat reached the bottom of the slope and began the final descent down the wooden ramp into the pit. As her foot hit the boards, Natalie felt unexpectedly lighter, as if gravity had freed her. She felt her spirit floating up and away. She was as high as the crane that cast its pale shadow on the ground, and she saw her life with penetrating clarity.

She saw herself driving from Michigan back to New York, full of hope for a future with Ray and confident in her power to gain him. She saw all the years she had passionately thrown herself into their filmmaking, hoping to elicit his passion. She saw herself leaving London and Geoffrey, crossing the Atlantic for Ray, hoping that if her presence hadn't changed him, then perhaps her absence had.

With startling panoramic vision, she realized that going back to Ray in hopes of fixing him was *always* her decision. He failed her again and again. And again, she decided to try fixing him. Using the forgotten press passes to save their relationship wasn't going to work. It was a flimsy bridge, the flimsiest she'd yet built. *What the hell am I doing?*

At the bottom of the ramp, Natalie again heard Burke's hammering. Evidently, the wall still held. Murat didn't lead her in Burke's direction but took the left path to the shrine's west aisle. Natalie held her breath; she was closing in on Ray. For years she'd searched his changeable eyes hoping to find that she'd inspired love in them. But she'd only found its shadow. Love was always elsewhere, endlessly eluding her. *Why? Why did it never work?*

Abruptly, Murat turned a corner. Natalie heard unfamiliar, angry voices, and then she saw Ray. Or she thought she did. But it wasn't him. It was only the image of a man—a smirking, dancing youth with bright, winking eyes. He held a golden bowl in his right hand, but the bowl appeared ready to fall as if he were tossing it like a ball back and forth between his hands. The youth was as large and colorful as life; his pose simulated motion. Natalie could easily imagine that his winking eyes followed her. Those eyes were an invitation, and staring up at them, she felt a peculiar urge to touch the golden bowl.

Slowly, she stretched out her hand ...

"Oh, hey, I wouldn't do that. They told us only to look." The voice Natalie heard belonged to Clark. She made no reply but stood unblinking, entranced by Panikos the Youth and by the golden bowl slipping from his hand. Her fingers were inches from touching it. Spotlights blazed down on the mosaic; its tiny cuts of glass shimmered in the artificial light. As the shadow of her hand fell upon the bowl, suddenly she stopped. *Nat, the third rule is that you can only play with my ball if I let you.* She closed her eyes and dropped her hand to her side. Finally, she knew the truth. She almost laughed because she'd always known. It wasn't a secret. She'd wasted her time searching for hidden depths in Ray. The truth was on the surface. *He's nothing but a child, a selfish brat. He can never love me.*

Natalie opened her eyes, becoming conscious of voices all around her, but she couldn't understand them. They sounded hollow and far away, like echoes. "You would say that—you're Catholic," a young man's voice said angrily. "But it was the end of the Byzantine Empire, and it was all your fault."

"Your history is deficient and partisan," another voice replied—a woman's. "These events are complex. There is no easy place to lay blame. It was a series of errors, misunderstandings, and miscalculations by multiple parties."

"She's right," an elderly man said. "History shows that the Byzantine Empire had made itself vulnerable long before the Fourth Crusade—infighting within the royal family, arrogant assurance in Constantinople's defenses, and an unremitting grudge against the Venetians—"

"But the crusaders didn't have to sack the city and set

up a regime," the young man heatedly interposed. "They didn't have to oppress the people and—and kill the Four Keepers."

"Look, I'm not defending it," the elderly man said. "I'm only saying that Prince Alexios made Constantinople susceptible. His uncle had usurped the throne, put his father in prison. He asked the crusaders to help him defeat his uncle, promising to pay them. But then he failed to do so. And he misjudged his popularity. Once he'd gained the throne, his own people revolted against him and threw him out. You could say the emperors had only themselves to blame for losing the empire. It was a classic case of self-sabotage."

"Please, please, these ancient quarrels!" It was Ayhan's voice. "What is to be gained by reliving them?"

At the sound of Ayhan's voice, Natalie's mind focused in. For the first time, she observed the tableau before her. Standing before the mosaics of the Keepers were the two preservation specialists from Rome. The man and woman were arguing with one of the Greek graduate students. Listening to the argument were Ayhan, Ray, and Hromadova. Filming the squabble (secretly, no doubt, by the grin on his face) was Clark. Ray was looking right at her. Gazing back at him, Natalie felt nothing. Her emotions had fled. It was as if she were watching a stage rehearsal. Ray seemed unreal, merely an actor awaiting his cue. *Why am I holding on?*

In her periphery, she saw Murat confer with Ayhan.

"Oh, of course," Ayhan said, peering at Natalie. "Do take Ms. Ashbrook wherever she would like to go." Ayhan spoke clinically and returned her attention to the preservationists.

Natalie's eyes bored into Ayhan's back. She was angry at Ayhan, at Ray, and at Reggie for tricking her back into this mess, but mostly she was angry at herself for falling for it. The Ray she loved was the sorry and heartsick man Reggie had described, not this dallier who endlessly toyed with her hopes. His flirtation with Ayhan, while surprising, had also been predictable. She chided herself for not foreseeing it. Ray had taken a step toward her the night before. Of course, the very next day, he would take three steps back. That's the way the story always went. That's why it could never be a great love story. Ray always ruined it. Self-sabotage was his favorite game. *He'll never change.*

"Where are you going?" Ray asked her apprehensively.

"To pick up our press passes," Natalie answered flatly.

"Oh. Right. I totally forgot about that."

"Of course, you did."

"Let me go with you."

"No. I don't think so."

"Well, then take Clark with you."

"No."

"But—but you're gonna come right back, aren't you?"

Natalie detected a hint of worry in Ray's voice. A smirk slowly cut across her face. *My God, do we have to play it this way again?* Begging her not to leave was one of Ray's favorite lines. So, she too had joined the stage show, and she too knew how the story went.

"I always do come back, don't I?" she said ironically.

"Wh-what does that mean?"

"Oh, c'mon, Ray," she said with as much sweetness as she could simulate. "You're a man of deep penetration.

I'm sure you can figure it out."

She backed away, taking one last look at Panikos the Youth. He was vivid and shiny but disappointedly one dimensional. His winking eyes appeared to be beholding a secret horror. Natalie sensed that his mouth might gape. Ridiculous, she thought, he isn't real. *Nothing here is real.* She spun on her heels and headed toward the exit ramp.

"Wait," Ray called after her.

But she didn't wait.

And he didn't follow.

At the bottom of the ramp, Murat caught up with her. They heard Burke shouting. "A breakthrough! Look, these flagstones extend beyond the wall. The apse continues beyond. I was right. I am always right!"

Natalie glanced in Burke's direction, glimpsing a corner of the altar and beyond it, Burke on his knees scratching at the dirt. At that very moment, she hated him because of his mania for a stupid bowl. He reminded her of Geoffrey, and she hated him too. She hated all of them—Geoffrey, Ayhan, Staci, Reggie, Ray, and every other person who had ever hurt her. How dare they lie to her. How dare they use and diminish her. If only she could bring them all to their knees.

The dark walls of the excavation pit loomed overhead. Their height oppressed her; she felt as though she were standing in a deep grave. The shrine had been resurrected, but its heart was missing. Something beautiful had been lost forever. She thought it would've been better for the shrine to have remained lost than for it to be exposed in its present ugliness. She rubbed her arms, feeling bits of the ruins clinging to her, feeling an urgent need to escape from them. Without further hesitation, she marched up the ramp.

Murat strode alongside. He didn't understand what he'd heard. Was Mr. Cozart angry? What is pen-e-tra-tion?

"Oh, penetration is—is—" Natalie broke off, feeling a sore spot near her heart. She thought of the insight she'd just had about Ray. "Penetration is the power to see into things. To see things for what they are, not as they appear to be," she explained dutifully. "When you penetrate something, you discover its secret. Like—like Burke breaking through the wall to find the Dish. That's penetration. He wants to find the shrine's secret. Do you understand?"

Murat nodded. "Penetration is good word. Is kind word. Is—how you say?—a compliment." He grinned. "I see the truth. I penetration. I penetration many things!" His face beamed at his new understanding.

"You penetrate many things," she corrected him. "Not penetration. In English penetrate is a verb. An action. Something you do. Penetration is a noun, a thing, an event. It's the result of something being penetrated. You use verbs and nouns differently in sentences. Have you ever learned the English parts of speech?"

"Ah. To penetrate. Is verb. I understand."

"Do you?"

"Yes. You explain well. Nouns are subjects of sentences. Not verbs. I remember my English class."

Despite herself, Natalie smiled at the compliment. Yes, she did explain things well. It was one of her many gifts. It only took someone with an open mind and a willingness to learn. *He's way ahead of Ray.* This thought instantly animated her, and as they ascended the dirt slope, she went on to differentiate adjectives and adverbs. Murat probed her with relevant questions, and she always had the right answer. Her voice rose; she gestured theatrically, gleefully relishing the power of her mind.

When they reached the top of the slope, for a moment, the clouds parted, and the afternoon sun hit her like a spotlight full in the face. Its warmth stimulated the sore spot near her heart, until, like a seed, it burst forth, releasing all its vital, hidden potential. She felt a rush of white-hot anger. In her mind she saw Ray's empty, uncomprehending, pleading eyes, and in the very same instant, the haughty gaze of Dr. Zainab Ayhan. She wanted to overturn buckets, to grab clods of dirt and crush the soil in her hands. As they approached the van, she thought of the altar in the shrine, an unembellished slab, much more like an altar for sacrifice than for worship. She regretted not lighting it on fire.

All her thoughts were bent on destruction. As Murat drove her to the Church of Saint George, she taught him prepositions, easily eliciting his interest by peppering her lesson with specimens from her favorite poets. "She dwells with beauty—beauty that must die. And joy, whose hand is ever at his lips bidding adieu, and aching pleasure nigh, turning to poison while the bee-mouth sips. With. At. To. They tie things together, you see. Prepositions. It's from Ode on Melancholy by the English poet John Keats, who tragically died from tuberculosis at only age twenty-five."

She couldn't stop talking. The burning anger drove her.

## NO ANSWER

She spat out her words with exaggerated precision: and, but, or, nor, for, yet (she'd moved on to conjunctions). Murat would be wholly fluent in English by the time she was through with him. She told herself that trying to fix Ray had been an act of grace and charity. Influencing his behavior for the good had been the noblest motive. Loving her would make him a better man, wouldn't it? What had gone wrong between them was not her desire to fix him but his inability to learn. Murat could learn from her. Murat wanted to improve himself. Her plan to inspire Ray's love had been foolproof. Except that Ray was a fool. She'd misjudged her pupil. She should've known—she'd accused him of stupidity often enough, hadn't she? *Because it's true. He's a dolt. As ignorant as dirt.*

They reached the Church of Saint George before she could teach Murat interjections. She threw open the door of the van and stepped out blindly, immediately stumbling on the curb. "Damn," she muttered, clenching her fist. Her mind was in chaos. Somehow, she found the right door to the Patriarchate. The bearded man in a black robe who let her in invited her to wait in a hallway. As she did so, she stared ahead as if in a trance. Tiny prisms from a crystal sconce clustered on a wall. The little lights seemed to wink at her invitingly, and she squinted at them hard, for she thought she detected in them the shape of a golden bowl. *A bowl slipping from his hand ...*

She neither saw nor remembered anything else at the church. Surely, the bearded man in the black robe handed over the press passes. She must've signed a form for them. She couldn't quite recall. The tiny prisms of light had channeled all her mental powers. At last, with absolute lucidity, she knew what she needed to do.

"Murat, take me to Hotel Amir," she said when she got back into the van.

They drove to the hotel in silence.

"Don't wait for me," she told him when they arrived.

Once inside, Natalie flung open the door to her room and let fall her audio bag. She strode to the window, yanked open the curtains, and jerked her suitcase up onto the bed.

The Mystic 8 Ball rolled to one corner. She unzipped her suitcase and grabbed it. "You lied to me!" she shouted, holding the toy with its inky window up. As if shame-faced, the white die did not appear. She shook the ball hard. "You—you have always lied to me!" As she spoke, she felt a fierce tremor down her spine. The tremor rose into her throat; her vocal cords trembled. Her ears started to ring. It was as though some force were shaking her. She'd been an instrument for cosmic play for far too long. But no more.

It was simply a matter of how to end it.

She glimpsed beyond her window the small fenced-in garden she had seen her first night in the hotel. It lay right across the street. No one seemed to be caring for it. There were bare-limbed trees and low, unshapely bushes. Beneath the barren trees, tall, dead weeds entangled a rusted bench.

Without hesitation, and with the Mystic 8 Ball in hand, Natalie fled her room. In the elevator, she punched the button that said ROOF.

When the elevator doors opened, she stepped out

under a golden sky. The twilight sun, succumbing to the horizon, lit only the tops of buildings, sharpening the shadows. An elderly couple sat facing the sea. Natalie retreated to the opposite side, to the side facing the garden.

Standing near the balustrade, she turned the Mystic 8 Ball over in her hands. It'd be so easy to drop it, she thought. She wanted to watch it shatter. Then it'd be true how she'd answered Ray three years ago: "I threw it away."

It was time. Far past time. The trouble wasn't that she always left Ray. The trouble was that she kept coming back.

It was time to leave—for good—time to stop reliving the same story. And not even a love story, at that. No, she could face the truth now. Ray had only been a simulation of love. Nothing she'd ever imagined between them had been real. And her hopes were an illusion. Ray didn't love her; he gave her just enough so he could keep using her. Likely, his interest in her had always been pecuniary, to turn her talent into profit. No doubt, Ray and Reggie had conspired to lure her back. Ray's fight with Reggie and big speech to her begging her not to leave had merely been an act akin to his performance at Midtown Studios. Probably, Ray did need money because living the big life with Staci had cost him.

Cautiously, she laid one hand on the balustrade and peered over the roof's edge. Directly below her stood a man talking on his phone. The sun sank lower, threatening to lose itself in clouds. She squeezed the Mystic 8 Ball. It wasn't real either. Just a worthless plastic toy. A

# THE DIE IS CAST

blind guide.

She looked down at it. The toy was a little museum; memories like a newsreel began to play in her mind, soundbites of all her work with Ray: *The Full Chester*, *Monica's Dress*, and *The Tent at Ground Zero*. They were like old newspapers, filled with obsolete stories. There would be no more stories. She would see to that.

The man below had moved out of the way.

She held the ball over the railing. One, two—

No. Not yet. She pulled the ball towards her. It had been part of her and Ray since the beginning. Destroying it felt like death. Was she killing them? Killing herself?

Gently, she shook it and turned it over. It was ridiculous to ask it a question. What had it ever done for her? Yet she couldn't help herself. "Should I? Should I?" she said.

The inner die floated up to the window. At least, she heard that it did, heard its edges click against the glass, just beyond her touch. Always beyond her touch. She shook the ball again, harder. Again, she heard the die. But she couldn't see it. For the first time, it had no answer for her. Like a raindrop in the sea, it had lost itself, drowned at last in the deep blue ink.

Natalie cried out. "I'm sick of shadows!" With great might, she cast the Mystic 8 Ball over the sidewalk and beyond the street, watching as it crashed through tree limbs. It struck the rusted bench and shattered.

*Gone.*

She peered down into the shadows until the sun met the horizon and the rooftop fell into darkness.

Scene 28

## The Dream of Istanbul

*The Raffles Istanbul, at Nennen Center*

*Sunday, March 14, afternoon*

The room was the hotel's best. Floor to ceiling windows granted stunning views of the Bosporus as well as access to a private terrace. Turkish carpets covered the hardwood floor, and an elegant chaise and spacious walk-in closet gave the room the feel of almost-home. Above the king size bed hung a spectacular mural—a cityscape—painted in bold, sweeping strokes of blue. According to a notecard on the bedside stand, the mural was the work of a celebrated local artist and was called *The Dream of Istanbul.*

On the chaise, free at last from the Comfy-Go Pet Tote, Baby Girl lay shivering, curled into a ball, its eyelids twitching in rapid-eye sleep. What visions might be passing before its little-dog mind, none could know. Possibly, the visions were harrowing, given that Jane's incessant traveling exposed the dog to sudden and inescapable olfactory assaults, among other things.

For instance, during their layover in Amsterdam the previous evening, Baby Girl had suffered the scent of cat dander for several hours due to the aggressive petting of an unidentified airport attendant in the VIP Lounge. Jane kept an open-door policy regarding the little dog and surrendered it to anyone who asked. "Baby Girl loves everyone!" she always said. Thus, Baby Girl often found itself borrowed. The lounge attendant had rocked the little dog in her arms like an infant, delightedly exposing its sensitive underbelly and nipples. With its one blue eye, Baby Girl had spied on the woman's shirtsleeves the unmistakable hairs of a Blue Point Himalayan, a notoriously stupid cat.

A limousine had conveyed Jane and Baby Girl from the VIP Lounge to their plane; Baby Girl was set on a floor mat coated in squirrel scat, a scent indistinguishable from the smell of gravel to an untrained nose, yet malodorous in concentrated quantities. The foul rodent odor had lingered in the little dog's nostrils long after takeoff, which had been suffering enough, but to add further injury, upon being secured under a plane seat, Baby Girl had detected a mutant fungus, which combined with Jane's perfume (Daisy Dream) and a trace of methamphetamine, had proven to be for the full three-hour flight a quite dizzying potpourri.

In a bathrobe, Jane entered the room trailing steam, toweling off her hair. At the sound of the bathroom door opening, Baby Girl lifted its head. When it saw Jane, it stood and re-curled itself so that it lay with its back to her, its face toward the windows. Jane observed this. "You silly little thing," she huffed. When Baby Girl didn't budge, Jane returned sulkily to the bathroom, wounded that her Emotional Support hadn't yet recovered from its rare mood. An hour previously, when Jane had tipped Baby Girl out of the Comfy-Go Pet Tote onto the bed, the little dog had snapped at her. And Baby Girl never snapped at her.

The Raffles, Jane's five-star hotel of choice, towered over the European side of Istanbul, half a mile from the Bosporus Bridge. A trendy, defiantly contemporary newcomer to the city, the hotel stretched its neck above the seven hills of Old Town Istanbul which lay to the south. In a matter of months, The Raffles had gained a reputation for its superior spa services and had also become a premier shopping destination, as the adjacent Nennen Center boasted several luxury firms, including Fendi, Lanvin, and Valentino. Jane had already booked a spa treatment, a detoxifying "Luxury Voyage" that included a volcanic mud facial and seaweed-sugar body buff. Her voyage would begin in ninety minutes.

Jane re-emerged from the bathroom and dragged her suitcase over to the bed. With regret, she set aside the portable shower. Such was the price of being a Disher—disappointing others for the sake of the cause, and this time it was Meena and Roxy. And Dominick. Meena had divulged that he'd flown all the way from L.A. to Cartagena just for her. Still, Jane had stayed strong, refusing to be swayed from her quest to find the Dish, even when Meena had voiced firm doubts about her sudden change of plans:

"Bitch, you're, like, not listening to me at all. Istanbul? I mean, if your family finds out—"

"They won't find out."

"But like, why take the risk?"

# THE DIE IS CAST

"Because it's the Shrine of the Four Keepers! Don't you understand? It's my destiny. I can feel it."

"But like, you could end up with nothing. Your Nana is, like, a total hater and Dish-denier, and y'know, can do anything she wants just like that." Meena snapped her fingers for emphasis. "See, if she had you arrested in Moscow, what will it be next? I mean, you've got Whitaker Corporation on one hand, and then there's the Catholic Church. You're up against, like, the whole freaking world. I mean, think of RATS, Jane. Think of us."

"I am. I do. But it's the Dish, Meena. The DISH!"

Roxy shouted from off-screen. "Tell them you're with us, Jane!"

"Shut up, bitch," Meena barked at Roxy, "I was just gonna say that." She turned back to Jane. "Look, send a text to your father, at least. Tell him you're here. You'll be back in a week. Don't make them suspicious. It's the best thing, believe me."

Jane agreed but her voice lacked conviction.

Meena didn't detect this and quickly transitioned, abruptly dropping her voice, "So, like, Dominick told me something. He's having trouble moving on. If he could only understand why you broke up with him."

"This again?" Jane snapped. "Do I need to have a reason? I dunno why. He just isn't for me."

Such had been Jane's conversation with her friends. Recollecting Meena's counsel, she picked up her phone on the bedside stand. Since fleeing Corporate Headquarters in Grandeur two days previously, she'd gotten and ignored several phone calls and a text message from her father. "Why did you run out?" Max had written. "You should've just left with me when I asked. I wanted to explain what Carlisle said about your Nana. Where are you?"

Reluctantly, Jane opened a text window to reply. "I'm in Cartagena," she typed, then paused, trying to concoct an adequate lie. Nothing came to her, so she deleted the message and tried again. "I ran out because—" she inhaled, hesitating again. Then she deleted this message too and tossed her phone onto the bed, despairing of being understood by her father, and anyway, what was there to explain?

She emptied her suitcase and threw all her bikinis and beach wraps into a dresser drawer, these fashions being ill-suited for Dishing. Given her circumstances, she also didn't foresee any use for her vintage Chanel cocktail dress, and as she hung it up in the closet, she lamented the absence of her white Barmah hat and her Versace gray-silk bomber jacket with the fox fur collar. Her silver kimono, she was shocked to discover, had suffered some violence in transit—a spot of red wine, like a pinprick of blood. She called the hotel's cleaning service.

From an inner pocket in her carry-on, she extracted her diamond headband, the golden locket bearing Baby Girl's picture, a couple Steve Finder novels, and the Saint Nil (or Saint Chrysostom) icon she'd bought in Göreme. The saint's face was aloof yet beseeching. Jane almost felt he might share a secret with her if she leaned in close. Why she'd brought it with her, she couldn't say. She wanted it to be real, that's all. But it wasn't. Everything she'd learned about the discovery of the Shrine of the Four Keepers from *TrueDishers.net* only confirmed

Dr. Carlisle's original assessment—Babu had sold her a forgery. The white-robed man holding the bowl looked nothing like the sober Kostas mosaic or the wizened Zoticus, for instance. During her layover in Amsterdam, she'd watched Professor Burke's press conference several times.

Still, something about the little haloed figure in her hands made her feel a pang of longing. It was a roving, unfocussed feeling, like restlessness. Jane didn't know why she felt this way. The image just seemed familiar to her somehow, like a first memory. She sighed and dropped the icon back into her carry-on. It was only an illusion. Her icon didn't have a secret. No secret she didn't already know.

On the chaise, Baby Girl uncurled and stretched.

"Are you through being silly?" Jane asked it playfully. She reached into her carry-on and pulled out the box of Grammy's Teeny Treats.

Baby Girl sniffed the air.

Jane patted the mattress invitingly and squealed in delight when the little dog leaped onto the bed.

"Look at you, you're so brave!" Jane searched the box for a treat. But it was empty. "Ooh no, we ran out." She shook the box in front of Baby Girl theatrically.

The dog stared at the box almost with an expression of betrayal. It jumped off the bed and returned to its curled-up position on the chaise.

"You fussy little thing." Jane scooped up the dog and carried it back to the bed. She reached for *Templars of Doom* and cuddled with the little dog under the bedsheets. She began to read aloud. When she'd last left off, Bucky Browne and Princess Calixta had just entered the Monastery of the Bitter Mount. Only the Emerald Peregrine could unlock the vault in the tower, and they were about to use the key when Cyril the Blind Seer turned to the princess:

"Are you ready for what awaits?" he asked.

"What awaits? The Map of Fortunatus is inside, isn't it?"

"No."

"No?" Calixta gasped. "What do you mean? It has to be."

"Cyril, we've got to get that map," Bucky said.

"My friends, you think you seek only a piece of parchment, but I tell you it is so much more."

"How could a map be more than a map?" Calixta asked.

"In the same way that the heart is more than its four chambers."

"Cyril, the Templars will be here any minute. We don't have time for riddles," Bucky said impatiently.

"There is always time for the truth, my friend." Cyril turned toward Princess Calixta. Though he was sightless, he seemed to study her face, his eyes boring into hers. "That is what lies beyond these doors."

"The truth?" Calixta asked.

"Yes, the truth. And with the truth comes much danger, much hardship. Do you understand?"

"I think so."

"Because there are many enemies of the truth. The path you are choosing will not be easy. And so, I ask again—are you ready for what awaits?"

Princess Calixta hesitated. She looked at Bucky, then back at the seer.

"I don't think anyone is ever really ready to save the world," she said.

Cyril smiled. "Ah, dear Princess, you have answered well. I can see your heart is true. For all that is true is seen by the heart. Therefore, be assured—you will save the world."

"Great," Bucky said, "now can we open this vault before the Templars come and someone has to save us?"

Baby Girl had not paid any attention to the questions posed to Bucky and Calixta. Instead, its face was turned toward the windows, where it watched the veil of evening fall.

"Isn't it exciting?" Jane squealed, bouncing the little dog on her knees. "Are you ready for your life to change with Mama's? Change forever? No more Whitakers. No more mean Nana and weird, fat Leenie. No more Whiningham and, oh, and everything with it. 'Cause tomorrow, my little Baby Girl, we're gonna find the Last Supper Dish!"

Scene 29

## Anathema

*Church of Saint Euphemia*

*District of Chalcedon, Istanbul*

*Sunday, March 14*

*You will regret this.* Archbishop Anthimos sat in his office at the Church of Saint Euphemia and gazed out the window at the darkening clouds that swept across the afternoon sky. *You have forsaken your oath to the Emperor, Papi. Not only you, but also Diogenes and Elias—even the head of our Order, Philotheos. I will make all of you regret it.* Anthimos clutched the golden, double-headed eagle that hung about his neck. Though he treasured this symbol of Byzantine greatness, of late he had grown more and more discontent wearing it as an ornament. Burke's discovery of the Shrine of the Four Keepers had stirred his deepest longing, the longing for Byzantine power restored—and unleashed.

*You are all unworthy servants. You only do your duty. But you do not love the Legacy.* Anthimos turned his eyes to his desk. Before him lay a legal pad and a pen. He'd been sitting contemplatively for hours, finding himself suddenly free from prior commitments. The American film company 8 Ball Productions had canceled their scheduled interview, citing "an extraordinary opportunity to film Adam Burke's excavation." Miffed by their snub at first, Anthimos had quickly discerned their cancellation to be a blessing—one that he did not need to reveal to Philotheos or the rest of the Andronicus Order. He now had time and the necessary privacy to devote himself to a far greater venture—betraying the Patriarch's plan to steal the prodokleis from Burke.

He picked up his pen and tapped it impatiently on the legal pad. He'd yet to conceive a counterscheme. The lines before him were bare. Although he would never admit it to Philotheos, he admired the Patriarch's desperate audacity to undertake a heist. The Order's plan even had a chance to succeed. Papi, the perfect spy, had reported that no cameras were in the hall outside Girard Lab, the room in the museum where Burke would take the prodokleis. Since Papi worked in the lab processing artifacts from Burke's excavation, he had given the Order the security code. The museum guards, so Papi said, were lax, and he would distract them as the initiates Leo, Theo, and Winnipeg Joe slunk away with the prize. Diogenes had offered a splendid idea for disguises, and Elias's suggestion to leave behind a false clue in case the initiates were seen by an outdoor camera was ingenious.

Once Leo, Theo, and Winnipeg Joe had seized the prodokleis, they were not to return to the Church of Saint George directly. They were to use the Order's tunnel system as their getaway. A fitting scheme, as the tunnels had been dug centuries before for the very purpose of secret escape. Gabriel had retrieved from the Secret Archives the Order's master map, a document miraculously preserved from Constantinople's destruction. With it, the Order had charted the monks' underground trek to Saint George. An Order agent would drive them far south from the museum to the Gate House beneath the Saint Helen Church in the Yedikule District. There, assisted by Deacon Dorian, a young Gatekeeper, the monks would enter the tunnels.

Anthimos scratched at his beard. At the Order's meeting, he had objected to the heist, arguing that the Order should be rejoicing to see Dish seekers on the cusp of discovering the truth of the Last Supper Dish's disappearance. "Burke is about to uncover Andronicus's Legacy. We should be helping him find and use the clues left at the shrine, not trying to snatch those clues away. Guiding seekers to the Dish is our ancient charge—not peddling stories on a website!" he had contended. But Patriarch Philotheos had overruled his objections, until finally, all that had been left to him was to sulk in silent protest.

*There must be a way.* Perhaps, after all, the way was easy. One phone call to the American professor would thwart Philotheos. All Anthimos had to do was tell Burke about the prodokleis, instruct him what it looked like and how to use it. He had to encourage Burke not to give up his search for the Dish, for secrets of far greater value awaited him. Anthimos almost reached for his cell phone, but then he shook his head. No, that was not the way. Papi had already ruined his credibility with Burke. At the previous evening's exhibition opening, Papi had tricked him into talking nonsense in front of Burke instead of talking about the prodokleis. As a result, Burke could have no other belief than that he'd been accosted by a trio of fools. He wouldn't believe that those fools had told him the truth.

Anthimos cringed, recalling his humiliation at Papi's hands. Papi's betrayal angered him afresh. He'd been too quick to believe the old man had joined him. Old dogs, he should've known, stick to their old tricks. And yet, Papi's action had saved him from revealing too much to Burke. They all knew what Andronicus's Legacy would do to Dish seekers. Even the man-child Leronymos had possessed the foresight to warn Anthimos about culpability, discerning that if Burke knew who had told him about the prodokleis, then that person would be held responsible if or when the final secret of the Legacy did, in fact ...

*Culpability is a dangerous thing. You should listen to your brother.* Those had been Papi's words. Much as Anthimos loathed to admit it, Papi had been right. Why be part of a Secret Order if he were to play show-and-tell with all its secrets? Even he needed a reminder of the important things. Meekly, Anthimos crossed himself and thanked Emperor Andronicus for giving him a second chance to prove himself to be his worthy heir. He vowed to do it right this time.

The best way to pay Papi back would be to learn the lesson. He would ruin those oath-shirkers' little heist in such a way that he wouldn't be held culpable. He wouldn't be too eager to act without considering the consequences. If he simply tried to warn Burke about the heist, then the initiates would be caught, and the Order would be exposed. *And I would be the obvious culprit.* That wouldn't do.

Anthimos tapped his pen on the legal pad. *I will not rush forward. Let me walk backwards. What is my desired outcome?* The question was easy to answer. If the heist must happen, then he, not Philotheos, must receive the prodokleis from the three monks. *How do I convince the initiates to give it to me?* The strategy formulating in his mind was intricate, and yet its basis was quite simple. At the top of the legal pad, the archbishop wrote one word:

FEAR.

*Who would help me create this fear?* He scrawled several names—names of longtime allies in the Order and those of other useful people.

His cell phone rang. *Ah, an ally indeed.* "Brother Chrys, what news?" Anthimos said. "Philotheos call off the heist?"

"Ha! I am afraid not," Archbishop Chrysanthus said. "It goes forward—and with haste. Papi's student Giulio reports that Burke has broken through a stone wall in the apse."

Anthimos sat up. "Burke listened to me. I urged him to dig under it. Has he found anything?"

"Not yet. But Papi confirms that the apse extends beyond the wall. That ashlar wall was a false face. Papi says they must tear it all down before a search can be done. It will take the rest of the day, tomorrow as well."

"I knew it! This proves I was right." Anthimos smacked his open palm on his desk. "I guessed the ancient Order had secured the Legacy before the Ottomans conquered the city. Ah, Chrys, think of what this means. Can you not imagine the possibilities?"

Chrysanthus chuckled. "So, you still intend to sabotage the heist, do you? What is your plan? You must move quickly. The Patriarch has already told the initiates to prepare themselves. All the pieces are in place."

Anthimos grinned. "Yes, but the game board is about to change. I will explain tonight. After the celebration of the Triumph of Orthodoxy, you and Lerry come to my office. I will tell you the new rules."

After saying goodbye to Chrys, Anthimos scanned the names he had scrawled on his legal pad. When his eyes fell on one name, he felt his skin tingle. He picked up his phone, considering for a moment how best to word his question. As he knew, there was only one way to change the game in his favor. He had to change the gate by which the monks would enter the Order's secret tunnels. *Gatekeeper Dorian is the Patriarch's tool, but Sander Minolas is mine.*

"Yes, Sander, this is Anthimos. Yes, I am well, thank you. Say, have you been following the progress of the American archaeologist, Burke? Ah, yes, I thought you would be. Yes, quite amazing, the shrine's discovery. In fact, I have just gotten word that Burke is breaking through a fake wall—naturally, you know what must be hidden behind it." Anthimos relished Sander's exultant reaction to this news. The Gatekeeper's desire for Burke to discover the prodokleis was as great as Anthimos's own. That desire must be stoked.

"What does Philotheos think? Bah!" Anthimos scoffed. "Of course, he should be pleased. But no. He wants to steal the prodokleis from Burke once he finds it. Yes, I am serious. Why? To lock it away so no one will come near the Red Gate. Laugh if you wish, my friend, but I was there when he and his spineless cadre planned the theft. The Patriarch's cowardice has infected the Order." Anthimos paused for effect. "He—he would have us all betray Andronicus."

Sander was outraged, as Anthimos knew he would be. He'd encouraged the Gatekeeper's complaints about Philotheos for many years.

"I agree, it's shameful," Anthimos said. "That is why I plan to stop Philotheos and help Burke. It is our oath to assist seekers of the Dish. If I were to call on you to support me in this worthy cause, would you lend me aid?"

Sander's reply was immediate.

"Oh, that is good to hear," Anthimos said quickly. "We must purge the Order of cowardice and uphold our ancient charge. We must stand with the Emperor, even if that means certain other sacrifices must be made. But such sacrifices would be small. We made no oath to Philotheos, after all. If aiding me forces you to resist him, I think you could do so with a clear conscience, do you not agree? The Patriarch breaks so many rules that do not suit him."

Sander hesitated, but his answer was affirmative.

"Excellent. I knew you were a man of wisdom. We live in extraordinary times. Extraordinary measures must be taken. We have no choice," Anthimos declared confidently. A great show of confidence would gain him the prize, he believed, and so he went on smoothly to say, "Although you and I—many of us—have longed for a seeker to reopen the Legacy, none of us dared hope it could happen. But now, an incredible opportunity is set before us. For the first time in over seven hundred years, a seeker might enter in. Just think of it, Sander. It is a miracle! Miracles always restore life as it should have been. They expand our vision of what is possible. We must seize that vision. We must participate in the miracle. We must be its instruments. I am sure you feel the significance of what I am saying. Oh, indeed? You feel the Emperor's spirit has roused itself? That is a profound way of putting it." Anthimos licked his lips, tasting victory. He'd come to his significant question and chose his words carefully. "We must let the Emperor's spirit guide us, even if we are guided beyond our limits, beyond those slight rules we must keep, the oaths that join us within the Order. Miracles upend the natural order of things. So, if aiding me necessitated that you set aside the normal rules, would you? We will act in secret, of course. I will protect you. No one will know of your involvement."

Anthimos held his breath, but he need not have been anxious. Years of stoking Sander's discontent had done its work. The Gatekeeper's reply sounded like a snake's low hiss. Anthimos grinned and stroked his beard. "You are a bold man, Sander. You will be rewarded by your choice. Say and do nothing for now. I will contact you again soon. This we keep until the wages of sin are paid."

Jubilant from his victory, Anthimos leaped from his chair and threw open the window. His office overlooked a courtyard where stood the shell of the former Church of Saint Euphemia—the wall of the apse—bound in brown, leafless vines. The old church had been built in the thirteenth century by Emperor Andronicus. The clinging vines stabilized the ancient wall and thus were never cut. Anthimos examined the state of the wall often as a private act of communion with the Emperor. Thinking of what he'd told Sander, he sobered. He'd said the Emperor's spirit was guiding them. He'd not meant it. But maybe it was true.

*Now for my first move.* The game board had been altered thanks to Gatekeeper Sander's loyalty. It was time for Anthimos to roll the dice. He retrieved an Istanbul street map from his filing cabinet and traced the route that the Order had planned for the getaway driver to take from the museum to the Saint Helen Gate. *Time for another call.*

"Mr. Pasa, thank you for answering. Yes, this is really The Archbishop. I know it has been some time. You are Rail Bureau Chief now—congratulations on your promotion—but I hope you still have some clout at the Department of Traffic where you once were? You do? Oh, excellent. What do I need? Street barriers placed at some choice locations—only for a few days. You know I make it worth your while. I can wire, say, $10,000 to you immediately. I need the barriers set up at soon as possible—tomorrow night even."

Pasa demurred at the timing. His contacts at the Department of Traffic would not appreciate a phone call on a weekend, even for a bribe. He was sure he could broker a deal, but the department had grown inefficient since his departure, a sad fact that would cause a week's delay. If The Archbishop's errand were urgent, then barriers owned by the Rail Bureau could be used instead, but that would entail factoring in the cost of transportation and union labor ...

"Double the amount I named," Anthimos said, not troubled by Pasa's haggling, as he'd started the bidding low.

Twenty minutes later, after Pasa had learned how many barriers Anthimos needed and where they were to be placed in the city, ten thousand dollars had become twenty-five. Anthimos winced at the sum Pasa had weaseled from him, but the profits from *TrueDishers.net* had been considerable for the year, and Anthimos's cut had been generous.

Having blocked Leo, Theo, and Winnipeg's escape route from the museum, Anthimos considered his second move. He was about to reach for his phone again when the sound of his office door opening made him start. Who would dare? Quickly, he laid a Bible over the legal pad.

A bright-eyed young priest popped his head in. "Your Eminence, I'm so sorry, I didn't think you were here."

"Father Tobias, it is quite all right," Anthimos answered. "I had an appointment, but it was canceled. You could not have known. But what is that giggling I hear behind you?"

"Newest members of our youth group," Tobias announced cheerily. "I am giving them a church tour before we celebrate the Triumph of Orthodoxy this evening. The children are curious about all the mysterious things here. But we are in your way." He turned to leave.

The sound of children's voices melted away Anthimos's irritation at being interrupted, and the thrill of successfully scheming for the glory of Orthodoxy spurred his desire to see the future of his church. He stood and walked around his desk. "Not at all," he said to Tobias. "What I am doing can wait for a bit. Bring the children in."

"Oh, I do not wish to trouble you—"

"It is no trouble. Please, I insist," Anthimos said. He smoothed the folds in his black robe and straightened his eagle pendant. Influencing young minds appealed to him immensely, and he sought to make a good impression.

Tobias beckoned to his small troupe—two six-year-old girls and a boy of ten. "I have a surprise," he said to them. "Here is an important man for you to meet. This is Archbishop Anthimos, the leader of our diocese of Chalcedon." Then to Anthimos, he said, "Your Eminence, this is Petronella, Edora, and Nico."

The children stared up at Anthimos with apprehension, but he bent down, touched each child on the head, and blessed them in a warm, gentle voice. Then he conjured up pieces of fruit taffy from the pockets of his robe, and the children were quickly won over.

"So, you are taking a tour of Saint Euphemia," Anthimos said to the happily chewing children. He gestured about his office. "What would you like to know about first? I will answer any question."

"Is your beard real?" the boy asked.

Father Tobias reddened in embarrassment. "Nico, what a thing to ask His Eminence."

"I want to touch it," Petronella said.

"Me too!" Edora chimed in.

"Children, please," Tobias admonished them.

Anthimos huffed theatrically and waggled his finger at the boy. "That is not what I meant."

Nico smiled bashfully but returned Anthimos's gaze.

Anthimos held his frown another moment, then burst into laughter. "Everyone gets one touch, but no tugging."

As they held Anthimos's beard, the two girls squealed with glee, but Nico remained quiet.

"Real enough?" Anthimos asked the boy.

Nico nodded. "One day, I will have a beard like yours."

"That's enough, children," Tobias said. "Let's leave His Eminence and start our tour."

"I shall give the tour," Anthimos announced suddenly, his eyes still on Nico. Before Tobias could object, Anthimos said, "These children are Orthodoxy's future. Shaping our future is a responsibility we all share." He grinned impishly at the children, pleased to lead a rapt, captive audience. "I know all kinds of secret things about this church," he said to them. "Would you like to know them?"

The children demanded to know everything, and Anthimos led the group through the narthex. "What secret should I reveal first?" he asked when they had entered the nave. The children were gawking all around.

"A man is on the roof," Petronella shouted, pointing up.

Filling the expanse of the dome above was a haloed man robed in indigo. His eyes were large and earnest, and his skin was luminous as if his face itself were a light. His right hand was raised, and he held a book in his left hand.

"Yes, we call that secret Christ Pantocrator. But it is really Jesus waving hello from heaven," Anthimos said. "Not many look up to see our Lord as you have. You are a girl who spots secrets easily."

Petronella pirouetted and chanted, "I found the se-cret."

"Does everyone remember our Lord's favorite book?" Tobias asked the children in a sing-song voice.

The three answered in unison, "The Biii-ble."

"I wanna know about that." Edora pointed to a high partition at the front of the nave. It was covered with colorful paintings of people stacked in two large tiers. The wood framing each portrait was brightly gilded.

"Yeah, the pictures are pretty," Petronella said.

"Very pretty," Anthimos agreed. "This wall is called an iconostasis." He repeated the name slowly, and Tobias tried without success to have the children pronounce it. Anthimos continued, "These are special pictures. We call them icons. All the people here are holy, and they did amazing things to help our church long ago. Here is Saint Euphemia." Anthimos pointed to a woman with a lion at her feet. "She was killed because she believed in Jesus. But she is alive in heaven. All these people are—they still help us now. These icons are like windows—they see us, and we see them."

"Like watching a video on the computer?" Edora asked.

"That's right," Anthimos said. "I will give prizes to anyone who can find Jesus." The children yelled and pointed. "Yes, he holds the book, just like on the dome," Anthimos said. "Now, show me his Holy Mother." More yelling and pointing. "Of course, Mary always holds baby Jesus. Now, who can show me the angels? Oh, that was easy, they have big golden wings." Anthimos passed out more fruit taffy.

# THE DIE IS CAST

"Today is special," he explained as the children ate their candy. "It is a holy day, the first Sunday of Great Lent. When you come back later the church will be filled with people, and we will celebrate the Triumph of Orthodoxy. Does anyone know what triumph means?"

The girls shook their heads, but Nico said, "It means, like, winning."

"Yes, winning," Anthimos said firmly. "Our religion has been through many bad things, and mean people have tried to stop us from going to church. They do not like the pretty pictures of Mary and Jesus. But God has always taken care of us. Tonight, we celebrate how God helps us win. But we also remember the mean people who are still out there. We pray that God will make them go away. Here is a secret." Anthimos winked mischievously. "The Triumph of Orthodoxy is my favorite holy day, even more than Christmas."

"Nuh-uh," the girls objected, "Christmas is the best."

"Your Eminence, what's behind those doors?" Nico asked curiously. He pointed to the center of the iconostasis. Two hinged panels between Mary and Jesus bore icons of the Twelve Apostles. "I have seen the priests go in and out of them," Nico said.

Anthimos nodded his approval. "Very observant. That door is the Beautiful Gate. Beyond it is the church's sanctuary—a very holy place. We take bread and wine to the altar and God transforms them into Jesus. When we share the bread and wine in church, we share God with everyone."

"Can we go back there and see?" Nico asked.

The girls chanted, "We wanna see, we wanna see."

"No, only priests like me and Father Tobias can go into the sanctuary," Anthimos said. "It is a secret place."

Petronella and Edora whined their displeasure.

"You said you would tell all the secrets," Nico objected.

"Er, that's enough, kids," Tobias interjected. "Be happy, Nico, that His Eminence has taken the time to teach you."

Nico was glum.

Anthimos appraised the boy. *Should I play a little show-and-tell?* Nico was young, but any chance to stoke his curiosity into a flicker of desire must be taken. The church—and the Order—must have a future.

They heard the groan of the church's large main doors opening. Friendly conversation echoed from the narthex.

Father Tobias glanced at his watch. "Time flies. The parents have arrived to pick up their children."

"Would you go out to meet them, Father Tobias?" Anthimos asked. "I would like to speak with the children a few minutes more. I do not want them to leave disappointed."

After Tobias had gone, Anthimos knelt and gathered the children close to him. "I cannot take you to see the altar, but to make up for that, I will tell you my *super*-secret." He dropped his voice conspiratorially. "It is so secret, not even Father Tobias knows. But you must promise not to tell."

"We promise! Tell us the super-secret!" the girls loudly urged him. But Nico remained quiet. Anthimos delighted to see the spark of interest in the boy's face. He glanced up at Christ Pantocrator. He'd not told the children that the image depicted Jesus as Ruler of the Universe, holding the destiny of all people in his hand.

Briefly, Anthimos imagined himself—not Philotheos—as head of the Secret Order. He imagined himself seated on the throne with young men like Nico all around him, men sharing his zeal for the Legacy. *Emperor Andronicus built a Beautiful Gate indeed. I will open it for Nico—just a touch. No harm will come of it.*

"I have been to another church," Anthimos whispered to the children, "a *hidden* church filled with secrets." His eyes shown with glee. "It was built by my favorite saint. It is called Saint Andy's Church of Secret Adventures. It is like no other church in the whole world. You do not stand in it to pray and sing. Oh, no! You play in it. Saint Andy's is like a big playground. Why, the first thing you see when you enter is a merry-go-round. You can spin it until you are dizzy."

"Nuh-uuuuh," the girls reacted skeptically.

"Yeah huh. I am an archbishop, so I would know. Remember Christ Pantocrator?" Anthimos pointed up. "The dome at Saint Andy's is sooo big—and flipped upside down. It is like a swimming pool where you can have a big party. And if you are extra-nice, there is a fireworks show, just like on Republic Day." Anthimos waved his arms about, simulating fireworks exploding. "Fwooosh! Boom!"

"Nuh-uuuuh!"

"Yeah huh! And the iconostasis at Saint Andy's is a big jigsaw puzzle, and you must move the pictures around until they fit just right. And if you solve the puzzle, then the Beautiful Gate will unlock. And guess what?" Anthimos looked directly at Nico. "You get to go inside and find Saint Andy's secret treasure. Do you know what it is?"

"The Last Supper Dish!" Nico yelled. "Just like in my Bucky Browne comic books."

Anthimos gaped and put his hands to his cheeks, pantomiming shock. He recognized the glow of fervor in the boy's eyes and smiled in satisfaction. "Maybe when you are older, I will take you on the adventure, and we will see. But I have kept your parents waiting." Anthimos stood to usher the children to the narthex.

"Is there really a secret church? Is the Last Supper Dish really there?" Nico asked Anthimos as they walked through the nave. "Or was that just a fun story?"

"Just a fun story, Nico," Anthimos replied. Then, out of earshot of the girls, he added with a wink, "But I did not lie."

As Anthimos and Tobias watched the parents leave with their children, Tobias said, "I couldn't help but overhear Nico mention the Last Supper Dish. Do you think it is really out there, waiting to be found?" His tone was skeptical.

Anthimos fiddled with his eagle pendant. "I prepare for the Triumph by praying near the ruins. Care to join me?" He strode with purpose through a side door in the narthex and into the grass courtyard. Tobias trotted along behind.

"I'm sure you've kept up with the news of the Shrine of the Four Keepers," Tobias said. "Pundits are saying it is the most significant excavation since the Egyptian pyramids."

"Indeed. Its discovery is amazing. Portentous even."

"You think it will affect Pope Boniface's visit? It'd be a shame if it marred the Dialogues of Love with the

Patriarch. Many expect the Pope to offer the Dish back to him."

Anthimos halted his walk, rankled to be hearing Latin propaganda on an Orthodox holy day. "What do you mean *the* Dish?" he said coldly. "That thing is *their* Dish."

Tobias raised his hands in a mollifying manner. "Oh, I know the relic the Catholics hold is disputed. I only meant that the Pope may offer it as a gesture to further heal our ancient schism—like he offered Saint Kosmo. I just worry about this shrine. It aggravates old wounds. But, like, peace is what we need, isn't it? I fear this discovery will hurt Boniface's attempt at reconciliation."

"It will." Anthimos resumed his walk but turned his face from Tobias to hide a sneer. The young priest was obviously a budding idealist, full of faith in humanity. Experiencing disappointment would do him good. "The shrine reignites the hope that the Dish was saved from Latin greed. Philotheos respects Orthodoxy's history. The Latins betrayed us. The shrine memorializes that. We must never forget."

"So, will Professor Burke find the Dish there?" Tobias asked in that same doubtful tone.

They arrived at the ruins of the former church. As Tobias looked on, Anthimos bowed three times and crossed himself. Then he inspected the wall. Some of the brown vines had begun to grow new green shoots.

"If Professor Burke is a man of truth, he will find what he seeks," Anthimos said. "You see, the shrine was built for people like him—seekers of the truth." He picked a withered tendril from the bricks of the wall. "Answers await at the shrine, ready to be plucked out."

"Oh, really? Why so certain?"

"It is written in the accounts—the Annals of Andronicus. The historian Metochites writes that the Emperor commanded an inscription to be carved on the altar—Ask, and it shall be given thee. Seek, and ye shall find."

"Oh. I haven't read the Annals," Tobias admitted. "Just a summary. Did Metochites say the Dish is at the shrine?"

"No."

"Huh. That's weird. Why not?"

"Very simple. The Emperor did not permit him. As court scribe, Metochites was the Emperor's mouthpiece. But he does confirm that all four icons of the Keepers were at the shrine. They were distributed to pilgrims—for a small fee."

"Like buying a souvenir." Tobias laughed. "Some things never change. You think the professor will find all four?"

Anthimos narrowed his eyes. "I think it very likely."

"Really? The icons contain those riddles. If they really are riddles. Some say they aren't. Do you believe solving them will reveal where the Dish is hidden at the shrine?"

"Not at the shrine. Why have seekers come to the shrine to get all four clues only to have the Dish be somewhere else in the same building? No, the clues lead seekers elsewhere."

"That's a popular theory. So, like, where?"

Anthimos smiled insincerely. Anger flashed in his eyes. He discerned that Tobias was merely humoring him with his questions. "I will tell you what I told Nico—only Emperor Andronicus knows."

"A treasure hunt with riddles to solve?" Tobias scoffed, his disbelief on full display. "No offense, but, like, how can people think that? I mean, I know a lot of people do, but seriously, it sounds like a Steve Finder novel."

Anthimos's face darkened. He lifted his chin haughtily, having had quite enough of the young priest's flippancy. Time to nip it in the bud. He crushed the dried stem in his fingers and said, "Let me tell you a story, Tobias. Once there was a great city, rich in gold, in history, in culture, and in religion. Its churches were filled with light and with prayer. This was Constantinople—the Queen of Cities. But there were many others who despised and envied her. They formed alliances and betrayed her trust, conspiring to besiege her, to plunder and despoil. And so, they did. On ships from the West they came. For three days Latins pillaged and sacked, murdering priests and raping nuns. They ignited a great fire that swept thousands into the streets, only to perish there by the sword. The Latins entered our churches, smearing frescoes with entrails, desecrating the relics of the saints, and smashing holy vessels to bits so they could more easily divide the spoils among themselves. And after this, they turned our brilliant jewel, Hagia Sophia, into a whorehouse, seating a prostitute on the throne of the patriarch."

Anthimos placed his hand on the ruined church wall as if he felt some pain within it that he could ease. He went on:

"Thusly, did the Latins begin their rule. And thus, it continued for fifty years, and we were without comfort. For where does one turn when betrayed by a brother? when forsaken by God? As an ancient prophet lamented—O City, thou hast drunk at the hand of the Lord the cup of his fury! But even while the rubble still smoldered, rumors were heard—the Lord's presence had not departed from the city, and so the Latins could not ultimately prevail. Our most holy relic, the Last Supper Dish, had been spared—plucked from the hands of the marauders, and as some said, by God himself. Into their hands instead was placed a worthless dog dish. The Latins, in their arrogance and greed, could not see the difference. Because, Tobias, spiritual objects can only be spiritually discerned, with the eyes of the heart. This was the message of Kostas, Zoticus, Panikos, and Nil, may their memory be eternal. And what do you think the Latins did when they suspected these monks spoke the truth?"

Tobias stared at the ground. His voice was but a whisper. "The Catholics killed them, Your Eminence."

"Well, you know that part of Orthodoxy's history at least." Anthimos narrowed his eyes, studying the young priest's face for signs of its former levity. He found none.

"Do you think, Tobias, that these four men would have died for a lie?" Anthimos asked sternly.

"No, Your Eminence," Tobias answered meekly. "I don't think anyone willingly dies for a lie."

"No, of course not. No one thinks that." Anthimos looked at the clouds. The sun was setting, and the sky blazed a brilliant orange. The clouds were streaked with crimson.

"I tell you this story to remind you to beware of any reconciliation with the Latins," he went on. "Recall the words of the great Saint Makarios. He says the heart bent on evil is a dragon's lair. It is filled with dark towers, brooding and aflame, and treacherous, forsaken valleys. There lions roam, and spiders spin their deadly webs. And the serpent devours its prey. That, Tobias, is the Catholic heart."

▼ ▼ ▼ ▼

That evening, as congregants assembled to celebrate the Triumph of Orthodoxy, Anthimos stood in the center of the nave gazing at the icons before him. His vestments were scarlet, and the ruby eyes of his eagle winked in the candlelight. The faces of the saints and angels seemed to shift and move with life in the flickering light, as if all the windows of heaven were open. The congregants gathered about Anthimos, and the choir sang, "Freely, You bore the cross to liberate Your creation from the enemy's oppression."

As Anthimos listened to the chant, gathering strength from the power of the people's voices, he glanced at an icon tucked into a corner of the iconostasis. The candlelight left it half in shadows. Anthimos could just make out the figure of a crowned man stepping into the light. He carried in his hands a miniature church, and genuflecting before an enthroned Christ, he offered it to his Lord. The man was Emperor Andronicus. Anthimos relished the heavenly vision. *As Christ frees us from sin's bondage, I shall free the greatest of your works from its shackles.*

While Anthimos and the congregants looked on, a procession of priests filed from the Deacon's Doors to the left and right of the Beautiful Gate. Archbishops Chrysanthus and Leronymos were among them. The priests gathered before Anthimos. Chrys handed him the Dikirion, and Lerry gave him the Trikirion. Long like swords, they were sacred candlesticks symbolizing the power of God. Anthimos pointed the candlesticks at the congregation and crossed the candles, forming the shape of an X—the ancient sign of blessing. *Andronicus has bequeathed to us a great weapon, my people. God has given it into my hands, and I fear nothing.*

Afterwards, Anthimos led the procession through the Beautiful Gate into the sanctuary. Chrys and Lerry placed the bread and wine on the altar. Anthimos intoned the prayers of consecration through which these earthly elements would become the body and blood of Christ. When he had finished, he was given a censer of burning incense. Twelve bells on the chain from which the censer hung began to ring as he moved around the altar, filling the chamber with the astringent aroma that sanctified the sacrifice of Christ. Only the twelfth bell, the bell of Judas the betrayer, was silent. He heard the choir sing: "O Lord, by your sacrifice you have saved your people. Bless all Orthodox Christians. Grant us victory over our adversaries." *Yes, my people, a sacrifice will be made. The wages of sin will be paid. This I will keep.*

The priests returned to the center of the nave. Normally, Anthimos led the ending procession, but today was a holy day, the Triumph of Orthodoxy. He stood at the chanter stand instead. "It is God who judges, throwing down one and exalting another," he prayed from the seventy-fifth Psalm. "In His hand is a cup with foaming wine. He will pour a draught from it, and all the wicked of the earth shall drain it down to the dregs."

# THE DIE IS CAST

"Amen," the congregation responded.

Anthimos touched his eagle pendant, imagining Professor Burke unlocking the mystery the Order of Andronicus had safeguarded for so long. The Emperor had left behind a grand adventure for seekers of the Dish. Anthimos prayed that if any joined the archaeologist's search, they would be Catholic. *Come, for unpleasant truths await you.*

The congregants stood still—hushed, waiting.

Anthimos began to sing. At first his chant was but a murmur. Slowly, his chant gained force, his pitch rising steadily measure by measure, until nothing could hold it back, and it burst forth in a mighty crescendo. "To those who scorn the mysteries kept by the Orthodox Church, Anathema!"

In response, like a sudden wind, the voices of the choir rang out. "Anathema, Anathema, Anathema."

Anthimos chanted, "To those who mock the truths revealed by our holy images and relics, Anathema!"

"Anathema, Anathema, Anathema," the choir sang.

"To those who in pride betray the true faith, Anathema!"

"Anathema, Anathema, Anathema."

The voices of the choir were like the tolling of a bell. The music carried unto the far corners of the church, enthralling every ear with its solemn beauty.

Deeply stirred, Anthimos raised his eyes to the dome and gazed at Christ Pantocrator. *O Sovereign Lord,* he silently prayed, *may the betrayers be trampled in the great wine press of your wrath. May they be slaughtered and their blood flow, their putrid carcasses burnt* with fire, and the stench of their melting flesh rise to heaven!

He raised his hands heavenward. On his chest, the ruby eyes of the eagle flashed like sparks. As he joined the final chorus with his own deep roar, calling down curses on his enemies, he felt as if the ethereal rhythms of the chant were lifting his own heart up to the throne of judgment.

"Anathema! A-na-the-maaa! A-NA-THE-MAAA!"

# THE DIE IS CAST

## 8 Ball Productions

Director ~ Ray Cozart

Producer ~ Reggie Lovett

Sound ~ Natalie Ashbrook

Camera ~ Clark Cannon

## Featuring

Anthimos ~ Orthodox archbishop of Chalcedon

Zainab Ayhan ~ curator, Museum of Ancient History

Babu ~ shopkeeper

Baby Girl ~ Jane's dog

Carlino Betori ~ Roman Catholic cardinal

Boniface X ~ Pontiff

Roxy Boscana and Meena Kim ~ Jane's friends

Adam Burke ~ professor and archaeologist

Calvino, Foo, Hromadova, and Stoltzfus ~ archaeologists

Frank Carlisle ~ curator, Summit Art Museum

Chrysanthus ~ Orthodox archbishop of Greece

Frederico D'Angelo ~ director, Holy See Press Office

Diogenes ~ Orthodox abbot

Eduardo Donizetti ~ Roman Catholic cardinal

Duffy ~ Burke's graduate student

## CREDITS

Nicole Dziedzic ~ homeless advocate

Elias ~ Orthodox archbishop of Boston

Steve Finder ~ novelist

Louis Fortier ~ Roman Catholic bishop

Gabriel ~ the Patriarch's secretary

Gloria Kilday ~ Jane's mother

Gordon and Sylvia Krayzel ~ retired ambassador and wife

Laomendon and Jakab ~ medieval monks

Leo, Theo, and Winnipeg Joe ~ Orthodox monks

Leronymos ~ Orthodox archbishop of Italy

Kitty Lightly ~ television show host

Giulio Makarios ~ Papadopoulos's graduate student

Toby Milto ~ Patricia's assistant

Michael Mistral ~ magazine reporter

Murat ~ Ayhan's assistant

Ahmet Öztürk ~ director, Ministry of Culture and Tourism

Papadopoulos ~ professor and archaeologist

Feredun Pasa ~ Istanbul Rail Bureau Chief

Geoffrey Peagram ~ professor

Petronella, Edora, and Nico ~ children

Philotheos ~ Patriarch of the Greek Orthodox Church

Victor Santorini ~ Papal secretary

Staci ~ fashion model

Tobias ~ Orthodox priest

Jane Whitaker ~ heiress and Disher

Kathleen Whitaker ~ Jane's aunt

Max Whitaker ~ Jane's father

Patricia Whitaker ~ Jane's grandmother

Acknowledgements

Heights & Woodhouse thank all the readers who have joined the quest with our characters—and with us.

This quest started for us seven years ago with a late-night conversation filled with laughs about some guy named Velvet Joe who stole a famous artifact. Lady Jane, our adventurer, chased him to a tropical island, while at the same time she was starring in a live-action TV show. We'd also concocted a love triangle with two professors pursuing the same woman who was killed tragically by a hippopotamus. Don't ask us how all that was supposed to connect. Heights wanted thrills, and Woodhouse craved romance. Thankfully, Velvet Joe and the hippo exist now only in our first composition notebook, along with our other shaky ideas.

We've learned much along the way about ourselves and about successful collaboration. Mostly we've learned that we need each other to make our ideas work. The story we ended up with is not his or hers but uniquely *ours*. We are happy to share our story with you. We hope you agree that we made some wise choices in revision.

If you were entertained by Burke, Ray, Natalie, and Jane's adventures, then we invite you to share your experience by leaving a review at Amazon.com or your preferred social media site. On Instagram, look for Heights & Woodhouse to follow Lady Jane's travel blog.

We have more adventure, romance, and intrigue in store for you in book two, *A Bold Move*. Check out the trailer scene for it on the next page. In addition, don't forget to snag your free copy of *When the Pirate Met the Princess*, the touching story of when Ray and Natalie first met, a story available at heightsandwoodhouse.com:

http://heightsandwoodhouse.com/get-pirate/

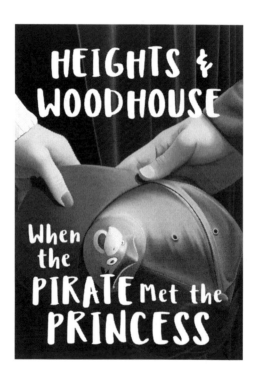

# Preview for A BOLD MOVE, Book Two of Lady Jane and the Last Supper Dish:

Along the service road behind the museum, in a parked black sedan, three monks slouched down in the back seat as a van drove past.

"Is that it? Is that the one?" Leo asked Gene, the driver. His tone suggested he hoped the answer would be *no*. He raised his head up just in time to see taillights disappearing around the corner of the building.

"It's white. Papi said it would be," Gene answered.

Leo tried breathing deeply. Beside him, Winnipeg Joe was chanting a prayer. Theo's head was bowed. "Brothers," Leo murmured, "it is time."

The three of them made the sign of the cross.

Just then twin beams of headlights lit up the back window, silhouetting their heads. They ducked too late as a second van sped by.

"What was that?" Winnipeg gasped.

"They saw us!" Theo moaned.

Leo felt dizzy. His stomach heaved. Papi hadn't mentioned a *second* van, as Winnipeg and Theo instantly pointed out. How many people were there? Were there more security guards than they'd accounted for? Were they armed? Did they have guns? Which van had the prodokleis?

Gene had no answers.

Nor did Leo, though his brothers turned to him with their panicked questions.

"Quiet! I need to think," he commanded. He shut his eyes, for the reality of the second van upset all their battle plans. Their scheme only accounted for Burke and maybe two or three others. But now? His own question needed an answer. "You know the way, Brother Leo," he heard a voice whisper to him. It was the voice of Zoticus the Wise. The Four Keepers had come to him.

*No, I do not know*, Leo replied to the voice.

"Will you run away?" Panikos asked.

*Winnipeg, Theo, they are too frightened.*

"You scold them, but you do not lead them," Nil admonished. "Go first, and they will follow."

*But how can I be sure?*

"For over seven hundred years the Order has withstood every calamity, even the fall of Constantinople itself," Kostas uttered. "And here you sit quivering because there are two vans instead of one. Bah! Use the element of surprise. Strike quickly. Their numbers do not matter."

"The Order will fail without you, Brother Leo," Zoticus said. "Move boldly, and you will gain your place among us."

Leo opened his eyes. His dizziness had vanished.

"Brothers, it is time," he repeated calmly.

Winnipeg and Theo shrank from him.

Leo observed this. "Come, brothers, will we be forever shamed? Will we return to His All Holiness with nothing?"

They stared wide-eyed at Leo.

"Let us at least scout the situation, see what we are dealing with," Leo insisted.

Winnipeg fidgeted and bit his lip.

Theo, however, lifted his chin. For a moment, the two monks regarded one another.

"The Dish of Christ reveals he who is true," Leo said.

He opened his door and stepped out into the night.

"Heights, what *is* this?"

"What? It's the next scene. You know, at the museum. All those bishops jumping and smacking each other—"

"I know what it's about. I mean, wow, you use the word *turn* in, like, every other sentence."

"It's an action sequence, Woodhouse. The bishops were turning around, and Ray and Natalie turned to look."

"Yeah. Here you write—*There was a turn in the conversation*. And here—*It turned out to be a mess*. You must have used every cliché containing the word *turn*."

"I was establishing a unifying theme."

"Ugh."

"What? You do the same thing in your scenes."

"Listen, Heights. While I edit your chapter, why don't you do something useful? Like, write an author bio for us. You can handle that. Probably."


Woodhouse is a writer who is picky about word choice, but the scenes do read rather nicely after she edits them. Heights admits he doesn't do much with narration, but he is clever with dialogue and can write something that makes Woodhouse laugh, on occasion.

Made in the USA
Columbia, SC
10 June 2021